IN THE MIDNIGHT HOUR

"I . . . have told you and told you—I am not Chantal! *Je ne comprend*—why will you not believe me?"

When she lapsed into French like that, she was a ghost resurrected, but there was another, even more basic reason why he would not believe her disavowals. He buried one hand in her lush black hair and pulled her head back. "Because of this."

Still pressing her against the wall, so that she felt every inch of his aroused passion, he swooped down on her mouth, seizing it for his own. Unlike the first time on the stage, or that time in his carriage, he exhibited no patience, no tenderness and no restraint. Tonight, during this midnight hour when wild things prowled, he was no politician, nor even a suitor.

He was a wolf marking territory.

She was his chosen mate.

And wolves mated for life.

Other *Love Spell* books by Colleen Shannon:
PRINCE OF KISSES
THE GENTLE BEAST

The Steadfast Heart

COLLEEN SHANNON

LOVE SPELL BOOKS ◆ NEW YORK CITY

LOVE SPELL®

August 1998

Published by

Dorchester Publishing Co., Inc.
276 Fifth Avenue
New York, NY 10001

ISBN 0-505-52271-3

Chapter One

On that sunny afternoon, few of the ton attended the King's Theater. Most found the Duchess of Derbyshire's Thames regatta more interesting than the London matinee debut of a little-known ballet, and a lesser-known prima ballerina. But of the two events, this performance of *La Vestale*, a tragic tale of forbidden love, would be the more memorable in years to come.

A gigantic chandelier suspended from the frescoed ceiling illuminated the gay scene. Fringe members of the elite flitted between the boxes that lined the sides and upper galleries in elegant semicircles. The boxes themselves were resplendent in John Nash's elegant new renovation, decorated as they were with gilded checkered woodwork on a pink background. Their crimson curtains and squabs made a brilliant backdrop for the men and women who perambulated between them, exchanging compliments and barbs by turns. All wore their finest to hide their chagrin at not being invited to the social event of the season.

Plumed in feathers, shrill of voice and as partial to sparklers as magpies, they chattered like a flock of birds. Doubtless, all agreed, the duchess's regatta would be a soggy, boring affair. It was much more pleasant to attend the theater, they opined, unaware that, after this afternoon, they would be sought after by even the highest sticklers for their knowledge of the season's most delicious scandal.

In one of the most exclusive boxes, a man stood surrounded by people. He had a confidence in his bearing, a discreet elegance in his person that drew admirers and detractors alike. He wore a yellow rose diamond stickpin and an emerald signet ring with a casual grace that said much of his heritage. When he spoke, he did so quietly, as one accustomed to being listened to.

Still, it was not his obvious nobility, nor even his pleasant face that one first noticed. His appeal was founded upon the spirit that emanated from within—a serene strength and gentle wisdom, an interest in those around him, whatever their station might be. His smiles at his visitors conveyed the confidence of one born to rule, and the initiative to do so wisely. Those who knew him well, however, and they were few, caught the melancholy behind the sunny blue eyes that was as much a part of him as his regal bearing.

He was not unusually tall, nor spectacularly handsome. His nose was too small to be imposing, his face too square for perfection. His mouth was strong rather than moody, his eyes too astutely aware of the foibles of humanity—his own included—to fit the sultry, Byronlike handsomeness that was all the rage. His hair was an unremarkable sun-streaked brown, the curly lock always a-tumble over his forehead giving him a boyish look. His physique was slim and lithe, his every movement as graceful as the Thoroughbreds he stabled. He was not a man to stand out in a crowd, yet the men and women squeezing into his box to offer their greetings gravitated to him.

Some were hangers-on, eager to be seen with this most elite member of an elite circle; others were admiring acquaintances hoping to further their friendship; and a bare few were genuine friends who wondered why he had attended the ballet this afternoon.

They knew what it cost him.

The eleventh Earl of Dunhaven, Vincent Anthony Kimball, smiled warmly at interloper and well-wisher alike. "In truth, had I known I'd stir up such interest, I'd have rented a larger box! Have I become so bookish that it's an event for me to venture out?"

A voluptuous, flirtatious young widow tapped him on the arm with her fan. "Any outing graced with your presence is an event, your lordship," she said, simpering.

Vince caught the hand she would have placed on his arm, bent lithely and brought it to his lips, thus hiding his grimace. Was he to be plagued until he was gray and goutish with importunate females? he wondered to himself. But his smile held no malice when he released her and straightened. "Then I shall have to socialize more and make it less so, for certainly a dull fellow like myself should not draw attention away from diamonds such as you."

While she was preening under the compliment, he turned to a young beau in a chartreuse waistcoat and orange jacket, with shirt points so high and stiff they stabbed his cheekbones. "Herbert, how good to see you again. Did you take my advice and buy that lively pair of chestnuts at Tattersall's?"

The young man swallowed, his prominent brown eyes both bashful and adoring, and stuttered, "Y-yes, sir. Sweet goers they are, t-too, just as you said."

"Excellent! And Jasper, has your new drainage system worked as well as we hoped?"

A rotund little man with the ruddy cheeks of a landholder who enjoyed overseeing his own property replied, "Exactly as you designed, by Jove. Haven't had a spot of trouble since. But deuce take it, man, why won't you let me repay you with that little filly I offered?"

The earl's smile was sweet as he shook his head. "Because you owe me naught. It's satisfaction enough knowing the rarefied atmosphere of the Lords hasn't stunted my brain. I enjoyed designing the system far more than you enjoyed paying for it, I warrant."

Jasper agreed fervently, "You've the right of it there, lad!"

Laughter rippled at this, for Jasper's clutch-fistedness was no secret in this gathering. And so it went, the earl greeting each visitor in turn with unfailing good humor, courtesy and an uncanny ability to address that subject which interested each person most. When they filed out, their faces were aglow with enjoyment. Each was convinced he was a prime example of humanity, a little more determined to prove it—and each admired more the man who incited such warm feelings.

Only two people remained as the orchestra tuned up. One was a small, majestic-looking matron wearing a diamond tiara that would have sparkled in Westminster at dusk. She watched her son with eyes as blue and direct as his own. "Why are you so patient with such social-climbers, Vincent? You should have sent them along forthwith."

Vince sighed at this old, old argument. "It costs me less to be pleasant than it would to snub them. And it's a deal kinder. Part of our family is no more aristocratic, after all, so what right have I to flaunt myself?"

She bristled. "My grandpapa at least had dignity and kindness."

"Exactly so. And I would be less than true to his memory and my name were I otherwise."

The other person in the box laughed softly and kissed the lady's offended cheek. "Dear ma'am, you know he's impossible to argue with when he's like this. You'd not have him different."

The matron relaxed and returned the tall, redheaded man's smile. "You're right, of course, Robbie. I should be happy enough that I coaxed him into attending today."

Vince snorted. "Coaxed, is it? More like coerced, madam."

"Talk to him, Robbie. Tell him how foolish he is to hold sacrosanct a boy's memory and condemn me to loneliness because of it." When Vince's mouth tightened, she said more insistently, "It's true. Were it not for that French chit, you'd be married with a brood by now . . ." Robbie's tightening fingers gave her pause less than the anguished flash of blue eyes that quickly looked away.

Silence stretched uncomfortably before Robbie said tactfully, "I've yet to meet a woman who would be

11

happy to play second fiddle to John Bull, ma'am. As long as Vince is so devoted to politics, perhaps it's best he not marry.''

Vince shot him a grateful look. "So I've tried to tell her. Some people were not meant to wed, and I, I fear, am one of them." As the lights began to dim, he relaxed into his seat, settling the issue.

Adeline, Countess of Dunhaven, gave a disgruntled sigh and turned her attention to the stage, but Robbie still watched his friend. He knew Vince better than anyone, and he worried at the white look about his friend's mouth. Adeline had no idea how much Vince had loved Chantal, so she didn't know how it strained her son to attend a ballet, any ballet, because of the ghostly ballerina that always haunted the earl, especially in such surroundings.

Vince's unfailing charm and tact even when he was not in the best of humors never ceased to amaze Robbie. This intrinsic decency made the earl a force to be reckoned with in the House of Lords. Many opponents had dismissed Vince as a soft ninnyhammer, only to find themselves gently but eloquently argued into silence, the bill they supported defeated by Vince's leadership.

Vince had need of some of that drive in his personal life. He'd kept himself sequestered for too long, bright memories his only solace. It had been almost ten years since Chantal's disappearance, but Robbie feared the wounds inflicted by their brief liaison would never heal. At least they wouldn't as long as Vince held himself aloof from the beautiful women who would have beggared themselves to win his interest. For his friend's sake, Robbie hoped Vince would lay Chantal's memory to rest. Thus, Robbie had added his persuasions to Adeline's that Vince attend the ballet tonight—though for a different reason.

He'd heard from a friend who attended this same ballet in Milan that the prima ballerina was of uncommon beauty. She was a wisp of a thing, as delicate and graceful as her namesake, Papillone. If she was as charming as rumored, then maybe here, at last, was a woman who could interest Vince longer than a night or, at most, a week. Robbie knew of no quicker relief for the dismals than a new mistress. As for the reports that Papillone rejected all admirers, Robbie dismissed them as rumors planted by the little danseuse herself to entice more bees to her honeypot. Who ever heard of a virtuous ballerina? he scoffed inwardly, settling back as the curtain opened.

Beside Robbie, Vince gritted his teeth to stem the gorge rising in his throat and told himself he was being ridiculous. Adeline and Robbie were right. It was high time he exorcised the ghost of his past. Chantal was either dead or married by now. If she had cared as much for him as she'd claimed, she never would have disappeared without a word.

And so he forced himself to watch, trying to deny the tearing anguish in his gut as the first dancers floated onstage. But the memories persisted, made poignant by his emotions: It was wrong for him to be here. It should be Chantal on that stage, dancing for him, only for him as she had so many times before. He was too busy grappling with his emotions to pay much attention to the stage as the first act began.

A mock Roman circus had been set up, complete with chariots, horses and spectators draped in togas. The games at an end, the Vestal Virgins entered to a slow, measured rhythm from the orchestra, bearing palms and crowns for the victors. Vince noted with vague appreciation that each Vestal was lovely and sinuous, both innocent and wordly, as they began a fluid dance that seemed inspired by the poses he'd seen on Roman mosaics.

They wore the briefest of togas, each baring a graceful shoulder, a golden cord tying white gauze about their waists. The material had been so cleverly draped that, though each dancer was covered to her ankles, details of each supple figure were quite apparent. So in tune were they as they arched, dipped and swayed that at first none stood out. Like a sonata, they blended into a harmonious whole. But then the corps de ballet faded into the background, leaving two people in the forefront.

Vince's wandering attention sharpened. He leaned forward.

Center stage stood Decius, the winning gladiator, clad in leather jerkin and helmet, with Emilia, the smallest Vestal. Unlike the other dancers, who wore their hair up, her long, blue-black tresses were braided with a golden cord, the braid falling over one delicate shoulder. Her waist was tiny, her hips as curvaceous as the legs glimpsed through the thin gauze. She lifted slim arms to place the crown on Decius's head. Their eyes met, drawing the gaze of the audience from the graceful movements of their bodies to that intense look. The gaslight centered on them, highlighting the emotional moment of two people falling in love at first sight. For the first time, the prima ballerina's face was clearly lit.

Blood rushed to Vince's head. He groaned and fell back against his seat, oblivious to Robbie's ''My word!'' or Adeline's shocked gasp. Vince gripped the arms of his chair so tightly, the worn material tore.

Pulling himself upright, he fixed his gaze on that small, brightly lit figure. He mouthed then the very name his companions had hoped today would erase from his lips. ''Chantal.'' And finally, in a hoarse shout, ''Chantal!''

Adjacent attendees looked into their box curiously in time to see Robbie put a staying hand on Dunhaven's shoulder.

Vince threw him off and bolted out the door. He leaped down the stairs three at a time, his pulse keeping time with each frantic step. He ran to the stage door, a prayer mumbling through his lips. ''Dear God, let it be, let it be, please . . .''

The stage manager turned at Vince's noisy entrance into the wings. He frowned, blocking Vince's passage. ''Yes, may I help you?'' His tone was nominally polite to this obvious member of the nobility.

''Please, I must see that ballerina.'' Vince cleared his throat and said more calmly, ''We are old friends. I'm certain she'd want to see me.'' He tried to push past the large man so he could see the stage, but a muscular arm barred his way.

''No one is allowed backstage during a performance, me lud. You must leave. You can speak to any dancer you fancy, but later.'' He tried to escort Vince away.

Vince shook off his hand. ''No, I'll not leave. Can I not wait here and speak to her between acts?''

The manager reddened at this flouting of his authority. ''You'll be speaking to the watch if you don't leave. Now!''

Vince threw a desperate look at the stage, which he

could barely see. He couldn't see her from here. Panic filled him. What if she left before he had a chance to verify her identity? What if he'd imagined her, conjured up the image he most wanted to see in the stress of attending his first ballet since she'd disappeared? He couldn't wait until the performance was over. He must find out *now*.

He looked at the manager's angry face. He looked back at the stage. For only the second time since reaching maturity, he acted on instinct, emotionally rather than logically. As if defeated, he turned and retreated a few steps. When the manager followed, he darted around the corner of the wing and stuck out his foot.

The man fell headlong. Vince leaped over him and ran out on stage, aware but uncaring that he would become the cynosure of all eyes. Uncaring that he, who assiduously guarded his good name, would make a spectacle of himself in exactly the way he abhorred in others.

The Vestals were pirouetting when Vince burst onto the stage. He searched frantically for that haunting face. A dancer noticed him and faltered to a halt, drawing the attention of the others. One by one they stopped and stared as this obvious gentleman walked slowly through them, searching, searching.

Vince didn't feel the shocked, fascinated gazes as even the orchestra whined to a stop, the musicians, too, pausing to stare. The audience buzzed as Vince wended his way to the front, his eyes riveted on a gleaming black head. He pushed through the stunned troupe, clasped the girl's arm and turned her to face him. The air left his lungs in a whoosh as the eyes he would never forget looked at him, myriad emotions in their lavender-gray depths. They were enormous eyes, vaguely slanted and fringed with thick, black, curling lashes. Eyes he'd despaired of ever seeing again.

Utter silence prevailed as every person in the theater, from maid to mistress, from footman to duke, stared. And, as the earl put up a shaking hand to touch her face, every person present caught the hunger and familiarity in that touch.

The theater owner put a staying hand on the angry manager's arm when he would have dragged Vince off the stage. "After this afternoon, the gentry will flock here," he whispered. Reluctantly, the manager subsided.

Vince knew nothing but the lovely, distressed face before him. With every pore of his body he absorbed the features that still haunted his dreams: high cheekbones, pointed chin, dainty nose, small, cupid's bow mouth and pearly teeth just visible between her panting lips. He would have been content to stare at her for hours, but when Chantal flinched away from the caress at her cheek, he was galvanized into action.

He jerked her to his lean length, groaning at the feel of her against him, substantial rather than the wraith he'd reached for in the interminable dark, lonely nights. He sensed the shocked gasps from the audience, but his only concern at the moment was Chantal.

He forced up her averted chin and looked into the eyes that were now veiled. "Why do you deny me, Chantal?" he whispered tenderly.

She bit her lip, refusing to answer, so he did then what his body had been urging him to do since he touched her. He lowered his sun-streaked head over hers and kissed her, swallowing her gasp. For the barest instant, she melted against him, as if familiar with the touch and taste of the mouth seeking hers so urgently. Then she stiffened and tried to push him away. He lifted his head and looked down at her, his blue eyes moist, but he would not release her.

She closed her eyes, a pained expression twisting her porcelain features, but when she looked at him again, her steely gaze matched her tone. "You mistake, m'sieur. My name is not Chantal. I insist you release me."

He did so, reluctantly, but kept within easy arm's reach. "Then why did you respond to my kiss?" His little smile deepened when a blush tinged her cheeks.

She patterned her worldly smile after his own as she looked him up and down. "You are a handsome man, m'sieur."

He frowned, for the Chantal he had known could never have been so bold, but his next question died unspoken as the theater owner, a satisfied look upon his cadaverous features, caught his arm. "Come, my lord. You may speak to Papillone after the performance."

Blinking, Vince finally realized where he was. He snapped his mouth closed and stalked off, delivering a look of blistering promise at Papillone over his shoulder. The ballet resumed, but it was almost the intermission before the prima ballerina recovered her former grace.

As for Vince, he coolly met every curious stare that followed him on the long walk back to his box. He sat grimly impassive through the remainder of the performance, his eyes glued to the small, raven-haired danseuse. After a few tentative questions that went unanswered, Robbie and Adeline didn't speak to him. Vince moved only once during the performance: At the interval, he went to the box door and bolted it, and then returned to his seat. When several knocks sounded, he ignored them. After a time, they stopped.

At this unwonted behavior, Robbie's blue eyes met the countess's bluer ones. He nodded slightly and said, "Vince, old chap, what say you to an early evening? I've the deuce of a headache."

"Take the carriage and go if you wish. I'll get a hack home." Vince's brooding stare never left the stage.

"Vince, it's probably not the same chit—" The countess's voice trailed off at the slash of the acute blue eyes so like her own. She rose with regal grace. "Very well, make more of a fool of yourself than you have done already. Pay me no heed, as usual. Robbie, your arm."

Sighing, Robbie stood and patted the stiff little hand that landed on his sleeve. "Shall I escort the dear lady home and return, Vince?"

"There's no need, Robbie. In truth, I prefer to be alone."

"As you wish." Wheeling smartly, Robbie and the countess left, marching in lockstep like practiced infantry.

Vince didn't even notice. His every muscle was rigid with self-control. By the time the interminable performance ended, he was so tense he felt he'd snap at a touch. He left his box shortly before the lights dimmed, but even so, he had to evade several people who would have waylaid him.

He was the first gentleman to reach the troupe's dressing rooms. A staring stagehand directed him to

Papillone's room. It was set slightly apart from the others, and he saw the door closing as he walked toward it.

Venting a rare oath, he hurried forward and banged on the door. When no one answered, he pounded harder. Heavy footsteps finally approached. The door cracked open. Vince had to look up, way up, before he could meet one storm-cloud gray eye. He glimpsed a thick, unruly thatch of copper hair and a broad chest.

A thick Scottish brogue snapped, "What is it, mon?"

"I want to speak to your mistress." When that hostile eye only narrowed, Vince snapped, "Now!"

"Papillone dinna speak to sassenachs sich as ye. Off wi' ye."

Vince stuck his evening slipper in the doorway, wincing when the man tried to shut the portal anyway, smashing his foot in the process.

Vince caught the savage glint of teeth, and when the pressure on his foot eased slightly, he wisely withdrew it. The door snapped shut in his face. Vince clenched his fists and thought about kicking the flimsy wood, but the gentlemen crowding backstage stared at him, one and all.

His muscles aching with tension, he wheeled and stalked off, pulling a stagehand aside. "Tell Papillone that Vincent Kimball looks forward to a quiet conversation." He gave the man a crown and hurried away.

His thunderous frown discouraged even the most avid gossips. By the time the hack delivered him at his townhouse, it was growing dark and he was uncertain with whom he was angrier—Chantal or himself. Never had he flaunted his feelings in such a way. But Chantal had always incited his deepest emotions.

After throwing his cape, hat and gloves at his butler, he snapped over his shoulder, "See that I'm not disturbed under any circumstances." He slammed his study door behind him, fetched his finest brandy and flung himself in the chair before the empty grate. He poured a hefty draft in a snifter, snapped down the decanter and drank the potent brew in two swallows. He poured himself another, leaned back and closed his eyes.

Breathing deeply didn't help. He tried striding about his study, nursing his brandy and his wounded feelings, but that didn't help either. He paused before the miniature of Chantal that he always kept on his desk despite his mother's protests. He picked it up in one hand and drained his brandy with the other.

So sweet, so innocent she looked, that lush hair flowing over her shoulders, that wistful smile that had never failed to move him upon her lips. She'd sat for this portrait at his request that last summer before she disappeared, and for ten years it had been all he'd had of her. If she had her way, it would be all he'd ever have of her.

His hand clenched so hard about the picture that he bent the expensive silver frame. How could she deny even knowing him? The man who'd held her image sacrosanct for nigh on a decade. His body trembled with the need to grind the miniature under his foot, but he forced himself to set it back down. His anguish grew until he felt he'd explode.

Growling like a wounded bear, he swiped everything off his desk and flung his snifter against the wall. A flying shard caught him on the cheek. He picked away the speck of glass, looked vaguely at the blood on his

21

fingers, groaned and slumped in his desk chair.

His foot knocked against something. He bent down, picked up the picture, stared blearily at it and then gently put it facedown on his desk. He closed his eyes, but the images crowding into his brain were not animated by sight. His heart was relentless, and at last he admitted defeat, buried his head on his arms and let memories take him away. . . .

Chantal had been a frail little ten-year-old the first time he'd seen her. Her mother, Annette, was a remote French relative persecuted by Napoleon because of her English connections. His mother and father had given her an abandoned cottage on their estate next to the lake after building a new one for their gatekeeper. Curious, Vince had ridden by the cottage the very day after, and glimpsed a small, dark-haired woman sweeping out dust and cobwebs. A little girl played next to the lake, feeding bits of stale bread to the black swans gliding there. Her hair had the same velvety luster as the swan's, her neck the same grace. She looked up at him.

They each paused—the boy in the expensive riding habit mounted atop a Thoroughbred and the girl dressed in a clean but patched pinafore—and stared at one another. Vince tipped his hat; the little girl curtsied nimbly and ran to her mother. Vince stayed where he was, staring at the closed door. He wheeled his mount and returned home, forgetting his intended ride.

Something about the child drew him. Perhaps it was her grace, or those huge eyes that stared at him as gravely as one of Hogarth's renderings of homeless street urchins, or perhaps it was because he was an only child and longed for a sister. For whatever reason, he questioned his parents closely about the new arrivals that night at dinner, only to receive a rare scolding.

He was to keep his distance from Annette and Chantal. He mustn't forget that his father worked in the foreign office. They'd hinted at a scandal that clung to Annette but refused to tell him details. In any case, open association with a penniless French ballet dancer, aristo or no, would do his father's political aspirations no good, he was warned.

However, as both his parents had made plain, Annette had nowhere else to go, and the Kimballs never shirked their responsibility, no matter how inconvenient. Vince was a responsible young man even then, and he tried to obey his parents' command; he truly did. But when he went fishing he spied a small face peeping at him from the bushes, and he couldn't resist inviting the child to join him. He fetched her a pole and taught her how to fish; a harmless pastime, he'd told himself. From his fourteen-year-old perspective, she was a tiny girl too fragile to play with and too young to flirt with. Where was the harm?

At first there was none. Chantal's shyness soon wore off, and to his delight, Vince found the delicate little girl to be a latent hoyden. She not only accompanied him on some of his roughest jaunts, she initiated many of them. How many times, in those golden days of youth, did they climb trees, then doctor one another's skinned knees so their parents would not know? How many nights did they sneak out their windows to spread a blanket on the vast lawn and tease each other with their knowledge of the constellations? How many meals did the growing girl cook for the maturing boy, only to be teased for her lamentable lack of culinary skill?

How many stories did they relate to one another, their personal favorite becoming the enchanting tale of the Steadfast Tin Soldier and the graceful ballerina he loved? How many times did the young lady, who was beginning to fill her revealing dancing costume in the most interesting places, dance for the young man?

It was those dances, Vince knew now, that had changed things between them. Annette had taught her daughter to dance, Chantal admitted to him during one of their many cozes, so she could support herself if she never found a man to love and marry. Annette was an unconventional noblewoman who believed marriage went hand-in-hand with love, and she instilled in Chantal the same belief.

Whether his burgeoning sexual impulses or Chantal's attraction to him changed their relationship, Vince could not say. He knew only that when she danced for him on one of his holidays from Oxford, the very air between them seemed to ignite. Chantal ended the evocative, swaying dance in his arms. The kiss they exchanged was their first as adults. Vince had played at sex with several tavern wenches, but the difference between their practiced movements and Chantal's awkward ones only whetted his interest. Here was the playmate of his youth, this kindred spirit and confidante, grown into a lovely woman who thrilled his heart as much as his body. How he longed to share the ultimate intimacy with her.

Ever protective of her, he broke their embrace, made a garbled excuse and fled. She lived on his estate; he was responsible for her.

Vince's father had died in a riding accident, and Vince attained his title at the young age of eighteen.

He'd been groomed since he was a toddler for the role, so he took to his duties with both enthusiasm and ability. His mother, long since aware of his jaunts with Chantal, changed from making broad hints to outright warnings.

How vividly Vince recalled the first time he heard the true story of Annette's past. His mother had been entertaining guests when he fled back home that winter day after Chantal's dance. On seeing his discomfiture, she coaxed the reason out of him. He'd never been able to keep secrets from her, but he was not surprised when her face tightened with worry.

"Vince, if you value your name and the trust your father—" her voice shook at the memory of her husband before she steadied it—"placed in you, you'll not see the chit again. Chantal's a pretty girl, but any connection with her would be disastrous." The countess rose to pace the chamber, and her unusual agitation told Vince how strongly she felt about the matter.

"It's time you heard the truth. Your father and I never told you before because we believed Annette's past was her own affair. She's been discreet since coming here, and for that we're grateful. But I can't have your infatuation with her daughter endangering your future."

She turned to face him. "As you know, Annette left France to escape Napoleon's influence. Since she was connected to a prominent British family, her every action came under question, and she feared for Chantal's future. When she came, she gave your father every bit of information she'd collected in her travels as a dancer, so we owed her much not only as a family, but as patriots. However, as you do not know, she had visited us here once before. You were only three at the time and would not remember. She took part only halfheartedly in all the gay affairs we held for her, and the reason for her lack of interest soon became apparent. Literally. You see, she'd met an English tradesman in France when he traveled there on business. They formed an attachment, consummated it clandestinely and then quarreled when Annette discovered that the wastrel was married. Unfortunately, she was already . . . *enciente.* She visited us in England to find and tell the father of his . . . issue."

Vince's gaze remained riveted on his mother as he listened. He knew she found the story distasteful by the way she stumbled over the tale, but he felt more sorry for Annette than appalled. This explained so much. Annette's rare smiles, her reasons for never marrying, her odd beliefs for a sheltered French girl. Not so sheltered, after all, he realized.

"She disappeared for a couple of days, and when she returned, she was distraught. Her gowns were loose for the style of the time, and when I visited her unexpectedly one morning, I realized why. She was already several months along. We offered, not enthusiastically I admit, to let her stay, for I knew how autocratic her father was. And with the Revolution, times were very uncertain for her in France. But she was proud. After she admitted the truth, she insisted on returning home. It wasn't until almost a year later that I discovered her father had cast her out. Fortunately, as it turns out, she took another name and made a place for herself on the stage—just before her entire family was beheaded. For a number of years she supported herself and her daughter, until Napoleon's inquiries into her affairs became too worrisome.''

The countess turned to her son and pulled him to his feet. Holding his hands, she said sadly, ''I'm sorry to pain you with the tale, my love, but you had to know the truth. Do you see now how impossible a future is for you and Chantal? She's a remote relative, true, but she's half-French, born on the wrong side of the blanket to a mother who is believed, wrongly, to have spied for Napoleon. If you wed her, you'll never have the political influence you want, and you might even be shunned by our friends.''

Vince stared unseeingly at their twined hands. Unwittingly, his mother had quieted his unease. Of course. He must marry Chantal. He'd been too young to think of marriage, but only through the sanction of God and church could he have all he wanted of the childhood love grown into an adult passion.

When he lifted his head to meet her gaze, his mother stiffened. ''Mother, you overstate the problem. Chantal is the ideal politician's wife: intelligent, educated, caring and tactful. Her background may cause problems at first, but none we can't overcome. Besides, you should know that I've applied for my colors. I can hardly ask her to wed me at the age of sixteen, especially since I'll soon be gone. But when I return, and she's old enough, I intend to give her my name. I'll never love another. I am a true Kimball in that.''

And that had been the end of it, as far as Vincent was concerned. At least he'd given his mother a new worry: his safety. But how could he lead England unless he was willing to die for it? He designed a ring he intended to have made for Chantal when she was old enough to become engaged. He ordered the family jeweler to watch for the unusual center stone: a large, perfect, heart-shaped ruby he wanted surrounded by diamonds. Like the tin soldier, he'd display a heart to prove his love for her. Like the tin soldier, he'd wait for her, but unlike the little toy, he'd not die of love for her. They were fated to be happy.

Or so he believed. While he was young and stupid, he thought now. But once begun, the rush of memories would not be dammed, no matter if they drowned him. His thoughts continued. . . .

He'd been determined not to compromise Chantal. He saw her only in the presence of others, so as not to tempt himself too greatly. However, a few months before his departure to join Wellington, Chantal herself proved the downfall to his chivalry. Tired of his evasions, she swam out to his little sloop, insisting she go along one last time. A quick squall forced them to tie up in a sheltered bay.

His frustration found vent in anger, and when Chantal laughed at him, rain plastering her dress to her ripening shape, anger found another kind of outlet. The elements raging without were as irresistible as those roiling within. The embrace he meant as a punishment soon became a gift.

Chantal, so she told him on that night long ago, was determined not to let him go away with no memories of her; she wanted to fill herself with him and memories enough to keep her while he was gone. Still, in a measure of her respect for him, she did not plead with him to stay. It was for his honor that she loved him, so why would she ask him to compromise it?

And other sweet things she'd said. Sweet, poisonous lies, they must have been. And yet . . .

The meeting of their minds was complemented that day by the melding of their bodies. There, on a reed bed in a deserted hut, rain pouring down the eaves, they knew one another in the last sense that remained to them. And they found, to their mutual delight, that their bodies were as compatible as their minds. When reason returned, Vince's guilt at stealing her virginity had weighed heavily upon him. Until Chantal kissed him, caressed him. Gave generously of her love, as she always had.

Vince squeezed his eyes closed as he remembered Chantal's teasing response to his apology for hurting her. "*Cheri,* if you had left me then, *you* would be the one in pain now. I have a mean right." She brushed a light fist against his square-cut jaw. "You only took what was yours, what I have wanted to give to you since I last danced for you."

He'd groaned her name against her lips and reveled again in the miracle of life, of love, in the wonder that was Chantal. And so began the happiest time of his life, the only truly happy time of his life, had he but known it then. He'd brushed aside her worries about what would happen when they wed and himself talked of arrangements for the day when he'd no longer need his mother's permission. She informed him that she had always longed to be a soldier's bride and would wait for the day she could follow the drum.

Their passion for one another was as infinite as their curiosity and, honor be hanged, as she'd succinctly told him, they had no reason to deny one another. Their stolen idylls were infrequent but heady as Vince learned that he, too, was like his grandfather and his father: He'd love only once, so he'd best have a care for the enchanting female God had blessed him with. Throwing caution to the wind, he made the engagement official even though Chantal was barely seventeen and he barely twenty-one.

However, his resolve was tested all too soon. Vince's first lesson of joy's fleeting nature came abruptly, brutally, on a rainy May day.

After Vince asked for her daughter's hand, Annette began long absences. They soon saw a glow about her, a happiness she'd never displayed before. However, before she could make the engagement announcement he and Chantal were anticipating, she disappeared. The day before the wedding, she was found in a carriage on the road to London, mutilated, her throat cut.

After comforting Chantal as best he could, Vince hied himself to London to hasten the authorities in their investigation. When, exhausted, he hurried back to his estate to their delayed wedding, Chantal was gone. She had taken only her clothes, and hadn't even left him a note.

To this day, Vince didn't know why. Why the only woman he'd ever loved, who had, he still believed, loved him, had left him.

The anguish he'd felt then came back in a rush, almost as sharp as it had been on that day nigh onto ten years ago.

Why? What had he done to drive her away? The suddenness, the finality, had almost driven him mad. When Bow Street had found no trace of her, and no word came from her in over a year, he'd done his best to forget. Told himself that a woman who could leave him so was unworthy of such devotion. Yet he'd rarely been attracted to a woman since, and he'd never given a thought to marriage.

The poignant fairy tale of his childhood had ended just as tragically in real life. His love for his dainty ballerina had almost destroyed him. He'd risked his life in the war a dozen times over, but God—or the devil—would not release him from his suffering. Though he'd been wounded and still carried scars, he'd not achieved the forgetfulness for which he'd longed.

Wellington had saved the day for England in one of the greatest battles the world had ever known, but the cost was high. He'd told his infantry in the midst of battle on the field at Waterloo, "Hard pounding, gentlemen, we'll see who can pound the longest."

And for days raucous with the screams of men and artillery, and nights lit by campfires and rockets, they'd pounded at the French. At first the French pounded back so hard that it seemed Wellington's men would have to fall back. But then, after exhausting days of advance and retreat, retreat and advance, Napoleon's Imperial guard, that most elite of the French fighting forces, broke and ran. They carried with them the French will to fight. Napoleon was captured, the tyrant defeated.

Vince was carried home on a victorious tide. His own hatred of himself was in inverse proportion to the adoration showered on the returning conquerers, for Vince knew that he was responsible for the death of many of his fallen comrades. Not because he didn't care about them; because he didn't care about himself. Without Chantal, he had nothing to go back to.

The pain of his own selfishness had never left him.

Even now his old wound throbbed, as if to remind him never to forget. The stench of the battlefield came back to him. It was a distinctive smell he'd always remember, a mixture of decaying corpses, acrid musket fire, the smoke of cannons and rockets, and mud slippery with blood and horse manure. Vince had slept little, eaten less, riding hard to battle, urging his men on to incredible feats of bravery. With every skirmish, and that last battery he charged, he'd hoped to be blown to bits. Many of his men were—some right beside him.

What sense was there in a world where Death took not the ones who wanted to die, but those who had the most for which to live? Vince had lost his best friend, who was newly married, in one of those charges. He'd fought on like a madman, taking the cannon battery with a motley assortment of men and turning it on the foe.

He'd been commended for his bravery by his superiors. He'd accepted their huzzahs with the same calm with which he removed the shrapnel from his leg. That eerie calm stayed with him to the end of the battle, past his arrival home, even to several years after his return.

But Death wasn't ready for him. Slowly, slowly, as the horrors of battle faded, as his wounds healed, his depression lifted. On the day he took his rightful seat in the House of Lords, he quit searching for Chantal. Peace, of a sort, was his reward. Happiness, no. But certainly a sense of purpose.

His thoughts come full circle, Vince raised his head. He stared at the bottom drawer of his desk. The temptation was irresistible. Raising his head, he shoved himself back from the desk, opened the drawer and lifted the false lining. He pulled out a small velvet sack and shook the contents into his palm.

An exquisite ruby glittered with the fire only the best stones possess. As he turned the large jewel this way and that, it shone the red of blood and broken dreams. Its perfect shape was emphasized by round diamonds: a heart. Vince felt as the little tin soldier must have when he burned for love of the uncaring ballerina.

This heart was all that remained of the man he'd once been—the young man who'd believed the world was his own, for he had the perfect lady with which to share it.

Vince laughed bitterly and clutched the ring. He felt a prick, opened his hand and saw that a sharp edge had drawn blood. A drop had fallen on the stone, indistinguishable from the jewel in color. The heart's brilliance shone through the blood. Vince stuck the ring back in the sack and put it away, vowing to sell it and give the proceeds to an orphanage.

Chantal had almost ruined his life. She'd certainly spoiled his hope for marital bliss and heirs. She owed him. Now that he'd found her again, he'd have his explanation at last. And, if he had his way, he'd have much more. But this time he'd not be such a fool. A woman who'd acted as she had didn't deserve to be put on a pedestal. If she was a professional dancer, she could be had for the right price. God knows he'd paid enough in emotional coin; any financial expenditure would seem cheap in comparison.

Vince opened his eyes, rubbed them wearily and then stood. He set the picture back upright on his desk, stoppered and put away the decanter. He climbed up to his room, ignoring the supper, long since cold, his servants had set on his vast dining table. His steps were as measured and firm as ever, but he stared dry-eyed into the darkness for a long, long time before sleep mercifully veiled his memories.

Chapter Two

Trembling, Chantal closed her dressing room door, longing to lunge for her huge trunk, throw all their things helter-skelter into it and get Hugo to hire them a boat to take them back to France. Instead, she sat staring at herself in the tiny cracked mirror in the only private dressing room supplied by the King's Theatre. When she first saw the tiny chamber, Chantal had not been pleased at the tatty screen or guttering candles. On the Continent, where her talents were lionized, she was accustomed to better.

But she wasn't on the Continent now. She was literally in the English lion's den. And unlike Daniel, she bore no purity of soul nor magical powers to save herself.

Or her son.

When the violent knocking came, she tensed despite herself. She forced her fingers to the familiar task of dipping into the face cream, smoothing it into her face and wiping away the heavy makeup. But she heard only Vince's beloved voice arguing with Hugo, visualized only the confused pain in his face when she denied knowing him. When he finally went away, she should have sagged with relief. She should have congratulated herself on her cleverness. She should be glad he was gone.

Why, then, did she rest her head on her arms to avoid seeing the tears in her own eyes?

Dear God, it had been ten years. How could he still make her weak with a touch? How changed he was, yet how much the same. The eyes, steadier, bluer than any she'd ever known. The nut brown hair, shiny with vitality. The exquisitely male form, muscled in all the right places, the straight, perfect legs she had once stroked with avid curiosity. The strong lips, the tenderness with which they had kissed her . . .

Groaning, she rose so hastily that the tiny stool tipped over. She flung off her brief costume to dress in street clothes. She had to get out of here, to breathe, to escape these tormenting images. But her fingers shook, making the tiny buttons into a conundrum as intricate and hard to untangle as the past she had to deny and the future she avoided planning.

It was the changes she could not bear in him. The betrayal, the rage, the pain in his deeper voice when he vowed that he would see her again. The lines carved from his nose to his lean jaw. Had she helped put them there? The smattering of gray hairs at his temples. She hoped they were not rooted in the same regret that had plagued her since she had been forced to flee. And most frightening of all—he was a boy no longer. Like the Vince of old, he would keep his promise and return. But unlike the Vince of old, this mature man was every inch the determined statesman, as determined and formidable in the House of Lords as his mother had boasted he would be.

She should have refused to follow the troupe to England and accepted a lesser role in a rival company. But she'd worked so hard to become prima ballerina, and it had been so long. . . . Truly, she'd expected Vince to be married, with his own brood by now. Furthermore, she'd had it from reliable sources that he never attended the ballet. She'd thought herself safe.

A harsh laugh almost choked her. Her hard-won composure, her fragile peace, had been lost the minute she set foot in England, for memories had almost overwhelmed her. One summer to last a lifetime, for the ten years would soon be twenty, nay, even thirty, and she would still be a pitiful figure pining for a man who'd long since forgotten her.

Or so she'd tried to tell herself. Until the ever calm, ever polite Vincent Anthony Kimball, scion of the House of Lords, burst onto the stage and interrupted her performance. Did she dare to believe that he was as tormented as she by their lost love affair?

Anguished pleasure flooded her at the thought. Part of her would like to believe that he had remained as true as the Steadfast Tin Soldier they'd likened him to all those years ago. But another part, the part that had kept her, body and soul, true to a memory for almost a decade, knew that Vince deserved better. If an illegitimate French bride who could not name her own father would have ruined Vince, how could a scandalous dancer known throughout the Continent be considered a better match?

"Maman," came a familiar young voice at the door, along with an impatient tapping. "You promised to buy me an apple at Covent Garden after the performance."

With a shuddering sigh, Chantal jerked a pelisse over her poorly buttoned high-necked dress. She wiped her eyes on a drying cloth, took a deep breath and glued on a smile. After she unlocked the door, she stepped back, for she knew what would happen.

As usual, it flew wide, banging against the wall. A whirlwind of energy and curiosity swept into the room, dissipating her black melancholy into a gray fog. "Come, *Maman*, or the apple seller will be gone!" cried the handsome red-haired little boy. His thick hair was a riot of curls about his round little face, and freckles sprinkled his mischievous nose. He might have been a street urchin, dressed as he was in broadcloth breeches, a stiff shirt and peasant clogs. But anyone who heard him speak would know that he was of Quality.

If it should ever become known that he was heir to one of the oldest, wealthiest seats in England, she'd lose him.

She'd die first, as she almost had having him.

He reached for her hand, felt its trembling, and stopped abruptly. His unusual eyes, a spring green as fresh and sweet as apple blossoms, widened with concern. *"Maman,* what is wrong?"

The grave respect and concern in his little face reminded her so much of Vince that she had to look away or burst into tears again. From the day of Tony's birth, she'd known he got his looks from his great-grandmother Callista Kimball. Adeline, Vince's mother, had shown her Callista's portrait those many aeons ago, before Chantal realized she was pregnant. But Tony's wit, his kindness, his intellectual curiosity, these came, along with his straight posture and perfectly shaped legs, directly from his father. She would give ten years of her life to see father and son together, for even a day, knowing of the bond between them; if the lean years of living hand to mouth had taught her nothing else, they'd taught her not to dwell on things that could not be. Squeezing her nails into her free palm, she mastered herself and her rioting emotions.

Then, for his sake, as she had done since she was little more than a child herself, she opened her eyes and smiled brightly, pulling her hand away to stuff it into her pelisse. "Tush, *enfant,* you know I am always *fatigué* after a performance."

"English, *Maman.* You told me always to speak English here because they dislike us so."

"*Ou*—yes, you are right." Always, when she was tired, or upset, she reverted to French. She would have to be careful, because Vince would recognize that habit. Her accent was much less pronounced now that she'd traveled to so many different countries, a change that was one of her few advantages.

Searching Tony's rough woolen jacket, she pulled out his cap and shaded his bright curls and green eyes. "Promise me always to wear your cap when you go out."

He scowled, pulling the too-big cap down over his forehead. "I detest hats."

"Well, detest heartily, my son, but obey me you

39

shall." She kept her tone mild, but her lovely lavender eyes were suddenly more steely than purple.

He peeped up at her and gave her that melting smile. "Yes, *Maman.*"

She shoved his cap back and tapped his nose for emphasis. "I mean this, mind. If you disobey, I will order Hugo to follow you day and night."

That disingenuous smile slipped. She watched him calculate having his exciting little jaunts about London spoiled by a very large, very dour and very imposing shadow. He sighed and answered sincerely, "Yes, *Maman.* Shall we begin our perambulation?"

"Indeed." She caught his extended arm and let him lead her to the door, hoping his latest hobby of confusing his urchin friends with his command of the King's English would not fall upon the wrong ears. He was distinctive enough. She'd have to tell his tutors to emphasize the sciences instead of literature—for a time, anyway.

As they entered the hallway, Hugo pushed his massive shoulders away from the wall beside her door and fell into step with them. "Where we be off to, mistress?"

A rebuke trembled on her tongue, but she bit it back. Many times she'd asked him not to call her that, given its rather more risque interpretation among the bucks of London, but she knew Hugo meant the appellation in the old, respectful way. Nothing, not storm nor pestilence nor cataclysm, would change his regard for her or his quaint way of showing it. And she was too grateful for that to try to change him.

Catching his brawny arm as they exited onto the narrow street, she walked between the two males in her life and answered, ''I promised Tony an apple.''

Two young dandies came roistering out of a corner tavern and spied Chantal. One elbowed the other, whispering something. Both came toward them, but when Hugo scowled and pushed up his shirt sleeves, they blanched and stepped off the cobbled walkway straight into a pile of horse manure.

Tony giggled. Chantal pretended not to see. Hugo put a tree-trunk arm as a wedge between the two and Chantal as she passed, but he needn't have bothered. The bucks had already stumbled down the street, their turned-up noses wrinkled as they rubbed their feet from side to side.

When they reached the Garden, Chantal inhaled deeply. This was one thing about England she enjoyed. The bustling market was not so different from the market streets in France, but it was larger, and boasted more varied commerce. The Covent Garden market district was a riot of color, a cacophony of noise and a bubbling melting pot of smells.

Here were the flower girls with their tempting, swaying hips and pretty posies; there stood an organ grinder putting his monkey through his tricks, both of them smelling equally bad. A child hawked nuts near a corner; a fruit cart was watched over by a woman with the nose of a banana and the belly of a watermelon. Chantal went up to her and bought apples for herself, Hugo and Tony, who had wandered off to watch a boy dancing for pennies.

Chantal had to admit that no French apple ever tasted crisper, sweeter or fresher than one purchased from a fruit vendor in the Garden. She eyed the flower girls with their baskets that exploded with colors and scents.

41

Munching her apple, she wondered how long it had been since she literally stopped to smell the roses.

Too long.

Too many cities ago, too many bad nights past—and too many suitors' bouquets returned unopened in memory of a love too long lost. She tossed the core to the organ grinder's monkey, who chirped in excitement and tipped his little cap to her before falling to his unexpected feast. She smiled at the monkey and his old master, unaware that, when she smiled, people, particularly of the male gender, stopped to stare.

A stout little man in a long black frock coat, plain white shirt and tradesman's hat paused as he left an apothecary shop adjacent to the market. The sign painted on the window beside him read CANFIELD'S APOTHECARY. And, in smaller letters, ELIXIRS, MEDICINES AND NECESSARIES. When he caught sight of Chantal smiling at the monkey's antics, his work-roughened hand froze on the gold-headed walking cane that was the only evidence of his prosperity.

The handsome popinjay exiting behind him almost bumped into him. "I say, Uncle, did you leave something?"

The older man didn't answer, still staring. The gentleman, whose distinguished graying hair and taller posture made him seem more a nobleman than a cit, craned his neck to see what his uncle looked at.

Unaware of the interest she'd aroused, Chantal opened her reticule, picked through the pitiful assortment of coins and pulled out several pence. She would be paid tomorrow night, so surely she could splurge on one rose. One rose to brighten her dingy dressing room. One rose so she could pretend that her senses, as she approached the ancient age of twenty-eight, were not blighted by responsiblity and resignation.

She dragged Tony by the arm to the first vendor, a young lass who looked not a day above sixteen. The girl had been watching her, almost as if she recognized her. When Chantal stopped before her, her thin cheeks flushed in a wash of color as pink and lovely as the flowers she carried. Her lively hazel eyes blinked rapidly, whether in embarrassment or shyness Chantal could not tell. Her patched dress hung on her tall, gangly frame as she bobbed a curtsy and a cheerful nod.

"Evenin', ma'arm. What's yer pleasure?" The girl started to put together an elaborate bouquet, but Chantal stopped her with a shake of her head.

"Just one rose, please. May I pick it?"

That distinctive face, when filled out and clean, would be striking. The even features fell, but brightened again when Chantal offered one pence too many. " 'Tis fitting. A rose for a rose." And she held out her basket, glowing a deeper pink and biting her lip.

Ridiculously, Chantal blushed at the compliment. She was used to more fulsome praise, but surely this flower girl, in her shabby dress and frayed straw hat, could not have been more sincere. Chantal passed over the fulsome blooms of bright yellows, pinks and reds for one simple white rose, tightly furled. She held it to her nose and inhaled.

"Sweet, ain't it?" The flower girl smiled, showing even, surprisingly white teeth.

"Yes. Like its former owner." The girl's full mouth fell open.

Chantal tapped her cheek with the flower. "What's your name, *petite?*" She bit her lip at her own turn of

43

phrase, but the flower girl didn't seem to detest the French, as so many of the English did.

"Lizzie Mayfield. And ye be that ballerina lady, from the theater."

Now it was Chantal's turn to be surprised. "Did you attend the performance?"

Lizzie grimaced. "Only in me dreams. No, I seen ye practicing when I brought the flower petals." Her full, sensual mouth pursed in a sigh. "I wanted to be a dancer, but me ma would have none o' that. T'weren't proper, says she. Well, says I, who cares? Has to be a sight more profitable. But I's all me ma had, God rest her soul, til she passed on nigh on a year ago."

"But who do you live with, Lizzie? Why, you're hardly more than a child yourself," Chantal said.

"On me own. I takes care of meself. The only dancing I does now is on the arm of me beaus, though I wish t'were more."

Hugo was eyeing the two approaching men with suspicion. He tugged on Chantal's sleeve. "Mistress, we must not tarry longer. It grows dark."

Chantal started as she realized that, indeed, darkness fast approached. With a last encouraging smile, she said, "Come visit me at the theater, Lizzie. If you wish to try out for the ballet, I shall try to arrange it."

Lizzie's pretty hazel eyes widened, but Chantal wasn't there to see it. Almost forcing her into a run, Hugo hustled her and Tony away.

The stout little man puffed as he tried to keep up, but he limped slightly and finally stood forlorn in the milling crowd. "Confound it!" He limped back to the flower girl.

"Lass, there's a quid in it for you if you tell me who that lady was and where I can find her."

Lizzie licked her lips as gold glittered on that rough palm. She closed her eyes, breathing deeply, and opened them to give him a vacant smile. "I dunno, guvnor. Never heard her name."

"Blast." The little man pocketed his money and stalked off.

His nephew, looking concerned, trailed after him. "But, Uncle, who was that and why did you want to meet her?"

"Never mind, John. She just resembled . . . someone I used to know. Come along, we've still a deal to accomplish before we rest this day."

Lizzie almost lost a customer, she was so busy staring after them mournfully. *A quid. Ain't seen one of those since Ned give me one when he took my virginity. But blimey, that somber little man and his peacock nephew had a set about their rig that didn't seem right. That there ballerina, who seemed so fragile a wind would blow her off, didn't deserve to have them pantin' after her.*

Lizzie plastered a smile on her face and turned to her irritated customer, wondering if she'd be brave enough to accept the ballerina's challenge.

Adeline strode up and down her son's dressing room, rubbing her elbows. "But Vince, what possible good will this do? Even if the chit *is* Chantal, there can be no future in it for either of you."

Vince tossed aside his third cravat, wishing irritably that the blasted dandies who'd made a man's necktie a

45

status statement were close at hand so he could choke them with their creation. At least that damned irritating Brummel was gone, fled to the Continent to escape his creditors. And good riddance! "Mother, I am far past the age when I need you nattering at me about manners and morals as I dress. I'm going back to the ballet, and that's the end of it. My reasons need not concern you."

Adeline's little hands dropped martially to her sides. She straightened so stiffly that someone might have poured starch down her spine; but then, she'd never been lacking in that.

Vince sighed, picked up his mother's hands and kissed both palms. "Forgive me, Mother. I am a bit . . . irritable. But surely you understand that, for good or ill, I must know if this Papillone is really Chantal."

"But why?" A cry so heartfelt, so concerned, that even Vince could not mistake it.

Precisely. All unawares, she'd expressed his reason. He had to know *why* Chantal had fled, *why* she'd never contacted him to set his mind at rest. What had he done to deserve that? His guilty eyes flickered away from his own reflection as he recalled a certain stormy day that had begun an affair he could never forget. Chantal had wanted it, too, demanded it, in fact. Still, that did not excuse his behavior; he had violated a virgin under his protection.

Adeline was staring at him with such anguish that he finally knotted the cravat, uncaring that the masterpiece had more the look of a child's fumblings, and caught his mother's shoulders in his hands. "I promise to do nothing that will shame my father's memory. I've caused enough scandal for one week." He made a face as he recalled the snide announcement in London's most-circulated scandal sheet that the King's Theater had enjoyed an unusually lively matinee yesterday, and that seeing the behavior of a certain "stuffed shirt" earl had been worth the price of admission.

Vince squeezed his fingers between his neckcloth and his shirt, reflecting that the analogy felt appropriate, for the nonce, at least. "Come with me, if you wish. I shall wait my turn, like a good little boy, to see the pretty ballerina."

She seemed to find his invitation as tactless as his sarcasm. Over her shoulder, on the way to the door, she tossed back, "I'll wait for the morning papers." And, on the threshold, she paused to glower at him. "Their account will, I warrant, be more complete than your own." The door slammed on his scowl.

He was not in the habit of being called a liar, especially by his own mother, but too many odd things had happened in the past twenty-four hours. He forgave her the remark, in particular because he hadn't been totally honest with her.

On the way to the theater, ensconced in his best carriage, he stared unseeingly out at the lamps lighting the cobbled streets. Here, next to his townhouse, Quality lived their lives surrounded by plenty and privilege. As if to personalize Vince's musings, a man in a greatcoat ushered a lady in fur and diamonds into an expensive chaise. Their liveried footman put up the step and climbed behind the carriage as the driver flicked his whip at the perfectly matched pair of grays. Yet, as Vince's carriage wended through the center of London toward the King's Theater, the buildings became smaller, meaner and shabbier.

No top-hatted gentlemen or fur-garbed ladies perambulated here; aproned women and men grimy with coal dust plodded through the streets with a calm desperation that bothered Vince. How many times had he argued over this very subject with his peers, both on and off the floor of the Lords? So great a divide between rich and poor tore societies apart, either in depression or revolution, as France had proved. Those who worked hard, scrimped and offered a hand to those even less fortunate should be able to climb out of poverty into prosperity, if not wealth. However, in the current system, many tried—few succeeded.

A portly little man, with a bulbous nose tipped with red and a booming voice that had cowed many a larger opponent, hovered before Vince's mind's eye. He shook a stubby, admonishing finger. "I tell you for your own good, lad—Parliamentary reform or nothing. Many of my friends are tired of waiting, trying to work within a system that makes them outcasts. You have influence in the Lords and at court. Use it or lose it."

At the time, Vince had bristled at the plain speaking. What right had Bartholomew Canfield, the richest cit in England and one of the best orators in the Commons, to threaten him? Especially when Vince's own sympathy for parliamentary reform was well known. Why, Canfield was a commoner without a drop of noble blood, yet he'd turned a lucky touch as a mining engineer into one small claim, then a mine, then a foundry and finally an enterprise so vast that it sometimes seemed half of England was owned by Canfield. Vince had pointedly looked about at the towering mansion in prestigious Grosvernor Square and at the army of servants. Furthermore, Vince knew that Canfield owned a block of office buildings on Lombard Street. Rumor had it he'd purchased the buildings at an exorbitant sum just so he could be close to the Royal Exchange.

"Your lack of privileged blood does not seem to have hampered you, my dear sir," Vince had pointed out at that quiet dinner at Canfield's mansion.

Expecting red-faced rage, Vince was shocked when Canfield chuckled. "By George, I knew you were a goodun. We have much to offer one another, my dear earl. We shall make far better allies than enemies." And then, as quickly as he laughed, he sobered. "And yes, I am vastly wealthy, but that is not because of, but in spite of, the obstacles mother England put in my way. And no one will ever know the price I paid in overcoming them."

Melancholy clouded those clear gray eyes, and he sighed and waved his butler over to the long dining room table. When that august fellow hovered respectfully at his side, Canfield crooked an imperative finger at him. "Tell the earl how much I pay you each annum, Renfrew."

Not a flicker of surprise at the rude question crossed his calm face as Renfrew replied obediently, "Five thousand pounds, sir."

Vince's fork clattered to his dessert plate. Why, that was more than the annual income of many of his peers in the Lords, a scandalous amount for any servant, no matter how valuable.

"And why do I pay you so much, Renfrew?"

"Because I am worth it, sir."

"And how much do my best maids earn?"

"Why, I believe you pay the chambermaid one thousand per annum."

Now Vince was beyond speech.

"You may return to your duties, Renfrew. Thank you."

"Yes, sir." And in his slow, dignified manner, the white-haired old butler returned to his post in the hall, guarding their privacy.

"Now, my fine young lord, do I advocate such largesse to every maid and butler in England?"

Helplessly, Vince shrugged. There was a method to Canfield's madness, and he was about to hear it.

"No, I do not. Only to those who deserve it. Not by an accident of birth, or by the whim of a monarch, or even by the grace of God." Canfield leaned forward, his gray eyes as acute as the sterling knife poised to slice his peach. "To those who labor, day and night, to learn a skill so well that they make themselves indispensable. If you wish the secret to my success, you've heard it, and I give you leave to pass it on. From my first position scuttling coal to my new idea of selling necessaries at my apothecaries, I live my life by one credo: to do the best I can with what I have. And anyone smart enough, diligent enough and decent enough to do the same deserves to be rewarded. Like Renfrew." Leaning back, Canfield had made neat work of the peach without wasting a drop of juice.

On this night several weeks later, Vince could still see those stubby fingers moving with a dexterity that should have been surprising. Vince could never eat a peach without making a royal mess, which said much of the industrialist's background. Here was a self-made man, indeed, one who had used his hands and the sweat of his brow to, as he had said, best effect.

And tonight, as Vince looked at the poverty about him, he saw it with new eyes. Not with the eyes of an earl who held one of the wealthiest seats in England, and not even with the eyes of a leading member of the Lords who advocated trying to improve these very conditions. No, he watched the narrow streets, only occasionally lit by a guttering lantern, with the eyes of a man who feared for the woman his heart had chosen.

Did Chantal have to traverse these streets late at night, after a performance? How many times was she accosted? How many pools of slop and open sewers did she have to sidestep? The dainty ballerina, whether she was Chantal or not, deserved better. Deserved the best, in fact. She should never have to walk these streets again.

Somehow, he'd protect her from this. . . . And, at the next meeting of the Lords, he must achieve new heights of eloquence and encourage his peers to do more than bewail conditions in London's poorer quarters. The ballerina had somehow put Canfield's arguments into very human terms for Vince. Indeed, every person of diligence and ambition should have a chance at a better life. With the winds of change and anger sweeping the political countryside, he had feared for his country for some time. Canfield had only articulated, in his usual blunt way, Vince's worst fears.

Either Vince and his kind shared their power, or they would have it wrested from them, as had happened in France. Vince smiled grimly, well aware that if he expressed his thoughts, he'd be accused of treason. But, he reasoned, he was merely concerned for the welfare of his country. After all, he owed his allegiance as an Englishman first to his country, and secondly to his sovereign.

As they finally drew up at the King's Theater, he

jumped down, a new determination in his step. He paused for the dozenth time to admire the elegant facade Nash had designed. The six columns were topped by Corinthian capitals, and the pediment with dentil molding was literally a crowning achievement on the Greek temple design. Then, with a brushing down of his jacket and a deep breath, Vince plunged beneath the portico, dodging several ladies who made a beeline in his direction and going straight to his box. Soon, very soon, he'd offer Papillone his protection and make it unnecessary for her to dance another step. Her charms should not be on display to every roisterer in London who could afford the price of a ticket.

They should be for his delectation alone . . .

Chantal had barely danced in the prelude before she sensed his presence. She did not dare look at his box, dead center in one of the best sections of the house, until she was floating away into the wings to allow the corps de ballet to come on. Sure enough, she saw the perfectly shaped head, the erect posture, silhouetted against the dim light in his booth. He was alone.

Sacre bleu, why could he not leave her be? She paced backstage, rubbing her elbows to stem the tide of gooseflesh. She should have followed her instincts and stayed in Italy, accepted the lesser role. But now that she was here, and he'd found her, she could only pretend to be something she was not: a stranger, a woman of loose morals who did not care for his charms because she was so involved with her other conquests.

It would be the role of a lifetime, far more challenging than any pas de deux or solo she'd ever worked years to master. Thus, when she was showered with roses at the end of the performance, she took special care to make her smile brilliant, sensual and inviting. Thank God only she knew what thoughts put that expression there. Thoughts she'd forbidden herself to recall for too many years. And if she now used her own memories of him against him . . . well, there was a certain rough justice in that.

The manager started to pat her derriere as she left the stage after the eighth curtain call, met her eyes and let his hand drop. "Excellent performance, little gel. I'll see about giving you a bit of a stipend if you keep the house packed for the next month."

Scandal had packed the house, as they both knew, far more than her skill. Still, their repeat attendees, and they were many, had returned at least partially because they enjoyed the ballet. "Thank you, *m'sieur.*"

He waved her off, his expression tightening. His dislike of all things French had been obvious to Chantal from the beginning. And so she took particular delight in exaggerating her accent every time she spoke to him. It was one of many tools she used to keep unwanted suitors at bay.

As the first knock came, she had a despairing premonition that all her handy little tactics would bounce off the armor of a certain indefatigable soldier. From behind her screen, Chantal shook her head when Hugo started for the door. "No. Not yet."

And she continued dressing, glad that no one else could see her shaking fingers. Deliberately, she had selected her most revealing gown. The brilliant emerald green taffeta rustled with every movement, making men wonder what she wore beneath it. The low-cut vee bodice framed magnificent breasts that were far fuller than they'd been before she became a mother. Her waist was not quite as small, either, but her continual physical activity had kept her stomach flat.

And her legs, slim and muscled, were much the same. The Empire-style dress was banded at the high waist with a black velvet ribbon. She wore at her throat another black velvet ribbon that usually held a cameo, which was all she had left of her mother. But Vince might recognize that, so she'd substituted a mother-of pearl brooch that she'd scrimped and saved to purchase from a friend. A mother-of-pearl comb held her abundant black tresses on top of her head, but just barely. The overall effect was of a woman in her sensual prime, who awaited only the right touch—and the right price— to doff her clothes and her morals. Hating herself, but knowing she had no choice, Chantal slightly rouged her lips and cheeks. She appraised herself critically. She'd been around enough harlots to know she looked like one.

When the knocking became more insistent, Hugo scowled. "That sassenach dinna give up easy, to be sure."

"Papillone, I insist on speaking with you," came Vince's grimly determined voice.

Chantal took a deep breath and whispered, "Hugo, above all things you must remember this: If this man, who is one of the most influential lords in England, ever discovers that Tony is his, I will never see my son again. It is absolutely critical that he believe me to be a flighty dancer, your lover, and the lover of anyone else with enough blunt."

Hugo frowned. "But ye not be that way."

"I know. But for Tony's sake, I must pretend to be.

54

Never refer to me as Chantal, or to Tony. Call him Edward, by his middle name. You know what to call me.''

"Aye, Papi." They pronounced her name like the poppy flower. She'd acquired the nickname when Tony was a baby, because he'd been unable to pronounce her stage title.

Taking a deep breath, Chantal reclined on her divan and waved a languid white hand. "Let him in."

Hugo opened the door a crack. A walking stick wedged between door and jamb, prepared to pry if necessary. A gleeful grin stretching Hugo's somber face, he pushed on the door just hard enough to make Vince think he intended to close it. The stick began to move as Vince started to use it as a lever. Hugo whipped the door open, throwing Vince off balance. He staggered into the room in a most undignified manner, falling to one knee beside Chantal before he caught himself.

She covered a smile with her hand. "Ah, is this not what every woman wishes for—a handsome man at her feet?"

Color tinged Vince's high, impressive cheekbones, but he scarcely missed a beat. "Perhaps. But every man wishes to position himself a bit higher." He raked her from head to toe with a heated, proprietary gaze that she'd neither invited nor welcomed.

So why did her heart flutter in response? Chantal was thankful for the rouge. Scandalous women surely did not blush. She pretended to simper, as if flattered, while inwardly she was angry. He never used to speak to her like that. "And what did you think of my performance, sir?" She spoke slowly and carefully so that her accent was barely discernible.

"It was magnificent, as usual." Vince stayed where he was, on one knee, his head cocked to one side as he appraised her, as if wondering if she were performing now.

Sitting up, Chantal offered him her hand. "Get up, my lord. You do not look comfortable on your knees."

Indeed, he stood quickly, favoring one leg. "An old war wound bothers me from time to time." He eyed her curiously. "Now why did you go pale at that news?"

Thinking quickly, she cradled her stomach. "I am *fati* . . . famished, 'tis all."

"Now that I can fix." He offered his hand.

Since his gaze kept returning to her bodice, she rose, though she pretended not to see his courtly gesture. The less she touched him, the better. "You are very kind, my lord, but I . . . am already engaged for this evening."

A scowl marred that handsome face. "Then where is your suitor?" He checked his pocket watch. "He's very late, if he's taking you to supper."

"Actually, he is already here." Chantal smiled at Hugo, who gazed back in his stolid, loyal way. Sometimes she wanted to kick him, for he was as immovable and unchangeable as his precious Highlands. He hardly seemed passionately attached to her, and acting was beyond him.

Disbelieving, Vince glanced between the two of them. "You accept him over me?"

"A prior commitment. You understand." She edged toward the door. When her back was to Vince, she frantically signaled for Hugo to offer his arm.

He looked confused until she reached his side and

snatched his muscular forearm. He patted her hand, trying to look courtly, but only managing to seem awkward. "Ah, yes, lass, 'tis off we be."

A dragon-headed walking stick blocked the door. Curious, Chantal studied the design. She knew it must be a legacy from his grandfather, Drake, but she'd never seen it before. The thought that Vince truly needed the support was horrific, calling up ghastly images of death and dismemberment. But it seemed she could not avoid them; he walked with a noticeable limp as he hurried to stand in the doorway, leaning heavily on the stick.

He must have seen something in her face because his tone became harsh. "I am not the man I used to be. But neither are you the girl I once knew." His gaze slipped disparagingly over her revealing attire, but a spark glowed behind those blue eyes that made them luminous. A needy, quintessentially male spark that both warmed her with memories of the past and tempted her to forge new links in the present.

The denial was forced, but she managed it. "I do not know what you mean. We had never met before last night. Please, sir, I shall perish from hunger if I stand here another instant."

And, from Hugo, a blunter warning, "Move, ye dolt, or I'll move ye meself."

Finally, Vince moved, even going so far as to open the door for them. But when they started down the narrow, dim hall, he trailed them. Surely he did not intend to follow them all the way to the private room at their inn?

But it seemed he did, for he followed them around the manager's office and past the stage wings. At the exit door on the back alley, Chantal stopped. Damn him, she'd forgotten how persistent he could be. His behavior required stronger tactics than her gentle rebuttal. Turning to face him, she glued a remote, cool look to her face, praying that her seething emotions were hidden. "Sir, I do not wish your company. Do you need plainer talk than that?"

Nothing but careful consideration showed on his face as he searched her lavender eyes. He did not seem hurt or angry. Unfortunately he did not seem discouraged, either, an assumption proved by his easy, "No. Prove to me you are not Chantal and I *may* leave you be." *If I so choose.* The latter he did not add, but he did not need to.

Even Hugo caught the inference. His huge hands balled into fists.

Chantal was frantically perusing her lengthy list of well used rejections when distraction came from an unexpected source.

The manager rushed up, shouting as he came, "Hugo! We need your aid immediately. Our new set is about to fall. We need you to hold it up while we reattach it."

Hugo still glowered at Vince. Vince stared coolly back, but his grip tightened about the dragon head.

Bowing to the inevitable, Chantal released Hugo and gave him a small push. "Go on. You know no one else is strong enough. I shall be fine."

The manager tugged at Hugo's arm. Hugo took one step, and then paused to glare at the earl. "See ye bring her back safe and sound, properlike, or I'll come a callin'." And off he went, his giant strides making the manager run to keep up.

"Where did you find this . . . mountain of a man?"

Vince asked, staring after his adversary with combined fascination and disbelief. "Wit he may not have, but I should like to find him on my side in a battle."

A bit of her tension fled with a misty smile. "In the mountains. And, indeed, the man has not been born who is more loyal and true of heart than Hugo."

Jealousy darkened his eyes at her obvious admiration, but he leaped at the opportunity to press, "What were you doing in Scotland?"

The smile fled. "I lived there, for a time." She pursed her lips as she appraised him. "If I sup with you, will you agree to leave me be afterward?"

He toyed with the dragon head, his gaze locked on her sensual, expressive mouth. "If I sense that your rejection stems from lack of interest," he said at last. He tendered his arm. "But I am glad you accept the inevitable. You are saving us both a deal of trouble. As much as I enjoy your dancing, I should not wish to be here every night."

A wish she fervently shared. Her hand rested lightly on his forearm as he led her to his carriage. Her fingertips tingled, as if she'd touched fire. In a way, she had. For with every meeting with this lover from her past, she danced closer to the flame, just as the ballerina in the story had, ending in a brief, glorious conflagration.

Such would not be her fate. She was not a young girl now, enthralled with the fairy tale of her youth. Aye, he was a soldier, wounded in one leg just as the little tin soldier had been, and aye, she was a ballerina, but there the similarity ended. She had not heartlessly rejected him, not willingly, anyway, and she would not be destroyed by their relationship. She was through with love. There were only two males in her life now.

But the rogue thought came: *As much as I love them, neither of them make me feel like this. Alive, wanted, cherished.* She forced the feelings into abeyance only by visualizing Tony's face.

The resolve steeled her as the coach lurched into movement. It kept her strong under that steady blue gaze that tempted her to come closer to the flame. . . . Thus, when Vince tried to sit beside her, she slipped to the opposite seat, staving him off with a gay laugh. "La, these streets could do with some new cobblestones."

At that propitious moment, they lurched into a hole in the street. Chantal grabbed for the seat edge, missed, and would have fallen if Vince hadn't caught her. His arms were stronger than they used to be, she reflected vaguely as he drew her onto his lap. His legs, wounded or not, were more muscular, as she felt them flexing beneath her buttocks. And the hand that came up to tilt back her head was rougher, more capable—and more determined.

Mesmerized by forbidden sensations, Chantal went limp. It had been too long. For a moment, surely, she could pretend that ten years had not passed, that this was her young lover, who would never hurt her. . . . The touch of him, the familiar scent of clean male and starched linen, the feel of his hand on her cheek, his other burning through her dress, all made mock of such paltry things as duty and honor and chastity.

Thus, when he tilted her head to his lowering one, she stayed still, unable to move.

Not because he didn't allow it.

Because she didn't want to.

This kiss had no audience. And, oddly, it had no beginning, for it was a continuum to their youthful passion, beginning light and shy, as new and rapturous as that first kiss so long ago. Vince's mouth barely brushed hers, making her arch for deeper contact. In that moment, lost in the presence of her past, she did not realize how much more skillful was this lover. The eager boy had become a man, with a man's patience and control. She knew only that his lips tasted divine, so soft and tender, and that she wanted more.

And he gave it, when she buried her fingers in his thick hair to hold his head close. The contact deepened slowly, his lips rubbing against hers with wistful persuasion until, with a strangled sound, she opened her mouth and gave him entrance. Now a groan shook him, too. His lips hardened and his tongue darted out to tease the sides of her mouth. He sipped and glided like a hummingbird, tasting here, dabbling into her nectar there, but not giving her the demanding pressure she wanted.

Another jolt made them both bounce against the seat. He fell sideways, lying down on the plush squabs. For an instant those strong arms released her, giving her enough space for reason. She began to pull away, but then he hauled her head down to his and gave her what she wanted.

Passion bloomed, fulsome and heady, at the touch of his mouth. He slanted his lips over hers, pulling, nibbling, tempting her tongue into his mouth. When she boldly accepted the invitation, she found welcome, for he rose to greet her with tongue and manhood. The proof of his own hunger stabbing into her belly delighted her. Their tongues twisted and writhed, neither dominant, but tangling with a joyful abandon too long denied them.

Chantal felt a coolness at her bosom before she realized that he'd loosed the back laces of her dress. The scrap of a bodice fell forward, leaving her aching breasts almost spilling free of the thin batiste chemise. He pulled her up to ease aside this last barrier.

Stop. Must stop. But the warning was a still, small voice amidst the clarion call of desire. It had been ten years since a man had touched her so, too long, in truth. Yet it was this man, and only this man, who could make her vibrate like a bow to his violin. Thus, when the cool fabric was replaced by the warm glide of male hands, she was helpless to resist. He cupped her breasts in both hands, his breath catching in wonder at the lush bounty overflowing both palms. He stared, his eyes almost black in the dim glow of the carriage lantern, as if she were a dream come true or a fantasy realized.

"My God," he rasped, his voice as needy as the hands that traced her, from the full, firm sides to the flushed and puckered aureoles. "I have never seen such beautiful breasts," he managed before his voice was muffled against her flesh. He licked and nibbled around one globe, cupping the other in his palm. Her breasts trembled like ripe peaches in his hands as, helpless to stay the tide of passion, she arched into his mouth. At last he took her nipple, suckling with a desperate need both old and new that made her womb contract with a stronger pressure.

His hands gently pulled up the hem of her gown, feeling above her stocking for the silken warmth of her thigh. She felt the gentle pressure urging her legs apart even as he turned his famished attention to her other breast. She felt him pressing urgently against her, his own need pulsing and hard, desperate for relief.

She was wriggling her hips to help, too far gone now to care about what she jeopardized, when the carriage jolted again, this time rolling to a stop. It bounced as the coachman climbed down, and then there was the rattle of steps being pulled from the boot.

They both froze, their hearts thudding a wild denial. With a scramble of arms, legs and clothing, they sat upright. Shaking, Chantal pulled up her chemise, her skin firing to crimson as she watched him button the top two buttons of his trousers. She had been so far gone that she had not even realized he had begun to disrobe. The reality of what she had almost done slapped her in the face, jolting her to awareness.

"Wait, Henry," he said as the coachman touched the carriage door. He had to clear his voice of hoarseness as he said softly to her, "Turn around and I will lace your dress."

Dumbly, she did so, and, indeed, never had she felt more stupid. In another reality, she might have been glad at the way his fingers trembled against her skin as slowly, laboriously, he managed to lace her dress. At least this passion was not one-sided.

But it would never see fruition. From this night forward, she could never be alone with him. He was not to be trusted. She jerked her dress down as his gaze strayed to her slim legs. Lie to him, she might, but to herself, she couldn't. *She* was not to be trusted. Whatever had drawn them to each other as youths was not dormant, as she had thought. It was an active volcano, rumbling and wild beneath the surface. It would draw her down and drown her in a river of fire if she were not very, very careful.

Thus, when he tried to catch her chin and meet her eyes, she jerked away and shoved open the carriage door. She stepped down, as haughty as if she were not a dancer but a lady born. She read ribald interest beneath the coachman's wooden expression, but Vince scarcely gave his man a glance. His gaze was glued on that erect little back as he said, "Wait for us, Henry. We shouldn't be above a couple of hours."

"Very well, my lord." Henry leaned back against the carriage, insolently watching the sway of Chantal's hips as she stalked away. But neither she nor Vince saw the liberty.

Chantal was so humiliated that she was ensconced in a private parlor in a very expensive, very exclusive and very private little inn before she realized where she was. She passed a mirror, wincing at the image there, and whispered, "Please, my lord. Give me a moment to collect myself."

Vince snapped his mouth closed, nodded brusquely and exited.

Almost, she crumpled where she stood. Perhaps she could melt into a pool of wax and be remolded into the strong, moral woman she'd been two nights ago. But she forced herself to peer into the huge mirror hanging opposite the damask-covered table for two that was set with the finest china and silver. The woman who stared back at her bore no resemblance to the Chantal she'd struggled so hard to become.

Where was the strength? She looked wild, as if she'd fly apart at a touch. She laughed harshly. But for the carriage stopping when it had, her legs would be apart at this moment as she accepted the thrust of Vince's domination. Nay, reveled in it.

For dominate her he had. Not with rough hands or superior male strength, but with a gentle, teasing ardor that had built slowly to a furious need that nothing but coupling could assuage. This was not the same man who'd worshipped her as a youth. This man was harder, smarter and stronger. He didn't need to use force, because his gentle strength was far more formidable. . . .

And he would be the end of all she'd worked for, stealing what remained of her good name, her freedom and her son, if she did not find a way to send him about his business. Chantal glared at her flushed face, the smeared rouge and throbbing pulse in her throat, and hated herself. She yanked a napkin off the table, dipped it in the crystal water goblet and scrubbed furiously at the paint. Then she wetted it again and scoured her face, shoulders and cleavage, as if she could wash away his touch, but she knew the memory would linger as long as she lived. The icy water quelled the last of the heated passion, at least. She tossed the napkin aside, pulled down her straggling hair and began to braid it.

Meanwhile, she glared at herself in the mirror with one minatory eye, lecturing herself in French. "Idiot! Send him away. It is your only chance." And *bon chance*, indeed, for it would take better luck than she'd had thus far to make him believe she had a distaste for him, especially after that interlude in his carriage.

Somehow, she would manage. She had to. For Tony's sake. For Tony's sake. She kept repeating the words to herself like a litany and, by the time Vince came back in, they'd given her strength enough to meet his searching gaze without flinching.

His lips twisted as he appraised her freshly scrubbed face and the tight braids piled atop her head. The sight of her own lip rouge upon his beautiful mouth almost undid her hard-won composure, but she looked away and sipped her water.

He went to the mirror, arched an eyebrow at his image, brushed his fingers through his hair, managing to make the curly locks even more of a seductive mop, and came back to sit opposite her. He was silent, his gaze upon her like a caress, until her defiant eyes finally met his. "Unlike you, I do not attempt to wipe away our kiss. It is a badge of honor I shall wear proudly." When she swallowed, his voice softened as he watched her throat move. "Until we share another. Which will be soon, I hope—"

"Never." The denial was a flat intonation, all the more determined for its lack of passion.

He paused in the act of lifting the wine bottle, but only for an instant. He appraised the label, nodded his approval at the vintage and pulled out the already loose cork. "I see. Another change of heart. But forgive me if I am a bit confused. Who am I to believe—the accomplished actress who disavows any interest in me or the woman who ignites in passion at my touch?"

Chantal willed away the blush. "You are a . . . virile man, *m'sieur*. And I have ever a weakness for men who know how to be men. Even if I do not find them, ah, intellectually stimulating."

Vince almost choked on his first sip of wine. "You tell me that you'd be glad to take me to bed, but you find me boring? Doing it a bit too brown, my dear." He set the wineglass down with an audible thump. "Then explain this—if you have a distaste for me, and

66

we have never met until recently, why did you react to me in the carriage as only one woman ever has?'' He hesitated, and then leaned across the small table until he could almost touch her. ''As the only woman who's ever loved me reacted. You have her eyes, her voice, her hair, her face, her . . .'' His gaze dropped to her bosom. ''Her legs. You dance even more gracefully, but I would expect that, since you are so much more experienced. But tonight told the tale, my dear. A woman can fake many things, but not the passion we shared. It went beyond the physical, and well you know it.''

Chantal accepted the wineglass he offered, taking a sip to give herself time to think. She had only one defense, but it was the only one that might disgust him. Weak armor was better than none. She made her smile avaricious as she eyed the yellow rose diamond stickpin glittering at his mussed cravat, and the emerald signet on his finger. ''You have charms aplenty, my lord. Upon closer, ah, contact, they are easy to appreciate. Especially the size of your . . . assets.'' She let her gaze flicker below the table before she looked back at him.

He stared at her, trying to delve deep into her soul, but somehow she kept her own gaze steady, artfully flirting with him. She heard his breath catch in disbelief; then his lashes lowered, but not before she caught the flash of disappointment. Still, his hand was steady as he reached into his inner pocket and removed a small box. He opened it and thrust it across the table under her nose. Even in the romantic lighting, the diamond earbobs glittered, dancing with fire as he turned the box this way and that. They were the size and shape of almonds, set in a plain gold chain-and-link design that set them off beautifully.

Colleen Shannon

Her dazed eyes lifted from the diamonds, but his own gaze was too busy wandering over her possessively to meet hers. His words both thrilled her and chilled her to the marrow. "Very well, my avaricious little ballerina. If I have so many . . . attributes you appreciate, then you should have no objection to accepting my offer of protection. For the nonce, it matters little if you are my childhood love. I want you, you want me. We are both adults. That will be enough for a beginning."

Hoisted by her own petard.

Fallen upon her own sword.

And what was that other amusing English saying? Something about a goose and a gander. The inane thoughts flickered through Chantal's head as the minutes ticked by.

That was it.

Her goose was cooked. . . .

Chapter Three

Vince wanted to kiss that flirty little smile away from her lips. He continued to turn the diamonds from side to side. Was she as flirtatious and vital as a skittish filly, or did she deny him like a calculated wanton to make him pant for more? He truly did not know. And the throbbing, needful ache in his groin informed him most adamantly that, at this point, her reasons, or even her morals, mattered naught. All that mattered was getting her into his bed. There, his long-lost love would have no clothes to wear and no artifice behind which to hide. No mask or pretense could ever survive the earth-shattering pleasure they alone could create. Tonight, in the carriage, they'd tasted a sip, but passion, like fine wine, was all the better for the waiting.

That passion would be even more delicious now he knew what to do with it.

Still, she stayed silent, but when he set down the box,

withdrew one earbob and knelt beside her chair to attach it to her ear, she caught his wrist and slithered from the opposite side of her chair in a supple movement that only a dancer could make. She shook her head at him gently. "I did not accept."

He rose slowly. "You will." He rounded the chair with soft, determined steps.

For an instant, wild fear flared at him, but her long, dark lashes shielded her eyes, and when she looked up, they were as brilliant—and as hard—as amethysts. "I will not. A ballerina I may be, with little money and less reputation, but my favors are still mine to give. And I say no. Now, do we eat, or do you wish to carry me straight home?"

She wandered to the dishes steaming at the sideboard, lifted one of the heavy silver lids and sniffed. "Hmm, Yorkshire pudding. It has been an age since I sampled it. Do you mind?"

Dumbfounded, Vince watched her load a plate with the pudding, steamed green beans, duchesse potatoes and fresh fruit. No other female of his acquaintance, either lady or ladybird, could so casually reject a king's ransom in jewels, and his person, with such insouciance, and then sit down to sup. Why, half the courtesans in London curried his favor. He'd had more than one duke's mistress bat her eyes at him. But this little ballerina, who looked as delicate and flighty as the fairy she resembled, had a hidden will as steely as his own.

Chantal had never been like this. Where he had led, she followed. Well, most of the time . . . He squelched the thought, snapping the box closed on the earbobs. Could it be that Papillone's protestations were true?

Maybe she merely greatly resembled his lost love. Regardless, why would a woman who made her living using her body reject him so out of hand, when she obviously wanted him, and wanted what he could give her? There was a mystery here. One that begged for solving.

She arched a dark brow at him and delicately wiped her mouth. "Excuse my hastiness, but I warned you I was hungry."

Finally, with a firming of his mouth and his own formidable will, he filled a plate and sat down opposite her. "So am I." But not for food. Mesmerized, he watched her beautiful mouth chew.

She pretended not to notice. "Tell me, sir, how is it that a man who professes belief in class equality, a man who lives an exemplary life, would wish to keep a scandalous dancer as a mistress? Does that not open you to political attacks from your opponents?"

His fork paused halfway to his mouth. Slowly, he set it down on his plate. "How is it that a dancer from the Continent, who claims to have no interest in me, knows so much of me and my reputation?"

Long black lashes lowered again. White little teeth nibbled at her lip before she shrugged in a very expressive French way that reminded him poignantly of Chantal. "I read the newspapers, like everyone else. You are quite a celebrity."

"And so are you. As you are doubtless well aware."

"If I am, you made me so." Their sparring might have lacked rapiers, but it was no less dangerous—or pointed. Hearts could be damaged.

Again.

He parried. "If I did, you incited it. And tell me, my dear, how is it that a flighty dancer is interested in politics?"

A flush tinged her high, lovely cheekbones, but she studied her empty plate as if fascinated by the porcelain. He could not tell if she was angry or embarrassed.

Finally she riposted, "I may lack an Oxford education, but I can think as clearly as the next woman. My country almost destroyed itself over this issue of class equality. I should not like to see it happen here."

"Why?" And he went for the coup de grâce. "Could it be that you feel a certain loyalty to your adopted country?"

He had to admire her aplomb; even backed into a corner, she refused to concede.

"Sympathy, yes," she responded softly. And then, with a conversational rebound that made him back off, she added, "But most of my memories of your country are not happy ones. Loyalty? *Mon dieu, non.*" And she rose to collect her tiny purse, as if she had declared herself the victor in their sparring match.

That desolate flash of memory in her eyes made him rein in his urge to probe further. However, it also made him more determined to get at the truth—one day soon, after he'd made her admit that she cared for him.

On the way back to town, he moved to sit beside her. This time, when he took her hand, she did not struggle. Her hand lay limp in his. And when he tried to engage her in conversation, he found her equally exasperating. Her body, with all its tantalizing curves, was here, but her spirit? It was far, far away from him and his petty desires. Or so she made him feel, this ballerina who led him such a merry dance.

By the time they arrived at her modest inn, he was fuming. No woman, indeed, no man of his acquaintance, had ever made him feel so inconsequential. How dare she lead him on in that carriage ride out, then treat him to this fit of the sullens as they rode back in? Did she expect to leave him panting for more and then just skip away? Apparently she did, for when he helped her down, shooing his coachman away, and caught her shoulders in his hands, she forestalled his invitation.

A soft, warm index finger covered his mouth. "Please, sir. Do not say it. We do not suit. And we have no future together, you and I. I shall be gone from England as soon as my performances end."

A chill crept over him at the thought. He could not lose her again. Nay, no matter if she were Chantal or not. He wanted her. He would have her. And he would keep her. However, as he had learned in the Lords, the direct approach was seldom the best one with an opponent. And he was dimly realizing that he faced an opponent more wily and invincible than any man who'd ever challenged him. In fact, her logical approach to conflict reminded him of someone, but he could not quite put his finger on whom.

Again, his gut warred with his head. Instinctively, he recognized the feel of her, the smell of her, the look of her. Yet his head complained that Chantal had not been so . . . indomitable. He glanced down. Nor so well built. His softening erection stood to attention again. Since he had little choice but to let her go, for the nonce, anyway, he released her.

"I will think on it, my dear." *You do not know how hard, nor how often.* He opened the door for her into the inn, adding lightly, "You may decide to stay, even after your performances end, though based on the nightly attendance, that shall not be any time soon."

She gave him a formal smile that put him even further at a distance. "Good-bye, my lord. I . . . wish you well." And, with an odd little sound in her throat, she flew up the stairs, rounded the corner and disappeared.

Just like Chantal. It took all his control to stand there and let her flee, but she was like the will-o-the-wisp she resembled: the harder he clutched her, the more she slipped away. Grimly, he retraced his steps, too involved in his thoughts to note the coachman's smirk as his servant held the carriage door open.

Desperation clutched him about the throat. If he lost her again, he would go mad. He had to know who she was, what motivated her, why she was running so scared. For frightened she was, and that thought was so insupportable to him that he literally felt nauseated. What had he done to put such terror in her eyes?

Using the head of his cane, Vince knocked on the carriage roof. When his coachman picked up the listening horn linking the driver's seat to the interior, Vince barked, "Take me direct to the Bow Street Runners." He glanced at his pocket watch. Almost one in the morning. Damn. But his inherent courtesy warred with deeper, truer feelings; the victor was one of which his grandfather would have approved. "I shall make it worth their while." Then, feeling only slightly better, Vince leaned back.

The gold dragon leered at him from the head of the cane. Vince used his sleeve to polish that grin and muttered, "Aye, no doubt Grandfather, roistering pirate that he was, would be ashamed of his descendant. I regret my namby-pamby actions, my dear revered ancestor, but I must suit my reactions to her actions or I shall lose her.'' Drake Kimball, the founder of their family dynasty, had swept his own heart's desire away to his lair, loving her and wooing her until she grew to care for him.

Heartily, Vince wished he had the same leeway. He was tempted, mightily tempted, but he had too much to consider.

Honor was not an idle word to him. And deep inside he knew that it was important to this ballerina, as well. In whatever guise she wore.

Thankful Vince couldn't see her as she really was— weak and needy—Chantal buried her head in her pillow to muffle the sobs so she wouldn't wake Tony. Their suite of four rooms was small but all they could afford, even adding Hugo's pittance of a salary to hers. Tony slept on the couch in the tiny anteroom near the kitchen, Hugo in the other bedroom. His looming presence had both quieted gossip and incited it, but tonight, along with her false rejection, mayhap it had helped to deter Vince.

Vince . . . Tears broke again, as hot and new as they had been those many years ago. Now that she had once more lost the only man she could ever love, the memories she'd successfully stifled rose up like wraiths of regret. They would haunt her until she exorcised them. And so, alone in the dark, aching for what was and what could not be, Chantal remembered. . . .

That year of our Lord 1815 saw the return of the spectre all Europe dreaded—Napoleon. Even now, this

April, he had reached Paris and was amassing his troops for one last attempt at glory.

And how many glorious young lives would he destroy in the process?

But on that unusually warm April day, Chantal was not thinking of war as she stared out the window of her small cottage at the lake where the black swans glided. She was, as usual in her seventeen-year-old passion, thinking only of Vince. Vince who, along with every other able-bodied young Englishman, rich or poor, was determined to join Wellington and repel, for good and all, this French upstart.

Annette rapped her daughter on the knuckles with her knitting needles. Dreaming, Chantal was too slow in helping Annette wind the wool for the sweater she was knitting for Vince. When Chantal looked at her, Annette squinted her eyes. *"Petite,* if I look very closely, I can sometimes glimpse that head of yours."

Chantal blinked, her lavender-gray eyes focusing on her mother. "What do you mean, *Maman?"* Quickly, she held her hands up so her mother could continue looping the wool.

"It is too far up in the clouds." Annette calmly continued her winding. "Vince may love you now, my child, but no good will come of your relationship, as I have told you times without number. He will be an important man someday. Adeline will never let him wed you, even when he reaches his majority in May."

"This comes from one who knows, *oui?"* Bitterly, Chantal pulled away as soon as the soft thread was curled neatly in a ball.

Sadly, her mother stared out at the swans. *"Oui.* This

is not the life I wanted for my daughter, who has the blood of kings in her veins, but nothing can change the facts: We are poor relations dependent upon charity. Driven from France by that monster, our loved ones beheaded, little more welcome in England than we were in France. And . . .''

''. . . I am illegitimate. Why will you not tell me who my father is?''

Pain wrinkled Annette's still beautiful face. Her eyes were blue, but it was obvious where Chantal came by her porcelain skin and coal black hair. She tossed her needles aside and stood to grip the curtains so hard that the white lace wrinkled in her hands. ''He, too, is an important man. Now, though he was not then. He is married, my child. Of what use would it be to stir up scandal?''

Chantal bit back the hasty words of youth, for her mother and Vince were all she had. ''Never mind, *Maman*. I . . . want to pick some berries. I shall be back before dark.'' Over her mother's protests, Chantal paused only to grab a bucket. Then she was gone, her feet winged and her spirit soaring high. She'd seen Vince ride by a few minutes earlier, and she knew where he was headed.

He'd been avoiding her of late. He'd told her it was best they not see one another much until they could wed. Next month, when he was twenty-one, he would marry her, then go off to join his regiment.

For once, Chantal agreed with Vince's mother. Vince was too young to go off to war. He was the last direct heir to the earldom of Dunhaven, and his life was too valuable to risk. However, unlike Adeline, Chantal understood why Vince felt that he had to go.

It was the same reason he refused to make love to her.

His cursed honor.

She reached the sheltered cove in time to see him rigging the little sloop for a sail. "Vince! Please, wait." Chantal kicked off her slippers and ran through the sand after him, her firm young calves flirting with the ragged hem of her old dress. She glanced at the greenish horizon. It was only three hours until dark, but she'd lived by the sea all her life. She knew when a storm approached.

He waved at her from his bobbing boat. "I'm not going far out. I shall be back soon!" And he returned to his rigging.

Putting her hands on her hips, Chantal glared at him. Since she'd ended her last dance in his arms, and they'd shared the kiss that rocked the earth under their feet, he'd let his prudish reserve interfere with their relationship. Honor, pah! If they loved each other, what matter that they were not yet wed? He would be of age soon.

She dug her pretty toes in the sand, debating, but then a totally feminine, totally French smile crossed her lips. After all, had he not promised her, on the day he gave her that lovely little tale about the Steadfast Tin Soldier and his ballerina, that they, too, were destined to spend eternity together? But no fire and doom for them; they would be happy.

And, in the absolute certainty of youth, she believed him, for, quite simply, she believed *in* him. He was not like her mysterious father, who had sired her, then deserted her mother. Vince was the playmate of her childhood, the hero of her youth, and now, her first, last and only love. She would trust him with her life.

And so, following her heart as she always did, she dived into the chilly April waves and rode them to her destiny. Vince saw her coming. He scowled, but his strong hands were still gentle as he pulled her over the side into the boat.

"Do you never stop to think? You could have drowned. Or you could catch your death of . . ." He trailed off with a gasp as he looked down at the gown plastered to her lithe young form. Averting his eyes, he pulled off his jacket and wrapped her up in it. "Chantal, I told you it is best we do not see much of one another until I get my mother's permission to marry you."

She snapped her fingers. "*That* for your mother's permission. When you join your regiment, Vince, I want to go with you. And I cannot follow the drum unless we are wed." She smiled wickedly. "Unless you want to cause a scandal. To me, it makes no difference."

His blue eyes turned as dark and stormy as the skies roiling over their heads. "I will not have you dishonored so. Do not speak like that again. I merely wish to try to please my mother first. I owe her that, in memory of my father. If she forbids our marriage . . . well, soon she cannot stop us. We must be patient."

Patient? Chantal's body throbbed with joy and passion, and misery when he was gone. He was the tempo, she, the melody; without him, there would be no music. And music was her life. "Can I not sail with you, this one last time? *S'il vous plait.* Then I shall be good. I promise."

His gaze drifted downward to the shapely young thighs his coat could not hide. A flush tinging his handsome cheekbones, he turned away with a curt nod.

Happy now, she helped him finish rigging the sails as she had done many times before. Soon they were soaring like gulls on a breeze that lofted them above the toils and tribulations awaiting them back on earth.

Here, with only the salt smell and the darkening sky and the smarting wind, her feelings made them one with the elements. Here, she could forget the murky smoke drifting in the back of her mind, the visions of exploding cannons and torn, bleeding flesh. Within the week after Napoleon escaped from Elba, Vince had purchased his colors, also against his mother's will, through his guardian. After May, when he attained his majority, he would leave to join his regiment. She intended to go with him, whether it was allowed or not, whether he forbade it or not.

She tried to tell herself that her fears were for naught, that Napoleon would be safely caught before he could persecute her family or her adopted country again, but her dreams were becoming more and more violent. And her fears sometimes choked her, even in the middle of the night. What if Vince really didn't love her as she loved him? He never introduced her to his friends. Maybe he was ashamed of her.

Only when she was with Vince could her nerves rest, and her heart know peace. And so, as she helped him with the jib and rudder as she had done countless times before, she was content in the moment. When they'd found a safe course through the breeze that didn't make them yaw too much, she asked, "When do you get your uniforms?"

"They are being made now."

"Does your mother know?"

"Yes."

Such tension in the single word. Chantal knew that Vince's relationship with his mother was difficult—and not just because of Vince's decision to buy his colors—but she also understood the deep love between them. If only things were different. If only she knew who her father was. . . .

"Chantal! Help me steer her in before the wind blows us out to sea!"

Vince's urgent tone finally penetrated her absorption. She looked up to see a great black cloud billowing down upon them like a giant sail. She helped Vince lash down most of the rigging. Still, for every foot they advanced to shore, the wind drove them back six inches. Lightning forked into the bloated black skies, dumping rain down upon them in sheets, until they could scarcely see the shore.

Finally, Chantal tossed off Vince's heavy jacket, picked up an oar and began paddling.

Vince's white teeth flashed. "That's my girl." He took the other oar, stroking as best he could while still guiding the rudder. When they at last bumped against the shore, Vince leaped over the side to tie them up and came back, holding his arms out for Chantal.

"Bah! What difference does it make? I am already soaked." And she jumped down next to him, caught his hand and walked with him through the waist-high water to the rocky beach. Sheltering under a large tree, they paused to look around and get their bearings. Chantal didn't recognize anything, but Vince did.

"It's old Boskie's place. There's a deserted hut up that path, unless it's been torn down!" He had to shout for her to hear him above the roaring waves and howling winds. "Come on!"

He tugged her up the path she could barely see, over the lip of the rise next to the beach, and into a ramshackle structure that looked as if it would barely sustain the storm. It leaked in numerous spots, but some wayfarer had recently occupied the place. The rush bedding smelled clean, and dry kindling still clustered in the firepit. But there was no flint.

Chantal shivered, rubbing her arms, for now she was freezing. Automatically, Vince started to put his jacket on her, watched water drip down his arm and tossed it aside in disgust. He investigated the shadowy corners of the hut by feel, triumphantly holding up an old fashioned tinderbox.

His fingers were shaking, too, so it took several tries, but he soon had a piece of rush caught, and then a twig. Chantal dropped to her knees beside the fire and held out her hands. It was soon a blaze. But she could not stop shivering.

Vince held up a tattered blanket. "I think a horse wore it, but it's all I can find."

Chantal sniffed it and wrinkled her nose. "I do not care for it. I shall dry, in time."

Studiously, Vince averted his gaze. As the fire crackled gleefully, casting a joyous blaze of light over her soaked form, he finally growled, "Then have a care for me. I am human, after all, and I love you."

After such a declaration, what could a girl do? Chantal was all too human also, and she loved this honorable young man with every wet pore of her body. She was so afraid of losing him to the war, as she had lost her home in France and the father she never knew. Chantal scooted next to him and raised her arms. "Then warm me, *cheri*. As God intended you should." And she caught his shocked face in her hands and kissed him.

For all of two seconds he resisted, but then, with a harsh groan, he showed her with lips and hands what he had been dreaming of. In that moment, the inseparable childhood companions made that last giant leap to adulthood with consummate ease. The affinity they'd always shared in tastes, values and goals was forged into a steely bond by this fusing of body and soul. Chantal had not understood it then.

But now, staring into the darkness, the adult knew why, over a gap of ten years of pain and loneliness, they'd never forgotten each other. They had been fated to be lovers, living examples of the little ballerina and the tin soldier. And, Chantal reflected sadly, holding her pillow close as she longed to hold Vince, they had also been fated to be separated by fire and tragedy.

She caught her breath between sobs, telling herself that this maudlin recollection only made the pain more intense, but once begun, the memories were tidal forces that swept all before them.

The blazing fire had been cool compared to their youthful desires. Vince's hands had shaken so badly that it was she, not he, who had removed her own clothes. And when she was naked, she stood straight and fit as only a dancer could, unashamed by the famished sweep of his gaze. When he stood to cradle her firm young breasts in his hands, she blushed but still leaned into him so he could know the heart-pounding he inspired.

"Chantal," he whispered. "My little love. My only love. Are you sure this is what you want?"

She stood on tiptoe to follow the rim of his ear with her tongue before she whispered back, "It is the only thing of value I have. Gladly I give it to you—''

And with a choked sound of need, he'd taken her gift, and all else she had to offer. Tenderly he laid her on the reeds, kissing his way from her ankles to her nape. She kneaded his shoulders with her hands, trying to pull him up, but even at twenty, Vince was a patient man. He held her wrists above her head and scraped his firm young chest against her nipples. When she gasped, he caught the sound with his lips, kissing her as he'd never kissed her before.

Deeply. With tongue and teeth and the need of a man. And she answered the only way she knew how: with the need of a woman. By the time he parted her legs with his knee and let her know him that first little bit, she was past fear. She cradled him between her legs, accepting the painful thrust as his right and her due, for only when that bit of flesh was broken could they each revel in this last, best intimacy.

At first the stabbing pain made her tense. It soon faded, replaced with the incredible sensation of feeling Vince deep inside her body. And even when, at the grand old age of twenty, he could not wait as patiently as she would have liked, she was so wrought by the wonder of the way they fit together that his own fulfillment brought tears to her eyes.

Vince collapsed atop her, his chest heaving. "Chantal," he whispered with an aching tenderness that echoed in her ears like yesterday instead of a decade ago.

"Vince," she cried back, stifling the sound of her own need with her hand. Had she known on that first blissful day what would come of that youthful passion, would she have been strong enough to deny them both? *Non.*

"*Non . . .* " she'd complained when he'd tried to move away. "You are not finished, *cheri.*"

Even as he tensed within the soft clasp of her body, he still refused to meet her eyes. "I . . . have dishonored you. Please, let's go home. We can wed tomor—"

"As we have planned in six weeks' time. We but anticipate the day a bit. Now, my fine young soldier, be strong. Show me what you so enjoyed." And she'd instinctively moved against him in a way as old as time, a way that she had not been taught but a skill she apparently possessed along with her fine bones and strong will.

Her indomitable soldier could not resist her long. And the next time, and the one after that, was pleasurable for them both. A pleasure that only grew better with the practice. And practice they did, in trysts at their fishing hole by the stream, in the meadow under the drooping embrace of a willow and, once, in the vast, remote ballroom at his estate where she'd always danced for him, that time all the more moving for its danger. Up to the day of his birthday they practiced.

Then, a day before they were to marry, two things happened that forever changed their lives. Her monthly flow was late, and her mother disappeared. Chantal had been so involved in her own new experiences that she'd thought little of the new flush in her mother's cheeks and the glow in her eyes. Her mother, too, had been gone a lot in the past month, but the one time Chantal asked her where she was going, Annette had laughed and kissed her on the cheek.

"I may be old, *petite*, but I am not dead. I, too, know what it is to love and be loved." She drew back to look at her daughter with wise and loving eyes. "Are you sure you are doing the right thing?"

Chantal loved her mother too much to pretend ignorance. "I love him, *Maman*. He leaves soon. I . . . could not lose him before I knew him. Whether we wed or no, I have followed my heart, and I am not ashamed."

They had shared hunger and poverty together. They had run from Napoleon's blood hounds, stowing away on a smuggler's ship. They knew the dangers of life and the follies of not living it to the fullest. And so Annette hugged her daughter again. "You will make a beautiful bride. I shall be back before the wedding. With a surprise for you."

Chantal followed her mother outside to the little carriage Vince had given them for their use. Chantal frowned as she watched her mother pull a carriage robe over her lap, hiding the old dueling pistol they'd brought with them from France. "*Maman,* what do you fear?"

"La, *petite*, the road to London is long and dangerous. I am but taking precautions." She lifted the reins in her gloved hands, pausing to wink at her daughter. "Behave. Do not do anything I would not do."

Laughing, Chantal nodded and waved her mother away.

It would be the last time she saw her alive.

Chantal was dressing in the gorgeous wedding gown Vince had purchased for her, wondering yet again why her mother had not yet returned, when Vince knocked on her cottage door. She opened it, the gown half on, half off her shoulders, and smiled joyously. "You have *Maman* with . . ."

Her voice trailed off when she saw the magistrate

behind him, his expression grim, his hat in his hands.
Vince entered the cottage and shut the door with his
boot. He looked resplendent in his red uniform, with the
gold epaulets on his double-breasted jacket and the
stripes down the form-fitting white pantaloons. He
caught her in his arms to cradle her as he gave her the
news.

"Darling, I ... well ..." He cleared his throat and
said rapidly, "Annette is gone."

"*Oui,* I know, but she promised she would return by
now. ..." Her voice trailed off because the look in
Vince's eyes told her what he really meant. Her hand
went to her throat. "*Non!*"

Gently, Vince explained the gruesome truth: Annette
had been found lying next to the overturned carriage,
her throat slit.

Chantal collapsed in his arms, barely aware when he
carried her to a chair and sat down with her on his lap.
When her sobbing eased to little gasps, he said gravely,
"Darling, I know this isn't a good time, but if we're to
find out who did this, we must work fast. Do you have
any idea where she'd been?"

"L-London. I-I think she might have gone to s-see
my father."

Vince lifted her chin to look at her intently. "And
she never said who he was?"

"N-no. But she seemed happier. I think she planned
to bring him to our w-wedding."

"Well, obviously we'll have to delay that until after
the funeral. We shouldn't wait any longer than that. I
want to do the right thing by you before I go away."

The time passed in a haze for Chantal. Vince was
away, making arrangements and trying to assist the

magistrate, but they could find no witnesses and no other clues. Whoever had killed Annette had picked his moment well.

And so, when her menses were late, at first Chantal assumed her emotional state had caused it. But by the time Annette was buried behind the cottage and their wedding was rearranged, Chantal was beginning to suspect the truth. Two days before Vince was due to leave for the continent, and one day before the wedding, Adeline called Chantal to her private salon.

Chantal had never liked Adeline, though in her private thoughts, she'd considered her future mother-in-law well named: Adeline the Chatelaine. The little woman was a martinet, all the more snobbish for the fact that her own grandfather had been a tradesman. Vince's mother had never hidden her disapproval of her son's choice of bride, but Vince had assured Chantal that his mother would come around.

A grossly mistaken assumption, as Chantal learned all too vividly that fateful day while Vince was in town at the magistrate's. Adeline rose to greet her, all that was polite. After she'd commiserated with Chantal over the loss of her mother, offered her tea and seated her comfortably with a wrap about her legs, she sat down in her own proper, uncomfortable chair. Her throne, more like. But Chantal had squelched the unkind thought.

Her blue eyes were more pale than Vince's, but equally astute. "Child, we need to have a talk before— well, before tomorrow. Tell me, do you believe Vince suited for politics?"

With an effort, Chantal squelched the urge to slurp her tea, just to live up to Adeline's poor opinion of her.

Instead, for Vince's sake, Chantal took one dainty sip and set her cup carefully in her saucer, putting both on the table beside her. "Yes, ma'am. Very much so. With his leadership abilities, he can do much for England."

"Yes. With the right connections."

The meaning was clear, but Chantal pretended obtuseness. "Yes, I am sure you know many influential people."

"Indeed. And they tend to be rather conservative in their notions." Adeline set down her own cup with a distinctive click. "Tell me, my dear, do you think they will invite a dancer into their homes? Or welcome the children of . . . an unsanctified mother?"

Chantal clenched her fists, but hid them in her gown. "You mean as a by-blow, I have no right to expect my children to enjoy such rarefied company."

Annette had the grace to look away from Chantal's obvious pain. "I did not set the rules, child. We can both but try to abide by them." She leaned forward to take Chantal's clenched hands. "Tell me, Chantal, do you truly love my son?"

More than my life. But she said dully, "Yes, madame."

"Then do right by him. Go, now, before he returns. He needs no distractions as he goes off on this confounded quest to stop Boney. I opposed it, but he's determined to go, and all I can hope for is to do what little I can to keep him safe. Do you not wish to do the same?"

"Of course." Adeline did not know that Chantal had planned to follow Vince. This was indeed a problem she'd not considered. If she were so close to the battleground, Vince would be thinking of her, not of his own safety. And even if she were safe in England, he'd be wondering how she was, if Adeline was supporting her, when he would see her again. However, if she disappeared, would not Vince be even more concerned about her whereabouts?

Chantal cradled her forehead in her palm, her head swirling. She was so tired, so confused, and the morning nausea was getting worse. Even without her mother to verify her condition, Chantal was almost certain she was pregnant. Now she had more than Vince to consider, though she did agree that he would be finished politically after their marriage. Those who led England needed to be above reproach, or at least not blatantly immoral. And she must be close to six weeks along, compounding the stigma of her own illegitimacy.

Why had she not seen this before?

Because she had been thinking with her heart and her body, not her head. Chantal rose, catching the chair arm to steady herself, and went to the window to stare at the vast promenade sweeping into the distance. The carpet on which she stood had been made in Belgium, and it was so thick her feet sank into it. The chandelier above her head was Austrian, the tea service Sevres.

The artificial lake with the little folly beside it was the crowning jewel of this luxurious setting. She'd seldom entered this mansion, not because Vince didn't want her here, but because she'd never felt comfortable. She knew nothing about running a house of this size, and Adeline would not be a willing tutor. Even worse, over time Vince would grow to resent his scandalous bride and her ineptitude.

Dropping one hand to her abdomen, Chantal closed her eyes to stem the tears. Most decisive of all, this innocent little life should not be punished for her sins. Chantal could not remember a time when she had not been lonely, whispered about, shunned for a background she could not help. True, if she stayed, the child would have a name, and if she left, he would not.

But at what cost? Chantal opened her eyes to see the black swans seemingly split in two by the haze of her tears, as if in sympathy with her grief. At least alone she could give the child love, as her own mother had raised her. She could concoct a husband who had died in the war, and, in a way it would be true. Far better to raise a child in humble, happy surroundings than in a cold fishbowl where everyone stared with disapproval. Chantal did not want this woman to help raise the boy. And a boy it would be, she told herself fiercely. A little boy who looked like Vince.

Adeline put a gentle hand on Chantal's shoulder. ''It pains me to have to say this, truly it does, but we must both think of Vince. You need not, of course, fear being destitute.''

''How much?'' Chantal dashed her eyes on her sleeve and turned to stare at Adeline, flinging off her hand.

Adeline took a step back. ''Why, ah, how does a thousand pounds sound?''

It sounded like a fortune, but Chantal knew she could get much more. However, had it not been for the child, she would have rammed the offer back in Adeline's teeth. It was all she could do to nod. And so it was that, before the noon sun peeked above the trees, Chantal was on the road in the carriage Adeline had hired for her. When the coachman asked where she wished to go, she merely told him, ''North.''

And north they kept going until Chantal discharged him and booked herself passage to Scotland in a public coach. She did not want the coachman, or anyone else, to know her destination, because she knew Vince would look. For a day, which was all he had before he left.

Those weary, jouncing miles were the most miserable of Chantal's life. Many times, she wondered if she'd done the right thing, but Adeline's words kept time with the iron wheels on the rutted roads. ''Think of Vince. . . . Think of Vince. . . .''

He'd forget her. He'd return safe from battle and wed some proper English girl who would be an asset to him, not a hindrance. The lecture could not stem the flow of tears. Her mourning garb had been her only shield, but even the heavy veil could not hide her grief, or her nausea. When they finally stopped in the Highlands, Chantal decided she'd gone far enough.

Vince would never look for her here. He'd assume she'd returned to the Continent. She rented a hut and was befriended by a crofter's middle son, a hulking but decent young man by the name of Hugo. And Hugo had literally been her savior. Without his assistance at Tony's birth, she would have died.

Her money lasted until Tony was seven. And when she had to find a way to feed them, it was good, and natural, that she took up her dancing again. Only when her feet had wings could she fly above her painful memories. She occasionally read in the newspapers about Vince's victories in the Lords, but she had been surprised that he never married. And when her skills took her beyond Edinburgh, she danced on the Continent. By the time she won the coveted prima ballerina position, she had to follow the troupe to England or accept a lesser role with a different company. She'd heard that Vince never attended the ballet, so she'd taken the risk.

Now, at the advanced age of twenty-seven, Chantal reflected sadly how little changed she truly was. She still soaked her pillow at night, dreaming of a man who'd long since forgotten her. Or so she'd thought, until a few days ago.

Could it be that Vince would never forget her either? Again, Chantal recalled the fairy tale, and how the steadfast little soldier had chased his ballerina through deluge and fire and tragedy, until they were at last united when it was too late for both of them.

Chantal punched the pillow, trying to get the foolish thoughts out of her head. If she'd known all those years ago what she knew now, would she still have left? She thought of Tony, of his lively curiosity and his love of practical jokes. Why, being groomed as the heir to the vast Kimball empire would stifle him. He was meant to run joyfully through life on his own path, not toe the mark and set an example for the generations after him.

No, for Tony's sake, she'd done the right thing. Vince merely wanted Papillone sexually. That was all.

Well, he could not have her. He'd taken her youth; well, perhaps she'd given it to him, but still, she could not risk giving more. She'd made the right choice, ten years ago and today.

They were not fated to live happily ever after. That sweet summer of her youth would have to last her a lifetime.

But when, near dawn, Chantal finally slept, she dreamed of sweeping along on a vast tide, trying to reach a safe harbor where Vince stood beckoning to her. . . .

*   *   *

Chantal wiped the sweat from her brow with a towel, glad that, in practice at least, she didn't have to wear all that heavy face paint. She was about to retreat offstage when she saw a tall young woman, willowy but imposing, stumble into the lights. Several other diffident young women followed her, and Chantal realized these were the new applicants for the corps de ballet.

Delighted, Chantal smiled at the new arrivals. "Lizzie! You did come."

Lizzie's high cheekbones were flushed, and her lovely hazel eyes darted about nervously. "Ah, yes, mum, but I feel nervous as a cat on hot bricks. Don't know if I can do this."

"Nonsense. Of course you can. Just pretend you are practicing in front of your mirror at home."

Lizzie answered wryly, "Don't have a mirror. Too dear, me ma said."

"Oh, well." Chantal glanced out at the theater manager, who was barking orders, and leaned close to whisper, "Then just watch me. I'll stand in the wings and show you what to do."

As it happened, Lizzie's competition was not formidable. The first girl had missing teeth and plump legs, though she moved passably enough. The second was apparently hard of hearing, for she stayed one step behind the orchestra. And the third was a stick of a girl whose every move seemed awkward.

Yawning, the manager waved Lizzie centerstage. Even from her position in the wings, Chantal heard his snide aside to his assistant, "If this is the best Covent Garden can send, then we'd best search our audience for rotten tomatoes."

Chantal bristled. She despised the man, but since he paid her salary, she tolerated his wandering eyes and rudeness. However, she'd not have Lizzie intimidated. She gave Lizzie a bracing smile and took the position the manager indicated. Lizzie did likewise, holding one leg behind her while she stretched her arms forward, yearning in her pretty face.

Her next move required a pirouette, which Lizzie managed in one unbroken spin, landing perfectly on both feet. Chantal was impressed. A short dancer had certain disadvantages. With some practice, she suspected that the tall Lizzie would one day dance her into a corner.

With age, Chantal would be relegated back to the corps, while Lizzie, a fresh sixteen, would be coming into her peak dancing years. Yet Chantal didn't feel threatened. She continued to show Lizzie each complicated step, and the manager was either too stupid or too indifferent to care that Lizzie's attention was centered firmly on the wings.

When he'd finished barking positions, he paused, scratching his chin. "Report to the theater early in the morning for practice. We'll give you a two-week trial."

Lizzie bobbed a curtsy. "Thank ye, sir." And she ran into the wings to hug Chantal. "And thanks to ye, miss, I get me chance."

Chantal patted Lizzie's back. "You *should* be thankful, my dear, for I declare I've just met my replacement."

Lizzie blinked. "Me, mum? Not hardly."

"I, Lizzie."

Lizzie nodded. "Aye. I'm right."

Chantal grinned. "No, no. You will meet many men

as a dancer, and they will treat you better if you speak like a lady. The proper pronoun is 'I.' As you would say, 'I am your replacement.' '' When Lizzie started to protest again, Chantal waved her imperiously to silence. She eyed her new friend critically, up and down, and sighed with envy. ''How often I have wished to be tall. Ah well, 'tis not the first time, nor the last, I daresay, that I have wished for something foolish. Now come along. I'll introduce you to our costume mistress. It will take her some time to fabricate a costume to cover a physique as imposing as yours.''

That Saturday, after the performance, Chantal tensed when a knock came at her dressing-room door. Vince had come once, but she'd sent him away, and it had been quiet for several days. She had hoped, even as she dreaded the prospect, not to have to see him again. She retreated behind her screen. ''Hugo, if that's Vince, would you tell him I'm engaged for the evening?''

She heard Hugo speaking. He came back inside, waiting respectfully for her to emerge from behind the screen, dressed in street clothes, before he handed her a card. In bold black lettering, it read, JOHN WHITMORE, ESQ., BARRISTER, 25 ST. JAMES STREET.

''The sassenach wants to sup wi' ye,'' Hugo said, his tone dripping with disapproval. ''What do ye want me to tell him?''

Chantal scribbled a polite refusal on the back of the card and gave it to him. ''Tell him thank you, but I am fatigued.'' She bent to put on her sensible half boots.

A few minutes later, Hugo was called away. Another knock sounded. This time, she could ignore it or answer the door herself. She opened the portal and had to look up, way up, into a handsome middle-aged face. Gray fanned out in a distinguished manner from the gentleman's temples, accenting his short, thick black hair. His sideburns were long, curving down a strong masculine jaw. His eyes were gray and intense as they examined her with equal thoroughness. "May I make my plaint in person, mademoiselle?" The gentleman stuck a well-manicured hand in his somber but tasteful vest and bowed low. "John Whitmore humbly requests your company at supper." He straightened before she could voice her refusal and added, "Among many friends, at a most respectable establishment."

Chantal was about to shake her head again when she saw a familiar figure approaching down the hallway. She accepted Whitmore's proffered arm and smiled. "Thank you, sir. On those terms, I accept."

Tucking her hand into the crook of his arm, he escorted her down the hall.

A smaller man, but one no less determined, blocked the walkway. "Where are you going, Chantal?" Vince asked.

"Why, not that it's any of your affair, but to sup with this gentleman."

Vince glared at the taller man. "Whitmore, since when do you frequent the ballet?"

"Since I heard of the charms of a certain dancer, Dunhaven," retorted the barrister. "Move aside."

Vince crossed his arms and planted his feet. "No." He didn't say, "She's mine," but he might as well have.

Whitmore gritted his teeth. His cultured tone slurred a bit. "Now see here, you ruddy—"

When Vince clenched his fists, Chantal drew away

from Whitmore and marched up to Vince until she was nose-to-nose with him. "I deduce I did not speak clearly enough at our last meeting. We do not suit. I will not see you again. I merely wish to sup with this gentleman. Please, do not embarrass us more. We are drawing attention."

Vince's clear complexion went a dull red as he saw half-dressed dancers peeking out of rooms up and down the hallway. Finally, with a choked sound of frustration, he stepped aside, flattening himself against the wall to let them pass.

Her nose in the air, Chantal pretended he was a giant blot upon the cheap wallpaper, but if she fooled Vince, she did not fool herself.

Nor, apparently, did she fool Whitmore, for he looked at her sympathetically after he had her settled against the plush squabs of his expensive chaise. "So the rumors are true," he said softly. "You *are* Dunhaven's lost love."

Chantal shook her head wearily. "If I were, I would be grabbing for every advantage, don't you think?"

"He certainly seems to believe so. As many times as I've seen him orate in Parliament, I have never seen him so discomposed."

Shrugging, Chantal responded, "I cannot answer for his state of mind. Now, why have you really invited me here?"

Whitmore leaned back, sprawling his long legs before him, but still keeping them respectfully away from her skirts. "Intelligent, as well as lovely. That is rare in a woman. Why, I thought you might be interested in a business proposition. I have watched you dance all week long, and I have observed that you rarely accept suitors' gifts or invitations. I do believe the only reason I wore you down this evening is because you wanted to spite Dunhaven." He paused, his head tilted against the cushioned wall as he appraised her reaction.

Chantal's smile slipped a bit. "Go on."

"And so I deduced, as we lawyers tend to do, that here is a lady of grace, stamina, intelligence and morals. A most unusual combination in a dancer." Whitmore leaned forward. "To come to the point, my dear—how would you like to open your own dancing academy?"

Back at the theater, Vince was about to burst outside and walk the long distance home, hoping to cool off, when a hulking man stalked down the steps ahead of him. Vince hesitated for all of a few seconds, and then he ran to catch up with Hugo. "Wait, Hugo. A word, please."

A bleak scowl lowered on Vince from a long way up. Hugo gave him exactly what he asked for. "No." And he walked faster.

Vince smiled wryly, hurrying to keep pace. "Perhaps I should elucidate. A few words. Maybe even a long string of sentences?" When there was no answer, he jibed, "Unless that's beyond your capability."

Hugo stopped cold, turned and jabbed a finger into Vince's chest. "No, but I dinna talk aboot the mistress, especially to a man she dinna want to see."

"Even if that man loves her?"

Hugo's finger sagged down, and for the first time, Vince saw a flicker of pity in Hugo's chilly gray eyes. "Even then, for she will no' have ye."

"But I will have her. One way or the other."

Hugo shoved Vince against a theater pillar and

growled, ''Then 'twill be the other, and the worse for wear ye'll be after it.''

Vince slapped Hugo's hands away. ''Beat me until I'm bloody and broken, if you wish, but I will not have done until I know the truth about this woman. Where she came from, and why she is so wary of me. She's hiding something—''

This time, Hugo caught him about the throat, choking Vince's vow back into his larynx. The theater had long since emptied, but the new gaslights springing up all over London lit the broad avenue. A night watchman, strolling down the street, saw the two men and came rushing up.

'' 'Ere now, none o' that on me watch.'' He was a tall, burly man, almost as tall as Hugo. He shoved Hugo away and asked, ''Be ye all right, me lud?'' He caught Hugo's shirt. ''I think I'd best take ye to gaol, ye scurvy 'ound, fer attackin' this fine gentmun.''

Coughing, Vince finally managed, ''I'm fine, my good man. We just have a slight difference of opinion.''

Glaring at Hugo suspiciously, the watchman stepped back. ''I'll follow ye fer a way, then.''

Hugo's broad forehead glistened with sweat, and his monumental swagger was a bit stiff-legged as he hurried toward his lodgings. Vince kept pace, determined to dog the fellow's steps until he wore him down. Hugo was obviously loyal to the bone, but he was also a poor liar. If the truth was to be had, here Vince would find it.

And so, when Hugo entered the quiet but respectable inn, Vince tailed him inside. He watched Hugo go upstairs, slam the door and lock it.

Vince knew better than to knock, but ten shillings in the right hand soon greased the lock. Instinct told Vince that a key to the mystery of Papillone dwelt inside. Vince winked his thanks to the chambermaid, took a deep breath, knocked once briskly and shoved open the door.

Stunned, Hugo stared at him, one arm in, one arm out of his coat.

Vince barely glanced at him, his attention firmly on the room's only other occupant. His curly red hair mussed, his light green eyes sleepy, a little boy sat up on the sofa, rubbed his eyes and said, "Hugo, who is that man?"

Chapter Four

Hugo, his bushy brows lowering on his broad forehead, his teeth bared in a snarl, more resembled a bear defending his territory than a man as he tossed off his coat and charged the door.

Unaware of his danger, Vince stared in mingled fascination and pain at this proof of Chantal's faithlessness. For the boy, despite his red hair and green eyes, had Chantal's winging eyebrows and perfect cupid's bow mouth. When the lad stood with ingrained courtesy and bowed slightly, he was the urchin Chantal brought back to life.

The slight child moved easily between Hugo and the man, putting his hands out to stop the avalanche of muscle and fury. Hugo quivered to a stop, blinking, and focused on the curious little face so far below him. "He's not fit fer ye to know, laddie. Let me send him aboot his business."

102

"At the opportune moment, good Hugo." The boy came forward, apparently not in the least embarrassed to be caught in his nightshirt. His legs were as well formed and straight as his hands and feet.

Vince collected his scattered thoughts, for the first time realizing how angry Hugo was with him. "Forgive my intrusion, ah . . ." Vince raised an eyebrow at the boy.

The boy opened his mouth, but Hugo rushed to insert, "Edward. Edward McFadden."

Tony cocked his head to one side and peered up at the huge Scotsman, but this time Vince's attention was on Hugo.

Softly Vince asked Hugo, as if he feared the response, "And your surname is . . ."

For the first time, Hugo favored him with a smile. "McFadden." When Vince gasped, he smiled wider, pulled the boy against his chest and settled a possessive hand on Tony's shoulder.

No answering mirth came from Vince. Instead, a red haze swam before his gaze as he tried to visualize Chantal in bed with this . . . this behemoth. The red haze widened. Vince had actually started forward before Tony moved and brought him back to his senses.

The boy shrugged out of Hugo's grasp and stepped closer to Vince. "Do you mean to take up residence upon my threshold, or will you come in? I permit you egress."

Vince blinked until he realized the boy actually meant *ingress*. Vince's mouth quivered despite his anger.

When Hugo growled a complaint, Tony sent him a shushing look. "Have you no etiquette? We should not be prejudiced just because he's an English nobleman. Are you here to see *Maman,* my lord?''

Curiosity grew, easing Vince's misery somewhat, as he nodded. Hugo was obviously a common man, but there was nothing common about this boy, from his perfect shape to his manners, his wit and his vocabulary. Vince's smile became full-blown as he silently repeated the boy's pronunciation of *pre-jud-iced.* Obviously the scamp's verbal grasp of English had not caught up with his reading ability.

Vince agreed, ''Indeed, that is most forbearing of you. I, being an interloper in your abode, am frightfully gratified at your inimitable kindness.''

Confusion flickered across the boy's face, but he hid it well. He went to a tiny table and picked up a decanter. ''Would you care for a tatty?''

Now it was Vince's turn for blankness. As the boy picked up a wineglass and held it up invitingly, Vince hid a smile. Oh, toddy. ''Your hospitality overwhelms me, kind sir.'' Vince bowed slightly.

Hugo had had enough of their nonsense. ''Laddie, yer mum will skin me hide if she finds ye above bed at this wee hour.''

Tony's mouth set mulishly, again in a way that reminded Vince vividly of Chantal. ''I am not fatigued, Hugo. And you and *Maman* have kept me so stifled, it's a wonder I have not perished from boredom.'' He offered Vince a glass of port.

Vince accepted it and sat down on the chair across from the couch. Hugo, still scowling his disapproval, plopped onto the couch, pulling the boy down next to him. The springs groaned in protest and then subsided.

And so the three males stared at one another, the

youngest, who should have been most restless, strangely calm. Hugo, on the other hand, leaned back, crossing his arms over his chest and shifting his weight on the couch.

Vince drained the wine, set the glass on the small table beside the chair and alternated shifting his weight from one side of the chair to the other. Hugo let his arms sag as he tapped one foot against the wood floor. Vince drummed a tattoo on the chair arm with his fingernails.

All the while, Tony peered between the two adults. His button nose fairly quivered with the scent of something strange, in that intuitive way children had of deducing exactly what one didn't want them to know.

A thousand questions quivered on Vince's tongue, but Hugo was simmering like a kettle about to blow, so he contained himself. For now.

Tony, however, did not. "How do you know my mother?"

Vince's fingers froze. "Ah, we met at the theater where she dances." Again. After many years apart.

"She will not accept your suit." Tony calmly met Vince's arrested gaze. "She does not grant her favors lightly."

"I would guess Hugo can vouch for that." Vince couldn't avoid the snide aside, but Hugo merely sat there stolidly, like a boulder one could break a toe on but never move out of the way.

Still, Vince's toes burned to try. This fellow was becoming a deuced menace. If he were this boy's father, he had an odd way of showing it. Why, the lad had the great fool flummoxed, as the boy would say.

"What is your name, sir?"

Vince started. He rose. "Pardon. I am Vincent Anthony Kimball, at your service." He bowed, so he didn't see Hugo's warning look when Tony started to reply.

Sitting back down, Vince searched for a way to put the question so as to get it past Hugo's alert but limited intelligence. "Um, and have you visited England before, Edward?"

"No, sir. This is the first time."

"And where did you live prior to this?"

"The Continent. Italy, Spain, France. Scotland, when I was small. My mother has danced on some of the greatest stages in the world, you know. Oh, and the sights we saw. Why, the Acropolis in Greece is the most amazing historical artifact I have ever encountered . . ."

And the boy continued to rattle on about the ancient Greeks, proving that he'd obviously had a classical education. Vince waited for him to wind down and for Hugo to yawn before he asked gently, "And what year were you born?"

"Why—" As Hugo stiffened, light footsteps sounded outside the door. Tony leaped up, his face glowing like a brace of candles, and flew to open the door. "*Maman,* see who has come!" He pulled Chantal into the room, but her back was to Vince, who sat near the wall behind the door.

She paused to brush his tousled hair away from his brow, "*Petite,* why are you not abed? You know I—" And then, as though she were attuned to his presence, as he was attuned to hers, she turned. If she had fainted, or tried to hustle the child away, he would have been more suspicious. However, though her beautiful mouth made an *O* of surprise, she took a deep breath, caught

106

her son's hand and drew him forward. "Have you made your bow to the earl, Edward?"

"Yes, *Maman*. Though he did not tell me he was an earl, it's obvious he's a lord. I tried to make him welcome while we awaited you."

"Yes, mademoiselle, we had a most interesting conversation. Edward was about to tell me how old he is."

Chantal quickly pulled her shawl over her head. Her expression was briefly hidden, her voice muffled as she answered, "Why, he's eight."

Tony puffed up indignantly, his skinny chest expanding as he drew breath to say something.

Hugo elbowed him in the ribs and mouthed a *shhh*.

When she laid the shawl neatly over the back of a chair, Chantal's expression was bright. Too bright. Vince peered back at Tony, but the boy was watching his mother curiously.

Another mystery, but one Vince could not solve at this moment. Of a sudden exhausted, too tired to wonder at the heightened color in Chantal's face, or even, at this hour, to tell himself that she *was* Chantal, Vince stood. "I regret my intrusion at this late hour, mademoiselle. Thank you for the wine, Edward. Hugo." Vince nodded curtly at his adversary. Hugo's lip curled in response.

The ballerina walked Vince to the door, where he paused. "And how was your supper?"

She smiled, a secret joy in her eyes that depressed him even more. This new suitor, apparently, was more to her taste.

"Illuminating," she responded. "Thank you for entertaining my son." She walked into the hall with him and paused on the landing, leaving her door ajar. Her voice had gone soft. "I fear I may not be seeing you again. I . . . have already given my notice at the theater."

"Oh yes?" He kept the query casual, surprising her. In truth, he was not overly concerned, because he had his own plans for her future. It was immaterial to Vince whether she danced, or even whether she intended to stay in England. If she tried to flee, she'd give him more reason to act as his instincts urged. Hang her foolish pride, hang her suitors and, by George, hang the law, but she would not flee him again. At least, not until he knew the truth about her.

Much as her son had done earlier, she cocked her head on one side. "I have been offered a chance to open my own dancing academy."

Now this *did* surprise him. "By whom?" She had no money for such a thing.

"That does not matter. We are to begin seeking suitable accommodations immediately."

Vince hesitated, but in this dark hour when he'd learned things about her that he'd rather not know, he had no patience for games, or for lies. He lifted her chin with his finger. "If you had told me you wanted it, I would have sponsored you."

Gently, she pulled away. "I cannot be beholden to you."

His barriers were so low that anger overwhelmed him much more quickly than normal. He did not know what to think of the boy, or whether to believe that Hugo really was the child's father. He did not even know what to think of her obvious excitement about operating her own academy. But this rejection that she'd tried so many times before, this, he knew how to deal with. Closing her suite door, he shoved her against the wall beside it. He planted both hands beside her head and leaned so close his breath brushed her lips. "Why is that, my dear? Could it be because you already owe me too much?"

She set her hands on his chest to push him away, but instead her fingers curled into the warmth of muscle and bone. Her breathing quickened, as if stroked to life by his own. "Wh-what do you mean?"

He lowered his head even more until his mouth was against her ear. "Chantal, did you think of me as you lay with that great hulking Scot?"

She shook her head, but since that made his lips rub against the side of her neck, she went still. "I . . . have told you and told you—I am not Chantal! *Je ne comprend*—why will you not believe me?"

When she lapsed into French like that, she was a ghost resurrected, but there was another, even more basic reason why he would not believe her disavowals. He buried one hand in her lush black hair and pulled her head back. "Because of this."

Still pressing her against the wall, so that she felt every inch of his aroused passion, he swooped down on her mouth, seizing it for his own. Unlike the first time on the stage, or that time in his carriage, he exhibited no patience, no tenderness and no restraint. Tonight, during this midnight hour when wild things prowled, he was not a politician, nor even a suitor.

He was a wolf marking his territory.

She was his chosen mate.

And wolves mated for life.

Indeed, a growl escaped him at the taste of her on

his lips. He nibbled and teased at her, pulling her bottom lip into his mouth so he could run his teeth along it. The stiffness eased out of her as slowly, hotly, wildly, he inserted the tip of his tongue between her panting lips and explored all she denied him. And then she was struggling to free her arms—but only to fling them about his neck and pull him closer.

He slanted his mouth over hers, lifting her off her feet to shove her flat against the wall and press his swollen need against the apex of her legs. Even through their layers of clothing, the contact shattered the last of his tenuous control. Rocking into her, uncaring, indeed, no longer even aware that they stood in a public hallway, he drank of her lips, parched like a wolf returned to his lair after a drought. Passion raged hotter and higher, high enough to consume them both. Still she answered with hands and lips. Her tongue answered every aggressive thrust as she ran her palms over his chest and sides, slipping them around his back to cup his buttocks.

His heavy need of her hardened further, until he wondered that it didn't sink them both on the spot, but he could not let her breathe, much less let her go. She had to breathe through her nose as he tilted her head farther back. He thrust his tongue deep into her mouth, moving his hips in concert with the hungry foragings.

From somewhere, an outside world intruded. He heard noisy footsteps and drunken laughter approaching up the stairs. *No,* go away, his fevered senses ordered, but even now, bent almost in two by this maelstrom of passion, he had a care for the woman in his arms. Whatever her name, he could not dishonor her so. They were in no state to see or to be seen, either of them.

Setting her on her feet, Vince dragged her by the

wrist to the first door he came to, pushing it. To his relief, it moved inward. He turned up the lantern burning beside the bed, slammed the door and locked it. He reached to grab her to take up where they had left off, but she was over the bed in a nimble flash of arms and legs he could not hope to match. Trembling, rubbing her elbows, she stood across from him. He couldn't reach her without a clumsy struggle.

He tensed to climb the bed, every male instinct in his body shouting, "Possess her! Prove to her she's yours!" but something in her eyes stopped him. The shadows gave them a crushed violet look that froze him in his place, for he sensed she was near her breaking point. By God, so was he! However, her bleak resolution was so close to what he was feeling, too, that astonishment slowed his heartbeat. His wild need of her softened enough to give him an instant of clarity.

With it came shame. He held a hand across the bed to her, vaguely noticing the emerald signet ring that had belonged to his father. The hand that ruled vast estates and coaxed passage of unpopular laws out of his peers in Parliament shook as he extended it to a penniless dancer. "Chantal, I'm sorry. I did not mean to . . ." What? Kiss you? Want you? Be so jealous of Hugo and any other man who's ever looked at you? Liar. He'd meant every action, but the smooth-tongued earl who'd charmed women since his cradle was speechless to explain how she affected him.

She shook her head in tormented denial. "You did not mean to humiliate me in front of others? Tell me, *m'sieur*—was it my reputation you were trying to protect? Or your own?"

"Yours, of course. I do not want people to talk about y—"

A harsh laugh cut him off. "It's a bit late for that. You should have thought of that before you accosted me on the stage."

"*Accosted* you?" His hand dropped and made a fist at his side. "Is that what you feel when I kiss you? If so, my prancing little ballerina, you adore being accosted. But then, I forgot the boy. You have obviously enjoyed a man's touch long before tonight." She gasped, and almost he wished he could recall the words, but she shouldn't scratch unless she wanted to be clawed back.

"You know nothing about me, or about him." She lifted her chin, and her voice steadied, icing over. "Nor shall you."

She marched around the bed, daring him with her eyes to touch her, or try to stop her. Reflexively, he reached out, but she swatted his hands away, continuing on to the door. She threw the bolt back.

The sound galvanized him, for it preceded her flight and his loss. He reached out one arm and slammed the door closed as she tried to open it. Then, pulling her to the bed by her struggling wrists, he set her down, stepped back and stood before her, his arms crossed over his chest. "No. You shall not leave until we come to some understanding. You are just like all women— you run when things get complicated. Not this time, whether your name be Papillone, Chantal or Cleopatra, Queen of the Nile."

She sat, stiff as starch, staring fixedly into space.

He sighed, the last of his passion fading to grim certainty. If he let her leave now, he'd lose her. Rubbing the back of his neck, he began to pace in the tiny space, trying to collect his thoughts. "I'm sorry if I kissed you a bit too . . . passionately." He swung around on her. "But that's the way you make me feel. No other woman of my acquaintance has ever made me lose control the way you have. Do you think I'm proud of this? Or happy about it?"

A bit of her stiffness softened as she whispered, "Why, then, are you ashamed of me?"

His mouth fell open. Was that what she'd thought when he hustled her in here? "We are already scandal enough without drunken roisterers bandying our names about from hill to dale. What we feel is surely our own affair." He winced at his unconscious turn of phrase.

The words apparently pained her, too, for she closed her eyes, nodding. "Yes. But it is true that a man in your position should not be . . . consorting with a ballerina, is it not? And that your own reputation has suffered since you saw me at the ballet?"

"To that I cannot say nay, but I have never lived my life according to any creed but my own sense of honor. My actions in the hall were more to protect you than myself. I swear it. Good God, my foolish girl, do you think I wanted to let you go?"

Finally, she looked at him, and the depth of shame and pleading in her eyes all but slapped him in the face. "No," she whispered, "and I admit I didn't want to stop, either. But I have too many things to consider besides my own desires. Must you keep tormenting me? Please, understand that my wishes here are immaterial, as, I fear, are your own. I am not free to accept your suit. Can that not be the end of it?"

A ghastly thought struck him. He felt himself go pale.

113

"Are you . . . married to that great brute?"

She blinked. "Hugo?" She shook her head. "No."

"But he claims to be the father of the boy."

It was her turn to go pale. Her eyes went even darker, as if she looked over far horizons he could not see, or even imagine. A chill swept up his spine as instinct told him that something bound this unlikely pair, a shared experience he could never understand.

He had to force himself to concentrate as she said, "In a way he is, for he was there when Edward was born, and has been the only father my son has ever known. However, Hugo was merely trying to protect me. The father of my child is . . . dead." She looked away as she spoke. He sensed that she'd lied to him, but at the moment, it was Hugo's lie that made him go weak with relief. The thought that she'd rejected his own suit in favor of that behemoth had been gnawing at him. But it was as he'd suspected: Hugo was, in the literal sense, her protector.

However, she tried to flee every time he reached out too fast. This time, he merely asked gently, "Then what else could keep you from me?"

Dignity sat on her proud, shining dark head like a crown as slowly she stood. At that moment, she was every inch a lady, whatever her calling or birth. "I am only a ballerina, 'tis true, with the reputation that comes with my profession. But me, *m'sieur,* it is myself I must look at in the mirror. I will be no man's mistress."

This time, he truly was speechless. "But . . . the child. You have obviously been with some man in the past, so why not—"

"Because I choose not to. Besides, as you yourself admit, I have done your own reputation no good. We should not blacken you further in the public's eyes."

"Hang the public!" He shifted from foot to foot, unable to be still. Deuce take it, why did this woman flabbergast him so? He'd been convinced that some deep, dark secret kept her remote from him. Was it truly only some puritanical moralizing?

He hesitated, but even if this woman was not Chantal, she'd gotten under his skin and wriggled her way into his heart. The words came of their own accord. "If that's your only concern, we can fix that easily enough. We shall marry. The sooner, the better."

She was goggling at him as if he'd suddenly grown an ass's head, with the idiocy to match, when the door opened in concert with a tuneless whistling. A man wearing a captain's regimentals froze on the threshold.

He peered at them, stepped back, looked at the number painted on the door and returned, frowning. "I say, this is my room. What are you two doing here?"

"Just leaving," Vince replied. He brushed past the captain, dragging Chantal with him. Vince tossed him a quid as they left. The officer's sputtering stopped in mid-spate as he nimbly caught the gold coin. Shrugging, he closed the door behind them.

At Chantal's door, Vince paused. "We cannot settle this tonight. May I have leave to see you tomorrow after the performance?"

She shook her head. "It will be my last, and the rest of the cast wish to take me out afterward."

"And no guests allowed?"

"No."

"Well, the next night, then. Here? At seven?"

She nodded this time, resignation on her face. He bent to kiss her, but she turned her head and his lips only brushed her cheek. "Good night," she said firmly, entering her apartment and closing the door. He heard it latch.

Frowning, he made his way down the stairs. She'd capitulated a bit too easily. This time, he was taking no chances. When he got home, he barked an order at his butler before he went upstairs. Then, while he awaited his caller, he looked around at his vast suite of rooms, imagining her there.

At the dressing table, brushing her hair. Helping him on with his jacket when his valet was occupied. Sharing a morning tea with him.

Waking beside him, the gold ring on her finger winking in the sunlight.

And suddenly, the heavy weight pressing on his chest was gone, leaving him free. Of course, he should have thought of it before. In the end, as with most complicated things, the solution to his dilemma was simple.

He wanted to vanquish his rivals for Chantal's favors; he wanted to bed her, not once, but often, for the rest of his life; he wanted to get to know that charming little boy better; he wanted to protect them both; and he wanted to send that detestable Hugo about his business.

The only way he could get everything he wanted was to marry her. After he met his caller, he prepared for bed, feeling that he could finally sleep. As the enormity of his plan overwhelmed him, he had to smile wryly. Egad, he was going to extremes to find out who she really was. This should certainly do the trick.

A stage name would not do on a marriage certificate. He'd be eager to watch her sign. . . .

* * *

In her rooms, Chantal looked about regretfully. This suite was the closest to a home they'd had in years. It would be a pity to leave, but Vince had left her no choice. Of his promise to wed her, she refused to think. He'd said it in a moment of passion, and even if he carried through, she couldn't allow it.

As she began to pack methodically, she listed the reasons.

They were as valid today as they had been ten years ago. He was just as important to England as his mother had warned her he would be. Why, only last week she'd read about a bill that had passed the Lords with his leadership, one that outlawed forcing orphans into workhouses. He needed a wife with a pedigree as long as her nose, one with the connections to further his career, not stifle it. If a penniless French bastard had been a liability, certainly a scandalous ballerina would be worse. Even through her misery, she had to smile as she visualized Adeline's expression should Vince bring her home as his bride.

Besides, Tony would despise the constraints of life as a little lordling. And Hugo! Her smile grew into a muffled laugh as she tried to picture Hugo wearing the Earl of Dunhaven's blue and gold livery, toeing the mark, pulling his forelock as he bowed to his betters.

No, this was best. Gently, she went into the other room and shook Hugo awake.

Groggily, he opened one eye. Both eyes widened when he saw the tears on her face.

Still, she smiled bravely. "Another adventure is upon us, Hugo. Can you arise and help me pack?"

*   *   *

The next night, the King's Theater fairly burst at the seams. From footlights to boxes, people of every station and nationality packed the house, most for the second or third time. A blind person from Outer Mongolia who'd never set foot in a city could have divined where the Quality sat merely by following his nose. Near the front, by the smoky gaslights, the scents of the stable and the fishery were strong. Farther back came the smells of cigars and wax, from the shopkeepers and candlestick makers. And farthest back, from the boxes high on the walls lining the gallery, came the scents of expensive perfumes and fine wines as corks were popped.

However, whatever their birth or creed, from dukes and marquesses to simple butchers and bakers, all agreed: Papillone was in uncommon looks tonight. She'd never performed her glissades with such grace, or extended her arms to her wounded love with such poignancy. It was almost as if she danced with all her heart to a dying art.

And who was this new girl in the corps de ballet? She was so tall, her legs so lissome and athletic that she seemed about to take flight with every athletic jeté. Those seated in front could see the sparkle in her lovely hazel eyes. Programs crackled as people squinted in the darkness, trying to read her name. There, the last one listed, for she was the newest member—Elizabeth Mayfield. Many a man made a note of the name.

In his box, Vince, too, saw the difference in Chantal. He knew every nuance of that expressive face and he'd memorized the height of all her leaps, so when she soared as she'd never soared before, landing gracefully in the arms of her partner, his heart leapt to his throat.

When she danced en pointe across the stage, kicking one leg in the air at the end to pirouette until he thought certain she'd fall, he understood what the rest of the audience only felt: She danced as if this were her last night on stage because, in truth, it was.

His late-night visitor the previous evening had returned early this morning, getting him out of bed to the displeasure of his valet, but following Vince's orders.

The Bow Street runner, in his distinctive cap and jacket, had come straight to the point. "Ye be a right strong bloke in the noodle, guvnor. She and the lad, and that great savage Scot, left 'fore daylight. We follered slowlike, like ye said, so they'd be none the wiser. They ended up on Dorset Street, only a stone's throw away from High Street. Fancy digs, they be."

Vince had frowned angrily. If Whitmore was her mysterious financier, how had they concluded the deal so quickly? "Are there teaching academies in the area?"

The runner nodded. "A fencing school and a boy's school." The runner handed over the exact location, scribbled on a grimy sheet of paper.

Vince gave the man a small, heavy pouch. "Good work, Jimmy. You and your men divide this, and there will be more to follow as long as you watch them, day and night. If it seems they're about to leave, one of you follow, and another notify me immediately. Also, I wish to see a copy of the birth certificate of one Edward McFadden. I believe you should start in Scotland, though he might have been born on the Continent, about eight years ago."

The runner put his hat back on at a jaunty angle. "Lick spittle and clean as a whistle, guvnor." Cheerfully pocketing the heavy pouch, the runner strode away as if it were not two hours before dawn and he'd just arisen, instead of spending the night on his feet outside a small inn.

Now, watching Chantal go into her last frantic pirouette before dying in her lover's arms, Vince clutched the scrap of paper in his pocket. It gave him comfort as he watched the audience rise as one, thundering their appreciation of a small Frenchwoman with more heart than sense. Flowers almost buried Chantal, and when she caught a red rose and brought it to her lips, curtsying so low her knee brushed the stage, the roar was deafening.

Chantal gestured her corps forward. The tall girl in the back seemed shy, but when one male voice called, "Lizzie!" and a score of others joined in, the newest troupe member crept forward. Applause rose high again, echoing off the soaring domed ceiling.

Chantal caught Lizzie's hand and urged her forward. She raised her hands for silence. "I am gratified by your warm reception, my dear friends, but I wish you to know that tonight I retire from the public stage to open my own dancing academy."

Disappointed groans sounded along with a few ribald suggestions as to what certain bucks in the audience wished her new calling might be, but Chantal ignored them. "Please, welcome Elizabeth Mayfield, new to our troupe, but very promising. Next week, she dances at the head of the corps. Please continue to honor all our talented dancers with the same attendance and approval you have offered me. I shall always remember this night fondly. I thank you, one and all." She curtsied again, and then danced off stage. And no matter how they roared and called for her return, she did not show herself again.

Vince hurried backstage, determined to catch her, for he didn't believe her claim that the cast had forbade outsiders at their party. But to his disappointment, as girls trailed out of dressing rooms, they were accompanied only by men carrying instruments or burly stagehands.

One of the last to leave, Chantal hurried out, dressed sedately in a midnight blue pelisse and pink walking gown. Vince hurried to catch up with her, but by the time he'd sidestepped all the traffic in the hall, she was already out the stage door. He threw the door open in time to see her getting into a carriage.

John Whitmore helped her up the steps. Chantal didn't see Vince stop at the stage entrance, but Whitmore did. He gave Vince a mocking salute and climbed in after his guest. Their carriage rattled off, the two of them laughing gaily, leaving Vince to make his solemn, solitary way home.

As always.

But not, by God, for long. She'd tried to run, never planning to see him again; he suspected she'd lied to him about the child's paternity; she'd lied to him about who could attend her party. He'd restrain himself no longer. If she played dirty, then so would he. She obviously preferred Whitmore's company, but that, too, he could change.

Pain pierced him to the quick, and he visualized himself sitting alone in his study, staring down at the ruby heart so symbolic of their relationship. Meanwhile, Whitmore would wine and dine Chantal.

On impulse, Vince said to his coachman, "Robbie

121

Tremayne's, please.'' Robbie had been pestering him to visit. Since that first night at the ballet, he'd been avoiding his friend. He and Robbie had spilled blood together on the battlefield, and they'd sipped their first whiskey together at Eton, in the shadows of the stables where no one could see them.

Unlike Vince, Robbie's weakness was women. Vince knew his friend would try to talk him out of his conviction to marry Chantal. Robbie believed marriage was for peasants and princes, and those in between owed it to society to keep John Bull's English stock both plentiful and diverse. Robbie himself had two children by two different mistresses, but at least he acknowledged and supported them, despite the fact that both women had long since gone on to other admirers.

As he knocked on Robbie's door, Vince wondered if he could be so magnanimous. The mere thought that Chantal could flit from man to man made him sick to his stomach. Vince had an intuitive understanding about people, and he'd stake his life on the fact that she was as fastidious with her sexual favors as he himself was. He grinned wryly. In a way, in marrying her, he would be gambling with his life. Certainly his reputation and his career would be in jeopardy if he were wrong about her.

Robbie's manservant opened the door a crack. When he saw who it was, his wary expression warmed. He pulled the door wide, grinning. ''My lord! The master will be so glad to see you at last.''

''He's in, then?''

A slight flush tinged the man's cadaverous cheeks. ''Yes, sir.''

Vince sighed. "Not alone, I perceive. Perhaps I should call some other time—"

But Robbie himself apparently had heard his voice, for he entered the small foyer from his sitting room, a lovely opera singer on one arm, a well-known actress on the other.

Vince had to force himself to stay put, for he'd had a brief fling with Moll Dupont, the most celebrated actress of the Drury Lane Theater, himself. Her lovely dark eyes widened at the sight of him, and then that full, sensual mouth formed a petulant pout.

"Vince, old boy! 'Pon my soul, I was beginning to think you'd deserted me," Robbie said, adroitly disentangling himself to come forward with his hand outstretched.

Automatically, Vince shook it, but he was already regretting the impulse that had brought him here. "I can see you're engaged, Robbie. Perhaps we can meet at White's tomorrow for luncheon."

"Nonsense. You know both my guests. We were just about to go for a late supper. I am quite certain they'd be delighted to have you join us. Is that not so, ladies?"

The opera singer nodded vigorously, but in the coy way Vince remembered with acute distaste, Moll said, "I should be even more delighted if the earl would honor me as my escort."

Robbie didn't bat an eye. "Quite. Two by two is such a nicer number than three. Even Noah himself would approve."

It was obvious Robbie was already a trifle bosky. Vince was about to refuse more firmly when Moll cooed, "The most fashionable little place just opened on the Strand. All the theater people go there after their performances. Why, I've heard that that clumsy little thing from the King's Theater is having a party there this very eve. Is that not so, Robbie?'' Her exotic dark eyes, almond shaped and as sultry as her voice, glinted as she arched a black brow at Vince.

Robbie wasn't so drunk that he didn't catch the undercurrents. However, since he'd made manifest his disapproval of Vince's obsession with Chantal on numerous occasions, he merely watched to see what Vince's reaction would be.

Vince hesitated. Chivalry and jealousy warred within him as he contemplated whether he should be so crass as to spoil Chantal's engagement with another man. But Whitmore was rumored to be ruthless in his business practices, and Vince was worried about Chantal's growing involvement with the barrister. He nodded. ''I shall be delighted to escort you, Moll.''

If Euclid himself had charted her course, the great mathematician couldn't have drawn a straighter line than the one she marked getting to Vince's side. He patted the hand she set on his arm. She tightened it possessively on his sleeve, and he hoped he hadn't made a mistake in accepting her challenge. He'd broken off with her precisely because she became overly possessive, and because her exotic charms had begun to bore him.

When she sat so close to him in the carriage that she was half in his lap, he *knew* he'd made a mistake. Too late to rectify it. Yet.

Besides, he was honest enough to admit that he'd like to see Chantal's reaction when, for a change, she had to watch a competitor clinging to *him*.

* * *

The Dove and Hawk public house on the Strand sent a blaze of light and gaiety unrivaled even on this late-night pleasure avenue of London. Theatergoers thronged the area, seeking food for the belly, conviviality for the soul and, in many cases, sexual relief for the body. Plush red velvet curtains lined the walls of the house, and a huge bay window thrust out into the street, as if to proclaim the mirth and rebirth that could be found here.

Merrymakers thronged in every corner, but it was the two round tables in the center of the room that held sway over the others. Here, the players laughed loudest, drank the most expensive wine and exchanged the liveliest conversation. And the small dark woman in pride of place next to a distinguished-looking man laughed when the other players laughed and frowned when they frowned.

Through her travels, Chantal had become expert at pretending attentiveness when her mind was elsewhere. And tonight, despite the fact that she knew she should be elated at the new opportunity Whitmore had granted her, somehow, surrounded by friends and admirers, she felt alone.

The die was cast, the Rubicon crossed. Still, she wished she could return to where she had begun. She felt an unreal sense of standing outside herself, watching Whitmore recount a ribald tale of a milk maid and a squire. He elicited gales of laughter, and even as Chantal smiled, she wondered why she was here.

She'd done what she had to, but oh, how she missed Vince already. She cursed the chance that had brought him to the theater that first afternoon. If only she hadn't seen him again, perhaps the distance of the years between them wouldn't be spanned nightly in her dreams. She'd never forgotten him and never would, but the raw pain had, with time, lessened to an ache.

Until seeing him again pushed aside old, painful memories for new, painful ones. The sight of Tony and Vince together had almost brought her to her knees. She hoped she'd hidden it well. When he kissed her outside the door, her raw emotions had welled up until he could have taken her like a trollop against the wall and she would not have made a peep of denial.

Now, when Whitmore reached the end of his tale, threw back his salt-and-pepper head and roared with laughter, Chantal could only wish he had a curly head of brown hair streaked with gold, a quieter laugh and dryer wit.

"Don't you agree, my dear?" Whitmore said, turning to her.

Chantal blinked. "Certainly." She hoped that she hadn't agreed that the world was flat and the sky was pink.

But Whitmore seemed to find nothing amiss. He attacked his plum pudding with a hearty enjoyment that Chantal wished she could emulate. She toyed with her orange, knowing she should enjoy the hothouse delight, but nothing tasted right. She was about to request that she be excused when four new arrivals caused a stir.

Silence swept the tables nearest the door, for it was rare to see such a well-known politician here, and on the arm of one of the most notorious flirts in England, to boot. Chantal glanced up in mild curiosity and froze, her napkin halfway to her mouth. Misery tightened a fist inside her stomach, winding her.

Vince, her steadfast soldier of refinement and loyalty, was seating the notorious actress, whom even Chantal recognized, with the same courtesy he'd shown her. Their table was adjacent, and Vince, either by accident or design, had sat down facing her. He gave her a look that made her chin rise and her spine stiffen. How dare he disparage her own choice of escort when he seemed happy to be with that . . . that harlot?

Apparently Whitmore had seen the new arrivals, too, for he whispered to Chantal, "Deuced bad timing, what? Shall we depart, my dear, for our own private party?"

Yes, she longed to say, but Vince had challenged her as surely as if he'd thrown a gauntlet at her feet. Stay she would, at least for a few more moments. Flirt, just as he was flirting.

Her melting smile showed her dimples to best advantage. "Certainly not. Would you care for more wine, my dear sir?" She held up the bottle.

Even as he let her pour him another glass, he shook his head admiringly, for he'd obviously deduced enough of Chantal's relationship with Vince to know that much remained unresolved between the pair. Mischief glinted in his eyes. Several of their tablemates had risen, yawning, so Whitmore called, "I say, Kimball, would you and Robbie and your charming guests care to join us?"

Chantal gasped. That was a bit too much of a challenge, but Vince had risen with alacrity. Robbie rose more slowly but joined them, seating the blond opera singer next to him. Vince sat on Chantal's other side, Moll next to him.

"What a cozy arrangement," he drawled, draping his arm around Moll. "As Robbie observed to me earlier, even numbers are so much nicer than odd, don't you agree, mademoiselle?"

"Oh, I don't know. One seems a rather nice sum at the moment." Enough was enough. She'd flee to fight another day. Chantal drained the last of her own wine, preparing to rise, but when a hand clutched her knee, she froze. She'd recognize that touch anywhere. How dare he touch her so intimately in such a public place? Even more infuriating, he still had his other arm around Moll. When had her moral young soldier become such a cad? She jerked her leg aside, knocking into Whitmore's elbow.

His raised glass sloshed wine over her bodice. Chantal gasped, but before she could lift her own napkin, Vince had dipped his spotless one in his water glass and moved it toward her bosom. Before it could land, she snatched it away.

"I can manage." The drips were few and the wine was white, but still, the stain made as good an excuse as any. She felt the acute attention of every gentleman at the table as she dabbed at the stain, and her bodice was much higher than those of most of the women. Chantal tossed the napkin aside and again tried to rise. "If you will all excuse me, I must—"

Again, that hand caught her knee. When she looked at Vince in outrage, he was smiling, but he hissed out of the side of his mouth, for her ears alone, "Leave, and I shall follow you and have this out on the street outside."

Slowly, she sat back down again. "What do you want of me?" she whispered in despair.

"Everything." And he turned his attention back to Moll, who was pouting and pulling at his sleeve.

Jolted, Chantal leaned back as if he'd slapped her. What was the matter with him? He did not comprehend the word no, or her repeated rejections. What did she have to do to make him understand that she did not want his suit? Abruptly, she understood why he was so resistant to her rejections. He knew they were as false as her protest that she didn't care for him. If she couldn't convince herself, how could she ever convince him?

While her mind was whirling, Whitmore said, "Kimball, I want to talk to you about the Combination Acts, and now's as good a time as any."

Vince demurred, "We shall only bore the ladies—"

"Are you speaking of the laws that Pitt helped pass in 1800 that forbade labor unions?" Chantal asked sweetly. Vince's mouth dropped open, and she was so pleased to see that at last she'd surprised him that she went on. "It was high time Parliament abolished such unfair laws, which I understand they did, partially, last year. However, they did not go far enough. Until workers can bargain collectively, the right to petition for better wages and working hours does not mean a great deal."

When she was finished, Whitmore whistled. "I'm impressed by your grasp of the situation, my dear. Never have I heard the problem stated more precisely, especially by a female. What say you to this, Kimball?"

Chantal had noted that Whitmore never called Vince by his title, and she could only wonder what bad blood had spilled between the two, a conclusion borne out by Vince's cool, "I do not deny the need for reform, but these recent riots and strikes have only strengthened the position of the naysayers."

"So speaks a member of the landed gentry," Whitmore said dryly. "England is troubled not by too much armed strife but by too little."

"And it is exactly that philosophy that makes the king and his lords so obdurate. Look what revolt has done to the economy of France."

"And look how throwing off the yoke of Tory dominance has rejuvenated America."

The two men exchanged a glare of antagonism that would have manifested itself in fisticuffs but for the setting and the company.

Alarmed, Chantal caught Whitmore's tense arm. "Please, John, I am quite fatigued. Will you see me home now?"

His muscles slowly softened. He patted her hand. "Certainly, my dear." He pulled her chair back.

Vince didn't try to stop them, but he did offer a parting shot across Whitmore's bow. "Does Canfield know his assistant's views are so radical?"

Whitmore stopped, his hands on the back of Chantal's chair. "He is greatly in sympathy with my opinion, actually."

Vince snorted. "Bartholomew Canfield is a reformer, true. But he is above all a pragmatist. And there is nothing practical about revolution."

"Who is this . . . Canfield?" Chantal asked.

Something strange flickered in Whitmore's eyes as he held her wrap for her without answering. She didn't see the shadow pass, but Vince did.

He removed his arm from Moll's shoulders and gripped the table edge. "Only one of the richest men in England. Whitmore is one of his chief business managers. Papillone . . ."

Armored by her cloak, Chantal responded, "Yes?"

Vince glanced at Whitmore, at Moll, who was scowling, then back at Chantal. "I have your new direction," he said only. "I shall call on you soon so we may continue our discussion."

Chantal wished she could say she looked forward to that, but she'd rather have her teeth extracted. Would she be forced to flee England to get away? In that moment, Chantal almost hated Vince. But when she looked at Moll, who was pressing her scandalously bare bosom against Vince's shoulder, she hated herself more for her own jealousy.

Masking her emotions and her head with her hood, she shrugged, took Whitmore's arm and strode off without a second glance.

But not without a second thought . . .

Chapter Five

By the end of the week, all London was abuzz with the opening of Mademoiselle Papillone's Dancing Academy. She was only a ballerina, true, and of course no respectable young woman could ever study something so scandalous as ballet dancing. Nevertheless, the discreet advertisement in the *Times* also stated that she'd include instruction in the more acceptable forms of dance, such as the quadrille and the waltz. Nothing so crass as the cost of the lessons was included, but the address given was respectable.

Indeed, on the day prior to the opening of the school, Chantal walked around the cavernous room with John Whitmore, appraising the job his workers had performed. She was immensely grateful to John; he'd not only found this property for her, funded the school and located the proper workmen, he'd even assisted her in the design, offering help when she asked, listening when she didn't.

Long floor-to-ceiling mirrors lined one wall. Comfortable seats sat opposite. Chantal counted. Twenty, twenty-one . . . good. The full thirty she'd asked for. They'd be prepared for the first musicale. A tasteful landscape adorned the end wall, and the thick carpet underfoot in the expansive foyer was forest green, sprigged with tiny white flowers. The walls were white plaster. The dancing floor itself was polished walnut parquet, gleaming under the chandeliers. The whole effect was clean, professional and inviting.

Exactly what she'd wanted. Chantal caught John's arm and stood on tiptoe to kiss his cheek. "I cannot thank you sufficiently, John, except to promise that you will receive every penny of your investment back, with interest, as agreed. But I do wish you'd let me put it in writing."

He smiled down at her, holding her close with one arm when she tried to move away. "Nonsense. I am a barrister by profession, and no one knows more than I that most contracts are made to be broken, anyway. A handshake between two honest business people is just as binding. Though I confess I'd much prefer an even more, ah, official union."

Gently, Chantal slipped away. This was not the first time he'd hinted at marriage. While she was flattered, she was also surprised; they'd only known one another for a few weeks. She'd allowed him one brief kiss in passing, but more she would not dream of. Not when her nightly slumbers were so erotically full of another man's image . . .

Turning away to hide her flushed cheeks, she said, "Do you know that we already have five people registered?" She hurried to the small desk he'd set in an adjacent closet they'd turned into a tiny office, fishing in the middle drawer to brandish several pieces of paper. "Two tradesmen's sons, who wish to learn the waltz, one official's daughter who wants to dance for her own family entertainments and a professional dancing couple who had retired who wish to take up the stage again. Is it not marvelous?"

"Marvelous." John glanced outside at the empty hall, closed her office door and took both her hands. "I understand that you are involved with your new venture, and am well satisfied that such should be the case. However, why will you not agree to attend the opera with me? Surely that is not so much to ask in return for such a hefty investment."

His gentle admonishment served its purpose. She blinked guiltily, but she couldn't explain her reasons any more thoroughly than she had heretofore. She did not want the tattlemongers busy again, just when the gossip had begun to die down now that Vince had apparently quit following her. A full fortnight had passed since their repartee at the theater party, and she could only suppose that she'd finally managed to convince him that her rejection was final.

Or she'd scared him off. Maybe when he saw her holding court over a table of drunks and libertines, he'd finally understood that a scandalous ballet dancer was not appropriate company for a promising leader in the House of Lords. The pang pierced through her stomach all the way to her backbone, but she only slumped for a moment. This was best, she knew it was best. Somehow, she'd convince her foolish heart that her head knew best. Tony must come first, as he always had.

When John's smile slipped as he awaited her answer, she forced a gay note into her voice. "La, sir, I have seen enough theaters to last me a lifetime. I will be too busy for some time to go on idle outings with anyone."

His hands tightened on her shoulders almost enough to hurt, but when she wriggled, he released her. "Very well, I concede. For now. But I shall ask again, and again, until I wear you down. You fascinate me, Papi. We are well suited, and I will devote myself to proving that to you. Mademoiselle, *a votre service*." He bowed and exited, stepping like the dignified gentleman he was.

Frowning, Chantal watched him go. In her twenty-seven years, she'd had more daily contact with men of every sort and station—from the aristocrats on two continents who'd courted her to the male dancers she danced with daily—than most women would in a lifetime. But John Whitmore, as Lizzie would say, was an odd ducky. He was a strange combination of politesse and intimacy, intelligence and opportunism, charm and coarseness. Yet, there was something about the way he sometimes looked at her that made her nervous. His pursuit had daily grown more determined, and she dreaded what would happen when he no longer agreed to their dainty dance of pursuit and avoidance. . . .

She was still wandering about her new enterprise, wondering about the man who'd funded it, when the bell at the door tinkled. She whirled, and a smile, bright as one of London's new gas lamps, flamed into life. "Lizzie! I am so glad you came. How is your practicing coming?"

Colleen Shannon

Lizzie, who already looked more the lady in her new blue serge walking dress and kidskin half boots, walked with her distinctive, graceful stride toward her friend. She spoiled the illusion with an infuriated, "It ain't coming, because I'm busy goin', if ye catch me drift. That tomfool manager played paddy fingers with me bum one too many times. I beamed him a good 'un fore I could stop meself. So he give me short shrift, and I can't say I'm sorry, none, neither. I come to see if ye need any help."

Chantal didn't know whether to shout with glee or frustration. All her lessons with Lizzie, for naught. Well, maybe not . . . She made a rapid mental calculation of what was left in her purse and threw caution to the wind. "Of course. I can't pay you a lot, at least not yet, but I have an extra bed in my room if you want to share with me."

Tears gathered in Lizzie's snapping hazel eyes, softening them to sea foam green. "Do ye mean it?"

"Of course. We shall be two single ladies together, turning up our noses at inopportune suitors." Chantal used her forefinger to tilt up her retrousse little nose and mince across the room, her other hand on her swaying hip. Her antics worked, she saw in the mirror, for Lizzie's tears dried as she chuckled.

"Aye, we can watch each other's backs."

"Or backsides, as the case may be." Chantal winked slyly, and Lizzie slapped her thigh, her chuckles turning to guffaws.

Chantal shook her head. "Ladies do not guffaw, Lizzie."

Lizzie's honking laugh stopped with a bleat. "I'm not sure I want to be a lady, mum."

136

"Call me Papi, Lizzie. And I assure you, it will simplify your life considerably. Do you not want to marry well?"

Lizzie shrugged. "Ye ain't, ah, have not, and it has not hurt ye none, I mean any."

Chantal's mouth drooped. "That is between me and my son and no one else, but I can tell you if I could live my life any way I wanted to, I would prefer a happy marriage over having to support myself and T—Edward."

Irritably, Lizzie tilted back her bonnet when it slipped over her eyes. "Then why don't ye? Ye must have had offers aplenty."

"Not from the right man, Lizzie." When her friend's mouth opened again, Chantal shook her head slightly, indicating that she'd had enough questions for now. "Enough roundaboutation. We must get you suitably attired. Do you not have any bags?"

Lizzie pointed to a wrapped bundle by the door. "Only me old dress and a few other things. I used all me salary for the sennight to buy this fancy rig."

"And a good investment it was. When we get you speaking correctly, we shall go shopping together and see what's available, *oui?*"

Lizzie eyed her suspiciously, as if realizing her mentor did not refer to clothes. But when Chantal led the way back to the office to rummage through her trunks, Lizzie followed meekly enough.

Vince tossed aside the political treatise on which he'd been trying to concentrate and rose to fling open the heavy velvet drape at his study window. The continual rains had stopped at last, and the September days had burst over the horizon in a blaze of glory. At the stately park across from Vince's townhouse, the variegated hues of trees and shrubs combined in a backdrop more magnificent than any a theater could devise, yet Vince stared blindly at the display he normally enjoyed with his morning tea.

Two weeks had passed since he'd seen Chantal, as he still believed her to be, and an eon it had been. He'd decided to give her time to set up her new enterprise, to let her feel secure, before approaching her again. And it wouldn't hurt to see what his investigation turned up. He had tried wooing her, and pursuing her, to little avail. Once he knew more of her past, he could productively plan for their joint future.

And so, when his butler knocked and ushered in the Bow Street runner Vince had hired, Vince let the curtain fall and bounded across the room more like an eager boy than a dignified peer of the realm. "Well, man, what news have you?"

The runner, with the usual dogged discretion that made Bow Street the most effective policing force in London, waited for the butler to close the door. He pulled off his hat, his expression grim. "Very little, sor. We could find no record of a boy born in Scotland, not by the name ye give us, nor here. As fer the laidy, little is known o' her until she moved to Italy and joined a small dancin' troupe. We're told she never became any man's mistress, despite many offers, and that she kept to herself, with that great Scotsman and her boy."

Vince's heart sank. If Bow Street couldn't discover the truth, he would likely never know it. "And what is Hugo's relationship with the lady?" He held his breath.

The runner shrugged, his shoulders broad and impressive in the distinctive red jacket. "Our sources ain't exackly sure o' that, either, but they did not believe him to be the boy's father." He pulled a scrap of paper from his pocket. "One thing don't fit so right and tight, though. Them namby-pamby theater blokes didn't remember the boy by the name o' Edward." He squinted at the paper. "They called him Tony."

Vince stiffened. His heart lurched back in place and began to pound. "And what last name did they know him by?"

The runner pocketed the piece of paper. "They didn't. Said that were odd, too. Papillone never gave her last name, nor the last name o' her son. Do ye want me to search more?"

Vince grabbed a sheet of paper from his desk, scribbled down a name, made some rapid mental calculations and added an age. He handed the sheet to the runner. "Search for a birth record under this name and approximate age."

The runner's eyes widened as he read: *Anthony Kimball, age nine.* "Ye think the lad is yours?"

"I rely upon your discretion, my friend." And to seal the bargain, Vince offered the runner another sack of gold, even heavier than the last one. "Time is of the essence. If the child turns out to be mine, it will explain much." And it will open a whole host of other nasty issues, but Vince squelched that thought.

The runner put his hat back on, tipped it and didn't waste any more time. As the door closed behind him, Vince slumped into his desk chair. His heart raced with hope and possibilities, even as his stomach churned with rage. If the boy was his, he was more confused than ever as to why Chantal had run. How could she deny him his heir? Surely she knew that he would adore the boy, even as he had adored her.

He leaned his aching head in his palms, the dilemma that had tormented him for almost a decade one step closer to resolution. But the truth it revealed might be one he could not bear. . . .

When the door opened, he glanced up with a scowl, wondering why his butler hadn't knocked. The frown deepened when he saw who stood there. "What do you want, Mother?"

"Some courtesy, to start," she snapped, closing the door with an audible thud. "This brown study of yours has gone on long enough, Vince. You are about to slip into a fit of black depression, if you are not very careful. I have not seen you like this since you returned from Waterloo. And over what? A—"

He slammed his palms down on his desk and stood. "Your opinion of my intended bride is no longer of moment to me."

She backed away a step, the lines in her still lovely face deepening. "So, it is she?"

"I do not know. Yet. But I shall. However, her identity, one way or the other, need not concern you. I still intend to wed her."

"But why?" She blinked rapidly and he realized she was holding tears at bay.

Blast it, he could never bear to see any woman he loved cry. Besides, she was not to blame for his mood. He slumped back down at his desk, too tired for more prevarication. She might as well begin to understand her new daughter-in-law now. "Because I weary of the nights alone, the days without laughter, the years that pile up like gravestones marking my life to pass unmourned. I want someone to love, even if she doesn't love me, and children, even if I must have them with a woman not of my own station. She is a good mother, kind to others, a charming conversationalist, well read and well traveled. Surely you can see that these are excellent attributes for a politician's wife?''

Neither her rigid stance nor the mulish set of her mouth softened.

He sat upright to finish, with the exact enunciation he used in the House, ''All I care about is that she intrigues me, she arouses me and she does not bore me. Three virtues that make her sterling beyond compare, no matter her past. And frankly, I should think you would treasure her for the same reasons. Is it not enough that I want her?''

The impassioned end to his speech finally made her relent enough to say in a wobbly voice, ''How many years I have longed to hear you say those words about a young woman. Any *suitable* young woman.''

''Mother, she is suitable to me. And with time, I believe she will be suitable to society. You do not know her as I do.'' Vince picked up the miniature on his desk. ''God did not grant me my wish to wed Chantal. But I was so brash and immature then. Maybe, in His wisdom, He waited until I had more to offer a woman of quality. And she is a woman of quality, through and through, Mother, in all the ways that matter, no matter her birth or breeding.''

When she looked as though she might disagree, he waved a silencing hand. ''I've had her investigated by the runners. She never, according to those who knew her, accepted any of the men who courted her.'' He smiled wryly. ''Even myself.''

''And that great Scottish person who dogs her skirts? What is he to her?''

''That, too, I shall discover. In time.''

She took a kerchief from her skirt pocket and blew her upturned nose. Then, with the decisiveness he recognized with dread, she straightened. ''Very well. I wish to meet her. I have heard that she's opened some sort of dancing school. I shall book lessons.''

He lifted an eyebrow. ''I thought you'd given up dancing.''

''Many a thing I've given up for your sake, you young ingrate. This will not be the first time I've done something scandalous for you, either.'' Regret shadowed the lovely blue eyes so like his. She seemed about to say something, bit her lip and turned to the door. ''You shall accompany me. On the morrow.''

For once, Vince didn't argue. Gently, he set the miniature back down, some secret instinct telling him all would be well. He smiled with anticipation, visualizing Chantal's expression when she saw him. . . .

A short distance away, in Grosvenor Square, another family squabble was brewing, though only one of the men present at the vast dining table knew it yet. Bartholomew Canfield, as he did every morning, breakfasted with tea, a coddled egg and dry toast. No kippers, kidneys or rashers of ham for the richest cit in England. He ate as he did everything else: with an economy of effort and expense to save both for when they were truly needed.

He spread his financial news out before him on the table as he ate, not dropping so much as a crumb on the pages, so dextrous were his movements. He started to skim through the society pages, as he always did, saw a small artist's rendering of a lovely face and froze. He flipped back to the page. Absently, he stirred sugar into his second cup of tea, missed the cup and dropped the spoon on the floor.

Arrested, John Whitmore glanced up from his own reading. His uncle by marriage was never so clumsy. Curious, John rose, set the spoon back on the table and snapped his fingers at an attentive servant to bring another. Canfield didn't even look up.

John rounded Canfield's chair to see what so fascinated his employer. He paled as he saw a portrait of Papillone. The caption read, "London's most celebrated ballerina retires from the stage."

Heavily, John sat back down. He'd been expecting this, but it was too soon. He wasn't ready yet. He toyed with the rest of his own breakfast, waiting for Canfield to speak.

Finally, after he'd obviously reread every word of the brief story, Canfield set the paper down with a thwack. He shoved his own barely touched breakfast aside. "John, I wish you to engage this ballerina to come here for dinner tomorrow night."

"Might I ask why, sir? Do you intend to take a mistress at last?"

"No, no, none of that. I'm too old for such nonsense. I lost the only woman I've ever loved, but I am curious about this girl. She sounds like a handful and a half."

Astute as ever, you old buzzard. You still don't know the half of it, John thought. But he merely nodded. "I

143

will seek her out and give her your message.''

Canfield stood with more energy than he'd shown in months. ''Do not take no for an answer, mind. Pay her if you have to. I do not care about the amount.''

''Quite.'' John departed, jamming his hat down over his ears. What would Canfield do when he discovered that his trusted assistant and nephew already knew the delectable Papillone, had in fact set her up in a new endeavor?

When Lizzie ushered Vince into her office later that day, Chantal revealed little of her reaction. She'd just ended her first series of lessons and her feet ached. The way her spirit soared on seeing him only irritated her more. ''What do you want?''

The dragon-headed cane, which he'd been idly twirling, went still. He kicked her office door closed with his foot, sat down in the straight-backed chair opposite and said mildly, ''If this is the way you greet all of your customers, you must not have many.''

She stared at him. ''Customer?''

''My mother and I both wish to be taught the waltz.''

''You both already know how to dance. And how to make others dance to your tune.'' She bit her tongue, wishing she'd withheld that last remark, for it showed how much she'd been affected by him.

''Odd you should feel that way, because I have found quite the opposite. You dance to no one's cues but your own, whatever they might be. You shall, in fact, make a master instructor in the fine art of the waltz, which is surely an analogy for the intricate and intimate relationship men and women share. We men suffer the illusion that we do the leading, and I confess that I shall be interested to see what new steps you introduce me to.''

They were no longer talking about dancing, Chantal knew. The thought of touching him, brushing against him hip to thigh, made her flush and go cold with alarm at the same time. Damn him, his moves were the dangerous ones. If he only knew the damage they could do, and not just to her. But that secret she would take to her grave, so she could only choose between accepting or rejecting him as a client.

But his mother . . . She was a different story. Chantal had often wondered if the old witch ever thought of the young girl she'd bribed and forgotten. Or cared about her shattered self-respect and loneliness. However, she had not the luxury of pride. The Countess of Dunhaven was almost on a social par with the likes of Sally Jersey and Countess Lieven; surely her patronage would give the new school the cachet it needed.

Still, practical or not, the words almost choked her, and her voice was husky when she said, ''I should be honored to tutor you both. How about nine o'clock, tomorrow?'' Lizzie would do the teaching, but he didn't need to know that.

Immediately, he rose, his watchful, suspicious gaze lightening with his smile. ''Excellent! Shall I write you a cheque now or in the morning?''

''Tomorrow will be soon enough. Good day.'' Before he'd even reached the door, she turned back to her accounts.

She felt him hover there, as if he wanted to say something else, but finally he gave her a curt little bow and departed. The accounts blurred before her eyes because she wanted nothing more in life than to call him back, kiss him and tell him who she was. However, she'd marked her path on a more tortuous course years ago, and she'd traveled too far to turn back now.

Still, no matter how she lectured herself, neither acceptance nor peace would come. The young ballerina passionate with life and love had, a decade ago, danced too close to the flame. She'd almost perished, but Chantal was beginning to realize she still slumbered somewhere beneath Papi's matronly dignity. The young girl wanted to laugh again, to love again, to know a man's touch again. And no matter how she told herself she had to be strong for Tony's sake, Chantal knew that, if she were not very careful, that young girl would break free in Vince's arms. . . .

Restless, Chantal tossed aside her boring tallying and stood to seek the only remedy that had kept her sane over the years. Unmarried women of her moral fortitude had dealt with these feelings in a variety of ways. Some pleasured themselves, others read, still others sought the forgetfulness of drink.

Chantal danced.

She dressed in her instructor's costume of loose but flowing purple smock belted around her tiny waist by a gold cord. She was covered from neck to heels, but the soft cotton molded lovingly to her form, and the deep color brought out the purple in her eyes. Chantal lit every gas lantern in the practice room, as if to dispel her own gloom, and began to dance.

She began slowly, swaying dreamily to an inner music, her arms weaving like flower stalks reaching for the sun. Her waist began to sway, then her hips, and finally her legs joined the dance. She was so caught up in her passionate affirmation of life, the only one allowed to her any longer, that she didn't hear the door open, or see John Whitmore enter.

He froze, staring in awe, and sank back into the shadows.

She went en pointe and minced across the floor, her arms arched gracefully above her head, and ended her trip before the mirrors with her hips arched forward. She rotated her hips a few times, watching herself in the mirror, lips parted and red, then she spun and bolted away in athletic leaps, as if frightened of her own sexuality. But she was soon back, as though she could not help herself. This time her stabbing steps alternated with vigorous kicks, higher and higher, until her loose smock bared her thighs.

Slowly, dreamily, she took the pins from her hair, tossed the thick black locks over one shoulder and ran her fingers through the curls, brushing down over her breasts. Then, in a burst of energy, she was off, twirling and kicking, kicking and twirling, higher and faster in a dancing climax as sensual as a sexual one would be.

Panting, she ended taut and graceful as a bow, her neck arched back, her heart beating at her throat. Then, wearily, she straightened and went limp, her head bowed. A movement made her lift her head. When John Whitmore emerged from the shadows, she went bright red.

The expression on his face and the bulge in his tight pantaloons told her how long he'd stood there. Chantal wanted to melt into the floor in her shame. She only danced like this when she knew she was alone.

"Sir, you should have said something." But her acid tone apparently had no effect on him, for he still advanced, the look on his face one she'd seen too often. She turned to run, but he caught her arm and whirled her back around into his grasp.

"I knew you were a hot one beneath that demure mask," he said huskily, hauling her against his rigid form. "Come with me, and I shall give you a bed big as a stage to revel in."

"No, John, you misun—" Her protest was muffled by his mouth. At first she stood quiescent. She owed this man a great deal, after all. But when he bent her back over his arm and thrust his tongue into her mouth, she began to struggle. When her genteel squirming had no effect, she tried kicking his leg. But her soft dancing shoes did no damage. In fact, he pulled her even closer.

Another woman might have panicked. Another woman might have screamed. And even the girl she'd outgrown would have waited for her handsome soldier to save her. But the new Chantal had the delicate power and fortitude of her namesake.

Butterflies flew across continents to reach their nesting grounds. Buffeted by the winds of change, preyed on by predators, they yet reached their goals with delicate wings intact. They achieved their end by the same advantages that saved her now: steely grace of form and sheer stubbornness of will.

Using both to good effect, she went limp, leaning back in his clasped arms until he had to bend over farther to hold her. Still more she leaned backward, pressing her feet firmly against the floor between his widespread legs. Finally, his own balance thrown off, he loosened his clasp and raised his mouth.

Swift and true as a Monarch butterfly, she ducked under his reaching arms and flickered across the stage, evading his clumsy grab. When he hurried after her, she ran to the hat rack beside the door and grabbed it, poking him in the belly with the bright, polished brass he'd helped her select from the curiosity shop down the street. "No, John. Be still." Her tone had much the ring of a schoolmistress trying to calm an unruly pupil.

However, while the tone might have had little effect, the jab in his belly made him blink. That blind, sexual urge to possess began to ease. The look that replaced it concerned her more: sheer, outraged male pride.

"Why the deuce do you dance like a tart if you do not wish to be treated like one?" He slapped the hat rack aside.

Anger flickered to life, replacing her guilty resignation. "I thought I was alone. I dance like that for no man." Save one. She slammed the hat rack down, shoving aside with equal savagery the poignant memory of the last time she'd danced like that for a man. And what it had led to. . . .

His red-faced outrage began to fade. "But my dear, there is no need for you to be so . . . unfulfilled." He approached to take her hand and kiss it, adding tenderly, "Wed me today, by special license, and I shall satisfy you in every way a man can satisfy a woman."

Uncomfortably, Chantal withdrew her hand. "Sir, you are most kind, but I have been an independent female for too many years. I am happy as I am." Well, as happy as it was possible to be, she amended.

"You did not dance like a satisfied female."

Even as she flushed again, she cocked her head with the distinctive, feminine strength she'd learned from her mother. "Please, let us not discuss the matter any longer. Now, how may I help you?"

He collected himself with visible effort and said curtly, "I have come to invite you to sup with my employer. He wishes to meet you."

Chantal was shaking her head before he finished. "Sir, I've already told you, I do not wish to ally myself with any man—"

"Even the richest merchant in England?"

That caught her off guard, but only for a moment. She shrugged. "I would not become the mistress of the king himself, no matter how flattering the invitation."

Grudging admiration flickered in those gray eyes, inciting her own lively curiosity. Sometimes he seemed almost prepared to dislike her, until she did something he considered unusual for a woman. Like rejecting a wealthy suitor. Indeed, he seemed to have a poor opinion of women in general; not for the first time, she wondered why. She squelched her own growing unease and politely listened to his explanation.

"I fear you misunderstand. Mr. Canfield has never, to my knowledge, kept a mistress. He is too busy with his various enterprises. He merely admires your dancing and your courage and is curious to meet you. I should hate to disappoint him, as he is a most generous man. In fact, you will make me look ineffectual if you do not accept, for he gave me most express instructions that I was not to take no for an answer. Very few people refuse Bartholomew Canfield."

Now where had she heard that name? That was it—John and Vince had discussed him that night at the party. Vince seemed to respect him, which was recommendation enough for Chantal. "Is he an old gentleman?"

"Quite old." His tone said, *Quite safe*.

"Very well. When does he wish me to come?"

"Tomorrow evening. At seven." He gave her the address in Grosvenor Square. "I shall be glad to escort you, if you wish. My presence is required, anyway."

"That will not be necessary. I shall take a hansom." And use the last of her cash to do it, but she'd be damned if she'd go to the home of the wealthiest merchant in England like a kept woman. That was one of the most expensive areas in the whole of London. She made a mental note to wear her most costly, most dignified dress. And since she only had one garment that qualified, the choice did not take long.

John tipped his hat to her. "Thank you, my dear. And . . . I regret if I gave offense earlier. I can only plead the force of my feelings for you."

Chantal shook her head. "Your behavior was no worse than my own, sir. The incident is forgotten."

"Excellent." He bowed deeply. "Until the morrow." He strode out.

Only when the door had closed did Chantal slump. God, she was tired. Why was life always so ruddy complicated, as Lizzie would say?

The next morning, exactly two hours before Chantal's first lesson appointment, an ebony carriage with scarlet silk hangings, led by a matched pair of blacks with ornate headdresses, drew up before her school. The school itself still had a closed sign on the door, but the rooms above on the second floor blazed with light in the early morning fog.

The carriage's occupant, heavily veiled, stepped down daintily on the steps her coachman set up. For a moment, she stared inside the school windows at the glimmer of light in the back. The lady, for such she obviously was, cupped her hands against the glass to peer at the office door, which was barely visible from the front. When Chantal exited to carry a plant out of the office, the lady shrank back so Chantal wouldn't see her.

Easing to the side, she nodded at her coachman.

He walked briskly up the steps beneath a small side portico to the flat above and banged the brass knocker on the dark green wood door. Hugo answered, scowling down at the smaller man.

"The Countess of Dunhaven wishes an audience, my good man," the coachman said with the loftiness only a nobleman's servant can display.

Snobbery bounced off the granite countenance so far above the coachman. "The mistress be not at home." Hugo stepped back to close the door.

A very well-bred, very icy voice preceded the lady's measured steps up to the door. "It is not your mistress I came to see. You are Hugo, I apprehend." The lady pushed back her veil to reveal a still pretty but lined face. "I am Adeline, soon to be your mistress's mother-in-law, I believe."

When Hugo only stared at her stupidly, she snapped, "Well, my good man, stand aside. I wish to meet my new grandson-to-be."

Sheer force of will moved the mountain aside. Slowly, still gaping, Hugo opened the door wide.

"You may have the rest of the day off, Robert. I do not want anyone to see my carriage, so I shall take a hansom home," said the countess. Robert was left alone outside, wearing the surly expression he was careful never to let his employers see. The door closed, and all was quiet.

He started when a faint scream sounded. Then a thump came as a body hit the floor. He heard faint Gaelic cursing, and the rattle of a glass being filled.

His scowl became a grin when a clear young voice asked, "Who is that lady, Hugo, and why has she fainted?"

Precisely at the appointed hour of nine, Vince arrived for his lesson, wondering irritably where his mother had got to. She had been impossible of late. But as he jumped off his powerful bay and tied up the gelding, honesty compelled him to admit that he'd hardly been easy to live with either. Not since . . .

Sighing, he shoved the door to the school wide. Several other people were already stretching before the huge mirrors, led by a tall young woman Vince recognized as the girl Chantal had introduced on her last night at the ballet. Of Chantal, he saw no sign.

Lizzie eyed him appreciatively, her smile growing wider as he removed his jacket and stood straight in his lawn shirt and tight pantaloons. He bowed slightly. "You are Miss Elizabeth, I believe. I am Vincent Kimball, at your service."

Dressed in a long smock, she made him a slight curtsey. "Thank ye, sor. And welcome ye be."

To whom? Vince wanted to retort, still looking around for his errant love. The other people gawked at his scowl. They were dressed in coarser attire, and obviously knew a lord when they saw one, whether he was incognito or not.

Lizzie clapped her hands. "Enough introductions, bloke—ah, laidies and gentmun. Continue with your practicing, if you please." And she led them through more stretching exercises.

Before joining in, Vince watched curiously. He'd seen men stretch so before duels or battle, but he'd never believed dancing was so strenuous as to require it. Indeed, many physicians scoffed at the need, saying it merely stressed the same muscles that would shortly be stretched. However, Vince had noted that when he moved about vigorously before riding or hunting, he usually came through the most tiring activity unscathed. He was even more intrigued that Chantal had apparently embraced the radical tactic. There were depths to the ballerina he couldn't wait to plumb.

Heaviness settled in his groin as another vision flashed across his mind's eye.

The door opened. Glad for the distraction, Vince glanced up. The man who entered with a lovely young girl on his arm looked vaguely familiar. He was an average-looking fellow of medium height and slim build, with mousy brown hair and unremarkable eyes. He had the bearing and body type of some of the best spies Vince had known during the war. Men such as he could slip in and out of the oddest places without being caught simply because, like chameleons, they could blend into every setting. As Vince stared at the fellow, trying to place him, the new arrivals joined him at the mirror.

The man smiled tentatively. "You are Lord Dunhaven, are you not?"

Vince nodded. "And I have the pleasure of . . ."

"Quincy Renner, my lord. We have met at the House of Commons a time or two, I believe."

"Oh yes, I remember now." Actually, what Vince remembered was not exactly complimentary, but he was too well-bred to say it. Vince held out his hand. "Good to see you again, sir. And this is . . . ?" Vince glanced at the girl next to him. She was a dainty little thing with striking blond hair and big blue eyes, a walking, talking advertisement for Dresden.

"This is my daughter. I want her to be instructed in the finer arts, and this seemed as good a place to start as any."

"Do you still work with Orator Hunt?" The famous speaker had fallen somewhat from grace a few years before, when rumors of his messy private life surfaced, and after that terrible massacre at Peterloo. The dragoons had slaughtered men, women and children impartially when Hunt's fiery oration about the evils of the corn laws caused a riot.

"Not often. I have been too busy with affairs of state."

Renner was the chief secretary to one of the more radical members of the Commons, and he'd been rumored to have unsavory connections with some of London's worst rabble-rousers.

However, as Vince had never been swayed by gossip, he smiled pleasantly and discussed that safest of all subjects, for it brought universal disapproval from rich and poor alike: the execrable English weather. Renner was agreeing that the recent rains had lasted even longer than usual when a door opened and closed and soft footsteps approached.

Every nerve in Vince's body awoke, and he didn't need to turn to know that Papi approached at last. He turned anyway, his breath catching in his throat at sight of her.

Like Lizzie, she wore a simple smock, but hers was purple, and a gold cord cinched her small waist. Another gold cord was wrapped through the thick black braid that looped over her shoulder to her waist. Her hair hadn't been so long when he knew her before, if she was indeed Chantal. It was getting harder and harder to remember that this ballerina might not be his lost love; it was getting easier and easier not to care.

Papillone was fascinating in her own right. More fascinating, in some ways, than the spirited young girl who'd won his heart. For this was a woman grown, the most formidable opponent Vince had ever faced, and he knew it would take every wile he possessed to win her.

However, when she greeted them, her gaze passing over him without lingering, he merely smiled and nodded with the rest. She went down the small group, ascertaining the interest of each person, and when only the theatrical couple at the end expressed a wish to be tutored in ballet, she nodded briskly. "My assistant will lead those of you interested in the waltz. I shall teach the ballet."

Ignoring Vince's scowl, Papi nodded at the nervous young man sitting in the corner. He lifted the violin he held to his chin, set bow to strings and began to play a lively measure.

The ballerina led the couple to the end of the room to show them the basic ballet positions. First she demonstrated the plié, then she stood back and watched them try to duplicate her effortless movement. She shook her head, moving about the couple, lifting the woman's arms, standing next to the man to show him how to place his feet.

"Sir, don't ye want to dance with the young laidy?" Lizzie's voice penetrated Vince's absorption. "We shall be even then, laidies and gents."

Flushing, he banished his vision of Papi leading their own children through the dance with the same patience and skill. "Yes, of course." Vince struck the proper pose with Lettie Renner, one hand lightly touching her waist, the other holding their clasped hands high.

Vince didn't bother counting with the laborious one-two-three Lizzie encouraged. He'd danced since he was ten, and he barely noticed when Lettie stumbled a time or two. He was too busy staring over her shoulder into the mirror, where he could just glimpse Papi dancing now with the handsome older man while the man's partner watched, nodding.

Dammit, he didn't like seeing other men touch her, even so impersonally. What the hell was he doing here, especially if she was going to refuse to dance with him? The lively music had ended with a crash, but he was still dancing when Lettie stepped on his foot as she stumbled to a stop.

Several snickers slipped out from the others as Vince froze, staring at himself in the mirror.

Lizzie smiled. "That was good, everybody. Shall we change partners, as ye would at one o' them fancy balls?"

Vince found himself hauling around a fat woman in enough pink lace to drape the bow window. And he was paying for this? During the next interval, he checked his pocket watch. He couldn't bear this torture

157

much longer. It was not like his mother to be late. Was something wrong?

For the first time in ten years, something was going right for the Kimball family, Adeline reflected as she sat next to her grandson. During the past two hours, they'd gotten to know one another. The boy was a delight. He was intelligent, kind and far more refined than she'd ever expected any child of that French guttersnipe to be. Still, despite her sordid background, Chantal was descended from royalty on her mother's side, and in the case of Tony, blood had told the tale. With one look at his red-gold hair, spring-green eyes and mischievous smile, Adeline had known the truth. She had seen the old miniature of Callista Raleigh Kimball when she was ten. And save for the difference in gender, the boy was the image of the great-grandmother he had never known.

Faced with Vince's ultimatum, she had come here to decide for herself whether she could bear to have this by-blow live in her house with his scandalous mother. A chore had become a delight, a duty a pleasure. For the tenth time, she hugged the boy.

He squirmed away, moving a bit farther down the couch, and wiped the kiss on his cheek away. "Aw, don't go all smarmy on me." He cocked his head, reminding her of his mother. "Are you really my grandmama?"

She nodded.

"Then you must know my father! Take me to him." He jumped up.

Adeline swallowed. She'd been too shocked and

158

thrilled to find the Kimball heir to think what damage she might do to the boy if he discovered the truth on his own. "Ah, I am not sure your mother is ready for you to know your father yet."

"My mother told me my father was dead." The flat contradiction was punctuated by flaring green eyes that proved the boy was indeed a direct descendant of his fiery ancestor. "I shall give her a firm talking-to, I assure you. But perhaps she didn't know how to find him."

"Perhaps," Adeline agreed hastily. Too hastily, for Tony sank back down beside her, looking woebegone. My, the lad was smart. Too smart to fool so easily.

"Will you take me to him or not?"

"Can we not get to know one another first? I am so honored to meet you, my dear sir. Would you like to go to the Palindrome?"

His nose wrinkled, but he was distracted for the moment, proving that she had once been the mother of a precocious boy herself. "No. I've already been there, but I should love to see Tattersall's."

She rose. "Then let us go. They have the sweetest goers, as my son would say. You appreciate fine horses, then?"

"I should say so! I want to have my own, one day. I shall wash up and be back directly." He disappeared into the next room. Hugo emerged, looking uneasy.

Vaguely, she realized the huge young man stood before her, but Adeline had to blink away tears. She was partly to blame for the way her grandson had grown up. Why, his own horse was the smallest of his inheritance, but he talked of it as if it would be his greatest joy in life. She looked around the clean but sparse room, and a pang of guilt she'd never known made her sway on her feet.

In bribing Chantal to leave, she'd paid for the loss of the one thing she and Vince could not win with power, wealth, prestige or charm. Someday she might grow to see the rough justice in that. For now, she could only grieve over the nine years in Tony's life that she'd lost.

Hugo caught her arm. "Steady now, milady. Where do ye take the boy?"

She dashed her tears away on her sleeve. "He wishes to go to Tattersall's."

When she was firm on her feet, he released her. "I must ask the mistress."

She caught his arm, unaccustomed to having to plead for anything from anyone, least of all a common Scotsman, but the words came easily enough. "I swear that I will do naught to hurt the boy, that I will bring him back after our outing and that I will not tell his father about him unless Chantal gives me leave to do so."

Resignation flickered on his face as she spoke that forbidden name. "Ye know then?"

"Tony is the image of Vince's grandmother. Chantal apparently doesn't realize that, nor does my son. He has met the boy?"

Hugo nodded. For once, countess and common man stared at one another, the same thoughts in their heads.

What would they do? And how could they protect Tony from being hurt?

When the interminable lesson at last ended, Vince hauled his jacket over his shoulder with irritation. He nodded at Renner, who smiled as he escorted his daughter out. Vince even managed a smile back at the fat woman. However, when Chantal threw Lizzie a meaning look, and Lizzie came over to escort him to the door, Vince balked.

"I have yet to pay for my lesson."

Chantal waved him away. "I give you one free. You obviously do not need them."

Vince's fraying patience snapped. He ripped off his jacket again, tossed it uncaringly on the floor and approached the dance instructor. "No? You, who dared to claim that I make you dance to my tune, you who have barely looked at me for the past two hours, *you* make a judgment on a skill you have not tested?" He stopped in front of her and held out his arms. "There is a better way to find out."

Chantal stared at him coldly. "I don't care to, thank you." She tried to turn away, but he caught her wrist and whirled her into his arms.

She scowled. "I've had enough manhandling for the nonce, thank you."

His touch immediately gentled. "What do you mean by that?"

She shook her head. "If you insist, I am certain Lizzie can lead y—"

"Whom do you fear, my little love? Me? Or yourself?" Vince stroked her bare arm from wrist to shoulder. He felt gooseflesh rise at his touch.

Her gaze had fallen to his mouth. "I . . . I . . ."

"Please, one dance. Then I shall torment you no longer."

When she saw her friend's obvious distress, Lizzie stepped forward, but Chantal shook her head, took a deep breath and accepted Vince's hand. Lizzie clapped

161

her hands at the staring young violinist. He screeched into action, so busy ogling the handsome couple that he was several stanzas into his music before his bow began singing instead of caterwauling.

At the touch and feel of her, Vince's breath began to quicken. She was soft and light as down in his arms, but more woman than he could ever hope to hold. Despair mingled with elation made his head spin even as he whirled her around, taking full advantage of the spacious room. He held her eyes, trying to convey how much she thrilled him, how much he wanted her.

Her own eyes had darkened to a purple to match her gown. She saw, she heard, she understood. Her hand trembled slightly as he drew her closer, but she didn't pull away. Where he led, she followed, their steps moving as one.

"See how well we are matched?" he whispered, pressing his chin against her temple. He could feel her breasts brushing against him now, and the heaviness in his loins grew until he knew she could feel him, too. To his delight, when he drew her hips closer with his hand upon her waist, she didn't draw away. She wanted him, too. Why did she fight so hard?

And then her head was resting on his shoulder and she was swaying with him, hip to thigh. He had to force himself to recall the onlookers, so badly did he want to pull her even closer. She would drive him mad if she didn't stop playing these blasted games. Her lips said one thing, but her body said something else entirely.

"Is it so terrible to follow a man, if he leads you well?" She stiffened in his arms. He cursed under his breath at his own stupidity, trying to ease her close again, but he'd spoiled his advantage.

She jerked free, her breasts heaving under their thin covering. Her nipples were hard. He raked her with his gaze, not trying to hide his own arousal. He held a pleading hand out to her. "Have dinner with me tonight."

With a brisk flip of her braid to her back, she seemed to collect herself. "I cannot. I am already engaged for the evening."

"With whom?" He expected her to bite his head off, but she merely smiled sensually.

"The richest merchant in England has invited me to sup with him."

Astonishment made Vince back up a step. "Bartholomew Canfield? I did not know you knew him."

"I do not. But I shall. Who knows? Before the evening is out, I may know him very well indeed."

Lizzie and the musician gawked at the two of them, but neither of them noticed, so intent were they on their battle.

Vince wanted to reach out and grab her. He wanted to carry her off and ravish her. But first, he wanted to paddle her. However, since he was too civilized to do any of those things, he merely arched an uncaring brow to hide his own rage and pain. "So, you've decided to become a dancer in deed as well as name. I confess I hoped you'd choose me, but as Canfield can buy me several times over, no doubt you've made a wise decision. And when he touches you with his stubby, age-marked hands, think of me. You can be assured I will think of you no longer."

He turned on his heel and stalked out, leaving his coat on the floor.

Chapter Six

Through a film of tears, Chantal stared at the coat on the floor. Dismissing the musician with a jerk of her head, Lizzie moved toward her, her hands outstretched, but stopped when Chantal bent to pick up the navy blue jacket. She pulled it over her shoulders and hugged herself, the sleeves trailing down over her hands. She rubbed the soft superfine against her cheek, inhaling deeply of the scent of the man who'd worn it. And then, as if her feet had the wings of hope she denied her heart, she ran to her office, slammed the door closed and locked it.

Her mouth working in sympathy for her friend, Lizzie stayed frozen in the center of the room, wondering what to do. Blimey, the Quality didn't act with the good sense God gave a goose. And though her employer had never spoken of her background, Lizzie knew a lady when she met one; that gent was obviously a blueblood, from his proud chin to his noble arse.

And a noble arse he was making of himself. Couldn't he see that the lady was trying to protect her son? No one had to tell Lizzie that Papi feared the boy's reaction if she accepted this lord's "protection."

Curious term, that. One more lie the Quality told themselves to make their debauchery less shocking. Lizzie worried at the cord about her waist, listening to those heart-rending sobs, but she sensed that Papi would not welcome sympathy, at least not now. There was unfinished business 'tween those two, Lizzie decided. Too much emotion, too strong an attraction. In fact, though Lizzie had little familiarity with that odd feeling herself, she'd seen the other flower girls act like regular ninnyhammers, sashayin' about with their beaus on their arms, mopin' when they weren't.

Love.

Lizzie wrinkled her nose, wondering if she'd ever be lost in that sweet madness. She shrugged, hoping she wouldn't. 'Twasn't proper, as her ma would say, to ever forget yer plaice in the world, or Him that put ye here.

But for Papi . . . well, the lady had herself admitted she preferred to wed, if she could wed the right gent. And, knowing exactly who that right gent be, Lizzie decided that mayhap she could help things a bit. For Lizzie Mayfield always repaid a kindness with a kindness. She gave Papi a bit longer and then knocked softly on the door. "Can I get me clothes, Papi? I . . . got an appointment."

A sniffle sounded, and then a nose blew fiercely. The bolt was thrown and the door swung wide. Lizzie entered hesitantly to find her friend hanging the dark blue jacket on the coat rack beside the door. She kept her face averted as she said, "*Excusez-moi*, Lizzie. Sometimes . . . never mind that. We have no further lessons today, so I think I shall go soak in a hot tub."

Lizzie nodded, pretending nothing untoward had happened, and tossed her clothes over her arm. "I'll help ye heat the water 'fore I leave."

As they walked toward the door, Chantal glanced at her taller friend. "Are you seeing a beau?"

"No, no, nothin' like that. Jest . . . someone who needs settin' straight about somethin'."

"I see," Chantal said, though it was obvious she did not. When she entered the flat, she called, "Tony! Hugo!" There was no answer. Chantal shrugged. "Tony's been begging to go to Tattersall's. I imagine Hugo finally indulged him."

While they heated water, they kept up safe chatter about their pupils, who had talent and who didn't. "That pretty little gel is light on her feet, right enough," Lizzie observed.

"Yes. She came to us on John Whitmore's recommendation to her father, I believe. I am told that Mr. Renner knows a great many people in Parliament, and that I should go out of my way to be civil to him."

As she poured the first bucket of hot water in the hip-deep copper tub, Lizzie nodded. Chantal sorted carefully through her clothes and pulled out a stunning but demure gown of watered gold silk. The low neck was fitted with cream-colored lace, gathered at the neck into a high-standing collar that would make a porcelain frame for the wearer's face. The same lace peeped at the long hem and puffed sleeves. A long cream silk sash tied at the high waist into a bow, meeting at the back where the cut left the wearer's back bare.

Lizzie poured in the last bucket, sighing as Chantal put out cream lace gloves, her mother's brooch and cream silk slippers. "You'll look like Cinderella in that fancy dress, Papi."

Chantal added a bucket of cold water to the tub, mixed the water with scented bath salts and removed her clothes to lean back with a weary sigh. "It shall be a very odd godmother I meet this night, then. I wonder if Canfield is my true financier and John just hasn't told me?"

Lizzie removed her smock to dress carefully in her own new dress. "Who is this Canfield bloke?"

"A wealthy man who's asked to meet me."

Lizzie scowled, one sleeve on, one off. "Fer what?"

"Curiosity, I'm told."

"Yes, well, just ye remember, as me ma always said, 'twas curiosity what killed the cat—and the butterfly."

Chantal touched the scented steam rising from the tub with a reflective, gentle finger. "If that's his intention, he will have a rude awakening."

"Then why do ye go?" Lizzie pulled up her other sleeve and stretched her long arms behind her back to button herself.

"I cannot afford to insult such a powerful man. A dinner costs me nothing." Chantal grimaced. "Besides, anything I don't have to cook tastes wonderful."

Lizzie laughed. She already knew how much her new friend hated to cook, but they'd both had enough of Hugo's haggis and oatmeal to last a lifetime. She contorted her spine to reach those last pesky buttons.

Chantal sat up. "Here, bend down and I'll help you with that."

Surprise flitted across Lizzie's face, for the thought of help had not occurred to her. But she turned her back and knelt.

Chantal dried her hands on a towel and buttoned the last buttons. "We are friends, are we not? We must count on one another, and help one another."

Lizzie stood, her face flushed, and went to the mirror to brush her hair. Aye, it was true. She weren't used to help in dressing, or in anything else. Her employer's warmth began to melt the ice around Lizzie's wary heart, and she became more than ever determined to help her new friend find the happiness she deserved.

When she'd pinned her hair neatly back and set that detested bonnet at a jaunty angle, Lizzie turned to smile at Papi, who was now washing her abundant black hair. "Then I guess I'll see ye later this evenin'."

"Yes. I'm not quite sure when I'll be back. I'll leave a note for Tony and Hugo if they do not return before I depart. You have your key?"

Lizzie patted her pocket. "Have fun, Papi."

"You, too, my dear."

Not bloody likely. And if the blueblood she went to see thought he could continue to pull at Papillone's wings like a spoiled schoolboy, well, 'twas time he was sent to the corner.

And so the residents of the flat above the new dancing school went about their business, unaware that separately they toiled for the same end: uniting Chantal and Vince.

When, shortly after seven that evening, Hugo unlocked the door to an empty flat, Adeline sagged with relief. She wasn't ready to face Chantal yet. First, she had to tell Vince the truth, for if he learned it from anyone else, he'd never forgive her.

She looked down at Tony's grubby, happy face, his curly red hair, and admitted that any words she had to eat, any sacrifice she had to make and any distasteful dancer she had to embrace would be a small price to pay to secure this delightful little boy as the rightful heir to the Kimball estates. Of course, Vince would have to legally adopt the lad, but that was a minor formality that would be easy enough. Aborting the scandal, should the truth out, would be much harder. . . .

Tony's solemn bow recalled her from her machinations. "Grandmama, I wish to thank you most effusively for the multitudinous joys we have shared this day." Tony cradled the new bag of marbles she'd purchased for him and set his bag of candy down on the table beside the couch.

Hiding a smile, she bent to kiss Tony's sticky cheek. They'd stopped at half the confectionaries between here and Tattersall's trying to satisfy the sweet tooth Tony seldom got to indulge. Adeline wet her clean kerchief in an ewer of water and knelt to clean his face. " 'Tis I who must thank you, my boy. But mind, now—keep our secret. At least until I can bring your father to you. I shall tell him about the gelding you liked at Tattersall's. We shall begin your riding lessons very soon."

Now that the grime was removed, Adeline could see the flush coloring the boy's cheeks, though his excitement was obviously greatest at meeting his father. "When will you bring him?"

"As soon as I can." Adeline rose, twiddling with her reticule, wondering how to thank the towering Hugo. One simply did not have physical contact with the lower classes, so she couldn't kiss his cheek as she wanted to—even if she could reach it. She sensed that Hugo was almost as much responsible for Tony's healthy, happy life as his mother.

Finally, she said simply, "Thank you, Hugo. You are a good man. You have my word that I shall be discreet until we get everything sorted out. I will let nothing harm Tony."

Bashfully, he stubbed his work-booted toe into the carpet. "Thank ye, me lady." He escorted her to the door, summoned a hansom and helped her inside. During the short drive home, she leaned weakly against the hard seat, trying to marshal her arguments, for she knew she'd have need of every wile she could summon if she were to appease her son.

The decanter rattled as Vince poured a second brandy. It was growing dark, which suited his soul, and it was getting cold, which suited his passions. Desire had brought him and Chantal together. Desire had torn them apart. His for her; hers for anyone but him.

Despite her continual denials, despite her increasingly cruel rejections, instinct persisted in whispering that Papi and Chantal were one and the same. But she'd never admit it, and even if it were true, whatever bond they'd shared in childhood was obviously long broken—by her choice. His devotion would end as sadly as that of the steadfast little soldier, who was rejected by his lovely ballerina, only able to join her in death.

Let her go. She doesn't want you. No matter how

many times he reiterated the words, they didn't ring true. Even today, when she'd danced with him, she'd desired him. A woman could not fake hard nipples and dilated pupils. So how could she leave him and go to an old man?

Visualizing those stubby fingers caressing Chantal's flawless skin brought him such torment that even the third brandy didn't help much. But the fourth began to numb him. By the time his butler knocked and came in, Vince's gaze swam and he had to blink to focus.

"Sir, a young woman begs an audience. She says her name is Lizzie Mayfield." The butler's tone dripped with disapproval as he added, "She is alone."

Vince set his glass down on the edge of the desk. "Sh—send her in," he said with difficulty. He tried to straighten his cravat, but even without a mirror he knew it must be hopeless.

Shortly after, Lizzie entered, tall and imposing despite her youth. She looked at the decanter, she looked at the glass, and then, she looked at him. The contempt in that knowing hazel gaze acted like a slap in Vince's reddening face. He bolted upright, knocking over the glass. The brandy that soaked his privates made him wince, but conversely the icy hot chill further revived him. Leaving the glass where it fell, he waved her into a chair and enunciated, "To what do I owe the pleasure?"

She shook her head and planted her feet. "Do ye love Papi?"

Slowly Vince sat back down. "You do get straight to the point, don't you?"

The girl responded dryly, "Someone needs to."

Chuckling ruefully, Vince propped his elbows on the

desk to peer at her. She seemed to be leaning sideways, so he moved his head with her until he blinked and refocused, realizing he was the one about to tip over. Blushing, he sat upright. If this girl hadn't obviously cared for her friend so much, and if he'd been less bosky, and less hurting, he'd have been more reserved. But under the circumstances, he responded before his normal barriers had time to rise. "That question is better asked of her, but I can save you the time. She doesn't want me. I've made it clear that I want her most acutely. I even offered to marry her. She's rejected every one of my overtures and is apparently about to enter a . . . business arrangement with Bartholomew Canfield."

Lizzie caught the back of the chair across from the desk and leaned foward to state, "She's only goin' to help the school. She told me herself that if he asked her to be his mistress, she'd send him about his business."

All of a sudden, the brandy seemed to take some of the chill away. Vince wrenched his cravat open, leaving it dangling about his neck. "The little minx, she gave me to understand there was more to it than that."

Lizzie nibbled at her sensual mouth, hesitating, but then she burst out, " 'Twas the only way she could stop ye from tormentin' her."

"I? Tormenting her?" Vince's laughter had a bitter ring. "You've the truth hind end first on that one, my dear. I cannot sleep, I can barely eat, I—"

" 'Tis the same fer her." Lizzie pushed back her bonnet and squinted at him, as if she had a hard time seeing him at such a distance. She seemed to be satisfied that he was properly tortured, for she nodded. "She would not thank me for tellin' ye this, but I believe she loves ye, me lord. And I do not know how, or when, but I think she's loved ye fer years.''

Vince's heart surged in his chest, sending more tingling warmth throughout his sluggish veins. He had to grip the desk harder to lever himself to his feet. ''Has she admitted she knew me before?''

''Not exackly. But why else has she rejected all them rich blokes for so long?''

''Indeed, but if I am her one true love, why does she continue to reject me?'' All of Vince's frustration rang in the question.

''I think it has somethin' to do with the little boy.''

Vince gasped. He sank back into his chair, stunned as the truth hit him. Good God, if the boy was truly his, Chantal probably feared he'd try to take him away.

Mission accomplished, Lizzie's satisfied expression said. She collected her reticule and straightened the bonnet she was apparently not used to wearing.

Vince collected himself enough to rush around the desk and open the door for her. And he must be sobering under the hopeful news, because he only stumbled once. ''How can I thank you for coming here and telling me the truth?''

Lizzie was so tall that their eyes were on a level, and he had no defense as clear hazel tested him for truth or deceit. He met her gaze steadily. Finally she said, ''By making her happy, me lord. Good evenin.' '' And she sailed out of the study, nodding regally as the butler opened the front door for her.

Weakly, Vince leaned against the study wall, wondering what the hell to do now. Unmask Chantal, and she might try to run again. Let her keep to her charade, and they'd go on in this hellish stalemate. Lizzie had brought him hope, but she'd also made the solution to his dilemma more problematic.

He had to see Chantal before he could decide how to proceed, and he needed an ally. A pudgy face and piercing gray eyes materialized before him like a genie from a bottle. Bartholomew Canfield was better at seeing through subterfuge and accomplishing the impossible than anyone Vince knew. Besides, what interest did the cit have in a penniless ballerina?

Feeling light-headed with nervousness, Chantal stepped down from the hansom, accepting the driver's helping hand. She gave him the fare, plus a small gratuity. "Would you return for me in three hours, please?"

He tipped his cap. "Aye, milady. Good even to ye."

"And the same to you." After he drove off with a brisk snap of his whip above his team, Chantal still hesitated. She turned and appraised the privileged district of manicured lawns, imposing statues and grand mansions. Gaslights had followed a circuitous route in London, springing up like wildflowers, without regard to geography or need, glowing first in the most expensive areas. And here, in Grosvenor Square, the entire neighborhood was a veritable night beacon, as if the lights understood what London's poor did not: neither grace, goodness nor generosity decided such matters.

Gold was the great determiner.

It elevated the low-born, celebrated the nameless and sanctified the wicked. And Chantal, who had been poor all her life, stood in the shadow of the tangible, towering proof of the power of gold, wondering why she'd been summoned like a heretic to worship at the feet of Baal. After her bath, she'd gone to the circulating library to seek more information about this man who seemed so interested in her.

From all she could discover, Canfield was a fascinating individual. He'd been born the son of a poor Welsh miner, the only surviving child of a brood of seven boys. Those who did not succumb to the coal dust died of accidents or disease, with the exception of this youngest son. Though his growth had been stunted by the cramped quarters and the foul humors of the mines, Canfield's small stature was apparently compensated by a lofty intellect. He had parlayed a lucky strike into a job as a mining engineer, conducting himself so skillfully that he began to be rewarded with first one small claim, then a larger one and so on until the poor coal miner's son not only owned the mine, he owned most of the mine owners after he bought them out.

When he conquered Wales, he moved on in a widening swath to the sea, north and south, like Alexander bent on conquest. But Canfield's methods were more subtle, for it was not the might of his sword that won him dominion but the glitter of his gold and the power of his persuasion. When he'd bought every coal, copper and silver mine he could, he bought the foundries. From there, he expanded into shipping, moving his refined ores to the great industrial ports of England, and from thence to the four corners of the earth, able to bargain for the best price since he controlled every aspect of the mining and distribution. He bought a seat on the exchange and made so many shrewd bargains and powerful contacts that he was rumored to be not just the wealthiest cit in England, but possibly the wealthiest man in all of Europe. His great enterprises expanded daily. His most recent interests were in retail, hostelries and steam engines.

However, as Chantal took a deep breath to steady herself and climbed those imposing steps, it was not his business acumen she admired but his apparent humanity. He'd instituted so many reforms in all of his many ventures that his employees, apparently numbering in the thousands, had not only refused to strike against him, they spoke of him in glowing terms even to the meanest reporters of London's most virulent rag sheets. Canfield not only paid a fair wage for a fair day's work, he scandalously based each employee's pay on performance, not seniority, or even need. Further, he refused to hire children. He'd instituted shorter working hours and paid holidays in all his enterprises. Many of his competitors were forced to do the same or lose their best help. Bartholomew Canfield was that most dangerous radical in a day of radicals—cool-headed, practical—and since he'd recently been elected to the Commons, he had a vast new forum for his ideas.

Admiring the four-story Palladian mansion, Chantal banged the lion-headed knocker against the huge mahogany door. She felt more secure in coming here after her research, for Canfield was not only old enough to be her father, he was reported to be a bit of a prude. He was not known to frequent bawdy houses or sponsor mistresses, and since his wife had died many years ago, childless, Canfield had been grooming his nephew by marriage to inherit his wealth. And that nephew, one John Whitmore, was already an admirer of hers, so Chantal concluded that she had nothing to fear in coming here. She suspected that Canfield's morals extended to his personal life and private passions, but tonight would tell the tale.

In fact, nervousness was quickly giving way to curiosity to meet the man who, unhappy with the destiny society decreed for him, had literally forged his own. Even without meeting him face-to-face as yet, Chantal already felt an affinity with this man so far above her station. And so, when the butler swung open the massive door, ushering her inside the domed foyer, she was able to give him her wrap and reticule without trembling.

"You are here at last!" John bolted down the carved marble steps that swept up the center of the circular entrance hall. One story up, they divided in opposite directions, rising to a lofty overlook above the black and white marble foyer. Alcoves, lit from above by gas, held Roman statues that she assumed were replicas until she moved closer. She gasped. That rich patina, the striking pose of Athena in her helmet holding her spear, could not be faked. And the next alcove held . . .

John smiled as her eyes widened to saucers. He nodded. "It's a genuine Michelangelo. But come, Bartholomew is eager to meet you." He held her arm and escorted her up the red-carpeted stairs to a vast dining salon that glittered with gilded molding, a king's ransom in sterling Sheffield silver, exquisite Austrian crystal sconces and a gold-rimmed bone china dinner service set for three at the long Chippendale table.

While Chantal studied the room, Canfield studied her. He stood at the head of the table, somber in a plain black frock coat from an earlier age and loose-fitting, comfortable breeches. His cravat was tied simply, but his buttons were gold, and his old-fashioned buckled

177

shoes glittered yellow as well. His pudgy, callused hand caught the chair back as she advanced toward him, still clasping John's arm. He might have swayed briefly as she came under the bright chandelier. His gray eyes closed, but by the time John led her across the vast room, Canfield's smile held only polite welcome.

As she made her curtsy, he bowed slightly, grimacing, and favored one leg. He lifted her up from her curtsy and seated her himself, saying, as if to put her at ease, "Don't ever grow old, dear lady. How unfair of life to imprison a young soul in a decrepit body."

Calmly, she spread her napkin over her lap as he sat down at the head of the table. "Indeed, but the reverse is even more distasteful. I have known my share of young people with old souls, and they are unhappy people indeed. After all, it is our souls that are remembered after we depart this earth."

Canfield burst into a booming laugh all the more startling in his small, pudgy frame. "By George, you've the right of it there! I knew you'd be as witty as you are lovely." His sharp gray gaze dropped to her bodice, but when she shifted uncomfortably, it moved back to her face.

Yet, as the first course of turtle soup was served, his eyes kept straying to her bodice often enough that she began to wonder if she'd been mistaken about his interest in a mistress. Their dialogue became more lively with every remove, for the minute John tried to shift the conversation to something innocuous, Canfield turned the subject on its end by saying something provocative. And each time, he avidly watched for her response, whether they discussed the shameful conduct of their new king, who had taken his libertine tendencies as Prince Regent with him onto the throne, or the shabby treatment of women in society.

He stabbed a piece of meat with relish as he jabbed at her, "And what think you of allowing women the right to vote, my dear?"

Chantal almost choked on a bite of pheasant. She coughed, swallowed and sipped the wonderful white wine to give herself time to think. Normally men avoided this subject like the plague. The mere idea was radical and seldom spoken of except by a few extremists, though Chantal had read that the American colonies had experimented, in their early years, with allowing free women to vote. When Canfield chewed methodically, still awaiting her response, she finally said, "I think we have earned it, but it will not be granted in my lifetime."

Defiantly, she lifted her chin and awaited condemnation. John Whitmore hid a frown in his napkin but deferred to his employer. Canfield's gray eyes took on a steely gleam as, once more, they dropped to her bodice before lifting to appraise her mutinous face. "And why is that, do you suppose?"

Carefully, Chantal placed her knife at just the right angle on her plate. "Why, I can only speculate, but I rather think it's the result of the same reason that children are treated so poorly in our society. Only men can own property, except in rare circumstances, only men can vote and only men can make our laws. Why should men do anything to limit their own power?"

John's fork rattled as he dropped it. He was obviously displeased with her honesty, but inwardly she shrugged. One shouldn't ask for an opinion unless one wanted the truth.

Canfield, however, seemed neither shocked nor disapproving. He wiped his mouth, calmly settled his napkin in his lap and raised a finger, indicating that they were ready for the next remove. While the attentive servants took the plates away, he let the tension build. Just when Chantal was squirming in her seat, he said gently, ''I confess to drawing the same conclusion, though I find it an odd one for a young woman. Most young women of your station have been so protected and pampered that they are quite content with their lot. . . .''

The way he trailed off invited her to fill the silence. She took another sip of wine, debating how to react. They'd had a different vintage with each course, but each wine had been of the finest quality, so smooth that it was easy to forget its potency. Assuming she'd never see him again after tonight, she admitted defiantly, ''I have been neither pampered nor protected. Such niceties as to whether women should think of these things are hard to distinguish when one is busy feeding and clothing oneself. From the time my mother fled with me from Napoleon to her death when I was only seventeen, I've had to fend for myself. In recent years, after the death of my husband, I've had a young son to support, so I've not had the luxury of debating this issue. I can only tell you that until women are allowed the right to vote, any gains society makes will be both transitory and superficial. A just society does not deny the rights of half of its citizens.'' She heard the ring of her own passion in the vast room and bit her lip to stem her diatribe.

John Whitmore's mouth had curled with distaste, but, again, he said nothing, watching his employer. She glanced at him and away, more than ever convinced that the front John Whitmore presented to the world bore little resemblance to the inner man. Which led to the logical question: Who was the real man?

As he clasped his hands on the table before him, Canfield's expression was unreadable. "So, you were born in France?"

Gladly she accepted the change in subject, thinking yet again that any man so perspicacious must be a force to be reckoned with in Parliament. "Yes, sir."

He lifted an encouraging eyebrow, but she pretended not to see. She'd made enough damaging confessions for one evening. She covered her wineglass with her hand when a servant moved to refill it and shook her head.

Canfield's cupid's bow mouth, an odd one for such a bulldog of a little man, flickered in a stifled smile. That might have been admiration deepening the color of his gray eyes to slate, or disgust. He had the best card-playing face of any man she'd ever come across. By the time the trifle melted in her mouth, Chantal was ready to leave. Whatever Canfield's purpose, her own had not been served in coming here. He'd not once brought up the subject of her academy, and she wasn't bold enough to hint.

As soon as she discreetly could, she pushed her half-eaten dessert away. "This has been a most . . . interesting evening, sir. I wish you the greatest good health and happiness." She set aside her napkin, intending to rise, but his next comment gave her pause.

"Young woman, I am not in the habit of being dismissed. Kindly be still and listen." Canfield tossed aside his own napkin with an air of decision.

Chantal tensed in her chair, liking neither his tone nor his arrogance.

That great booming laugh rattled the cutlery again. He shook his head admiringly. "You're a feisty little gel. I like that. I cannot abide people who never disagree with me. How would you like to work for me?" His gaze dropped to her bodice again.

How could she have misread him so? Chantal wanted to sink under the table in shame, but she mastered her flush and said evenly, "I am not a lightskirt, sir."

"Did I say you were?" he tossed back. "Do not flatter yourself. Not even your abundant charms are enough to perk up these weary old bones. Your position would be perfectly respectable, I assure you. I need a new secretary."

Her hackles lowered. "But sir, I have no experience in such matters. All I am really skilled at is dancing—"

"You've a sensible head on your shoulders, you are well read and have traveled extensively. That is all the experience I require. I shall be glad to train you. You may bring your son and your servant here to live. I shall assign you your own suite of rooms, and your salary will be very generous." He named a figure that stunned her.

Helplessly, Chantal shook her head. "I am flattered, truly, but I must beg the press of previous commitments."

For the first time, he scowled suspiciously. "Are you about to wed?" He said the words as if they lodged in his throat like a canker.

Again, she wondered at his interest in her. "No, no, it's just . . ." Pleading for help, she looked at John, who stared at his lap. Canfield obviously knew nothing of her dancing academy, or of his nephew's part in financing it, so John must be her sole financier. "I have begun my own business enterprise. I cannot desert my clients or my benefactor so capriciously.''

''And who is that?''

From the corner of her eye, Chantal saw John tense. ''That is not of moment. Now, if you'll excuse me. . . .'' She rose.

Canfield levered himself to his feet with effort, glaring at her. His lined face abruptly showed its age. He opened his mouth, but before he could speak, a discreet knock preceded the appearance of his dignified butler.

''Sir, pardon the intrusion, but the Earl of Dunhaven is below, begging an immediate audience.''

Whitening, Chantal dropped back into her chair.

Canfield's open mouth snapped closed as he eyed her shrewdly. He sat back down and clasped his hands before him again. ''Show him in.''

''Sir, I must leave,'' Chantal whispered, casting a hunted look about her for another exit. But there was none. She couldn't face Vince again. Every leave-taking grew harder than the last. Why must he keep following her?

Her whirling thoughts found little organization or surcease as Vince entered. He was dressed like what he was: a titled member of the landed gentry. His brown jacket and cream waistcoat set off his broad shoulders perfectly. His buff pantaloons molded every inch of his masculinity in a way that made her mouth go dry. His cravat's waterfall was intricate and framed his chiseled, solemn features in a way Brummel would have applauded. That he had dressed so carefully before he came here said much of his mission.

His gaze skimmed over her, paused on John and finally settled on Canfield. He came forward, stopping at the end of the table to bow. "Forgive the intrusion, Bartholomew, but I..." He shrugged, as if even the silver-tongued orator couldn't think of an excuse bold enough to justify his barging in like this.

Anger made the perfect bromide for Chantal's panic. "You've nosed your way into my affairs once too often, sir."

"Affairs?" He zeroed in on the word, scowling.

Canfield's pudgy nose twitched as he watched the byplay. John glared at Vince, but Vince had eyes only for Chantal.

Abruptly, Chantal stood and said with great dignity, "Since your business is so urgent, I gladly leave you to it, my lord. I was departing anyway." She turned a cold shoulder to Vince, whose gaze had dropped to her bodice and stopped there, and made Canfield an even deeper departing curtsey. "I have much enjoyed our evening, sir. Good-bye and godspeed."

Canfield came around to catch her hand and raise it to his lips. His beautiful mouth lingered there.

Craning his neck, staring fixedly in the area of the pin on her breast, Vince had an odd look on his face. Canfield was so short that he topped Chantal by only half a head. His thick dark hair was streaked with silver but gleamed black as the coal in which he'd made his fortune.

Whitmore, too, seemed uneasy at the strange tableau of the lovely young woman and rich old man. His long legs shifted restlessly under the table.

Finally, Canfield lifted his head to say, "I shall see you again, never fear, child. My coachman will see you home."

"That is not necessary. I have already engaged a hansom—"

"Necessary or not, such is the case. These deuced cabbies are charging too much, in my estimation." Canfield rang a bell beside the door. A footman in dark green livery materialized to escort Chantal downstairs. "Good even, child. And godspeed to you as well."

Never had any Cinderella fled with such alacrity or blessed relief. However, as she dashed down the marble steps, Chantal was careful to keep her shoes and her wits firmly about her. Something about this odd man made her nervous, she decided as she watched the butler dismiss her cab driver with a handsome tip. Canfield's interest in a young woman he'd never seen before this night was a bit too pronounced, and, if that same young woman had her way, he would never see her again. The way he kept staring at her bodice, plus his agitation when he'd thought her married . . . well, suffice it to say that Mr. Canfield's motives were as devious as he was. He would not be the first aging man, yearning for youth, to seek a celebrated mistress. Best to give him a wide berth. Papillone would not be the latest stepping stone on his search for the fountain of youth.

When she stepped out of Canfield's plush carriage, Chantal was glad to find familiar ground under her feet. She nodded regally, thanking the coachman, not noticing as he scribbled down her address, and ran up the steps to her flat. Inside, she was relieved to find Tony and Hugo there.

She hugged her son. "Where were you, *mon fils?*"

Tony glanced at Hugo for guidance. Tired she was, but her motherly instincts were alerted. Putting one hand on her hip, she turned to glare at Hugo. "Where have you two been?"

"We went to Tattersall's," he said, but his eyes never quite met hers.

"Hugo . . ." She tapped her foot, waiting for more.

Guiltily, Tony whipped a sack from beneath the couch cushions. "And he took me to the confectionary, even though he knows you do not like me to eat candy."

Relieved, wanting to laugh at her own lurid suspicions, Chantal smiled. She must still be shaken from that odd dinner party. "Once in awhile, *petite,* you can indulge yourself, but where did you find the money?"

"We . . . saved it." Tony opened his bag wide. "Pick something, *Maman.* The sweets are all—" he kissed his fingertips, looking very French just then, despite his decidedly English looks. "And how was your own engagement?"

Chantal was too busy munching and talking about the odd little cit to note the conspiratorial look that passed between her less than ingenuous son and her all too guileless servant. You let me handle her, Tony said wordlessly.

Shrugging, Hugo sought out his bed, where, his expression replied, he could get a little needed peace from all these sassenach stratagems. . . .

When Chantal was gone, Vince couldn't maintain his dignity any longer. He sank into a chair and wiped his sweaty brow. Canfield chuckled, his amusement more muted, and took his own seat again.

"In faith, she is a spirited little gel, isn't she? What have you done to put her nose out of joint?"

Vince grimaced. "Everything, apparently. I'm a living, breathing thorn in her side. She's all but set fire to me to rid herself of me. That will be next—"

"With little success, apparently. I'm flattered at your visit, dear fellow, but we are not such good friends to warrant these cozy little fireside chats, are we? At least, not yet. Could your visit have a mite to do with my pretty guest?"

Vince glanced at Whitmore and quickly away. He accepted a glass of wine from a hovering servant and sipped.

Raising an interested eyebrow, Canfield jerked his head at his nephew. "You were unusually quiet tonight, John; must not be feeling quite the thing. I give you leave to seek an early night."

"I'm not tired, Uncle."

"Yes, tired indeed," Canfield said as if John hadn't spoken. "See you in the morning."

Resigned but not happy about it, John stood, made a curt bow and closed the dining room door with quiet but audible offense.

"How do you abide that devious sycophant?" Vince burst out before he could stop himself. "Do you know with whom he consorts?"

"You mean Quincy Renner and his ilk in the Commons, and those on the streets, who would wrest by force what they cannot win by guile?" Canfield stirred a generous measure of cream into his coffee, quite unperturbed at Vince's revelation.

"If you know, why do you still employ him? Do you not know that he can ruin you if he crosses the bounds and drags you into his style of revolution?"

Canfield sipped his coffee and made an approving

187

sound. "My dear chap, allow me to worry about my nephew and his actions. He thinks he's quite the barrister, with his secrets and his ploys, but he hasn't wiped his butt since the age of four without my guidance."

Vince shoved back his wineglass. "Oh, yes? Did you know that he's used his generous salary to tie Ch— Papillone to him in a trumped-up business enterprise?"

"You mean the dancing academy? He's been at great pains to see I didn't know about it, even enlisted the little gel's sympathy. Her loyalty was quite touching actually, but she's too sensible not to see which side her bread's buttered on. She didn't mention it either, not wanting to offend him."

Vince plunged his hands in his pockets to keep from shaking the pomposity out of the old boy. "But why? He'll never get rich financing dancing academies. What is his interest in Papillone? For that matter, what is yours?"

For the first time, Canfield's self-satisfaction was deflated a bit. "That's the question, is it not? John has apparently figured out my interest in her, hence his as well. . . . Tell me, lad, did you see the brooch she was wearing?"

Vince's eyes widened. His wineglass tipped over in his hand, but he was so shocked that he didn't notice the port stain spreading over the priceless Irish linen tablecloth.

Conversationally, Canfield continued. "Unusual piece of jewelry, that. Never seen one before or since with mother of pearl of that quality, surrounded by such fine black pearls. Only the South Seas yields riches like that. Most appropriate that they should adorn one so richly blessed in all that matters—just like her mother."

Under the impact of Canfield's admission, Vince rocked in his chair, feeling his world go topsy-turvy at the description of the brooch he'd not been able to get a good look at. If Chantal had known he was coming tonight, she would not have worn what was probably the best piece of jewelry she owned. The proof of Annette's brooch at his beloved's bosom would have been hard enough to deal with, but this . . .

He blinked, seeing the little cit standing next to Chantal, kissing her hand. No wonder they had the same gleam to their raven hair, the same cupid's bow mouth, the same small stature, the same steady gaze. In fact, if one combined Canfield's pale gray eyes with Annette's almost violet ones, one would come up with the lavender gray of Chantal's. "Great God in heaven. *You* are Chantal's father!"

In the room next door, John Whitmore put down the listening horn he had been holding inside the fireplace flue both rooms shared. He leaned his forehead against the expensive silk wallpaper, his teeth gnashing together. He wasn't certain which infuriated him more— this certain proof of his suspicions about the haughty little bitch's paternity or Canfield's disparaging description of the nephew who'd served him faithfully since he was out of shortcoats.

No wonder the little dancer was so haughty; she came by it naturally. But this time Canfield had been a bit too canny for his own good. He was making these heart-felt confessions to the wrong man. If the little heiress persisted in preferring that damned interfering Kimball to a man of twice his mettle . . . well, she'd make the wrong choice.

A deadly choice.

Didn't wipe his butt without guidance, eh?

Wonder what Canfield would say about John Whitmore's ingenuity when the old buzzard found his new heiress with her throat slit?

"Took you long enough to figure out," Canfield returned, with a placid sip of his coffee. "I declare, I thought you a more perspicacious fellow than that. Or do I flatter myself unduly when I say that I resemble my daughter at least a little?"

"More than a little, sir. I suspected it when I saw you kiss her hand, but my mind could not accept the shock." Vince rubbed his dazed eyes. "But . . . I do not understand. Why have you waited so long to come forward?"

The saucer rattled as the gold-rimmed cup was set down with enough force to chip the base. "Because Annette died before she could tell me where to find my daughter. I only stumbled onto the truth after I saw Chantal by chance in Covent Garden buying a rose; then, later, I saw her picture in the newspaper. She has much the look of her mother, too. I told John to set up this dinner so I could learn the truth myself. Even without the brooch, I would have recognized her anywhere."

Another revelation rocked Vince back in his chair. "It was *you* Annette was visiting that last night of her life."

"Of course." Pain shadowed his strong features. He rested his forehead in his hand, his face twisted as if spikes were being driven into his skull. "Sometimes I think God punished me for my sins that night, taking from me the one thing money and ambition could not buy.''

Literally on the edge of his seat, Vince listened as one more mystery of his boyhood was solved.

''Annette saved my life, you know, the first time I saw her,'' Canfield mumbled, staring at the tablecloth. ''During the Revolution, I made a run to France, intending to trade my ore for brandy which was, as you may recall, more valuable than gold at that time. I had succeeded, and was loading my cargo aboard to return home when a mob discovered my nationality and attacked. Annette had come to Calais with her family, and she shamed the ring leader with nothing more than her wit and her tongue, backed up by her servants who were, then, at least, still loyal. The mob dispersed, slinking into the darkness like the dogs they were. Over the protests of her family, Annette stayed at their seaside chalet, tending my wounds. My men grew frightened and sailed back to England, but a week passed before I was strong enough to be told this news. The mob stole my purse, so I had no money, no ship and no means of buying my passage home. And the violence was growing worse, the resentment against Englishmen by then almost as bad as that against the nobility.''

''How did you escape?''

''Her father would have nothing to do with me. Annette sold some of her jewels to buy me passage. We were in love by this time, but I was too much of a coward to tell her that I was already married to the daughter of the man who owned the foundry I was interested in buying. It was not a happy alliance, but I knew that all my ambitions would be for naught if I divorced her to wed Annette. Still, I encouraged Annette to flee to England with me, fearing for her life, but she refused to leave her family. We did not know then that she was . . . *enciente*. I promised to return when I could. She wrote to tell me of her pregnancy, but because the mail packets were so sporadic, I didn't receive the letter until her family had already been beheaded. I was like a madman then, resolving to divorce my wife, no matter what, if God would only grant me a second chance, but my best sources could not tell me whether she lived or died. Then, I knew nothing of her English relatives, or that she'd escaped by becoming a dancer.'' Canfield's monotone spoke of feelings too painful to remember, much less voice.

Vince shuddered, reciprocal pain setting up a dull pounding in his ears as he recalled his own bleak torment, wondering whether Chantal lived or died. Why had she made the same mistakes her mother had? Was it something in Frenchwomen that made them so insanely proud? He had to force himself to listen as Canfield went on.

"Then, years later, when I visited France again, I attended a ballet and saw Annette dancing. It was a shock, let me tell you.''

Vince didn't need to be told that. He stared, feeling a chill run down his spine at the similarity between Canfield's fate and his own. "And you confronted her?''

"Yes. Asked about the child, of course. She lied, told me that she'd lost the infant in childbirth, probably fearing I would take Chantal away. She had never forgiven me for not telling her I was married. She found out by chance, shortly after she wrote me the letter about her pregnancy, when she was apparently visiting your own family in England. She hurried back to France, but when her father discovered her condition, he threw her out—just in time to save her from the guillotine. That's why she took up dancing, though it would be many years before I knew this.''

Vince's heart was pounding so hard now that he felt sick. It seemed the Fates themselves had frowned upon the two Englishmen, decreeing that they love and lose like some of the more tragic Greek heroes. Hurry! Hurry! his instincts whispered, 'ere you lose her. His urgency to confront Chantal with the truth and force her into marriage almost overwhelmed him, and he had to make himself listen as Canfield dully concluded the tragic tale.

''When it seemed Chantal was going to be safely settled with you, Annette called on me again. My wife had died, you see, and I was free. God forgive me, but Annette never stopped loving me, even as I never stopped loving her. Those few weeks of happiness were the greatest moments of my life.'' Canfield's voice broke, and he hung his head, as if he couldn't bear for Vince to see his pain. ''Annette planned to surprise Chantal by bringing me to the wedding, but . . . she . . . she . . .'' Canfield's eyes squeezed shut, and he didn't have to go on.

Vince said grimly, ''I want you to know, sir, that I did all I could to find out who killed Annette. I was with the magistrate the day Chantal ran away, but we never found a clue to the bastard who did it.''

His fingers trembling, Canfield drank deeply from his cup. When he spoke again, his voice was stronger.

"I sent a legion of Bow Street runners to comb the countryside, and they turned up nothing. But I can tell you from experience, lad—cherish those you love, else lose them you will and live a lifetime of regret."

Vince shifted restlessly, not needing that particular little homily. What would Canfield say if he knew it was Chantal who was the coward, not he? "I love your daughter, sir. I loved her when I was a boy. I love her even more now that I'm a man. I even loved her when I wasn't sure of her identity. I had quite determined to make Papillone my wife, long before this night."

Canfield slammed the tabletop with his palm, making the dishes rattle. "Deuce take it, must you always have the last word?"

Vince stared.

As if he could not be still, Canfield stood to pace the elegant room. "How can I be happy that you're taking my daughter from me before I've ever had a chance to know her?"

Ah, that was it. Vince hid a smile behind his napkin. "Sir, you are welcome to visit whenever you can. She can even spend some time with y—"

"It is not the same, you smooth-tongued young devil, and well you know it. I want her all to myself."

Vince tossed his napkin aside. "Then resign yourself to disappointment. She ran from me once, giving me a decade of misery."

Understanding flickered in Canfield's gray eyes. "And you will not let her do so again?"

"No." Flatly. "We shall wed with unseemly haste, with or without her cooperation."

"And how do you propose to get her to agree, if she is not willing?"

How did one tell a loving father that one planned to seduce his daughter? Vince shrugged.

Canfield sighed, the whoosh from his lungs fluttering across the air like the wings of regret. "I am too old, but I confess I shall be delighted to watch the battle. She's confoundedly proud, you know. Like her mother."

"I know. I would not want her otherwise."

Canfield's melancholy lightened in a smile. "By Jove, I believe you wouldn't. And the lad?"

"I shall love him, whether he is my child or not. I am currently investigating that."

"He's yours."

"How do you know?"

"I know Annette. And, after tonight, I know my daughter. She loves you, just as her mother loved me. She could never betray you with another man, especially so soon after leaving you."

"If you're so prescient, then kindly tell me why the hell she left the first time?"

Canfield's smile faded to that haughty look that had silenced some of Parliament's loosest tongues. "No doubt something you did."

Vince bristled, but then he sighed and backed down. This man would be his best, and perhaps his only ally, in winning Chantal. He could not afford to alienate him. "Perhaps." Vince strode forward to offer his hand. "I welcome you, sir, as Chantal's protector, and formally request your approval for my pursuit of her hand in marriage."

Canfield shook his hand once, briskly, and then waved him to the door. "Given, though reluctantly. And I expect to see her often."

At the door, Vince paused. "Do you intend to tell her?"

"In good time, when she knows me better. She will be an extremely wealthy woman someday, so she needs to be taught how to manage her money." Canfield gave him a challenging frown. "Or are you one of those gothic-minded noblemen who believe once she weds you, her money is your money?"

"You can tie up her funds to a fare-thee-well, for all I care," Vince retorted. "It is Chantal I want." He exited, leaving Canfield to brood alone over his cold coffee.

All the way home, Vince brooded over the little flask of brandy he kept for emergencies inside the saddle pouch. He gave the stallion his head, knowing the beast would loiter over every mare he passed. He needed time to think.

The first thrill of elation had passed, leaving only his quandary to accompany his recriminations and fears. Why had she resisted so strongly, lied so often and so well? Surely she knew he would never take away her child. Maybe she blamed him for something he was unaware of. That must be it. She thought he hadn't sought her mother's killer hard enough, or she resented his going off to war, or she feared being a politician's wife, or—

—she doesn't love you anymore.

He tightened his hands on the reins so hard that the stallion tossed his head. No amount of supposing could answer the tormenting questions. Chantal herself must supply the explanation. Unless . . . there were times when his mother seemed reluctant to talk about Chantal. Could she know more than she let on? It wouldn't be the first time she'd taken a stand, opposing him for what she believed to be his own good.

Vince clucked to the stallion, urging him to a faster pace. When he reached his townhouse, he jumped down, tossing his reins to a footman instead of going back to the stable. Despite the late hour, he entered calling for his mother.

Their butler, wooden in unspoken disapproval, stated, "I believe she is in her rooms, sir. She was looking for you earlier."

Vince loped up the steps, knocking once on his mother's door and then bounding inside before she could answer. "Mother, I—" He stopped, shocked. His mother, her head bowed on her arms, was sitting at her dressing table, weeping. He had not seen his mother cry since his father died.

Sometimes he teased her, saying that if he looked up the word *indefatigable* in a dictionary, he'd find her picture. Nothing ever flustered or frustrated her. She was a veritable dynamo, and yet she was sobbing as if she were broken in heart and in spirit. Dread tightening his throat, expecting to hear something awful, Vince crept up to her and put a gentle hand on her shoulder. "Mother, what is amiss?"

"Oh Vince," she sobbed, burying her face in his chest, "how can you forgive me?"

Dread became acute anxiety. They had only argued bitterly about one subject. Vince patted her shoulder, searching for a gentle way to put his questions, when she sniffled, leaned back and thrust something up at him.

It was then that he saw the picture clutched in her

hand. Limply, he took it, intuition telling him that the most jolting realization of a shocking night was upon him. He stared.

His son stared back at him.

Chapter Seven

Weak at the knees, Vince sagged down on the dressing bench next to his mother. It barely held the two of them, but he scarcely noticed the discomfort as he stared at the lovely young girl of about ten who wore Tony's face. "Who is this?"

His mother blew her nose fiercely. "Your Grandmama Callista. When she was a girl."

As the implications sank in fully, Vince braced himself for the next blow. Anger was slowly rising, so he measured his words with great care. "So, you know about Chantal's child?"

"Yes."

"For how long?"

"Today. I arrived at the dancing academy early with the intention of viewing her son myself, to see if I could bear to have him in my home."

"And?" It took all of Vince's control not to shout

the one word, for the truth was rearing its ghastly head.

"He is obviously your son. He not only greatly resembles Callista, his mannerisms much remind me of you when you were a boy."

Vince closed his eyes so he wouldn't have to stare at that vibrant young face any longer. Nine years. Nine years of his son's life stolen from him. "Did Chantal admit that Tony is mine?"

"I didn't see her. I . . . spent the day with my grandson. That's why I never came to our lesson. Vince . . ." She held out a pleading hand, but he knocked it away and stood.

"It's because of you that she left, isn't it?" So quiet the words, but they were the lull amid a hurricane, the dead silence after a stampede—or the quiet of a calm man on the verge of a rampage.

And so, in her twilight years, for the last and worst time, the countess rose like an aging diva to face the music of her own orchestration. To her credit, she did so without flinching, head high to accept rotten tomatoes instead of roses. "Yes."

When Vince stared at her blindly, she apparently saw the nightmarish progression of years in his eyes, his fears for the family she'd stolen from him, his anguish at the deprivations and indignities they'd suffered. She reached out to him again, but he didn't give her the grace of a response. He stared through her as if she had become inanimate to him, of no more consequence than the bench, or the rug upon which he stood.

Agony on her proud face, she whirled and began to pace. "You must listen. At the time, it was so clear to me. She was not only illegitimate, she was such an impetuous child, and half French to boot, with an unknown father. On his deathbed, your father made me promise to guide you well. He knew you had such gifts that one day you could even be prime minister, and he was determined that I aid you in that ambition. So I could either accept the girl as your wife or be true to my promise to my husband. Was I so wrong for the choice I made?''

Vince's eyes had begun to clear of that dreadful blankness, but the bleak anguish in his soul felt like a wound draining his life's blood away. His mother had betrayed him and condemned both him and Chantal to a decade of loneliness. Nothing she said, indeed, nothing she did, could compensate for that fact. ''Yes. Because my life was not yours to mold, no matter what my father said.''

She stopped, rubbing her hands on her elbows. ''Time without end I have told myself that very thing. Had I realized you loved the girl as much as you did, enough to die being true to her memory, I never would have bribed her. But you were both young. You were about to go to war, and I knew you would be different when you came home. The man would not be happy with the pretty young wife a boy wanted—''

''Enough!'' Vince clenched his hands into fists and took two strides toward her, but when she flinched, he turned away, sickened at his own near loss of control. His heart was rotting in his chest, and somewhere at the back of his mind he knew an even uglier truth waited to be faced, but he wasn't strong enough for it yet. ''You did not know Chantal as I knew her. How many times did you invite her to the house for tea? How many times did you visit her in the cottage? How many of the manners and mores that mean so much to you did you try to teach her?''

Adeline hung her head. She had no defense against his accusation, and she knew it.

''You sicken me.'' Vince clutched his stomach, where he did indeed feel nauseated. He'd had too much to drink today, too little to eat, and too many shocks for a nightcap. ''Leave me. I must think of what to do.''

At the utter contempt in his voice, she reared back up. ''Whatever I have done, I am still your mother, and you will not speak to me as if I were a servant.''

''Henceforth you mean no more to me than that. Some officious nursemaid who thinks I'm a child. Who wants to make the most important decisions of my life for me.'' Vince leaned toward the woman who had borne him and gritted between his teeth, ''Well, how is this for a mature decision, madam? I want you out of my home. When I bring my bride and my son back, you will not be welcome.''

All the remaining color drained from Adeline's pale cheeks. She swayed, not as if she'd seen a ghost, but as if she'd become one. ''You cannot mean that—''

''Not mean it? As if I couldn't really be devoted enough to that 'French chit'? As if I don't know my own mind? Or heart?'' His voice broke at this last word, and he had to turn away from the look on her face. ''Go, before I say even more I'll regret.''

Regret. Her gasping breaths filled the silence of the room, and Vince felt regret wash over him in waves. It wasn't enough. Forgiveness was salvation, but some actions were beyond saving. What she had done was unconscionable, and perhaps irrevocable. The Chantal he'd loved had died in those ten years as surely as if his mother had smote her down like an Old Testament matriarch.

Sounding very old, her steps shuffling, Adeline finally departed, leaving him to his dilemma and what new life he could resurrect from the old. Some remnant of Chantal's youthful passion remained, for the feelings she'd once borne for a much younger man burned deep beneath her disdain. He'd felt it in her touch, heard it in her voice, seen it in those unforgettable eyes. And yet, even as he tried to clear his head for the most critical military campaign of his life, truth came knocking.

She'd accepted money to leave him.

The nausea he'd swallowed back again rose up to choke him. He barely made it to the chamber pot in time. He had little in his stomach to lose, and the dry heaves seemed to rip away his last shreds of dignity and restraint, leaving him a shuddering mess upon the floor.

And that was exactly what he felt like: leavings. The two most important women in his life had used and betrayed him. His mother, living her own twisted ambitions through her son. And Chantal? She must have dallied with him, grown weary and, rather than wed him, accepted money from his mother to flee. Had she known then that she was pregnant? If so, he could never forgive her, just as he could never forgive his mother.

He debated asking his mother for more details, but he couldn't bear to see her again. Besides, he had to hear the truth from Chantal, face her with her own cowardice and avarice. She'd ripped from him something precious, something as irreplaceable and unique as the life she'd taken from him and then hoarded.

That idealistic young man who'd marched off to war,

hurling himself before cannon balls and horses' hooves, had returned home with scars that went far deeper than a wounded leg. He'd lost his boyhood and his innocence the day Chantal had disappeared, before Waterloo. In the dark of night, when the sky was lit by rockets and the fires of the battlefield, he'd faced something even more devastating than his own mortality: apathy. He didn't care if he lived or died. He didn't even much care whether they beat Boney.

Life held no joy, no meaning and no hope. A young man who'd believed in the old-fashioned values of honor and love and chastity had returned believing in nothing. Caring for nothing and no one. Deliberately he let the memories sweep him away, hoping to put them behind him forever.

Tears came to his eyes as he remembered those agonizing years that had passed in a perpetual fog. All the men he'd hired to look for her. The despair that ate away at his sanity, day by day. The horrific dreams, not of friends being blown to bits, but of Chantal, frozen and starving, alone. The uncertainty was the worst, for he didn't even know if she lived or died, much less if she mourned him as he mourned her.

And then, three years after he came home and could still find no trace of Chantal, a friend had invited him to sit in during a session of Parliament. Here, he found a spark of interest. He began reading again, going out again, and the spark soon became a hearth where he could warm some part of himself.

Finally, he quit looking for Chantal and tried to accept with grace the decision God had made for his life. He laughed bitterly, his face buried in the carpet. God? No, two interfering, selfish women. But he forced himself to finish the progression of his thoughts, knowing he couldn't mark a new path until the old one was trod.

The Vince who had resurfaced could still laugh, still charm the ladies and even still have sex. But love? Marriage? Children? They were foreign concepts to him. And they would have remained so for the rest of his life but for a trick of fate.

Or God's unfinished plan? Some higher power had led him to that ballet. Perhaps the same power could lead him through this new path of pitfalls and morasses. He'd been stumbling blindly, feeling his way for the truth of who this ballerina was and what they meant to each other.

The blindfold was off. And if the truth was both more devastating and less palatable than he'd hoped, at least he'd found Chantal again. Feeling slightly better, he pulled himself to his feet and rang the bell rope.

When the servant came, he said, "Bring me some of that hearty chicken soup the cook made for lunch. Bread. Cheese and fruit. Immediately."

"Wine, your lordship?"

"No." Vince changed his clothes while he waited. When he was dressed, he stared at himself in the mirror. The black garb had not been necessary since he'd slipped behind Boney's lines with a fellow spy, but it still fit the same. He pulled his stash of guineas from his bureau and put them in his pocket. Then, deep in the chest at the end of his bed, he removed a wrapped bundle. The paper was dusty and tattered with age, but he peeked inside. The brilliant red seemed as bright as ever.

He was packing a few of his things and the bundle in a portmanteau when the butler himself brought the tray. "Here, my lord, let me call your valet—"

"Nonsense. I'm perfectly capable of packing. I'll be gone for some time. Could be days, could be weeks, could be months. My mother will be moving out. While I'm gone, I want you to see that the house is cleaned thoroughly from top to bottom. I'll be bringing back a lady. And a child."

The butler, despite the lively curiosity in his eyes, bowed solemnly. "Shall I call your coach?"

"No. My curricle. I'll drive myself. You may go."

"We shall miss you, sir." The door closed with the same quiet dignity of the man.

I'll miss me, too. The curious thought left as soon as it came. But even as he forced down the hearty meal, knowing he'd need strength, Vince was grimly aware that he was endangering the new Vince even as he pursued the old. He wanted back the idealistic, passionate young men Chantal had destroyed. But in finding him, he might have to sacrifice the careful, courteous statesman.

Because what he planned to do tonight was neither careful nor courteous. It would scandalize every member of the Lords if they learned of it. It might even have shocked his ancestor, Drake Kimball. When he'd wiped his mouth and swished it clean with water, Vince stared at himself in the glass.

The blood of Drake the pirate ran hot in his veins tonight. He knew better than to ask Chantal for an explanation. She'd just send him about his business, more determined or frightened than ever if she discovered he knew the truth about Tony. She might even flee again, and that he simply could not allow. No, it was time to

give the little French tease some of her own medicine.
Just as they'd begun their old romance in bed together,
they would begin their new one with no clothes and no
subterfuge between them. When he had her naked,
screaming with arousal and need, she would admit the
truth. And when she admitted it, he would take her
straight to the parson.

He smiled, resembling Drake Kimball, legendary
beast of the illuminated fairy tale that had been passed
down within his family. The black silk shirt whispered
against his skin like broken promises about to be
mended. The tight black leather breeches both cupped
and cradled his arousal like the feather bed of dreams
and desire they'd soon share.

Hefting the case over his shoulder, Vince stalked out.

Hugo started awake, staring into the darkness. What
was that faint sound? He strained to hear. There it was
again, a stealthy footstep. Hugo rose, wearing nothing
but his nightshirt, and hefted the water ewer beside his
bed, stealing into the sitting room.

He saw a blur of movement, and then a knife was
held to his throat. A silky, refined voice he recognized
said smoothly, "Put the pitcher down, Hugo."

Stunned, Hugo complied, peering at the dim figure
dressed in black. "What ye here so late for? Does the
mistress ken?"

"Not yet. But she will." The knife was removed and
sheathed.

Hugo's muscles bunched.

"And to save you the energy and the aching head,
dear fellow, my intentions are of the most honorable.

I'm taking Chantal with me—and yes, I have it on indisputable authority that she *is* Chantal—and when I bring her back, we shall be married.''

They'd kept their tones to fierce whispers, but when Vince turned toward Tony's room, Hugo raised his voice. "Now see here, ye blasted sassenach—''

"Hush! I know that Tony is my son, so just whist, me lad. I only want to look at him.''

Hugo stood there in his nightshirt, making futile fists with his big hands, wondering what to do. He followed, watching as Vince pulled the curtain from the tiny window so he could see his son.

Tony lay peacefully, sleeping on his side, facing the door, his bounteous vitality humming even in his utter stillness. Hugo adored Chantal, but Tony was like the son he'd never had, and he was fiercely protective of him. Devil take the hindmost, he'd send this fine lord about his business if he thought to hurt a hair on the wee laddie's head.

But Vince knelt, staring at his son in the moonlight with a stillness that spoke of many things, but not menace. Hugo saw the emotions twisting that handsome face as Vince gently stroked the tumbled hair away from the boy's brow. Awe. Regret. Fierce pride. Love.

And since Hugo had known all of these same emotions, the last of his fears faded. For the first time, he felt a common ground with this top-lofty earl. Aye, a proud one the lord might be, but he loved the lad, 'twas plain as the pattern on yer kilt. And so Hugo retreated to the sitting area to give father and son time alone.

Vince came out of the room a few minutes later, his eyes sparkling too bright in the moonlight. "Watch over him for me." He set a heavy pouch on the table. "We shall return as soon as we can."

Hugo's open mouth snapped shut. They needed the money, and it was right for the boy's father to offer it. "What do ye intend to do with the lady?" Chantal had always been, and always would be a lady to Hugo.

"Love her."

The simple response made Hugo's brawny shoulders lift in a heartfelt sigh of relief. He knew what Vince meant, but he also knew that Vince's desire had the proper basis. And he understood Chantal well enough to realize that the path past her pride was in her bed. He'd seen her dance when she thought herself alone. So, man to man, the Scot and the Englishman shared a glance in the dark of night that was the first tentative handshake between them.

As he watched Vince enter Chantal's room, Hugo smiled slightly. He heard drawers opening, the sounds of clothing being stuffed into a pouch and then Chantal's sleepy voice.

"Hugo? Wha—" A gasp, and then a little screech, "Vince! What are you doing—" that ended on a wail.

Vince exited with the pouch over his shoulder and Chantal, sheet and all, tucked safely in his arms. Rubbing her eyes, Lizzie trailed after them into the light glowing from the candle Hugo had lit. When she got a good look at what was happening, her hazel eyes narrowed into slits and her hands clenched into claws. She flew at Vince's back, spitting like a cat.

Hugo stepped between them, catching her arms. "Dinna fash yerself, lassie. 'Twill be all right."

"Hugo, get out of my way! He's kidnapping her, you

209

dolt!'' Lizzie kicked his shin, but since her foot was bare, she hurt herself more than him.

Vince was at the door now, having a time opening it under Chantal's struggles.

She raged, "I won't go with you, I'll send the constables after you, I'll—"

"You've done enough damage to me for one lifetime—*Chantal.*"

The way he said the name silenced both women immediately. Vince still scrabbled at the door latch and finally sent a pleading look over his shoulder.

Hugo reached around them, respectfully tucking the sheet about Chantal's bare legs, and opened the door. Chantal's teeth were grinding together now. "I'll never forgive you for this, Hugo. You . . . you . . . man!" She said the last word like a curse.

Hugo hunched his shoulders, unable to squelch a twinge of guilt even though his generous, loyal heart knew Vince was doing the right thing. A fine lady Chantal might be, but she was a wee bit too stubborn. He contented himself with a last glare and a warning as he trailed the couple down to the street. "Treat her right, mon. Or ye'll have me to answer to."

"I'll give her exactly what she deserves," Vince replied somewhat ominously, plopping her down in the curricle next to him. He wrapped the sheet tightly around her struggling arms and legs, knotting it over the seat so she couldn't get away without sacrificing modesty and dignity.

Hugo bit his lip, but by then it was too late. The high-strung matched pair were off at the snap of the whip.

Lizzie stood beside him in the night wind, looking resigned as she watched them round a corner, skidding on two wheels, and disappear. "Well, if ye arsk me, he ain't decided yet if he's going to rape her, beat her or marry her."

"Mayhap all three."

Lizzie peered up at him. "Ye don't sound worried none." Then she shrugged. "But I agree. 'Twon't be rape. She's ripe for it. Still, she's been alone and independent fer a long spell. 'Twon't be easy fer him to get past that." Lizzie wrapped her arms about herself in the brisk fall breeze and shivered. "And we're barmy in the noodle if we don't get out o' the street in our unmentionables." She hurried back up the stairs.

But Hugo still stared after the curricle, mingled hope and worry in his strong face. Why had he not taken time to warn the lord that his love had almost died in childbirth, that the doctor had advised her never to have any more children?

By the time they left the turnpike, Chantal gave up pleading. He'd gone mad. That was it. No sane person dressed up like a pirate, kidnapped a matron from her bed and tore through London in a curricle, scraping curbs and scattering dogs along the way. She would have jumped and taken her chances but for the dangerous speed of the vehicle, which was probably why he rushed so.

But the way he'd said her name . . . She shivered, pulling the sheet more closely around her neck. Like a mingled curse and a blessing. Like Aladdin, who'd stumbled upon riches using *Chantal* instead of "Open Sesame."

Could he know? But how? She'd seen him tonight, and he had seemed no different. Except . . . She stiffened. Her mother's brooch! She'd been so confused by Canfield's odd behavior that she'd barely taken note of Vince staring at her bodice. But he never got a good look at it, she told herself. No, it must be that he was tired of wooing her and had decided to take the direct approach of his piratical ancestor.

Well, she was no Callista Raleigh, to tame a beast. If he tried to touch her, she'd bite his hand off. She looked at that hand, guiding the curricle so easily. It was perfectly shaped.

Tony's hand.

Gulping, she looked away, telling herself that her heart raced in fear. She'd foresworn men and all the treachery and joy they offered. For Tony's sake, this man could never find out that she was really his lost love. Even if by some miracle the adults managed to work through their towering difficulties, what of the boy they'd created when they were all but children themselves? Tony would have a home and wealth beyond dreams, yes.

And responsibilities he would despise.

The future Earl of Dunhaven was a rapscallion boy who hated his lessons and was never happier than when he wandered around London with his ragamuffin friends. She tried to visualize that boy sipping tea with his grandmama, surrounded by doting dowagers, and a laugh escaped her.

"Something funny?" But Vince didn't sound amused.

Somehow, that struck her as even funnier. She giggled uncontrollably, winning a glare before he turned back to the dirt track of a road. It was three in the morning, so they'd passed few carriages, and the moon was often behind clouds, so the ones they did pass barely checked before continuing on. "In the gothic novels I've read, the villian is always elated to get the heroine in his clutches. You sound as if you'd like to shake me senseless."

"I want you senseless, all right. Beneath me." But his tone sounded grimmer, if anything.

A giggle lodged in her throat and almost choked her as she figured out why he sounded so strange. He was grim, all right. Grimly resolved, like that villian Lovelace, to bed her before the night was out. And would he then cast her aside, ruined?

No, his mother had already done that. She caught back an even sillier laugh and knew she was on the verge of hysteria. She clamped her hands on her knees, squeezing until her knuckles went white, and forced a measure of calm. She'd escaped Napoleon's autocracy, she'd supported herself and her son for years, and she'd survived a labor that had killed many a weaker woman. She could handle a domineering earl, she told herself. She couldn't take a chance on losing Tony. Once she admitted who she was, Tony's identity could not long remain secret.

Her stern self-lecture fell on attentive ears, but her other senses were more unruly, eager for the power of the forbidden. The strong arm brushing against her as it mastered the high-spirited horses; the thigh crowding her as Vince deliberately bumped against her on every curve; the scent of healthy male sweat and arousal—all were heady temptations.

Gritting her teeth, she admitted that she wanted Vince. Badly. Forever. Even more than when they'd been young, for now she knew what she was missing.

But it would not be the first time she'd denied herself for her child, nor would it be the last. She closed her eyes and took a deep breath. At last, her voice was steady. "Where are you taking me?"

"Perhaps it will do you a bit of good to wonder. As I wondered. To worry. As I worried." Strong white teeth clamped together as he snapped the reins on the horses' rumps to urge them faster.

"Why are you so angry with me?"

He opened his mouth, pressed his lips together and shook his head. "Not yet."

Many silences they'd shared, some comfortable, some not, but never had she felt doom hovering over her head like the sword of Damocles, ready to cleave her in two no matter which way she jumped. Dear God, was he going to rape her and then kill her? Certainly not. As much as he'd changed, Vince Kimball was still very much a gentleman. But was he still a gentle man? She glanced sideways at him. His jaw flexed as he tried to control his emotions, with little more success than she'd had with her own.

Something had happened tonight. Something that convinced him she'd been lying to him. If she continued with the charade, she might push him beyond what he could bear. After all, the gallant soldier of her youth never would have kidnapped her this way. But then, she was no longer the innocent little ballerina, either. They were both adults now, with all the skills of evasion and denial they'd had to learn to survive. He, on a battle-field; she, on a stage. A sudden poignant longing for the simple joy of her girlhood almost overwhelmed her.

Nonsense. It was forever lost. But perhaps, came the forbidden thought, something even more rapturous could replace their childhood passion. But no, that too, was idle dreaming. She was a woman grown, a mother with responsibilities, not a young girl free to fling herself recklessly at a man.

The rapid succession of emotions had led her up hill and down dale into a nadir of depression. Anger, excitement, joy, fear and, finally, sadness. This dramatic flight into darkness would lead them . . . whence, she knew not.

And why?

That was most terrifying of all.

By the time Vince pulled off the main road, Eos was dancing on the horizon, cavorting with a golden riband. The curricle lurched into ruts as it followed a desolate track. The path led through tall trees that hadn't seen a pruning in years, if ever. A muted roar sounded as they followed the track, and misty light formed a nimbus up ahead.

Despite herself, Chantal leaned forward, excited by the scent of salt and the cry of a gull. The sea! The trees thinned, opening onto a whitish rocky plateau overlooking a gray tempest of crashing waves. A cottage clung tenaciously to the rocky peak, just out of reach of the foaming spray. The wind had risen, and gulls circled on the gusts, crying raucously.

The cottage, with a thatched roof and white-washed stucco walls, was charming with its bay mullioned windows fronting onto the sea. It had green shutters and a sturdy green door with a fanciful wrought-iron door knocker in the shape of a smiling dragon. Immediately Chantal realized where she was. This was the Dover summer cottage of the Kimball family.

Drake Kimball had bought it for his bride so they

could escape the humors and ills of London during the warm months. It had been handed down through the generations. Some of the Kimball women had spent their confinements here; others had honeymooned here. Chantal had heard Vince speak of it, for he'd promised to bring her here the summer after he returned from Waterloo.

It was seldom used in the fall and winter, however. The winds were too cold, and it was extremely isolated where it stood on the rugged, windward side, away from the city. Chantal's heart, which had sunk in her breast, lurched and began to patter an alarm. Why had he brought her here, isolated from human contact, if he had good intentions?

Vince's teeth flashed in the gloom. "Frightened, my lovely?" His teeth snapped together as he jumped down and stalked around to lift her free of the clutching sheet. "You should be."

As soon as her feet touched the ground, she slapped his hands away. "Of you? I think not." She almost said she wasn't the poor relation any longer, but she caught herself in time. If he was deliberately trying to infuriate her, he was doing a wonderful job.

He pulled a large key from his pocket and opened her clenched fist to drop it into her palm. "Everything should be in readiness. Go, fix us a fire. You do remember how I taught you to set a fire, do you not?"

She turned a haughty shoulder to him, not dignifying his taunt with a response. She let the sheet drop where she stood, uncaring that the whipping winds wrapped her thin lawn night rail about every inch of her body. For a moment, she stood there, knowing the morning sun beamed through the thin fabric. Only when she heard his sharp intake of breath did she walk to the door.

He'd set the rules of this dangerous new game, but she was a fast learner. Taunt for taunt. Threat for threat. And insult for insult.

Caress for caress . . . She shoved open the door, infuriated that her body could turn traitor even when she was so angry. She slammed the door behind her, narrowly eyeing the strong dead bolt, but she reluctantly turned away. No reason to encourage him to act the uncivilized savage. In his current ill humor, he'd doubtless knock down the confounded door.

Chantal drew the curtains back from the mullioned windows, swung one open and turned to appraise the cottage. A thick sheepskin rug that looked new lay before the empty grate, its lanolin making the pelt gleam even in the muted light. A cozy settee sat across from a plush wing chair by the fire, making an intimate seating arrangement. The small kitchen boasted a pump handle that would give them running water, and when she opened the wooden buffet she found it stocked with food.

Even the small table was set for two with gleaming china and silver. Chantal's heart started an urgent knocking at her ribs, but she had to know. She stalked to the two side rooms and found them both warm and intimate with their own fireplaces, massive beds taking up most of the space. Fur rugs lay across the ends of each bed, and when she flung open the armoire, she found it stuffed with clothes that would fit a woman of about her size. She slammed the armoire shut and went to the bedroom window, wrenching it wide to inhale the salt breezes and stem her rising panic.

This cottage had but one purpose. Here, the statesman would have congress of only one kind, and it involved only two people. How often had he brought a woman here? And why, after accepting weeks of rebuff, had he finally decided to force the issue?

"You don't follow directions any better now than you did when you were a girl." Vince dropped the bags next to the bedroom door. "Where's my fire?"

Startled, she whirled. "I'm not a servant. You may have this room. I shall take the other." She walked toward him, but the Earl of Dunhaven had died a quick death, apparently, at the hand of the pirate's grandson.

Instead of moving aside for her to exit, Drake's progeny blocked her and caught her shoulders in his hands. She turned her head aside from his lowering mouth, and his warm lips brushed her temple. She felt emotion quivering through him just in the touch of his hands, but for the life of her, she couldn't decide what it was. It was more than desire, however.

"No, Chantal," he whispered, burying his nose in the sweet curve of her shoulder and neck. "We eat together, we talk together. And we sleep together. As we should have on the honeymoon we never got to share."

She caught her fingers in his thick hair and lifted his head to meet him, eye to eye, will to will. "And if I refuse?" She held her breath, expecting him to fly into a rage, but the slow, sensual smile hit her squarely where he aimed it—below the belt.

"I shall convince you otherwise. And enjoy every moment of the . . . persuasion." As he drawled the last word, his tongue came out to rim his perfect white teeth.

She stepped back so hastily that her knees brushed against the bed and buckled. She went sprawling. She hastily scrambled to her feet, fearing he'd take advantage, but he'd already left, whistling a martial tune she recognized as one all the rage during the war years.

If he'd pulled out a trumpet and heralded *"Charge!"* he couldn't have made his intentions clearer. They were at war, and this pretty cottage would be the battlefield. When the contest was over, whoever stood firm on principle would win. He would attack her virtue with everything in his powerful arsenal, and unless she could repel his desires—and her own even more unruly ones—she would be the spoils of war. Victorious, he'd cart her off and rule her ever after.

As the enormity of the task before her penetrated her mind, she sank onto the bed. If she lost, she could only become his mistress, admit Tony was his and that she still loved him, had always loved him. Even worse, she'd become another woman succumbing to the superior will and intellect of man.

Eh bien! She might not be as strong as Vince, but she could teach him a thing or two about wit and endurance. She bounded up again, dropped the night rail to her feet and went to the armoire to pull out appropriate armor.

When she came out ten minutes later, Vince was still whistling as he carved a leg of mutton and hunks of bread, adding cheese and fruit to each plate. A cheerful fire crackled in the grate, percussive accompaniment to the brassy calls of the gulls circling outside.

He set down the plates on the table and picked up the glasses, turning. His eyes widened. One of the glasses slipped from his slack grip to the floor and rolled, unbroken, under the table. "What in God's name . . ." His gaze ran over her hungrily.

She lifted a long, slim leg encased in a tight pantaloon, tucked the thin wool stocking in her slipper and did the same to the opposite leg. She shoved the lace-trimmed shirt more snugly into her belted waist and tried to push back the sleeves from her fingers. Scowling down at her small hands, she used them to good effect and turned back the cuffs of his dress shirt. Finally, she lifted her head, tossed her long braid over her back and put her hands on her hips.

In warfare, a surprise attack always gave one the advantage, she told herself as she said loftily, "I merely thought that if you were going to challenge me to a duel I would dress appropriately." In anything but the low-cut, scandalous gowns that were all she'd found in the armoire. However, judging by the look on his face, the pantaloons clung too tightly to her richer curves and the shirt fell off her shoulders too far, lending her anything but a proper air. She sat down at the table, picked up the knife and fork and began to eat, ignoring him.

He lifted an eyebrow at her deliberate rudeness. With exaggerated courtesy, he bowed, pulled out his chair, folded his napkin on his lap and sipped his wine with one pinky in the air.

His perfect manners contrasted so with his wind-blown hair, flushed cheeks and rumpled shirt that she had to laugh. But she swallowed it behind her napkin and took a vicious stab at her mutton, telling herself that mirth, too, was an enemy. Anything that got past her armor must be avoided.

What, then, would she do when he touched her?

"My, we're bloodthirsty today," he said in a simpering voice. "My very dear lady, calm yourself. I do not wish to fear for my virtue."

A giggle escaped her at the picture he evoked.

His nose and pinky lowered to their accustomed positions, but the flash of his teeth could only be described as wicked. "See? I can still make you laugh."

Her smile was wiped clean. "And cry." She took a quick sip of wine.

His own smile faded as rapidly. "Not willingly. I want to give you nothing but happiness. The joy that was stolen from us can be ours again. If we allow it."

She set down her glass so hastily that the red wine splashed down the white shirt, dripping into her cleavage. Shocked by the cold dash, even more frozen by the look on his face, she went still.

Earnestness was replaced by something far more dangerous. To both of them. She bolted to her feet, but she was too late.

With a guttural growl of something that went beyond need, past pain to a fate that beckoned even as it repelled her, he caught her in one arm and swept clear the table with the other. She found herself flat on her back on hard wood with an equally hard, equally resolute pirate's grandson licking the wine from her bare flesh.

At first she tried to push him away, but he'd earlier unbuttoned the first two buttons of his own black shirt, and her scrabbling hands caught in the old silk. The tearing sound mingled with her own moan at the dart of his tongue into her heated flesh. And then her hands felt the sensual reality of hard male muscles and soft male hair. Her hands flattened against his chest and savored the touch.

Here was man, offering to satisfy all those feminine cravings denied for too many years. Even more shattering, here was Vince. No wraith that haunted her dreams, no forbidden love of her youth. Vincent Anthony Kimball, her first and only love, kissed his way down her neck, nudging the cloth of his own shirt away from her shoulders. She felt it slipping along with her control but had no strength to grasp either.

And then he was muttering with every kiss—words that enthralled her, words that alarmed her, words that tore at her last shreds of self-control. "So long," he murmured as he stabbed his tongue into her throat. "How could you deny us?" He licked his way from one collarbone to the other. "Why didn't you tell me?" He pulled the shirt down over her arms to kiss the exposed curve of her bosom. "I will never let you go again." As if unable to stand any more barriers, he ripped open the shirt and exposed her to his eyes and touch.

The sea breeze coming through the open window cooled her heated flesh. She tried to sit up, but he muttered something incoherent. His cheeks flushed red in the rising sun, he bent her back over his arm to satisfy a hunger that owed little to the body and much to the soul.

When his warm mouth closed over her flushed nipple, she gasped and melted in his arms. He tugged at her breast, not like a hungry infant, but with the poignant need of a man who'd been denied the right to watch his child suckle on this breast that should have nurtured them both. And yet, there was a tender awe as he laved her torso, first one breast, then the other, a gentle plea that bypassed her sensitive loins and lodged straight in her fragile heart.

Give to me, and I will give you all that I am, he said in a manner more eloquent than words. *Only together can we be what we were meant to become.* He cupped her full, aching breast and lifted it to his mouth, kissing, licking, nibbling, until she was squirming with the need to answer him with the fullness of heart and body.

Stop, she told herself sternly, but what came out was, "Oh God, don't stop." And then, oddly, he did. He panted as if he'd run a marathon, and the bulge stabbing into her belly was as hard as the table. Still, he paused, lifting her chin to force her languid eyes open.

His own eyes were so dilated that the pupils almost consumed the blue, but he gritted out, "Chantal, tell me who you are."

She blinked, trying to tug his mouth down to hers, but he gently resisted. "Chantal, my lovely lost love, tell me why you left me."

Reality crashed back with a vengeance, revealed by the blinding light of a rising sun. This new day could foretell the loss of her son, and the merciless glare of her own weakness shamed her. The fulsome give-and-take they'd just shared became sordid. As tawdry as the ripped shirt and the wine splotched on a man's garment that no decent woman would wear.

She wrenched herself away from him. When her back was safely turned, she managed, "I am not Chantal." And she stalked to the bedroom, slamming the door shut behind her. The painful silence was filled only with the beating of her own heart. Then she heard the shatter of thrown crockery, and the outer door opened and closed hard enough to shake the cottage. She wanted to sink into a ball of misery on the bed. She wanted to pound her fists on the wall and scream her frustration. She wanted to dance until she dropped of exhaustion, too tired to think and much too tired to feel.

But Chantal had not the luxury of losing control. Taking several deep breaths, she stood and took out the first dress she found. Revealing or not, it couldn't offer any less protection than these ridiculous garments. Maybe if she looked more the lady, she could act more the lady—and be treated more the lady.

Still, as she dressed, she knew the hope was as futile as the fleeting thought that maybe his own frustrated desire would make him give up and let her go . . .

Desire clawed through his loins, eating into his gut, mawling his male pride. By sheer physical effort, he kept it at bay and resisted the need to rush back and toss her on the bed. Too soon. She wanted him, indeed, but not enough to give in. Not enough to admit that she was as mercenary as she was beautiful. And yet, even in his anguish, he frowned. If she were so mercenary, wouldn't she gladly marry one of the wealthiest peers in England? Even more curious, if she couldn't give up her cursed independence, why wouldn't she become his mistress? And why the hell had she accepted a bribe to leave him?

No, if she were mercenary, she would not be willing to bed him for nothing more than transitory pleasure. He could have had her just then, and they both knew it. But he didn't want a quick toss on a table, or even a long laze in a bed.

He wanted the lifetime she'd stolen from him.

He'd be satisfied with nothing less.

If he had to continue this blasted stalemate until they

were both screaming from frustration, then so be it. But neither of them would leave this cottage until she admitted the truth. Truth could bridge the chasm of years and regrets. Truth could answer the questions that tormented him day and night. Truth could establish a foundation on which to build, and truth could forge a new bond between the parents of a willful young scamp who needed a father as much as a mother.

Only by reiterating these homilies to himself was he able to master the painful ache in his loins. It would be so easy to take her, to ease them both, but he sensed that once he did, one of his few advantages over her would be lost. She was almost as frustrated as he was. If he withheld himself, he still had a tool that might be useful.

He smiled ruefully, adjusting himself in his breeches. If that tool didn't sink him to perdition with the weight of its own arousal . . .

By the time he returned, Chantal had cleaned up the mess and calmed herself enough to face him without cringing. She was making a peasant stew on the fire, and it filled the cottage with a homey smell that eased some of the tension between them. She was dressed in the most demure gray wool gown she could find, which was just shy of scandalous. The fine inset of gray gauze exposed gleaming skin and deep cleavage. The gauze made an upstanding ruff about her face. It was woven into a gleaming ribbon about the high waist to tie behind her back and trail to the hem. A maid's dress it wasn't, but the color suited her mood.

He nodded at her somberly and went to set the table without being asked. Since they'd barely touched breakfast, both were hungry, and so little was said until the steaming bowls of stew were empty.

Then, shoving back her bowl, Chantal gripped the table edge. "Vince, this serves nothing. I truly regret that I can't admit to being your lost love, but surely you can see that holding me against my will only makes me angry."

Resting his chin in his palms with his elbows on the table, he stared at her without blinking.

She cleared her throat and continued calmly, "While I cannot deny that my body finds you attractive, my mind resents your . . . coercion. However, if you release me now, we can agree to let bygones be bygones." Expectantly, she looked at him, proud of her calm attempt to defuse an inherently explosive situation.

Letting his elbows drop, he folded his hands in his lap and watched her with the bucolic contentment of a cow. Stupid, phlegmatic, serene.

She gritted her teeth but kept her tone cool. "Come now, help me pack and drive me to Dover. I can catch a stage from there."

All she won was one blink from those long-lashed, mellow blue eyes.

Frustrated, she grabbed a flower from the pot on the table and handed it to him.

His lips twitched, and finally he showed enough life to take the flower. "My funeral wreath?" he asked.

"No, your cud."

He blinked, and then laughed heartily. "My dear, I have ever adored your wit. Pity you don't use it to equal effect in your own self-appraisal."

She stiffened. "You know nothing of me."

The mellow look disappeared in a snarl. He crushed

the flower in his hand. "Mayhap not. At least, not of the heartless woman who could disappear without a trace, leaving me to grieve for the rest of my life without knowing whether you lived or died."

She reared back as if he'd struck her, astounded that he could change so quickly from a cow to a wolf. A lonely, snarling wolf, hungry for flesh. She was poised for flight, but the waiting stillness in his posture warned her not to flee or he'd be at her throat. She nibbled her lip, wondering what to reply. His gaze dropped to her mouth and darkened. "I . . . I . . . agree that what your lost love did to you was wrong. But perhaps . . . she had no choice. Or at least it seemed like no choice to her at the time."

Some of the wildness eased from his eyes, but the great sadness that replaced it made her throat feel as if he did indeed squeeze it in his jaws.

"I know what my mother did. And while I shall never forgive her, your behavior was hardly exemplary. You should have at least come to me and told me what she said, Chantal."

Chantal waved her hand in the air, but the denial was weak and she knew it. She stared down at her napkin, folding it intricately, one way and another, anything not to have to meet that predatory stare that saw through her subterfuge and fear.

However, the tumbling emotions she'd experienced in the past eight hours had left her dizzy, unable to hold herself upright with her usual pride and control. She felt as if she were falling down a well with no bottom; once she tried to plumb the depths of what she'd lost, she'd never surface again. At least Papillone, mother of Tony, woman of independence, would not resurface. And sweet, innocent Chantal, lover of Vince, had long ago died.

Which left . . . whom? As if he'd ripped blinkers from her eyes, she saw again the image she'd strived to forget. That parlor, black swans gliding with the placid contentment she forever forfeited on that day. She remembered Adeline's impeccable manners, and the last cruel cut that had torn her from Vince's side. "Do you truly love my son?"

"Yes, madame."

"Then you must do right by him."

Do right by him . . .

Painfully, Chantal lifted her head and made herself stare at Vince. Many excuses she could make. *What should I have done—ask you to choose between your mother and myself? Beg you to teach me all the things I needed to know to be a politician's wife when you were hardly a man yourself. Ask you not to worry about me when you were about to go away to war and should worry about no one save yourself.*

She almost tore the napkin in two, she worried at it so, but she came no closer to a solution. One thing, however, was clear: She'd been given a second chance. Was it truly too late? If he had not loved her as deeply as she loved him, surely he wouldn't have fought so hard to win her now. He could have taken her earlier on the table, and he had not. Instead, he'd tried to get her to admit the truth. Why was it so important to him if *she* was not important to him? Maturity was a curse and a blessing. Even as she could admit how much she still loved and desired this man, she also knew that love was seldom enough to mend the past or forge a future.

Now, faced with Vince's need and her own, she had

to look at herself in a different light. Perhaps she'd told herself she must be brave for so many years that the notion of her own cowardice had been unfathomable. Mayhap she'd resisted so hard not solely because of Tony, but because it was easier to march alone than in tandem. Easier to sleep at night in a single bed. Easier not to fear being hurt again because no man came near, least of all this man who'd devastated her life. She felt as if she were seeing through a glass, darkly. The image sickened her, for she was not accustomed to thinking of herself as a coward.

His ferocity softened as he stared into her anguished eyes. He caught her hands, still fumbling with the napkin, and said gently, "What is it, petite? Do not cry. I want to keep you from sadness, not cause it."

And then her own version of truth almost knocked her from her chair. She snatched her hands away, trying to find strength for the charade, but the fear fed on itself, almost consuming her. If Adeline had told him the truth, then he must know. . . .

"And Tony? What of my son?"

Chapter Eight

Vince probed those lovely, lavender gray eyes that had haunted him since the first time he saw her. What to answer? That he knew she'd lied to him? That Tony was his son, that even if she refused to wed him, he'd never allow her to take Tony away again? Or let her continue this infernal charade, give her more time to feel secure before he snapped her in the parson's mousetrap?

Vince stood to move before the fireplace. He put one hand on the rough-hewn mantel, staring down into the mocking, dancing flames. Either way, he risked scaring her off. He was in such a brown study that he didn't hear her rise and come to him. He started when her soft hand touched his shoulder. He spun around.

"From your silence, I deduce that Adeline told you some nonsense about Tony being your son," she said lightly, the consummate Frenchwoman. No anguish in

this sleek, sophisticated coquette now. Wide, disingenuous, those eyes fluttered long lashes at him. "But it is
not so."

Vince clenched his fists at his sides. "No?"

"No." But she backed away a step at the look on
his face.

The conniving little tease made the decision for him.
He took one step toward her, easily closing the distance
she'd marked. "Odd, don't you think, that Tony is the
image of my grandmother?"

She paled but gamely lifted her chin. "Redheads are
not uncommon in England. I assume Tony gets his coloring from my father's side of the family."

"No."

She backed away another step. "No? How would you
know? I don't know who my father was myself."

"Because if you had seen my grandmother's features,
you'd know that such a likeness could not be coinci-
dence. The unusual spring-green eyes, the chin, the very
bone structure are the same."

This time, she literally refused to back down. "I do
not believe you. This is a trick, to get me into your
bed."

He'd been reaching out for her, but at this he dropped
his hands. Even for a tigress defending her young, this
was a savage attack. He swallowed his hurt and lashed
back. "You put a high value on your person, madame.
Why do you not value our son as highly?"

She gasped. "How dare you—"

He stuck his face into hers. "Do you have any idea
of the estates, the wealth, the opportunity you are self-
ishly denying Tony merely because of your own mis-
placed fears?"

Chantal the girl had never been able to keep still when she was upset. Chantal the woman couldn't either. She twined the folds of her skirt about her fingers, twisting his words with equal ease. "Even if Tony were your son, do you think he'd want these things? Or be happy with them?"

Rearing back, Vince couldn't hide his own shock. "Are you telling me Tony is happier as a guttersnipe living hand to mouth?" Immediately, he wished he could call the words back, but it was too late.

Her fingers stiffened in her skirt. "I admit that I have not always been able to provide well for Tony, but this I tell you, *m'sieur.*" Leaning forward, she poked her finger into his chest with every point. "My son has never gone to bed hungry. He has never gone to bed alone. He has never gone to bed afraid. He has never gone to bed unloved. Had he grown up on your vast estates, the latter two could not be assured."

Vince tried to catch her hand, but she snatched it away, continuing passionately, "I vowed when he was born that no matter how I had to deny myself, Tony would never grow up with my insecurities. Far better for him to wander the Continent with me, learn about the great civilizations, the arts, the sciences, tolerance and respect for people different from himself, than to be such as you and your kind. To look down on those less fortunate, uncaring of the starving poor while he cedes all decency and tenderness to his inherent right to rule. No thank you, *m'sieur.* I prefer that my son be poor and happy rather than wealthy and miserable."

The contempt in her voice stung him to the quick. How dare she sit in judgment upon him? "I never treated you like a poor relation."

She started to retort, caught the slip and replied, "No doubt others treated your ballerina as exactly that."

Her continual denials were driving him mad. His passions—and his fears—flared hotter with every deceitful word from that lovely, lying mouth. Still, a last time, he tried for patience. "My mother is no longer welcome in my home. After she told me the truth, I told her to leave. You will never feel that way again, Chantal."

Her porcelain features twisting in pain, she closed her eyes. "That was not right, Vince. No doubt your mother was trying to protect you when she sent that girl away."

Patience blew off the top of his head like a lid, leaving him a bubbling cauldron of warring emotions. She resented his mother on the one hand and lectured him about being cruel on the other. There was no pleasing her. And all through this distasteful confrontation, she refused to admit the truth. Before he'd put thought to action, he grabbed her up in his arms. "You persist in speaking as though it is not me you loved, me you left, me you betrayed. Until we settle this one lie, we cannot settle Tony's future or anything else."

As he spoke he carried her, ignoring her kicking legs and pounding fists as though he did not feel them. And indeed, compared to the emotions tearing through his gut, her puny strength affected him not in the slightest. "Very well, Chantal. You want proof? One place still remains where you cannot deny me." He veered toward his bedroom.

When she saw their direction, she froze, but only for an instant. Her fists beat him about the shoulders. "*Non!* I do not wish it—"

He tossed her on his bed and fell on top of her. "You don't know what you want anymore." He held her head still between his hands and kissed her. She writhed beneath him, furious. Her rage fired his own into a driving need to possess and dominate. Here, in his bed, she could not lie, or smile her false smiles. They had to go back to the beginning of their relationship before they could form a new, lasting one. "Be still," he muttered against her mouth, stopping her struggling legs with a strong thigh.

She bit him, but he barely paused, using the tactic to slip his tongue between her lips. He felt her heartbeat accelerate and knew the instant her emotions changed from rage to desire. Her fingers, pulling at his shoulders, dug into his arms. Her mouth opened to his invasion. Her legs relaxed. And, finally, her sweet little tongue began to answer the dance of his.

Immediately he loosened his grip. The cage of his arms opened, but she didn't spring free. With a despairing groan that sent a glad tingle through him, she wrapped her arms about his neck, pulled his head down and kissed him. Deeply, passionately, as if here, in his arms, the Chantal of old revived, cowing the formidable new Chantal.

And then . . . he couldn't think. He could only feel. He ran his hand up her silken leg beneath the skirt. Their tongues dueled in a passionate fandango, thrusting, retreating, imitating the greater intimacy to come. She shoved his coat off. He untied her sash and the buttons at her neck.

She worked on the buttons of his shirt; he tugged her stockings down. Shrugging out of his shirt, he kicked his shoes away and jerked off his own stockings. She sat up and pulled the dress over her head. When she was down to her chemise, and he was garbed only in breeches, they stopped and stared at one another. He reached out to touch her, saw his hand tremble and jerked it back in disgust. Almost, he climbed back atop her to deprive her of time to resist. But just as the old Chantal still slumbered inside the mature woman, the gallant young soldier still hid, wounded and sad, inside Vince. He waited. He had a feeling that most of the decisions of her life had been made of necessity; he wanted her to come to him by choice.

The passionate glaze cleared from her eyes. She looked down at her heaving bosom and then back at him. She drew a deep, shaky breath. "If I sleep with you, will you let me and Tony go?"

If she'd taken a knife and stabbed him in the heart, she could not have wounded him more. He bolted to his feet and turned his back. He clenched and unclenched his hands, wondering if he shouldn't take her now, since this was the only hold she allowed him over her. His gaze fell on his portmanteau. He dived into its contents, throwing his shirts, stockings and unmentionables over the sides until he found what he was looking for. He removed a paper-wrapped dress and shook it out.

He pulled her to her feet and jerked the crimson dress over her head. She was too stunned to struggle. She moved docilely as he slipped cap sleeves onto her shoulders and smoothed the tight-fitting satin down over her hips. Tiers of gold-spangled lace started at her hips, widening in a graceful fall to a short train. A slit up the side allowed the wearer movement. He unbraided her hair and ran his fingers through the thick waves until they fell over her almost bare bosom.

Chantal touched the silky fabric. "Why are you giving me this dancer's dress?"

Vince buried his mouth in the sweet hollow of her throat to whisper, "It was one of my wedding presents to you. I wanted you to dance for me in it. Many things you took from me, but this I will not be denied." He set her from him, grabbed something from the small closet and exited, locking her in.

He returned in a few minutes and flung open the door. She gasped at the sight of him and didn't resist when he dragged her out before the large mirror on the wall opposite the divan. "Deny this," he said softly.

Pain twisted her features as she looked at the lovely dancing girl standing before the handsome soldier in scarlet regimentals. She closed her eyes, shaking her head slightly, but he squeezed her shoulders and bent to nip her neck. Her eyes were purple when she looked again. For once, he read her thoughts, for they were the same as his.

A wish, a dream, a heartache stared back at them.

Ghosts of happier times awakened from their rest to haunt the cottage and the proud hearts who'd tried to exorcise them. How many times she'd danced for him and ended up in his arms. Her dancing had been the bridge between their youth and their adulthood, for it was then he'd realized she was a woman and treated her accordingly. How many times they'd remembered and dreamed of one another dressed as they were now. Vince, gallant soldier; Chantal, passionate dancer.

Praying the memories were as powerful for her, Vince cupped her head in his hands, running his thumbs over her high cheekbones, winging brows and straight nose. When he touched her mouth, barely rotating his thumbs at each sensitive corner, she inhaled sharply.

The words came easily, for truth was the only beacon that could lead them home. "How many times I reached out in the night for you, missed the sight of this face, grieved over your loss. It is not me you persist in denying, Chantal. It is yourself. I admire your strength and independence. You will not lose them in becoming my wife. You merely turn them to a greater good: making a home for a family who needs you."

"And how can a dancer be a good wife for a politician?" Her voice was husky.

She was wavering. Vince smiled. "You leave that up to me. I can assure you that once my peers in the Lords are exposed to your charm and wit, they will not care about your former occupation any more than I."

"And my dancing academy? What if I do not wish to close it?"

Vince bit his lip, but he could hardly demand truth without giving it. "I do not wish my wife to work."

She started to shake her head again, but he buried his fingers in her hair and bent to whisper in her ear, "We can talk more later. Now, I want you to dance for me." He stepped back, shoving the divan to the wall so that she had a clear space in the middle of the room.

"As Chantal?"

Feeling her resistance, he shrugged. "As a woman."

She looked from him to the cleared space to her image in the mirror. And then, as if she couldn't help herself, she lifted her arms and began to dance. She swayed gently at first, a reed in the soft breeze of her rustling skirts.

Vince leaned back against the side of the fireplace to watch, propping a booted foot on the masonry. Melancholy joy filled his heart, an odd mix, to be sure, but Chantal had always incited his deepest emotions. As he watched her begin to move faster, going on her toes in a spin that made her skirts bell around her, the realization he'd been ignoring overcame him. This Chantal, the one who'd lived apart from him, matured apart from him, given birth apart from him, was a better woman for it.

Like steel that becomes more tensile the hotter it's fired, this woman had grown strong through the perils and deprivations from which he would have sheltered her. Chantal held her arms above her head in a graceful arc, her spine bowed backward as she stabbed across the floor on her toes. Her hips rotated at the end of the step. Then, with a lithe movement so quick that he blinked and missed it, she kicked one leg out to balance herself as she spun on her other foot to face the other direction. A leg pointed behind her, she hopped on the grounded foot, her arms stretched before her to their full lengths, her lovely face a picture of yearning. Her cheeks were flushed, he assumed from the exertion.

What did she reach for? What did she want? He honestly did not know.

As she danced, spinning in a series of leg kicks now, his mixed feelings grew stronger. What right did he have to deny her such a God-given gift? Even if she agreed at last to become his wife, how could he make her give up a talent such as this? And his own career could only be hurt if he chose a working woman as a wife. A woman who was not only a ballerina, but one who owned her own dancing academy. Despite his insouciance earlier, he'd not be human if he didn't worry that marrying her could ruin his own career. But he had little choice. She and Tony were more important to him even than England.

The next time she spun, her bodice fell down her arms. Unanchored, the tiers of lace at her hips sagged. She stumbled on the train. He leaned forward to catch her in his arms. Her breath came rapidly between her lips. He could see down her bodice almost to her nipples as she leaned against him. He was astounded yet again at how much larger her breasts were than when he'd known her before. He couldn't wait to get his hands on her. His own breathing went ragged, and not from exertion. He expected her to pull away and jerk her clothes up modestly.

Instead, her cheeks flushed hotter. Holding his eyes, she stepped back two paces. With a supple shimmy, she let the dress fall. She stepped out of it and laid it carefully over a chair.

Vince waited, his heart thundering in his ears, holding his breath. The gulls crying outside, the pounding waves close beneath the cliff called to something wild and free in both of them. When she lifted her arms to untie her chemise, his erection came into full bloom, potent as the wild climbing roses on the cottage walls. He wanted nothing in life more than to be fruitful and multiply with this woman. She owed him another child, one he could watch grow inside her, suckle her, learn at her knee.

She stepped out of the chemise and stood naked before him. "I have always wanted to dance this way. Do you mind?"

An aching groan caught in his throat. Mind? He'd not have one left if she didn't take him to bed. He could only shake his head, propping his trembling form against the sturdy stone to keep himself on his feet. And then he watched as a literal dream-come-true danced before him, as skillful as Salome but surely more tempting.

Her neck arched as she crossed her heels in the classic dancer's stance. Long, lovely arms lifted over her head. Her breasts, firm and round, rose as she minced across the room on her toes. Her hips were fuller, too, and tiny white marks low on her flat stomach testified to her maternity. Somehow they added to the allure of a woman in full maturity, and hinted of how much more she could offer to a bedmate than could a young girl. Yet, strangely, her face glowed with all the youthful vitality she'd forfeited to raise his son. It was as if, unburdened by clothes, the spirit she kept in check had burst free.

She moved across the floor on her toes toward him and then stopped, her hips arched forward, yearning for a release only he could give her.

Vince tried to keep his eyes on her face, he truly did, but . . . The apex at her thighs became the focus of his being. He swallowed harshly. Many coarse things the men in his social circles called that portion of a woman's anatomy. But with Chantal, Vince instinctively realized that the vee between her legs was the fulcrum of her being. Any man who breached it was also being admitted to the workings of her heart and mind.

Was she really telling him this, or was he wishing it so? His eyes lifted to hers. She panted now, and this time, when she stretched her arms toward him, he lunged away from the fireplace and accepted their invitation. He shuddered at first contact but forced himself to touch only her shoulders and ask hoarsely, "Are you sure this is what you want?"

The look in her eyes as she fixed her gaze on his mouth made his passions flare hotter.

"Yes, Vince. Make love to me. This, I owe myself, no matter the dangers, or what the morrow brings."

The feel of her burned him, inside and out, and he was almost afraid to let his hands wander. What if she was nothing but another dream? Yet, when his tentative touch drifted down her arms, the goose bumps that sprang up were surely those of a mortal woman. Vince clasped her hands, lifting one to kiss the knuckles, drawing out this agony of anticipation. For ten years he'd waited. Chantal, the love of his life, had come home. He'd tempt her, tease her, torment her, and then he'd give her such pleasure that she'd never think of leaving him again . . .

Vince tossed his jacket over the chair. Then slowly, carefully, he lifted her arms and put them around his neck. His hands glided down her back, caressing the strong musculature of a dancer. Her own hands tugged his shirt free of his breeches so she could caress the planes of his back and waist. Then she lifted the shirt over his head, leaving his torso bare, and pressed up against him. Fire trailed the gentle brush of skin on skin. Vince shuddered at the feel of her breasts. He caught her waist, grasping tightly at his own wavering control.

When her eyes closed and she sighed deeply, pressing her breasts fuller against him, he rubbed back. She bit her lip, her nipples growing hard, burning where they touched.

Lower her to the rug. Take her now. But he shushed the male demands and used his body to continue the head-to-toe intimate caress. He brushed his trousered legs along hers, rubbing torso, arms and face against her softer, matching parts. He was delighted when her breath quickened. He could not forget that this was Chantal. After ten years of dearth, there was plenty. He could have stood here for hours, luxuriating in this contact that nourished instincts so starved they'd almost died.

But, as usual, Chantal had other ideas. She tugged at the straining buttons on his pants. "Off."

Groaning, he kissed her, free to run his hands over her silky skin. The taste of her, the scent of her, the feel of her, mocked the power of thought that had always guided him; primitive impulses mastered him now. Gently, he lowered her to the sheepskin rug before the crackling fire.

Chantal lay before him, watching him with a hunger almost as great as his own. She ran her hands over him, relearning the whorls of soft hair and muscular contours.

She felt the scar beneath the hair at his breastbone and stiffened. "The war?"

He nodded, skinning out of his breeches and unmentionables. Shyly, she looked away, but when he ran his palms down her arms, circling his way in gentle patterns to her full breasts, she gasped. When he kneaded the bountiful handfuls, her mouth fell open, ripe with passion. She kissed the scar on his bosom hidden beneath his chest hair and then circled his nipple with her tongue.

Biting back a groan, he caught his hands in her hair. Her hands slipped behind him, kneading his buttocks. Carefully, he brought their torsos closer, so close that his proud desire stabbed her in the abdomen. She stiffened at the heat and power of him, but then his head lowered and he lavished kisses on her breasts, leisurely pulling one nipple into his mouth to suckle. Her head fell back, and all resistance left her. Boneless, she melted to the rug in a puddle that invited him to dive into her essence and frolic there.

Vince needed no second invitation. Shoving her knees wide with his hands, he positioned himself carefully at the gate to her body, entering her that first bit. The feel of her against the hard, hot head of his sex almost overcame his control. But he honored her too much, and he had too much at stake to give in to desire. She tensed at the feel of him, spreading her legs and trying to arch to meet him, but he caught her hips in his hands and held her still.

An iron control he'd had to learn the hard way aided him now. "What is your name, woman?"

Dazed, her eyes fluttered open, the pupils so dilated they almost consumed the purple. She blinked at him and started to answer, but her own control was formidable. She bit her lip and turned her face aside.

Vince used his weapons to good effect. He rotated his hips into hers, nudging that throbbing button of flesh above her opening. Chantal gasped, trying again to lift her hips to his, but he held her still, teasing, slipping up, down and around. He was careful not to press hard enough to give her relief.

With a frustrated growl of sheer lust, she caught him in her hands, trying to pull him inside. Every other muscle in his body went as rigid as what she held, but with supreme effort, he managed to pull away enough to break contact. Lifting her over one arm, he lowered his head to feast on her bounty. He licked and teased, rotating his tongue around each globe, circling tighter and tighter to the nipples but not touching them.

Chantal squirmed beneath him now, her kittenish sounds of need soothing that tormented part of his soul that even this melding could not mend. Conversely, her own need heightened his determination. Her nipples were two hard points of desire when he finally brushed them lightly with his tongue. She shuddered, trying to hold his head still. He suckled her deeply, then lifted his head and asked, "What is your name?"

She tossed her head from side to side. "No, no, no!"

He shoved her thighs wide again. "Yes. Yes. Yesss . . ." On the last word, he slipped into her one inch. She was so moist that the movement was easy and slick. She sighed with relief.

That tight grip on the most sensitive part of his body almost mastered his wavering control. But he wanted more than a night with this woman; he wanted a lifetime. One built on truth, forgiveness and love—not lies and fear. Aching, his baser impulses screaming in outrage, he managed to pull out. He rested his glistening erection against her throbbing belly. "What is your name?" he gritted through his teeth.

Chantal glared at him, her eyes glittering. She looked elemental, primitive and passionate, far different from the sweet girl he'd fallen in love with so many years ago. But this woman was a far more fitting mate for the man he'd become. Vince clenched his teeth, cupped her head in his hands and tilted her head back to ravage her mouth. She kissed him back with equal savagery, consuming him, pulling at his erection, trying to win this battle of wills.

A shaky laugh was startled out of him when she nipped his lower lip and pulled it into her mouth, even as her hands pulled him toward that lower mouth. He kissed her back, hard, thrusting his tongue between her lips to hint at what she missed. "Your name, damn you," he growled against her mouth. He drew back. "Or so help me I'll take a swim in the sea and let you lie here experiencing the torment you mete out so well." He nudged her again, his body a beautiful, powerful inducement for truth.

She must have read the remnants of his pain because her panting breaths slowed. Her fierce expression relaxed. Her eyes softened to a lighter hue as she lifted a soft hand to cradle his cheek. "Ah Vince, *mon cher,* my stubborn darling. I can resist you no longer. You are the only one I have ever wanted in this way. The only one I ever shall."

He held his breath, but still he waited.

The smile she bestowed on him made his head spin with gladness. She pulled his mouth down to hers and whispered, her French accent strong with her emotions, "Of course I am your Chantal. Take me home again."

Joy exploded like fireworks in his heart, all the more festive for the somber dark nights preceding it. Vince took her to his breast, and his loins, and his heart. She wrapped her legs around his waist as, with one vital thrust, he ended their separateness forever. She gasped at the manly invasion, and he felt her tightness. Even snuggled in her silken purse, with the ravenous hunger of ten years of denial riding him, he made himself pause for control. He could never hurt her, but why was she so tight? It seemed as though she'd not made love since . . .

Blinking, he tried to focus on her lovely, flushed face. "Am I hurting you, love?" he gasped out.

Tears started to her eyes. Her hand shaking, she reached up to cup his cheek, caressing his face as though she could not believe he was really here, making love to her. He kissed her palm. "Shhh. I am fine. Take what is yours." Relaxing, she formed a supple bow about the arrow of his body to help him fly free.

The feel of her after so many long, lonely years made the debate of her chastity less weighty than the iron need pulling at his groin. She was here. She wanted him. That was enough.

Vince buried his face in the thick curtain of her hair, luxuriating in the tactile sensations of the silky curls above and below. Gently, slowly, he withdrew, testing her readiness by witholding himself until she arched her hips to urge him back. Laughing softly, he wrapped her hair into a coil, binding them together physically as this joining would bind them emotionally. He thrust deep. This time she opened to him, moaning her pleasure as he nudged the tip of her womb. Her hair slipped loose, changing from a coil to a curtain, teasing him by veiling and revealing the silky curves so decadently spread for his pleasure.

Closing his eyes, Vince gave himself over to the only woman who'd ever made him lose control. "Chantal . . ." And then even that whisper of breath took too much effort. He could only plunge, shoving her hair away from her breasts to cup them in his hands, squeezing them in tender concert with each thrust. He felt her tension rising with each upstroke high at the opening to her body, and a barbaric growl of joy escaped him. He was no boy now. If it killed him, he would wait for her, use his body like a drug to sate her and make her beg for more.

When he increased the tempo of the dance she'd initiated, she gladly followed, dipping and swaying to the rhythm of his gyrating hips. Higher they reached, their pas de deux approaching climax. She arched beneath him, and he took her cry from her lips as she clenched around him, her hips suspended in a final flourish. Her nipples hardened, stabbing him in the chest. For an instant longer, he held himself back. He would revel in this moment.

Time was suspended, physical laws subjected to lovers' rules. Ten years ended by a touch; motion not of reaction and opposite reaction but of two bodies in perfect synchronization; the distance between two planes traversed by a vow . . .

"I'll never let you go again," Vince groaned, pouring his essence into her. Spasms shook him.

"I'll never leave you. . . ." Chantal held herself tight against him to take his all, her eyes purple as his face twisted in an agony of joy.

Slowly, slowly, they returned to themselves, creatures bound by earthly deeds and duties. And yet, as their dazed, pleasured gazes met, they knew they had only to merge to achieve this ephemeral flight again.

Spent, Vince withdrew and pulled her head down on his shoulder. Sated, they still touched each other, exploring the changes a decade had wrought. "Your skin is so much softer, your curves fuller," he told her.

Her gliding touch stopped at his waist and pinched his hard belly. "Are you telling me I'm fat?"

He laughed, squeezing her buttock. "Delightfully womanly. You were slim as a reed before. I much prefer you this way."

"Good. I prefer you this way, too. You never had so many muscles—" Her voice drew off with a gasp when her hand glided down his thigh to his knee.

He tensed as she touched the hard scar tissue, knowing what would come next.

She sat up and gently turned his knee so she could see the outside of his leg. Her mouth trembled as she touched the scars that stretched from his upper thigh past his knee to his calf. "So, this is why you sometimes limp. A bullet?"

"Shrapnel." Before she could voice the other questions trembling on her tongue, he pulled her down atop him. "It seldom bothers me anymore. But you have already tended to my wounds in the best way possible. Come, nurse me again." He pulled her down until her breasts hung above his face and put deed to word.

Only much later, when he'd tucked her into bed and cradled her in the protective curve of his body, did he allow himself to sully the sublime with hard reality. What would he tell her when she asked for details of the wound? That he'd played cat and mouse with cannon fire, leading his regiment to the hottest parts of the battlefield because he didn't care if he lived or died? That he'd spent most of their years apart in a slough of fear and sorrow? That he'd pursued her so hard, and been so possessive, because that same fear still nagged him? If he lost her again, he could not bear it, especially now that he knew about Tony.

So many things they needed to discuss. Damaging admissions and difficult choices had to be made before they could set aside the pain and distrust of the past.

Still, for the first time, he felt optimistic. Vince smiled sleepily into the darkness. Like her namesake, Papillone had fluttered free before the gales of life, traveling far and wide in her search for home. Where would she light? Did he have the right to catch her, cage her, hold her in his hands for his own enjoyment? And yet, as she had twice proved beneath him, she needed him almost as much as he needed her. He had flowers aplenty for her to dally with.

But he was wise enough to know that no nectar, no matter its sweetness, would hold her indefinitely. Lovemaking was a start, and a good one, but trust would be harder to earn. He had to become as important to her as she was to him—in bed and out of it—before the butterfly would land on his hand.

Over the next week, he devoted himself to that end. He brought her tea and toast in bed. He wined her and dined her, feeding her off his plate, licking his fingers after she'd taken food from his hand. He told her tales of Parliament, and the fisticuffs he'd witnessed between two peers fighting over the corn laws. To his delight, her mind was as fully developed as her body. She could argue most subjects with both confidence and conviction. They did not always agree, but he had to admit that her logic had merit. He began to see that in many ways she was much like her father. He couldn't wait until she learned the truth about her parentage.

However, during that exploratory voyage of discovery, he deliberately withheld discussing their most divisive issues: why she had left; Tony; his mother; her dancing academy. He felt her discomfort any time the conversation drifted to those treacherous waters, so he ably steered them to leeward. Once she had his ring on her hand, then he would brave the storm.

However, there were other ways to navigate the waters with this fascinating new Chantal, and those he used aplenty. The next afternoon, as they peeled vegetables together for a huge stew, he looked at her slyly. "So, do you believe women should be given the right to own their own property, free and clear of their husband's control?"

Her knife slipped, clattering to the tabletop. "Why do you ask me this?"

Because you will one day be a very wealthy woman, and I need to know your thoughts on the matter. For himself, he'd be perfectly happy if Canfield tied up everything in trust for Chantal and Tony, but he was curious to see how liberated his shy ballerina had truly become. "I should think you'd have strong opinions on this matter, since you've obviously refused to wed the many men who have asked you."

That distinctively French shrug rippled through her lithe body before she picked up the knife again. "None of them were to my taste. But yes, I do believe England's laws in this regard are both archaic and wrong."

"So if you should suddenly become wealthy, you would want sole rights over your money, even if you should wed, say, someone trustworthy?"

Her eyes narrowed. She peeled the potato she was holding down to a nub, staring unseeingly at the woe-begone little thing. "Men do it all the time, do they not? Decide what to buy, where to live, which bank to use, what crop to plant, what charity to—"

"Some would argue that women are incapable of such weighty judgments." He hid a smile, calmly peeling his carrot but watching her from the corner of his eye.

"We are capable of rocking the cradles that hold the new leaders of the world, but we are not capable of business sense?" She made a scoffing sound, tossing the remains of the potato down in disgust. "I did not expect such arrogance from my gallant soldier." Her chin high, she stood to dust the room she'd dusted yesterday, leaving him to his even more mundane task.

Stung, he opened his mouth to retort but bit his tongue instead. Not yet. He let her flit around like an angry bee while he finished the stew. When he'd set the huge pot over the fire, he went to her and gently pulled the rag from her hand. "I did not say that such were my views. I merely wish to understand the new Chantal."

While he used his handkerchief to dab the dirt away from her lovely face, she shifted her feet, as if uncomfortable, but she allowed the touch. When he was done, he tossed kerchief and rag aside and caught her shoulders in his hands. "I could never quash the spirit or the initiative of any woman I loved. Her money will remain her money."

She relaxed, but a smile flirted at her lips, displaying her dimples. "Then you don't object to my dancing academy?"

His hands tightened on her shoulders. Damn the little minx. He'd walked straight into that one. He hesitated, but the image in his mind was so compelling that he blurted, "You shall look deuced odd teaching dancing while you're great with my child."

She whitened. Her pearly teeth showed in her gasp. She seemed to struggle for words, but then she pulled away, tossing over her shoulder, "I can still do the administrative work, even then. But I will never again bring a child into this world out of wedlock." She walked over to stir the bubbling stew.

For a long moment, he stared at her. Was it too soon? Shrugging, he decided she'd had enough time to grow used to the idea. He sat down before the fire and drew her gently to his lap. "I want to marry you, Chantal." He felt her tense on his lap but continued doggedly, "I have a special licence in the other room, and I know a vicar nearby who has already agreed to wed us. The sooner, the better." He put a gentle hand over her stomach.

She caught his wrist with both hands as if to pull him away. Instead, she made a strangled sound of either pain or joy, or mayhap a blend of both, turned on his lap and hauled his head down to hers. She kissed him as she'd never kissed him before: openly, joyously, like one not with just the right but the honor to do so.

That tight lump of dread, his constant companion for ten years, melted. Warmth and happiness streamed through his body. Everything would be all right. His ballerina, who'd led him through fire and turmoil and torment, would stand by his side at last. . . .

But then her fingers pulled frantically at his clothes. Before he had time to do more than gasp, his shirt was open and she was licking his nipples. He clenched his hands in her hair, shocked at her aggressiveness, but she wasn't long satisfied with that. Next she fumbled at his breeches, pulling him, hot and growing, into her hand. She stroked his length, slipping her hand up and down until he was like steel, aching for more.

She supplied it.

She untied her own peasant blouse and pulled it and her chemise down, baring her full, lovely breasts. He caught her about the waist and tried to pull her up to his mouth, but she held his wrists. "Be still. This, I do for you." And with a feminine grace and hunger that left him stunned, she caught his aroused wand and slipped it between the cleavage of her breasts, squeezing herself together with her own hands. The essence of woman enjoyed the essence of man in the most intimate, selfless caress he'd ever known.

Boneless, Vince dropped his head back against the chair, his eyes slipping closed as he gave himself over to sheer sensation. From far off, he felt her fumbling beneath her skirts. Then that warm clasp was released for an even more intimate one. Propping her knees astride him on the chair, she positioned him. With one supple twist, she used her dancer's body to good effect and sheathed him fully.

Great effect. Wonderful effect . . . Vince stiffened beneath her in an agony of pleasure as she began to ride him. She had never been so moist or needful. When he tried to cup her hips and move with her, she slapped his hands away. "No."

And so he sat still and let her pleasure him. She was so warm, so soft, slipping up and down upon him, her movements quickening with her excitement. He felt her silken purse begin to tense. He longed to thrust back in his own wild excitement, but he sensed that his quiescence was important to her. One last time she slipped up, freeing him to the tip, and then she dropped down, down, engulfing him more deeply than ever in a seering bath of passion. Meld, mingle with me, her muscles urged as she flexed upon him.

Crying out, he arched his hips into her and gave her what she craved. For a full minute, they shared the intimate flow of life in that unique bonding only lovers share. And when she collapsed upon him, her face on his shoulder but still cradling him in the depths of her body, he felt the wetness on her cheeks. He ran his fingers over the perfect shape of her head, feeling his own tears running down his face.

The other times had been wonderful, but this was intimacy as God intended. After this coupling, nothing could ever break the bonds they'd forged, Vince told himself. He rocked her in his arms, his throat so tight with emotion that he couldn't speak. They both shook slightly in the aftermath, little stabs of pleasure still darting through them. Only when she relaxed did he gently lift her chin and run his thumb under her eyes to wipe away her tears, unashamed when she stared in wonder at his own emotion. *I love you, Chantal.* The words rang so loud and true in his heart that at first he thought he'd spoken them.

Instead, he contented himself with a teasing, "I very much enjoyed the way you say yes. No man ever had a more enthusiastic acceptance to a proposal."

She blushed, trying to slip away, but he held her still, refusing to let her escape the intimacy of touch and thought. He delved equally deeply into her eyes, but this one question could not wait. "Why are you agreeing to wed me, Chantal? For Tony's sake?"

Again, she tried to slip away. Again, he caught her hips to hold her still.

Finally, she took a deep breath, flipped her loose hair over her shoulder and admitted, "Partially."

His heart skipped a beat. "Partially?"

"I . . . am tired of being alone. And besides, our . . . activities, well, uh . . ." She blushed deeper, biting her lip.

He bumped his hips up into her, amazed that he was growing strong again already. "Indeed. I cannot wait to see you great with my child." He cupped her breast and raised it to his mouth, tenderly reverent at her nipple.

She tensed, catching her hands in his hair, but he merely turned his attention to her other breast. "It's my turn to pleasure you, my dear." And standing, holding her anchored to him because he could not bear to break their bond, he lowered her to the sheepskin rug.

The stew bubbled a merry accompaniment as Vince showed her again, wordlessly, poignantly, how much he loved her.

By the time they left the cottage, several days later, Chantal needed their frequent couplings as much as he did. Some part of her realized that Vince had waged a careful campaign upon her, with his beautiful body and skillful hands the vanguard. What victory he sought, she was not certain, but his need for her was genuine. She was beginning to believe that, possibly, he did still love her. Possibly, he wanted to wed her not only because of Tony and the new heir they were likely to create, not only because he was lonely, but because he still wanted his Chantal. Twice she'd awakened in the night to find him watching her in the darkness. His arms always clasped her tightly, as if he feared losing her.

But when she questioned him, he gave a wry laugh and pretended he merely enjoyed looking at her. On their last night at a posting inn before their return to London, after the vicar had married them in a private ceremony with only his wife and son as witnesses, Chantal's suspicion became certainty.

They celebrated their union with the inn's best champagne and roast loin of beef. They stayed in the best—and only—suite of rooms. The innkeeper watched them walk about, hand in hand, as if they could not bear being separated, even for a moment.

" 'Twas rumored Sir Walter Raleigh himself used to sleep in this room," he said, winking slyly. "Without benefit of . . . respectability, if ye catch me meaning."

Vince smiled intimately into Chantal's face. "Are you suggesting, my good man, that my esteemed ancestor brought his lovers here?" He leaned close to whisper into her ear, "He obviously believes we're too amorous to be married."

She giggled, snuggling into the curve of his arm.

Vince arched a supercilious brow at the portly hostelier and lifted Chantal's ring finger. "We are as repectable as you please, my good man."

The innkeeper's smile slipped. He bowed unctuously. "Sorry, me lord, I did not realize ye was related to the bloke." He squinted at the huge diamond sparkling on Chantal's hand. "And congratulations to you both."

Vince had to smile at the man's melancholy air. "I apprehend you've been married for a goodly time?"

The innkeeper's bulbous, pink-tipped nose twitched and his eyes darted out to the corridor. "More's the pity." He coughed, pounding himself on the chest, when a sprightly but shrewish woman poked her head in the door.

"Henry, we've other guests who need seeing to." She sniffed, eyeing Chantal and Vince with suspicion, but since Vince had paid in advance with good English gold, she was obviously willing to give them one chance. "Good evening, sir, madam. Henry..." She flung the door wide.

He ducked out, giving her a wide berth as he went.

Vince and Chantal collapsed upon the huge fourposter bed in mirth. "Poor fellow," Vince gasped between laughs. "He obviously finds his marital duties somewhat tedious. Not that I blame him, being married to that shrew."

Chantal sat up and pretended to scowl down at him. "And will you someday be referring to me the same?"

His smile faded. He reached up, caught the back of her neck and pulled her down for a flaming kiss. When she collapsed upon him, he said, "No, whatever our marriage brings, pity will not be part of it." *Or regret. Come to me, and be my love.*

After they'd consummated their vows, they shared a plate of hearty English fare. Then, before a roaring fire, Vince opened a small black case, pushed her lawn nightgown down on her shoulders, and slipped something about her neck.

She craned her neck to see, gasping when she saw golden fire sparkling at her bosom, brighter, purer than the flames on the hearth. "The Yellow Rose," she whispered, touching it in awe. "Vince, are you sure you wish to give this to me?"

He leaned back on one elbow, eating her up with his eyes. "My grandmama would wish it. She said it should only be given in ... marriage."

What Callista had actually told him when she passed the priceless jewel down to him was, "And I hope you someday find a woman who will wear it with the same joy and love that I have always felt for the man who gave it back to me.''

Vince recalled the stormy story of Callista Raleigh and her dreaded lover Drake. The mysterious beast, the Dragon, had won the stone from Callista's family, only to reset it in more perfect form and give it back to her again. The lesson Callista had taught him that day was one he'd never forgotten—giving, not receiving, is the true test of love, and the true joy of togetherness. He wondered if Chantal remembered the tales he'd told her as a boy.

She obviously did, for when she looked at him again, her mouth trembled. ''I shall honor you when I wear it. You will never have reason to be ashamed of me.''

Touched, he kissed her brow. They climbed into the huge bed and fell asleep in an intimate tangle of arms and legs.

Hours later, Chantal awoke with a start. Vince tossed and turned next to her, moaning. ''No, please. . . .''

His voice held such pain that she assumed he must be dreaming about the war and how he'd gotten the wound he avoided discussing. Gently, she shook his arm. ''Vince, wake up.''

He grabbed her arm. ''She's starving . . . and cold. Mother, what will I do? How can I find her?'' He twisted in the bed, wrapping the sheets about his hips.

Chantal sat back on her heels, her eyes wide with shock. Dear God, he was dreaming that she was starving and freezing. With all the horrific memories he must carry of the war, it was her welfare that had troubled him? She rubbed her elbows, watching him toss and moan, and for the first time, guilt assailed her. She'd been too busy surviving and trying to make a home for Tony to torment herself overmuch with Vince's reaction to her disappearance. She'd assumed he'd get over her quickly and marry some lovely, well-connected young girl who could further his political career rather than impair it as she would have.

But his persistence in pursuing her, his deep sexual need of her, his gift of the Yellow Rose and, now, the proof of a ten-year-old pain she'd thought hers alone ... these reactions told her what? Did he still love her, deeply, truly, as she'd always loved him? If so, why did he not tell her?

Another thought struck her like a blow to the head. She cradled her stomach. And if he did love her that much, what would he do when he learned that having a second child could kill her? Even now, Chantal suspected she was pregnant. She would not know for certain for another week, but the timing had been right; her breasts were tender, and not just from their frequent lovemaking. She'd known full well the dangers in their uninhibited coupling, but she hadn't cared. More vital, more powerful even than her love of life was her need to create new life again with this man.

They'd both been robbed of the most bonding experience men and women share—nurturing a child together. She wanted to give Tony a brother, Vince another child to make up for the one he'd almost lost. Poor she might be, but this gift of inestimable value only she could give. Maybe then his mother would accept her, as the mother of her grandchildren, even if she couldn't accept her as the wife of her son.

Vince's tossing subsided as his arm found her in the darkness. Chantal lay back down beside him, glad he'd not awakened and forced them to face yet another obstacle to happiness. Mayhap she was a coward, but she couldn't bear to threaten their fragile happiness. And once they faced the issues that had held them apart, they could no longer pretend to be newlyweds without a past.

Miserable, Chantal closed her eyes. If her suspicions were true, and Vince had always loved her as deeply as she'd loved him, then she'd done him a great wrong. In leaving him, and accepting a bribe to do so, she'd betrayed all the ideals for which she'd loved him. They'd suffered ten years of pain and loneliness because she was a coward. And at least she'd had Tony, her one ray of light.

Chantal stroked his silky hair back from his brow, staring for a long time into the darkness. Whether it meant her death or not, the time had come to make amends. . . .

The next morning, when they left the inn for the short drive to London, Vince felt a difference in her. He was tired, and he vaguely sensed he'd had the dream again last night, but Chantal must not have awakened. Surely she'd ask him about it. But she was unusually pensive as they drove through the streets to his townhome. Finally, he decided she must be nervous at seeing his mother again.

He covered her hands, which were clasped in her lap. "Chantal, my mother will not trouble us. You need not fear seeing her."

She frowned down at her hands. "Vince, my son has had only me for ten years—"

"—our son," he said firmly. Pulling the curricle to the side of the road, Vince turned her carefully to face him. The flash of fire on her finger gave him courage enough to say, "So, at last you admit Tony is mine?"

She averted her head, nodding silently.

He waited, but when she said nothing more, he railed, "Why did you not tell me at the time, give me a chance to know my child? No matter what drove you away from me, you had no right to steal my heir without so much as a by-your-leave."

Silence.

Vince clasped her hands tightly enough to make her wince, but once exposed, the raw nerve quivered with such pain that he blurted, "I shall never forgive you for that, Chantal. You could have eased my torment with one letter telling me of the boy and that you were fine—"

"What then?" She snatched her hands away. "We would have been the poor relatives all over again, not good enough for the Earl of Dunhaven. Besides, I feared that you and your mother would take Tony away from me."

Snapping his mouth shut, Vince closed his eyes to temper his response. "I would never have done that, and it hurts that you could even suspect I would." He clucked to the horses, wondering if he should press the issue of why she'd left, but he'd had enough truth for the nonce. For now, he only wanted to get home, to see his son and have Chantal openly acknowledge his paternity of the boy.

When they arrived at last, Vince tossed the curricle reins to his surprised footman, lifted Chantal down and bustled her up the steps. He bellowed as they entered, "Tony, where are you?"

Chantal went stock still, nibbling at her lip. Like a hunted thing, she glanced at the door. "Tony is here?"

Colleen Shannon

"Of course. The day you agreed to wed me, I sent word for Tony, Hugo and Lizzie to join us. Now that my mother is gone, we have plenty of room." Vince walked to the bottom of the stairs, yelling with most uncharacteristic rudeness, not even waiting for his butler, "Tony, we're home! Come here, lad!"

A door opened above. Light footsteps ran down the hall. Tony paused at the top of the stairs, beaming down at them. Late afternoon sunlight streamed through the tall casement window beside the stairwell, turning his hair to molten fire as he ran to meet them.

With an extreme effort of will, Vince managed to stand aside to allow the child to go to his mother. Over Tony's head, he met Chantal's frightened eyes.

His mouth tightened as he glanced meaningfully at his son, then back to his wife. He didn't need to state the demand; from her expression, she heard it loud and clear.

Will you tell him, or shall I?

Chapter Nine

Tony launched himself down the last few steps to throw his arms about his mother's waist. *"Maman!* Come see. My room, it is so big, and there are dogs here, and horses, and the food is soooo good. . . ." He trailed off when she didn't respond, moving back to look at his mother with concern. "What is amiss? Are you not happy to see me?"

Chantal hugged him tightly. He was growing so tall that she only had to bend a little to rest her cheek on his bright head. *"Oui, petit chou.* I missed you greatly. You like it here, *hein?"*

Glancing at the silent man behind his mother, Tony nodded. He stepped away from Chantal and confidently strode before the master of the house. *"Bonjour, m'sieur.* I am most gratified at your hospitality. I promise not to be incorrigible."

Vince's mouth twitched, but he gravely shook the

small hand. "I am honored to have you here, lad."

After Vince released the boy's hand, both males looked at Chantal with an air of expectation.

Seeking some excuse to delay this most difficult conversation of her life, she glanced about. But the servants had apparently read Vince's stern expression and made themselves scarce. Chantal clasped her son's hands, took a deep breath and said rapidly, "Tony, sometimes life forces us into unpleasant choices. I grew up not knowing who my father was, a poor relation scorned by almost everyone I knew. And so, when you were born, I wanted you to feel secure in your heritage. I told you your father was a brave English lieutenant who died at Waterloo."

Chantal felt Vince's intense concentration on every nuance of expression in Tony's face. The boy listened attentively, but he didn't look upset. Yet. She measured her words with care. "It was only half a lie. You see, ah, the earl, that is, this man who has been so kind to you, ah, he is—"

Tony squeezed her hands. "You do not need to continue, *Maman*. I know he is my father."

Astounded, Chantal sat where she stood, her rump hitting the bottom stair with a thud.

Vince took a step back in equal shock.

And so both parents watched the matter-of-fact little boy continue, "I have known for some time, you see. My grandmama showed me the picture of my great-grandmama, and I have had a long talk with both her and Hugo."

Vince's eyes narrowed. "She did, did she? Have you spent much time with her?"

Tony nodded vigorously. "Every day. I do not quite

understand why she had to leave this house, but she said you would explain that to me.''

Vince's scowl grew blacker.

Tony caught his mother's lifeless hands. "I understand why you lied, *Maman*. It was quite wrong of you, but I can see that you thought you did not have a choice. But that is past." He twiddled with the huge diamond on her ring finger, making it sparkle in the sunlight. "Hugo said you would be married when you returned. This is so?"

She could only manage a nod. She'd always known that Tony was wise beyond his years, and countless times she'd thanked God for blessing her with such a wonderful son. But his equanimity in the face of such a shocking revelation shamed her. Would that she could have reacted so calmly to Vince's return to *her* life.

Tugging Tony to her bosom, she closed her eyes to stem the tears. "It is so. This is your Papa, *petit*. I am sorry for not telling you sooner. Go make your bow."

Tony stepped away smartly. He put one hand behind his back and started to bow before his father, but Vince made a strangled noise in his throat, knelt and hugged the boy tightly.

Tears streamed down Chantal's face as she saw the brightness in Vince's eyes. He blinked rapidly.

"Dear boy, I . . ." He had to clear his husky throat before he could continue. "I am the luckiest man in the world. I have such plans for you. So many things we can do together. We shall fish, and sail, and ride, just as your mama and I did."

Awkwardly, Tony patted his father's shoulder. He began to squirm in the tight clasp. "Indeed. But first—is it not time for dinner?"

A husky laugh escaped Vince. "Ah, a man after my own heart."

Only Chantal caught the depth of feeling behind the light remark. While Tony skipped ahead to the dining room, all right with his world, Chantal remained sitting on the steps under Vince's searching gaze, wondering how to right the wrong she'd done them all.

"Are you coming, wife?" He lingered over the last word, as if savoring the world's best caviar.

She nodded and waved him on. He hesitated, but when Tony called out to him, his expression emanated such joy that he seemed not much older than his son. He bounded after Tony, leaving Chantal alone to contemplate the miracle of a second chance.

The realization of the great mistake she'd made glowed amid the other murky uncertainties of her life. How could she make amends for the ten years she'd stolen from Vince?

One way. The only way. Her hands stole to her stomach. She bit her lip over a watery smile. And a most pleasant way. At least until . . . She shoved away the memory of that ghastly twenty-four-hour labor with Tony. This would be the greatest gift she could bestow on the two most important males in her life. A gift only she could give. If she lost her own life in the process, so be it. . . .

But no. She stood, hopeful for the first time in a long time. The old Scottish doctor had been wrong. She wasn't too small to have children. Tony needed a brother, Vince another son to fuss over from birth.

"*Maman,* come, I am hungry!" Tony called.

Chantal wiped her tears on her sleeve and went to join them.

After dinner, while Vince and Tony retired to the salon to get to know one another, Chantal ran upstairs to find Hugo and Lizzie. Hugo sat silently before Lizzie on a stool, his great arms outstretched as she wound her knitting around his hands.

Chantal's lips twitched as she watched Lizzie's tongue rim her lips in concentration at the task. She'd taught Lizzie the skill, and hadn't been surprised when her young friend showed a knack for knitting. Hugo sat glumly, this task obviously not to his liking. Chantal had to admit that he made a lugubrious contrast in this cheerful, ladylike sitting room papered in pink roses, his arms buried in pink yarn.

"Good evening, you two," Chantal said, closing the door behind her.

The ball of yarn flew across the room, unraveling as it went. Lizzie hurried over to her friend, leaving Hugo woebegone, tangled in the female nonsense. He gave Chantal a weak smile, but grinned in genuine warmth when she blew him a kiss.

Lizzie hugged her friend. "Aye, ye be glowing, as I knew ye would. Kidnappin' was the thing for ye." She picked up Chantal's left hand and showed the ring to Hugo. "See? I tolt ye they'd be wed."

He shrugged, hastily moving his arms apart again when the loop of yarn began to sag. A piece of lint floated up to his nose. He sneezed. "I dinna doubt it, missy. But is she happy?"

Chantal considered the question. Hesitantly, she nodded. For now, she resolved to enjoy the present and let the future worry about itself. "And I want to thank you, Hugo, for helping Tony to understand that I . . ." She trailed off, swallowing.

"Aye, lassie, 'twas but the truth. Did ye talk to the lad?"

She nodded. "He's with Vince now . . . but where is Adeline?"

Shaking her head, Lizzie sat back down before Hugo to continue her task. " 'Tis a criminal shame that the poor woman was made to leave her own home. I can understand the lord's anger, but he were wrong to send her away."

Chantal sighed. She sat down in the chair opposite Lizzie. "I agree, despite the pain she caused both Vince and myself. But I don't want to come between them. I've caused enough damage. Somehow, I must get Vince to forgive his mother."

Hugo smiled slightly. "As ye obviously have. Forgiven her, I mean. Ye have a grand heart, lassie."

Chantal's answering smile held more than a hint of mischief. "I thank you, kind sir. And how do you like it here, laddie?"

Hugo's smile wilted. He looked away.

Lizzie wrinkled her nose at Chantal. "He and the butler don't get along, ye might say."

"Might as well have a poker up his stiff rump," Hugo growled.

"And you, Lizzie?"

Lizzie's eyes widened. "Do ye have to ask? I've never been waited on in me life. I could get used to this in a trice, I fear."

"Get used to it, then." Chantal stood. "For you are welcome here as long as I draw breath." She bit her lip when she realized what she'd said.

The stool toppled over, sending Hugo and the yarn flying. He sat up, panic in his expression as he glanced

268

from Chantal's serene expression to her flat stomach. "No, lassie, ye must remember what the doctor said—"

"He was a sawbones of old." Chantal waved a dismissing hand. "It will be fine, Hugo."

Lizzie gave the tangled yarn a mournful look before she glanced between the pair, obviously catching the sudden tension that had invaded the room. "What do you mean?"

Chantal nibbled her lip. "When I had Tony, I almost died. He . . . wouldn't come out. His head was too big. If not for Hugo, we would both have died. He forged a tool that allowed the doctor to turn Tony's head and pull him free, but only after I'd been in labor for a day. I was so exhausted afterwards that if Hugo hadn't nursed me so tenderly, I never would have survived."

Clutching the arms to support herself, Lizzie sank back down in the chair. "Are you pregnant already?"

"I think so, though it's too soon to know for certain."

"Do the lord know ye almost died?"

"No. And neither of you are to tell him, understood?" They both nodded reluctantly under her commanding gaze. "The child will probably be small this time. Now, is the academy prospering? Have we many new students?"

While Lizzie talked, Hugo worked on untangling the twisted yarn. But that darkling look glimmered deep in his eyes as he watched Chantal. His lips moved in soundless prayer.

Those first few weeks flew by. Parliament had recessed for the year, so Vince was free to spend time with his new family. They played games together, rode together, shopped together. Vince seemed to delight in showering them with gifts, and Christmas was still weeks away.

Bartholomew Canfield was a frequent visitor, and the more she was around him, the more Chantal admired him. Being one of the richest men in England had certainly not spoiled the old gentleman. Lord or not, he truly was one of the most gentle men Chantal had ever known. However, she was bothered by the apparent secrets he and Vince kept from her. On several occasions, she'd enter a room to find the pair breaking off a hushed conversation to give her too-wide, innocent smiles. On one occasion, Chantal spied something small and glittering red in Vince's palm, held out to show Canfield, but Vince pocketed the trinket before she could get a good look at it and quickly changed the subject.

Other secrets lurked between them. Old hurts still remained, festering beneath the healing wounds. Chantal knew that, unless they addressed the painful issues, they could never banish the ghosts of the past.

One ghost loomed largest of all. In this season of joy and family, Chantal keenly felt Adeline's absence. The old martinet's touch pervaded the townhouse, from the dignified arrangement of the furniture to the perfect blending of color and form between wallpaper and accessories. To Chantal's dismay, she liked the townhouse very much as it was, and had changed little despite Vince's encouragement to decorate as she pleased. The fact that her taste and Adeline's were so similar gave her some encouragement, but it was growing increasingly obvious that Vince would probably never forgive his mother on his own.

Adeline had taken a small flat near Mayfair that had

passed to Vince from a remote relative. Chantal had tried twice to see her, but Adeline had been out on both occasions. Chantal had left the spanking new card with gilded edges Vince had insisted on procuring for her, but Adeline had not responded to her overtures. Chantal was growing worried. Confused as to why he was not allowed to see his grandmama since they'd returned, Tony had begun asking questions. So far Vince had distracted the boy with light remarks, but the time would come when the entire sordid history between herself and Adeline would have to be aired like dirty linen. She had to do something to prepare for that day.

When the time of her menses came and passed, Chantal was certain of her pregnancy, but not so certain of Vince's reaction. She'd been convinced he'd be delighted at her gift of another heir, but he was so possessive, jealous even of her time with Hugo and Lizzie, that she'd begun to wonder when she should tell him. Surely he'd begin to suspect soon, given the daily passionate lovemaking that made the huge old fourposter shake.

And her dancing academy complicated their relationship greatly. Despite Vince's feelings on the matter, Chantal wasn't willing to desert the enterprise entirely. She'd been so busy settling in, ordering wardrobes for both herself and Tony that would not shame Vince, making slight changes to the running of the household and planning for Christmas, that she'd only gone by the dancing academy once. Lizzie seemed to have everything running like a top, and the new dancing master she'd hired performed admirably, on the dancing floor and off, as one of Lizzie's many admirers. And so Chantal told herself that it was time enough to take over the reins of her new enterprise after the new year dawned.

If truth be told, she wasn't eager to force the issue of her employment with her new husband. She'd known too many years of loneliness to jeopardize her precious new happiness, especially given the added responsibility that would, literally, soon weigh her down. That revelation, too, she resolved to hoard until after the holidays.

Two weeks before Christmas, Chantal's fragile tapestry of life and love snagged on the horns of a new dilemma.

Cozy before a roaring fire, she, Vince and Tony sat stringing popcorn while an enormous yule log was wrestled into place by several footmen. Chantal listened with amusement as Tony discussed his new teachers with Vince. Tony's accent was becoming distinctively British, losing that charming cosmopolitan air that had hinted of his heritage. Given his new station in life, Chantal didn't know whether to be glad or sorry at the change. He would fit into English society, the better to take his proper place, but the old Tony of mischief and joy and curiosity had his sterling qualities, too. And so she watched the dynamics between father and son closely, wondering why Vince had not begun adoption proceedings to make Tony his legal heir.

"Mr. Twitter is well named, Papa. He twitters about, his hands fluttering, never landing long on any one subject. Latin and Greek are difficult enough without them being tweeted at one."

Vince frowned. "Do you want a different tutor in these subjects?"

Under his long eyelashes, Tony gave his father that

calculating look that was all too familiar to Chantal. "Perhaps. After the holidays."

Tony despised Latin and Greek. If Socrates himself came back to life to teach the subject, Tony would be bored, but Vince could apparently deny his son nothing.

"As you wish, my boy."

"And the history and philosophy teacher actually tells me that Homer likely made up *The Odyssey* and *The Iliad,* not basing them on history as we are taught in school. He also said that the library at Alexandria probably never existed and that—"

Angrily, Vince tossed down the string of popcorn. "I shall discuss this with my secretary at once and find you new tutors."

When Vince was gone, Chantal tied off her string, nipped the end with her teeth and draped the popcorn over a chair back. Then she stopped before her too-innocent son, crossed her arms over her breast and said, " 'Twill not work, you know."

"What, *Maman?*" Tony pretended interest in his own popcorn.

"You cannot get out of your lessons for long. Indeed, you should not. You have a responsibility to more than yourself now, Tony. Someday you will own this house and many more even grander. You must be taught the skills you need to manage them. Can you not see that?"

Tony stabbed his needle through a kernel so hard that the corn split in half. "But I don't care about them, *Maman.* Why can I not explore London with my friends as I used to? When Charlie came to the door, the butler sent him away. It's boring here. Tony, finish your lessons, Tony, don't slurp your tea, Tony, sit up straight,

273

Tony, pronounce that word properly. . . . Why, I shall run myself ragged trying to be an heir to an earldom. I'd rather be Tony, son of a famous ballerina, again.''

Just as she'd feared, Tony found the life of privilege as constricting as she did. Chantal knelt before her son and took the needle from his stabbing hand before he hurt himself. ''Do you love your new papa, Tony?''

Big green eyes lifted to hers. Some of the resentment faded. Tony nodded.

''Then you must accept what being his son means. It means all the things you just said, but it also means security and warmth and someone to always love you even if something should happen to me.'' Tony stiffened, so Chantal went on hastily, ''Not that anything shall. But you want to make your new papa proud, do you not?''

A firmer nod this time.

''Then study hard. And remember, your tutors have families to support. Unless you truly find them impossible to learn from, you should keep them. Unless you want them to starve in this season of giving?''

Biting his lip, Tony shook his head. ''I . . . did not think of that.''

Kissing his cheek, Chantal whispered, ''*Oui, mon fils. I know.*'' She leaned back and said briskly, ''Besides, once you learn Latin and Greek, just consider all the wonderful books you can read and all the new words you can impress your friends with. I shall talk to the staff and tell them that your friends are allowed to visit, with supervision.'' A visit that would require very strict supervision, indeed. Two of his best friends were pickpockets, and Chantal's rich imagination visualized them leaving the house with pockets bulging.

Tony sighed, his skinny shoulders lifting with the effort, but he was a sensible child. "Very well, *Maman.* I shall tell Father I wish to keep my tutors. May I go now? Harry and I are supposed to purchase roasted chestnuts from a lady he knows, then take them to Bow Street to resell them."

Chantal didn't bother to point out that his current allowance made such enterprises unnecessary. She still remembered what it had been like to be a child. It was far more fun to roam about London selling chestnuts than to ask one's father for money. "Very well. But dress warmly, and take Hugo with you."

Tony kissed her cheek. "You're a right'un, *Maman!*" And he scampered off.

By the time Vince returned, Chantal was on a stool wrapping the first string of popcorn over an archway. He came up behind her and hugged her, startling her so that she dropped the string.

Turning her to face him, he picked up the string and wrapped it about their waists. "Our son is as mercurial as you, my love. He's decided he wants his tutors after all. With a little help, I suspect."

Chantal didn't respond to his needling look. She was so tiny that even on the stool, she topped him only by half a head. Still, when he had to reach up to kiss her, she teased him by leaning back.

He pretended offense. "I always knew you were a sham. You've wanted to lord it over me from a pedestal for years now."

Haughtiness wasn't so difficult to pretend after all. "Anything worth winning is worth fighting for."

His smile faded. "I've proved myself several times over on that particular field of valor, I believe. The only

275

mistake I made with you years ago was giving you too much time to think. I should have whisked you off to the parson long before we planned. My tactics now are so much more successful, wouldn't you agree?'' He grabbed her about the waist, unwrapped the popcorn and tossed her on the settee, landing atop her. ''You're too busy being my wife to think of leaving me, right-o?''

Chantal's arms crept about his neck. Always, he teased on this subject, but she'd witnessed another of his nightmares and knew that his lightness hid darker fears. *''Oui,* darling.'' She cleared her throat. ''You have me exactly where you want me, now. The past is over. Let us not discuss it again.'' She pulled his mouth down to hers, as she did every time he hinted of the past. She knew he still wanted to understand why she'd left him, but she'd been afraid to broach the unpleasant subject, especially given his anger toward his mother. Time enough for that when they were comfortable together. Right now, they were more like lovers than an old married couple.

An advantage, Chantal reflected as she nibbled at his full lower lip, that they should savor while they could. They were in the process of doing exactly that when someone said from the doorway, ''Excuse me, dear boy, do I have the time wrong?''

Vince lifted his head and scrambled away from his wife, his cheeks flushed. He straightened his loose cravat and met Bartholomew Canfield's amused gaze. John Whitmore and Quincy Renner stood beside him, staring at Chantal with what could only be termed polite lust.

Immediately, Vince became the cool aristocrat. His fumbling hands dropping, Vince turned, helped his wife to her feet, blocking her figure with his back while he straightened her disarranged bodice. Satisfied, he tucked her hand in his arm to take her to meet their guests.

"Good afternoon, gentlemen. Excuse our tardiness, but I'm afraid we both lost track of the time. Darling, I'd invited Mr. Canfield for tea. I regret I forgot to tell you."

Chantal's feet dragged. She didn't miss the fact that Vince didn't include the other two men in the invitation, and she wondered why Canfield had brought them. Wondered, too, why Canfield looked at her so searchingly, as if her happiness were not only his concern but his duty to question.

But she curtseyed politely. "Welcome, sirs. I shall see to our refreshment. Pray, be seated."

She fled, ordering tea, scones and sweetmeats. She paused before the mirror in the dining salon to straighten her mussed hair and smooth her wrinkled clothes. Her day gown was all the rage, cream velvet trimmed in lace, but it was cut too low. If Vince had warned her, she'd have selected something more demure. Again, she had to wonder why he hadn't. He wasn't forgetful.

But she set aside her curiosity, glued a smile on her face and entered the formal salon again. The drawing room maid had just set the formal silver tea service down on the table before Chantal's chair.

Under interested male gazes, Chantal flawlessly performed this peculiarly English ritual that was the duty of every chatelaine. She poured the tea without spilling a drop, offering sugar and cream to each man, stirring the redolent brew with the right motion, not allowing so much as a scrape against the side of the cup. She served herself last, adding cream with a liberal touch. Vince didn't need to know, but she far preferred chocolate over tea. Meanwhile, she listened to the conversation.

Vince finished his amusing rendition of their marriage before the aging parson, suggesting to Chantal, "Show your ring to Mr. Canfield, darling. He knows a thing or two about stones, I'm told."

Obediently, Chantal stood, offering Canfield a plate of scones with one hand, showing him the large diamond with the other. Canfield's hand shook slightly as he caught her hand and peered down at the ring. She wondered at the emotion emanating from him. Why did he hold her hand so tightly? Chantal eased away as soon as she could, returning to her chair. Some strange emotion vibrated from this man every time she saw him, and it made her uncomfortable because she couldn't understand its provenance.

"Magnificent, indeed. But what of that pretty red ruby ring you showed me, lad?" Canfield asked. "I assumed that would be your wedding gift to her."

Under Chantal's curious gaze, Vince looked away. "Ah, no, not yet."

Ruby? What ruby? Chantal filed the question away for future reference.

"And where is my-ah, the boy?" Canfield asked.

"Indeed, where is Tony, darling?" Vince asked Chantal.

"I let him go out with his friends for a while." Whitmore had been grimly silent, so Chantal tried to engage him in conversation. "Have you visited the academy lately, sir?"

"No. As apparently you have not, either."

Whitmore's hostility could be sliced with a knife. Why was he angry with her? Their enrollment hadn't suffered during her absence, so he shouldn't care whether she'd been there or not. Confused, Chantal piled another plate with treats and took it to him. He accepted it, snapping his teeth down on a scone as if he wished he held her neck in his jaws.

Suddenly, Chantal understood. He felt she'd deserted him, putting his investment at risk. Under Vince's watchful gaze, she hesitated to reassure him, but finally decided she owed him too much. "I shall begin teaching at the academy again after the new year, John. You need not fear that I have deserted it."

Whitmore shrugged.

Vince stiffened.

And Renner's nose twitched like a bloodhound's as he scented a delicious whiff of scandal.

Only Canfield moved to fill the uncomfortable silence with a hearty, "I wish to celebrate your wedding. Might I inquire as to a suitable gift?"

Chantal protested, "That's not necessary—"

Vince shook his head at her slightly. "That's most gracious of you, sir. Anything you choose shall be much appreciated. You have exquisite taste, as you have proved time and again."

And to Chantal's mystification, both men looked at her as if they'd carved her out of solid stone and were standing back to appraise their Galatea. She set her cup down hard enough to make the fragile bone china ring. She was about to stand and make her excuses when Renner spoke.

"My lady, my daughter is a graceful tribute to any drawing room now. Please accept my deepest thanks."

279

It took several seconds before Chantal realized he was speaking to her. She blushed. She'd never once considered that she was a countess now, but her visitors obviously had. "Thank you, sir. But we taught your daughter only to use her natural gifts." This man's oily obsequiousness troubled her, and she could only wonder how he'd produced such a charming daughter.

Whitmore set down his cup in the saucer and put both on the exquisite inlaid table beside him, apparently not noticing that he left a tea stain on the glossy wood. "If you don't object, my lady, I've given Quincy leave to use the academy at night for meetings. They will leave everything as they found it, of course, and disturb nothing."

Vince inhaled sharply, choking on a sip of tea.

Chantal rose to pat his back. "What type of meeting?"

Vince wiped his mouth on a napkin and set down his cup.

"Oh, just a society we're both members of. Nothing of consequence," Renner replied.

Chantal sat back down, wondering at the undercurrents in the salon. Vince glared at her, obviously willing her to refuse, but without John she wouldn't have an academy, and she saw no reason to deny his request. She nodded. "You have my leave."

For the first time, John relaxed enough to smile.

Vince's brows met above his aristocratic nose. That imperial blue gaze lowered on John.

Again, Canfield jumped into the fray. "So, how does the lad like it here? And that great Scot?"

Gratefully, Chantal accepted the change in subject, explaining the conflict between Hugo and the butler.

"Hugo refuses to wear livery. He doesn't like the food here, and when he went into the kitchen to prepare his beloved haggis, the cook had a tantrum. The butler had to soothe him for over an hour. And Hugo's got the chambermaids in a dither. They're afraid to go near him. They say he looks like he's about to don kilt and bagpipe and behead everyone in the household with his claymore."

Vince and Canfield chuckled. Even the other two men smiled at her vivid description.

"It's hardly any wonder the butler doesn't like Hugo. His job has certainly become more difficult since we arrived, but I don't doubt, with time, we shall all contrive." Chantal opened the lid to the teapot to check whether there was enough. "Would anyone care for another cup?"

They all demurred.

Renner and John stood. "Well, we just wanted to congratulate you both," Renner said with false heartiness.

John nodded his agreement, but his gray eyes had an icy sheen as he shook hands with Vince. He gave Chantal a bow so short it was barely courteous, and looked at his uncle. "Quincy and I have an engagement, Uncle. I shall be home late this evening."

Canfield shrugged and stayed put.

The moment they were out of the room, Vince exploded, "How do you abide that viper in your home, Bartholomew?"

Canfield patted his mouth with his napkin and folded it neatly. "We use one another to mutual good effect. He needs my money, I need his managerial skills. Despite your obvious dislike of John, he has many good qualities. Besides, I owe it to his mother, God rest her soul.''

When Vince looked as if he might argue again, Chantal stood. ''Sir, would you care to see our solarium? It's one of the finest in London, so I'm told.''

Apparently gratified, Canfield set aside his napkin and rose to offer her his arm. ''I would be delighted, dear lady.''

However, they'd scarcely made the entry before the door burst open. Tony, his face smeared with soot, his velvet knee breeches torn at one knee and his white shirt dirty, scampered inside. A shrieking monkey was perched on his shoulder, his little red cap askew, his eyes wild in his ugly little face. Tony's eyes, equally wide and scared, held the same fear. He scooted behind the vast entry table where guests left their calling cards.

''Tony? What is—'' Chantal pulled her hand from Canfield's arm, intending to hug her frightened son, but she never made it to his side.

The mystery was soon solved when a very large, very angry and very ugly man threw back the front door without so much as knocking and stormed into the mansion. He wore the bright tunic, vest and cap of an organ grinder. ''That's my monkey, ye little divil. Give him me, or I'll set the law on ye!''

Ignoring the shocked stares of the Quality, he tried to round the table, his beefy arms outstretched. As agile as the monkey on his shoulder, Tony scrambled under the table to the opposite side, keeping the sturdy mahogany between them.

''No! You're cruel to him. I told you I'd pay you—''

''Two pounds? Ye scurvy little scum, I make more'n that on him in a day.'' The organ grinder faked a lunge in one direction and moved in the other, but Tony read his intent and sidestepped neatly. Hugo and Lizzie appeared at the top of the stairs, drawn by the commotion.

Just as Vince entered the hall from the salon, Chantal found her voice. She stalked toward the organ grinder. "I'm certain we can come to an equitable agreement. How much do—"

Without turning his head to look at her, the organ grinder reached out a long arm and slapped Chantal with the ease of long practice. She flew sideways, but Canfield caught her before she hit the ground.

In a trice, the confrontation changed from chaotic and slightly amusing to dangerous. Everyone froze, staring in shock at the bruise already appearing on Chantal's cheek.

Even the crude organ grinder seemed to realize that he'd overstepped himself, for he blustered, "Stay out o' this. Ye can't buy me off so easy, ye rich bitch. The little bastard stole my monkey, and he's going to pay fer it." He started to climb over the table to get to Tony.

The monkey followed his instincts and went higher. Perching on the top of Tony's head, he seemed to feel safe enough to shriek monkey profanities at his tormentor. Tony ducked behind a tall, inlaid secretary, peeking out with one wild eye.

Canfield looked about for his cane, presumably to beat the fellow with; the butler disappeared to fetch his burliest footmen; Vince picked up a marble figurine and stood between the organ grinder and his son.

The man stomped up to Vince, snatched the figurine away as Vince tried to raise it, tossed it aside and, with equal ease, picked Vince up and threw him against the wall. With a sickening thump, Vince's head banged against the sturdy plaster wall. He slumped sideways, dazed.

Now only Canfield and Chantal stood between the infuriated organ grinder and Tony. Chantal spared a tormented glance at Vince, who was shaking his head, trying to clear it, and at Tony, who crouched in a corner.

Dear God, no wife and mother should have to make such a choice, she thought. But Tony was in more immediate danger. Chantal clenched her fists and stood on her strong dancer's toes, preparing to launch herself at the mountain of a man. He was an avalanche of fury about to descend on her son.

From up above, a keen wail sounded like a bagpipe blowing the call of battle. Hugo galloped down the stairs like a mastiff trained for combat, bristling with strength, fury and blood lust. In four long strides he bounded down the steps, leaping the last few feet to tackle the organ grinder as the man reached out for Chantal.

Crash! Both men went sprawling, knocking into a spindle-legged chair. Under their combined weight, the gilt legs split like kindling. The two men fell to the marble, punching, kicking and biting without regard to safety or Marquess of Queensbury rules.

Vince made it to his feet and looked as if he might try to join the fray.

Jerking her head at Tony, Chantal sidestepped the two brawling men and went to her husband, catching his arm to keep him still while she felt the lump on the back of his head. She pulled her hand away, but it was clean. No blood, thank God.

Meanwhile, Lizzie hustled Tony upstairs and spirited him to safety.

Footmen crowded into the hall, but Vince shook his head at them when they moved to enter the fray. "Fetch the watch," he told one. The man disappeared.

Yelling a Scottish battle cry, Hugo landed atop the organ grinder, systematically beating the man about the head and shoulders.

Vince moved past Chantal and caught the organ grinder's arms, which Hugo held in an iron grip. Vince tied them above the man's head with his own cravat. Canfield finally found his cane and started beating the man about the legs, but the organ grinder still struggled, kicking with a burly leg.

With a last powerful punch, Hugo knocked the organ grinder unconscious. Wheezing, Hugo stood, favoring one leg, his nose bloody. Canfield offered a kerchief with one hand, leaning heavily on his cane with the other.

Vince moved carefully, as if he feared his head might fall off his shoulders, and patted Hugo on the back. "I knew there was a reason you Scots are so surly. You save your strength for when you really need it."

Hugo dabbed at a cut lip, glaring down at his fallen foe. "The mon's daft, that's what he is. He should be taken to Bedlam straight away."

Pulling Chantal to his side to appraise her cheek, Vince said, "No doubt the magistrate will agree with you."

Canfield sat down in the first chair he came to, one hand cupped over his heart. "I feel as if I've run a race. Tell me, dear chap, is this an amusement you save for guests? If so, next time I shall come better prepared." He cocked his head on one side to appraise the gigantic, fallen man. "A catapult and cannon should do the trick, I think."

Chantal giggled. Vince chuckled. Even Hugo grinned reluctantly.

When the magistrate entered, his cheeks puffed with exertion, he stopped and stared at the merry group. He scratched his head under his cap. "I thought there was murder at the least, from what this blighter tole me. What's amiss here?"

By the time they'd explained everything and the organ grinder had been hauled away, supper had come and gone, growing cold in the chafing dishes in the dining room. With his usual sense of fairness, Vince had given the magistrate twenty pounds to pay the organ grinder for the monkey. "He'll need it by the time he gets out of gaol," he said grimly.

Chantal perched on a stool before him while Vince rubbed her cheek with salve. She'd tried to look at his bump again, but he'd waved her away. "Tell Tony it's safe to come down now," he said to a maid.

She disappeared. Light footsteps dragged down the stairs a few minutes later. The monkey still perched on his shoulder, Tony entered the room. His cheeks were flushed. He had the same hunted look as the creature, and he looked equally helpless in this civilized jungle.

Sternly, Vince straightened away from Chantal and beckoned to his son. Canfield's gray eyes glowed, reflecting the gaslights in the salon, but Chantal wasn't watching him. Nervous, she glanced between Tony and his father. This would be the first test of their relationship, and she was worried, for she knew how stubborn Tony could be.

"Tony," Vince said calmly, "you were wrong to

take this animal away from its master—''

"But, sir, he was beating him—''

"—no matter how poorly he was treated. It's theft, pure and simple. Do you understand?''

"But, sir, I offered to pay for Rufus—''

"If he didn't wish to sell the creature, that should have been the end of the matter. How would you feel if some man offered to buy your pony for a paltry sum, you refused and then he took your pony anyway?''

Tony frowned. "But I don't beat my pony.''

"There is a difference morally, I grant you, but none under the law. If you are to be master of my estates, you must learn the finer points of such matters.''

Tony's lips trembled. He wrenched off two grapes from a bunch on the sideboard and offered them to Rufus. Rufus gobbled them greedily, seeds and all. And then, his mouth set mulishly, Tony mumbled, "Then maybe I don't wish to be master of your estates.''

Chantal closed her eyes, unable to bear the stricken look on Vince's face.

Canfield rose and came over to Tony. "May I see the little fellow?'' he asked.

Scuffing one toe into the thick carpet, Tony hesitated. But finally he released the monkey's lead rope. As if he'd found his home, the monkey scampered into Canfield's raised arms.

Canfield patted the hunched back and gave Rufus another grape. "He's a fine specimen. Tell me, lad, do you think this little man is better off here, where he's fed and watered and has a warm, safe place to sleep without having to fear predators, or would he be better off free, where he has to watch his back constantly?''

Tony nibbled at his lip. "Here, I suppose. As long

as he's with me, because I won't beat him.''

"And do you think the transition was easy for him? Don't you suppose he missed his old friends and surroundings? That he found the rules he had to follow hard to learn?''

Chantal's eyes opened to stare at this strange little man. She knew what he was doing. How had he grown so wise? And why did he care so deeply about her and her son? Why, he'd risked his life to protect Tony when he'd used his cane on the irate organ grinder.

Tony shrugged. "I suppose.''

"You know, I have friends in Africa. If you wish, I can see that he returns home to the jungle.''

"No!'' Tony moderated his panicked tone. "I wish him to stay with me.''

"I see. Then he'll have to learn to follow the rules, won't he?''

Tony's green eyes darkened. He glanced from his father's watchful expression to his mother's hopeful one. Finally, he nodded reluctantly. "I understand, sir. I shall try harder.'' He went to his mother and softly, delicately, kissed her bruised cheek as if to make it better, as she'd done countless times for him when he was growing up. "I'm sorry my actions caused you harm, *Maman*. And you, too, Papa. Does your head hurt very badly?''

Vince opened his arms to Tony. Hugging him tightly, he met Canfield's eyes over Tony's head. "Not anymore, son. It will be fine, now.'' To Canfield, he mouthed, "Thank you.''

Canfield nodded gravely, set the monkey down on a table and fetched his cane. "These weary old bones have had enough excitement for one day. Good even, all.''

"Let me escort you to the door, sir," Chantal insisted, holding the salon door open for Canfield.

He didn't argue. At the front door, she waved the hovering footman away.

That strong emotion she'd occasionally glimpsed flickered in Canfield's gaze as he reached out to tenderly cradle her bruised cheek. "What would you have done, my girl, if Hugo hadn't come to the rescue?"

Chantal shrugged. "Bitten, kicked below the belt, whatever was necessary to save my son."

He smiled. "I thought so. Will you come have lunch with me soon?"

"Just me?"

"Just you."

Chantal backed away a step. "It wouldn't be proper—"

The warmth faded from his expression. "Bless my soul, you silly goose. I have no designs on your body."

"Then why do you want to see me?" Indeed, Chantal had the feeling that once she understood that, she'd solve the mystery of his interest in her.

And mystery it was, for she'd never met the man until she had dinner at his home.

"To . . . get to know you better. Speak to Vince. I make no doubt he will not object." Gravely, Canfield gave her a dignified nod and exited to get into his waiting barouche.

That night, as she and Vince got into bed together, Chantal broached the subject. "Mr. Canfield has invited me to have lunch with him. Alone. Do you think it proper, Vince?"

Vince seemed occupied in pounding his pillow into the desired shape. "He's not a womanizer, Chantal. You'll be perfectly safe."

"I . . . see." She didn't. Why did he object so strenuously to John, but not at all to his even richer uncle?

Vince drew her unwounded cheek to his breast. "Now, about Tony. Why did you not tell me he hates his duties so much?"

Chantal's heart skipped a beat. Vince must have felt it, for he clutched her tighter. "I was hoping he'd grow accustomed to them. He can keep the monkey, can't he?"

Vince wrinkled his nose. "As long as he changes its diapers. My housekeeper is not happy, but I pay her generously. And by the by—I take back every harsh word I've ever said about Hugo. The man's a nonpareil."

Rubbing her cheek against Vince's chest, enjoying the feel of his skin and chest hair, Chantal said dreamily, "I would be dead without Hugo." Immediately, she wished she could call back the words, for she felt Vince stiffen.

He sat up against the headboard, pulling her with him. "Would you care to explain that statement?"

To distract him, Chantal tightened her arms about his neck and pulled his head down to kiss him. "Later."

"No. Now." Burying his fingers in her thick hair, Vince pulled her head back to bend a stern gaze upon her. "We've issues to settle, woman, as you well know. The sooner, the better. For both us and Tony. Now . . . how did Hugo save your life?"

Chantal pulled away. "Very well. You want straight

talk—why have you not begun adoption proceedings with Tony?''

"How do you know I haven't?"

"Well, obviously I shall have to be involved. Your barrister has been here several times, but he hasn't said a word to me about the subject.''

Blue eyes could be sunny, they could be hard and they could be sad. But when they filmed over with ice, they could freeze one to the soul. Chantal shivered as Vince's gaze drifted over her bare shoulders, leaving gooseflesh as it passed. She knew they'd both changed, matured from the young lovers they'd been a decade ago, but she'd assumed they had basically the same personalities, with the same strengths and weaknesses.

Not so. For just as she withheld the truth of her pregnancy from Vince, he was withholding some information vital to their relationship from her. Neither of them could have been so cagey ten years ago. Unlike those young lovers, they'd both known pain and betrayal, and sadness so deep it had no bottom. One learned artifice from such trials and tribulations, and politesse to hide one's fears.

Sadness almost overwhelmed Chantal. Would they ever be able to plan a future when every act of their present was haunted by their past? Refusing to back down, she awaited an answer.

Finally, he said, "I have my reasons, with which I will acquaint you when you learn to be open and honest with me."

And he turned on his side away from her, pulled the covers over his shoulder and promptly went to sleep.

The sandman took far longer to visit Chantal. When

she slept, she dreamed of herself, bloated with child, tramping barefoot through a raging storm, trying to reach Vince and Tony. Somewhere, she could hear them laughing, calling to her, but they were just out of reach. . . .

The next day, Chantal was still troubled by the dream, hoping it was not a portent. Vince had arisen without waking her, and when she went downstairs, she found him closeted with his barrister. She was tempted to listen at the door but couldn't quite bring herself to do so. She glanced at the watch pinned to her breast. Only nine in the morning. A scandalously early hour to go calling, but that, too, was just as well.

She lifted a finger to a hovering footman. "Call my carriage. I'm going out." She sent a darkling look at Vince's study. She still hadn't forgiven him for being so obdurate last night. It was plain to see where Tony got his stubborn streak.

She tapped her foot, waiting.

Lizzie came into the entry hall from the dining room, her cheeks rosy. She'd always been lovely, but now, with good food and pretty clothes, and her speech improving daily, she might have been the daughter of a duke rather than a poor girl who'd lost both her parents. Chantal already had in mind for her an acquaintance of Vince's. He was the heir to a prominent baron, a kind and intelligent young man who blushed every time he looked at Lizzie.

Smiling, Lizzie interrupted her thoughts with a cheerful, "Good morning, Chantal. How is your cheek?"

With an imperious little hand, Chantal waved away the concern. "Fine. And Hugo? Did his nose quit bleeding?"

"Ay, uh, yes it did. He's promised Tony to take him to Tattersall's today. With your permission, of course."

Chantal nodded her approval. "Is the monkey enjoying his new home?"

"Like a bug in a rug. Tony's trying to train him to use a box for his, uh, necessaries."

"Good." Chantal pulled on her gloves, drawing her ermine-lined pelisse over her shoulders. It was red velvet and made a striking complement to her red-and-green-plaid woolen gown. The gown was laced with red satin ribbons. Another red ribbon was woven through Chantal's dark hair. She'd worn the ensemble hoping to put herself in a more cheerful holiday mood. So far, the dress had done little for her spirits.

As the footman opened the front door, Lizzie followed Chantal down the steps. "Where ye, uh, you off and about? In case the lord asks."

Chantal's nose lifted into the air. "I have business in town. That's all he need know."

"But . . . Chantal, he—"

Chantal pulled the carriage door shut herself, punctuating her rebuttal, and said through the carriage window, "When he sees fit to share his business with me, I shall do the same. Drive on, coachman."

The coachman kept his eyes down as he took his seat, but she saw from his tight mouth that he didn't approve of his new mistress. Or her orders.

As they jolted off, Chantal tried to calm herself. She'd never been able to abide ladies who abused their servants, verbally or physically. Her irritation with Vince gave her no excuse to be rude.

When he helped her down at Adeline's, she gave him a pound. "I regret my rudeness. I do not expect to be long. I would appreciate it if you would wait.''

Pocketing the tip, he bowed deeply. ''Yes, milady.''

The brass door pull was stubborn in the chilly morning, but Chantal managed to give it a good tug.

A maidservant opened the door a crack. ''The mistress isn't home to callers this early.'' She started to close the door, but Chantal stuck her card in the crack.

''Give her this, if you please.''

The maid opened the door, glanced at the card and gave a startled look at the woman standing on the stoop. She hesitated, but a sleepy voice called from up above, ''Who is it, Hetta?''

Hetta slammed the door in Chantal's face.

Surely Adeline wouldn't toss her off her doorstep. Chantal's determination wavered slightly. If Adeline had disliked her ten years ago, how much more she must hate the woman who'd unknowingly caused such a rift between her and her only child.

Her leather half boots hadn't been designed for prolonged standing about on icy surfaces. Chantal stamped her frozen feet, slipped and fell to her rump.

The door flew open. Adeline, obviously hastily gowned because her collar was crooked, stared down at her.

Humiliated, Chantal tried to get to her feet and slipped again.

Tentatively, Adeline offered her a hand. ''It's a bit late, my dear, but we could both use a helping hand, do you not agree?''

Chantal took the hand, surprised at the strength with which Adeline pulled her to her feet. ''Thank you, your ladyship.''

Adeline squeezed her hand tightly, her ascetic features softer than Chantal had ever seen them. "Tush, child, you are the countess now. I'm but an old dowager, lucky to have a roof over her head after the mistakes she's made." She blinked, her eyes brighter in the morning sun, before she pulled Chantal inside.

That was doing contrition a bit too brown, Chantal thought, but she didn't argue. Adeline led her into a small but tasteful parlor. She sent the maid away for tea, toast, fruit and eggs.

When they were alone, Adeline twisted at the kerchief in her lap. "How is my grandson?"

Chantal smiled and told her about the monkey and the fierce battle that had ensued over its ownership.

Adeline gasped, covering her shocked mouth. "I wondered where you got such a horrid bruise."

Chantal's smile faded. "Vince has a lump on the back of his head. I'm considering giving him a matching one on his forehead."

Adeline's cup hit her saucer with a clatter. "Oh, my dear, never tell me you two aren't happy?"

Adeline's regret sounded sincere. Chantal eyed her hostess. This woman had once been her worst enemy, but her love for Tony and Vince was almost as deep as Chantal's own. She badly needed an ally, someone who could understand Vince. "Ma'am, I have never told him why I left—"

"No, my dear. You didn't need to. I told him."

Shocked, Chantal sank back against her chair and stared at her mother-in-law.

Chapter Ten

Would she ever understand these Kimballs and their stratagems? Vince had hinted he knew something of Adeline's actions, but Chantal hadn't realized he knew everything. A thunderous frown darkened Chantal's delicate features. "Do you mean to tell me that Vince knew, all this time we've been back together, that I left because of you?" How difficult it had been to keep silent under his verbal jabs. She'd not wanted to cause more pain between mother and son, so she'd bitten her tongue even during their worst arguments. Again, Chantal had a sense that this new Vince kept secrets too easily and grudges too close.

Rising, Adeline crossed to Chantal and stood in front of her. She rubbed her arms, her head bent, as if searching for the right words. "The Kimball men are strong, Chantal, even pig-headed at times. They have a fierce sense of possessiveness and commitment toward their

families. But when they love, they love once and forever, and they want the same from their chosen lover.
Vince is no doubt waiting for you to come to him, to
tell him the truth.''

The words made sense, but Chantal was not ap-
peased. Vince wanted her unremitting surrender, her
deepest fears and hopes bared for him to see and probe
at his will, but he would not so much as tell her how
he got that terrible leg wound. Or how their ten years
of separation had tempered the sweet young soldier
who'd adored her into a steely politician who wielded
words like weapons. Chantal set her cup and saucer
aside. She debated asking the question that dogged
her, but if anyone understood, it would be Vince's
mother.

"Vince obviously loves Tony, but I am troubled by
the fact that he's apparently not begun adoption proceedings. Does he intend to leave our son a by-blow
and let any new son I might birth become his heir?''

Adeline stiffened. "I cannot believe you can think
such a thing, much less say it. Vince could never be so
harsh to someone he loves.''

"Then why does he wait?''

Wavering slightly, Adeline sought her chair again, as
if her knees would not hold her. "I do not know. No
doubt, in good time, he will tell you.''

Time had a way of making such matters moot, Chantal reflected grimly. She wasn't certain how much
longer she'd be able to hide her pregnancy. She was
already growing nauseated in the mornings, and she
wanted Vince to adopt Tony now, before he knew.
Abruptly, her head began to ache, and she still had another errand to run before she went home. She stood.

"I have taken enough of your time. Please forgive my unannounced visit."

Adeline rose with her. "Not at all. I am honored you can . . . that is, I was wrong to ask you to leave, and, well, Tony—"

Touched, Chantal took mercy on her mother-in-law's pain. She caught Adeline's hands. "In the many years I have known you, ma'am, I have never seen you at a loss for words. Do not be ashamed on my account, for I forgave you long ago. I did not have to leave, after all, so I am not blameless. As for Tony . . . do you believe he would be the lad he is today if he'd been raised the son of an earl? *Vraiment?*"

Adeline gnawed at her lip but shook her head reluctantly. "But at what cost? If you knew what Vince went through—" She pressed her lips closed.

Again, this hint of dark days. "Enlighten me."

Adeline pulled away, walking to the door. "I cannot. I have already interfered enough in my son's life." But once she reached the door, she paused to give Chantal what could only be described as a pleading look. "Please, come again. I am so hungry for news of Vince and Tony, and my . . ."

Home. Chantal's flickering anger at Vince burned brighter. How could he have evicted this elderly woman from her own home? Were there not enough shameful secrets and thoughtless acts to set right? Impulsively, Chantal kissed Adeline's powdered cheek. The fact that the dowager had taken time to make up her face before facing her daughter-in-law touched Chantal more deeply than anything Adeline had said. For the Adeline who'd so intimidated a nameless young girl never would have cared what she thought.

This Adeline obviously did.

"Oui, madame. And I shall bring Tony." And I shall make it my mission to make Vince let you move back. Tony finally had a family. Vince's stiff-necked pride could not be allowed to rend it apart before it was fully formed.

Adeline's blue eyes filmed over with tears. She looked away and said huskily, "You are a sweet child, Chantal. May the good Lord forgive me for my hasty actions, even if Vince never does."

Stepping over the threshold, Chantal pulled her pelisse hood over her curls with a determined air. "He will, ma'am. That I can promise you." She nodded briskly and accepted the coachman's gloved hand into the carriage.

As they jerked off, the matched bays stepping carefully in the icy street, Adeline still stood on the slippery stoop waving until the coach rounded a corner.

In her eagerness to confront Vince, Chantal almost dismissed her other errand, but she was not one to neglect her obligations. She used the speaking horn to give the coachman their next direction, wondering how Vince would react when she told him she'd been to the academy. She missed her dancing, and intended to teach some of the lessons herself before she became too big to do so.

No matter how Vince reacted . . .

"What do you mean, she wouldn't tell you where she was going?" Vince demanded of the footman who'd assisted Chantal into the coach. The footman and the butler stood before Vince's desk in the study.

299

The brawny young man pulled at his tight neckcloth. "Well, ye see, yer worship, the laidy was in a right rush, she were, and I didn't think it proper fer me to question her, ye see. She wouldn't even tell the other young laidy where she was off to."

Sighing, Vince waved the servant away. "Very well. But next time, I want to know where she's going, and when she'll be back."

The footman made himself scarce with an alacrity startling in such a large man.

Defensively, Vince met the butler's stern gaze. He'd been their butler since Vince's earliest dim memory. No one knew better than Vince that the stiff-necked servant's forbidding air was a papier-mâché casing for a deep, tender heart. "I know, I know. I have been short-tempered lately. But she's hiding something from me, dammit. And I can't risk anything happening to her."

That stern gaze softened slightly. "Indeed, sir. I have told all the servants to be vigilant about both her ladyship and the lad. He's a fine boy, if you don't mind my saying so, sir."

"And if I did?" Laughing, Vince rounded the desk and slapped the old retainer on the shoulder. "You know I value your opinion as much as any man's."

Encouraged, the butler softened still more, unbending enough to hint, "Then might I say that the dowager countess is deeply missed belowstairs?"

Vince's smile disappeared. "You may, but that will be the end of it. My mother has caused me ten years of grief by her busybody machinations. I will not have her interfering with my new family before we are comfortable with one another."

When the old fellow opened his mouth again, Vince

imperiously waved him silent. "Enough. My mind is made up on the matter."

Sighing, the butler desisted. Glancing around to be sure they were unheard, he lowered his voice. "Very well, sir. But purely in the interests of a smooth-running household, might I suggest that the good Hugo would be happier back in Scotland?"

"Well, Hugo might be happier, but Chantal wouldn't. You shall just have to muddle along with him. Give him some duties about the house."

Those hollow cheeks went even more concave, giving the thin butler a positively cadaverous air. "I've tried that, sir. He breaks the china, bends the silver and frightens the maids. Even the housekeeper is afraid of him. We can't find any livery to fit him, either."

"Nonsense. Hugo wouldn't hurt a fly. He looks ridiculous fitted out so formally, anyway. I shall see what I can find for him to do."

"Very well, sir." He turned to leave.

"Wait a moment."

"Yes, sir?"

"The moment the countess returns, I wish to be informed."

"Yes, sir." The butler retreated with all the dignity of his exalted station.

Vince pulled back the heavy velvet drape to look out into the street. It was late afternoon, and the ponderous skies looked about to deliver boisterous triplets: snow, ice and wind. And both Tony and Chantal were out in the elements instead of safe at home, where they belonged. With him. Vince clenched the drape as images of that recurring nightmare returned. Chantal, starving, wandering in the snow. He forced himself to release the drape, taking deep, soothing breaths. He was being ridiculous. Chantal was safely wed to him. Nothing would ever harm her or Tony again.

But the fear hammered at the back of his mind a bit more insistently with every tick of the clock. When Hugo and Tony entered on a gust of wind, Vince met them in the foyer. "How was Tattersall's?"

Tony ran to meet him. "Wonderful, Papa. Hugo says if I am very good, I may be able to get one of the foals out of Raven's Roost."

"He does, eh?" Vince met Hugo's eyes, but that stolid gray gaze didn't flicker with a hint of embarrassment. Hugo knew that Vince could deny the boy nothing, but on the other hand, Vince didn't want Tony spoiled. He was such a delightful child as he was. . . . Vince shied away from the ramifications of that thought and ruffled his son's thick red locks. "Maybe someday. For now, your pony is all you need while you learn to ride."

Tony pouted. "He's like a rocking horse. He knows but two speeds: stop and go. Slowly."

Vince laughed. "I shall keep it in mind, my boy. Now, don't you think you should go study your lessons?"

Tony's lower lip jutted out like the prow of a ship. "Now? But I am tired, and hungry—"

"I shall have the servants bring up chocolate and biscuits. Go, lad."

Wrinkling his nose, Tony went. Hugo tried to ease away in the opposite direction, but Vince said, "Hugo, wait."

That broad back paused.

"Come into my study, please. We need to talk."

Inside, Vince waved Hugo into a wing chair opposite

the roaring fire and sat down in the other chair facing it. The chair legs groaned slightly, but they took Hugo's weight with no more protest. "Hugo, Tony is roistering about London entirely too much. As my son, he needs to display more decorum. He would be a rich target for the unscrupulous—"

"But ye havena adopted him, so what's the use in spoiling the wee laddie's fun? No one but us be the wiser aboot his real da."

Trust Hugo to get straight to the point. Vince debated telling Hugo the reason behind the delay but decided against it. Not even Chantal knew, because he could hardly explain without letting slip the truth of her parentage. And Bartholomew wasn't ready to tell her yet. "In due time, I shall. Besides, his behavior is inappropriate for—"

Hugo stood with a curt, "Fer who? Ye? Or him? He's a braw lad, and if ye smother him with a pile o' do's and don't's, he'll be miserable." Hugo turned on his heel. "That's all I have to say." And he exited quietly, ignoring Vince's command to stay.

Leaping up, Vince started to go after the impertinent fellow, but he took several deep breaths, picked up the poker and instead stabbed savagely at a blazing log in the hearth. The log split, spewing embers and smoke into the room. Vince jumped back, patting the sparks out of his breeches and stomping more out on the rug.

Fool, will you never learn to keep your head? he castigated himself. But why did he always carry this creeping sense of dread? Even when Chantal and Tony were safely underfoot, he feared losing them. And his obsessive concern obviously felt more like interference to his loved ones. They were both used to independence.

Vince knew he walked a fine line, and his fears were exacerbated by the fact that he and Chantal still hid secrets from one another. Aye, she slept nightly in his bed, ignoring the great fourposter in the adjoining room, and aye, their lovemaking was frequent, and wonderful.

But it wasn't enough. Every time he entered her body, he resented her self-contained mind more. She told him naught of her concerns, or her time away from him. And he couldn't quell a fear, unspoken to anyone, that once she realized she was heir to the wealthiest cit in England, she would not need him anymore. Tony wouldn't need him anymore, either.

Lastly, his towering concerns were topped by one dread that, sooner or later, he'd have to climb: Did Chantal still love him? This one question overshadowed all else, like a mountain he could conquer, if he only had the courage to try.

Every day, he walked around the hulking shape, trying to pretend it wasn't there. Not yet, he told himself.

However, Chantal apparently was not so conflicted. When he heard the front door open, he rushed into the foyer. The sight of his wife, her cheeks flushed from cold, her eyelashes dusted with snow, enticing in red and green like a Christmas package tied up for his pleasure, allayed his unease. He walked toward her, hands outstretched. "Good evening, my dear. And what have you been doing today?"

She squeezed his hands and then dropped them, turning to remove her pelisse and hand it to a footman. "Vince, may I speak with you?"

"Certainly." Vince tucked her hand in his arm and led the way into the study, seating her before the fire, and tucking a lap robe about her knees.

As soon as he was sitting, Chantal tossed off the robe. "Must you always fuss so?"

Hurt, Vince stared into the fire. A thousand retorts came to his tongue, but he bit them back. Too soon.

Chantal sighed deeply. "I'm sorry. I am . . . fatigued and cross. It's just . . . truly, sometimes I feel smothered. But that's not what I wish to discuss. Vince, I went to see your mother this morning."

Vince clenched the arms of his chair. "Indeed? I should think she'd be the last person you'd ever want to see again."

"Then I guess you do not understand me as well as you think. Ten years ago, I thought she was an old harridan, of course. But now I'm older, and much wiser, the mother of a son myself. I understand that she was acting as she thought best for you. Can you not see that and forgive her?"

Her tone was soft and pleading, but it sliced through Vince's ragged nerves like a scalpel. "My relationship with my mother is no concern of yours." When she reared back, he stood and knelt in front of her to cup her knees through her warm skirt. "Chantal, can *you* not see that my mother's presence here would complicate our new life together? She's been mistress of this household for many years. I want the servants to look to you."

A thoughtful look pursed that cupid's bow mouth. "I had not thought of that. But have you not considered that this rift is bad for Tony? He's already asking why his grandmama does not live with us."

Vince sat back on his heels. They stared at one another, the crackling fire and the scent of pine wreaths lending warmth and aroma to their domesticity. Hearth, home, happiness. All lay within reach. Yet both of them feared to grab.

"I shall think on it, Chantal," Vince finally allowed, standing to pull her to her feet. "Now, the dinner bell will sound soon. We need to discuss arrangements for the ball."

Graciously, she accepted the conversational shift, but a tightness about her mouth showed that the subject was not settled.

He longed to ask her how she could have accepted money to leave him, why she never wrote to inform him about Tony, why she fought him so hard before admitting her identity. But, as they discussed the New Year's Eve costume ball Vince was planning to introduce his new wife to society, they again avoided sorer subjects.

Time enough to press these issues when they were settled in. Soon, Vince told himself.

Yet, as Christmas came and passed, soon somehow was pushed farther and farther into a future that never arrived. The present was problematic enough. Vince knew Chantal was teaching at the academy again. Tony still tried to wheedle his way out of his lessons, and he still brought unsuitable critters, of the two-and four-legged variety, into the house. Vince's patience with the boy was growing strained. Adeline's name was never mentioned, but he knew that both Chantal and Tony visited her.

Chantal had lunched several times with Bartholomew, and the expression she wore after the enjoyable engagements could only be termed wondering. Vince suspected she was beginning to see the resemblance between herself and the cit. She said nothing to Vince about her curiosity. This reticence hurt him as much as her other evasions.

Resentment and fear had become a simmering stew that needed only one more added ingredient to boil over. The night of the ball, Chantal supplied it.

In abundance.

They had debated whether she should dress as a dancer, since it was this past that had made her scandalous to his peers at the Lords, but Chantal had suggested that they have the tale of the ballerina and the soldier printed on the backs of the invitations. Vince had looked at her admiringly. "What a stroke of genius, my love. How could anyone condemn such a romantic tale?" Chantal had a way of turning a liability into an asset, an invaluable talent for any political wife.

Really, he should take time to tell her so, he thought as he tied his cravat, but there was no time now.

And so, at the stroke of eight, Chantal was dressed in the red dress and lace-up dancing slippers. Vince wore his regimentals, carried a cane and had his wounded leg bandaged over the knee. He'd hesitated to feign injury out of deference to his fallen comrades, but Chantal shrugged in that distinctively French way of hers.

"Pah! How does it insult their memory to remind these spoiled darlings of the ton how many men suffered to save them from Napoleon?"

Shrugging into his jacket and buttoning it, Vince then bowed deeply. "I concede to your logic, my dear. May I say you are in looks tonight?"

She dimpled at him, pirouetting gracefully. Her hair was loose, swept up and to the side by a simple nosegay of hothouse red roses. She was both his old love reborn and his new one, made even more poignantly lovely by her trial by fire.

"And so are you, my handsome soldier. I much prefer you this way to the stuffy earl."

Vince cast a longing look at the bed, but he'd called this party, dash it, and it would not do for the host and hostess to arrive late. He offered his arm.

Chantal was reaching out to take it when a strange look passed over her face. "Excuse me, please." She disappeared to the water closet.

Sounds of retching ensued, and when she came out, she was wiping her lips.

Vince frowned, concerned. "My dear, are you ill?"

She gave him a pale smile that mimicked her former joie de vivre. "I shall be right as rain in a moment. I . . . haven't been eating enough lately."

Indeed, he'd noted that she'd picked at her food the past week or so, and that she remained abed until the maids brought her chocolate and toast. A suspicion crossed his mind. Since their marriage, she had not had her menses. No one knew that better than he; they rarely passed a night without making love. Yet surely if she were pregnant, she would have told him. No, he told himself. Her regularity had been disrupted, along with her lifestyle.

He yearned for another heir, but not yet. A baby would complicate their already difficult relationship. He watched her munch on the biscuits beside the bed and drink a glass of milk. She wiped her mouth and smiled at him, standing to kiss his cheek.

"See? Better already."

"I think we should retain a physician—"

"Nonsense. My stomach has always been susceptible to nerves. Don't you remember?"

Immediately, he felt better. He grinned. "Indeed, I remember the time you threw up all over the vicar when he was leading us through our wedding rehearsal. And the time your, uh, upset stomach disrupted my mother's garden party. That time, I believe you were serving punch. Rather spoiled my mother's soiree."

She crossed her eyes at him. "Now that you've done a wonderful job reminding me of my former insecurities, will you escort me downstairs to play hostess to some of the most important people in England?"

He pulled her hand through his arm and patted it contritely. "Forgive me. You are such a paragon of strength and virtue now that I feel a certain wistfulness in recalling that young girl, so eager to please."

Soft lips tickled his earlobe as she stood on tiptoe. "Ah, *cheri,* I have never been so eager to please you as at this moment."

Guests be hanged! Vince caught her in his arms and kissed her with all the desperate yearning he could communicate only with his body. She responded with open mouth, but when his lips wandered down to her shoulder, she pulled away, slapping his hands playfully.

"Do you wish your guests to know what we have been doing?" She went to the mirror to straighten the roses in her hair.

"Deuced if I care." Vince straightened his cravat, meeting her eyes in the mirror as the front door pull clanged downstairs.

"But I do." Chantal stood back and led the way to the door. "I want your colleagues to like me, Vince. I should never forgive myself if I hurt your political career. I know the ton is abuzz about me. Many will look for the slightest flaw in my behavior, and it is up to me not to supply it. You will help me with this, *oui?* And hint to me if I make any faux pas?"

"Oui."

However, from the first guest she greeted to the last she waved good-bye to, Chantal was a flawless hostess. To open the evening, she and Vince stood in the reception line, shaking hands with a motley assortment of harlequins, courtiers and pharaohs. Many of them looked at her askance. Some of the primmer dowagers, disguised only by proper dominoes, made so bold as to appraise her head to foot through lorgnettes.

Chantal gave them a winsome smile and let them look. "Madame, who is your couterier?" she asked one.

The lorgnette dropped. The graying dowager, who had the hanging jowls and stout build of an English bulldog, unbent enough to bestow a frosty smile on her. "No one to signify."

"Nonsense. May I?" Chantal asked, before touching the filmy watered silk sleeve that clung all too tightly to a plump figure. "Why, I must have the name. I have seldom seen finer stitchery, even in Paris."

Smiling now, the old woman gave Chantal the name of her dressmaker before a judicious nudge from behind sent her on down the line.

Her next interrogator was none other than the Countess Lieven herself. This doyenne of Almacks didn't need to intimidate Chantal with a lorgnette, for she wore her haughtiness like a crown. Her condescending look, pretty face and finely gowned, shapely form had cowed many a young girl before her.

But Chantal was not a girl.

The patroness enunciated, "I expect we'll receive your application soon, but I should warn you, my dear girl, that the Committee has become most discriminating of late."

"Indeed?" Chantal said, her smile firmly in place. "I have not quite decided whether to apply, actually. Perhaps in the summer, when I am not so besieged by invitations." And then, as those slim shoulders stiffened, she soothed the ruffled feathers with, "But ma'am, may I make so bold as to tell you that, as a new countess myself, I wish only to emulate your abilities as a hostess? They are famed, even on the Continent."

That imperious chin lowered a trifle. "We can perhaps have a chat before I leave this evening, if you truly wish to hear my opinion."

"Oh, I do," Chantal said sincerely.

"As you wish." The countess gave her a glacial smile and moved on, not quite certain whether she'd been snubbed or complimented.

As he greeted an old school chum, Vince watched his wife out of the corner of his eye. Her constant references to her heritage were a master stroke. It would do no good to pretend that she wasn't French, so, as with her dancing, Chantal had accented—literally—that very fact. The English, almost ten years after the war, were once more in a rage to imitate all things French. Their food, their wine, their clothing, their furniture styles, all began in Paris. And Chantal let slip enough famous French names for her guests to know that, despite her somewhat dubious history, she knew her way around a drawing room with the best of them.

Next in line, disguised only by a somber black domino and half mask, Bartholomew Canfield clasped her hands warmly. "You did a masterful job putting that social climber in her place," he whispered for her ears alone.

Chantal's smile deepened. "Thank you, sir. From a master of the polite snub, I consider that a compliment."

Bartholomew harrumphed. "Well, I have many an enemy who would disagree with you about that, but you're a sweet child to say it."

John was next. He held her hands too long, and already smelled of too much revelry. He raked her with a heated gaze. "Delicious. Just as you should look, a dancer with but one—"

"—many skills," Vince interrupted smoothly, clasping John's hands and pulling him along so forcefully that John stumbled. Hatred gleamed in his dark gray eyes like blood on a stiletto before he turned to an acquaintance who had tapped him on the shoulder. Vince dismissed his momentary unease, though he had started to become concerned about what John would do when Bartholomew officially made Chantal his heir.

Vince had his hands full seeing to his guests, and the press and flow of humanity parted him from Chantal for most of the evening. He occasionally glimpsed her, dancing in the arms of a stocky prince or a slim young knight. Whatever her partner's age or size, she had a way of making their pairing look graceful and natural.

A hand touched his shoulder. He started, spilling champagne on his sleeve, as he turned to the greeter. Even behind the black mask, he'd recognize those blue eyes and that crop of red hair anywhere. "Robbie! I hadn't heard you'd returned from abroad. How was Italy?''

"Very . . . Italian. If I had to eat one more bite of pasta, I swear I would have turned into a noodle.'' After Robbie verified that no one stood within earshot, he paused beside Vince, watching Chantal. "I was delighted to hear you'd wed the fair Papillone. But tell me—is she really Chantal?''

Vince nodded.

Robbie clapped him on the shoulder so hard that the last of Vince's champagne splashed onto the floor. Sighing, Vince set the fragile crystal flute onto a side table out of harm's way. His boisterous old school chum would never change.

Ever optimistic, Robbie proved it by beaming. "By Jove, your luck's held. It was a long time coming, but true love found a way.''

True love? Vince's heart lurched in his breast as Chantal noticed him and winked. If only it were that simple. It should be. They'd been reunited against great odds, but, unlike in fairy tales, true love did not always prevail over pain and mistrust.

Robbie raised an eyebrow at Vince's expression. "What's amiss with your wedded bliss?''

Vince noted staring eyes and shook his head. "Not now. Why did you come back early?''

Again, Robbie looked stealthily over his shoulder. He lowered his voice to a whisper. "Since the Peterloo massacre, there's been more boldness among the agitators for reform. With my contacts amid London's less, ah, desirable set, I was asked to see if I could figure out what their next move will be.''

Robbie had always run with a wild set. Surprisingly,

313

however, in a crisis he had the coolest head on his shoulders of any man Vince had ever known. Robbie had spearheaded many a mission behind enemy lines during the war, so Vince wasn't surprised that the former soldier's derring-do was equally indispensable in quieter times.

"Is there anything I can do to help?" Vince asked.

"Well . . . this Whitmore fellow's name keeps coming up, I don't mind telling you. Hints of some scandal he's organizing. Keep your ear to the ground about him, since he's associated with Chantal. He helped set her up in business, did he not?"

Vince grimaced. "Yes. And I offered to purchase his interest, giving him a tidy profit, but he refused."

Robbie shrugged. "Don't necessarily mean a thing. He'll be rich as Croesus when old Canfield kicks the bucket."

Not anymore. Again, Vince's gaze strayed to his wife. She was in the process of teaching a green young jester the finer points of the waltz. Vince merely replied, "I'll keep my eyes and ears open."

Later, Vince circled the drawing room, where they had set up card tables. Various games of whist and faro were in progress, and he noted that Bartholomew and John were sitting at the same table.

That was enough to give him pause, for John was obviously unhappy about losing. Bartholomew had said that John seldom opposed him in anything, so his mere presence in the same game made Vince curious. He stopped at their table on the pretense of asking if they needed refreshment.

All the card players refused. John pulled in his new hand, arranging his cards with a sour look. Bluffing was

314

apparently not one of his skills. Vince was turning away to another table when a shriek made him pause. Rufus scampered into the room, holding a lady's hairpiece of flowers and fruit in one nimble little hand. Tony, wearing casual knee breeches and a stained white shirt, was hot on his heels.

Inwardly, Vince groaned. He'd deliberately set up a masquerade ball, making the festivities too late for Tony's bedtime, to avoid the complication of explaining the boy's parentage. Chantal had accepted the excuse without question, thank God.

So far.

Rufus sought out the tallest spot in the room—a jester with a towering cone-shaped hat. The monkey scampered up the jester's full pants leg, climbing the startled man's shirt, over his shoulder to the hat, which promptly went askew. Half on, half off the jester's shoulder, the monkey clung to his perch, his fierce monkey face wearing near human defiance.

Meanwhile, Chantal and a lady dressed as a naiad, who'd obviously lost the hairpiece, ran into the room. Chantal put her hands on her hips when she caught sight of her son. "Tony, that animal will not be allowed to remain if you cannot keep him under control."

"I'm sorry, *Maman*," Tony said, reaching for Rufus.

Startled murmurs circled the room. Vince gritted his teeth, but the truth was out. Few in the ton had known that Papillone had a son.

Until now.

The few players who had not dropped their cards in favor of the simian drama did so now. Curious guests crowded into the room from the outside, trailing the commotion.

315

Shifty eyes darting about, Rufus circled around to his unwilling tree's other side, trying to gnaw at a shiny-looking apple. He spit out the wax confection, hitting John Whitmore in the back.

Grunting in surprise, Whitmore dropped his cards and sprang to his feet. "Get that little brighter out of here, or I shall make mincemeat out of him." And he grabbed a sword from a startled knight.

Feeling threatened, Rufus and Tony closed ranks. Tony dashed in front of his pet, his hands outstretched to ward off John. Rufus chirped in alarm and tried to climb his odd tree, but the cone hat was hopelessly crushed. When the unfortunate jester again tried to grab the monkey, Rufus bit him. The beleaguered man yelped, cradling his wrist.

Vince grabbed a plate of fruit and cheese from a table and carried it over to Rufus. "Shh, there now, little lad, this is more to your taste. Here, try an orange. Much better than wax apples." Vince held up an orange section.

Rufus glanced suspiciously from it to Vince and back. He had to lean out to snatch it, dropping the hairpiece in the process. He ate the succulent fruit greedily, his attention diverted. Chantal snuck up behind him, holding up the domino Bartholomew had given her. She tossed it over Rufus and tightened it like a sack. The monkey shrieked, struggling, but she managed to pull him away from the jester.

However, Rufus was surprisingly strong. The domino started to slip. Vince grabbed it from the other side. Between the two of them, they shouldered through gawkers and carried Rufus out to the larder, where they set him down and bolted the heavy door. Panting, they exchanged a speaking look, but they heard raised voices from the card room and hurried back. Guests parted before them, giving them a smattering of applause.

"Great show, old boy," came Robbie's amused voice. "Was that part of the planned entertainment?"

"Yes, and tomorrow it will be monkey soup," Vince said, only half teasing.

But then Tony's raised voice came, pure and outraged as only a little boy's can be. "—a bounder, that's what you are. Rufus won't be shot, by you or anyone else. You . . . interloper." Tony mispronounced the accusation.

Vince and Chantal struggled through the colorfully garbed guests. The Countess Lieven stood just inside the drawing room door, watching with glee to see how Chantal would handle this ugly scene.

"Interloper, am I?" Whitmore shot back, his words slurred from anger and too much wine. "Better describes you, you little bastard. For that's exactly what you are, isn't it?"

Shocked silence descended on the whispering guests like a mantle of snow. Everything went icy still and quiet. Avid gazes went from Tony to Vince and back.

Who was the child? He looked nothing like Vince. Where had the red hair come from? Some by-blow from Papillone's past, no doubt. The women who had begun to look more kindly toward Chantal curled their lips in disgust.

Many of the men looked salaciously between Vince and Chantal, obviously wondering how many men had had her before Vince.

Sensing their avid interest, Tony caught his mother's outheld hand and for once bit his tongue. Vince clenched his fists, wishing he held Whitmore about the throat, and with equal force quelled his urge to jump into the fray in defense of his family. He'd been in the political arena too long. If he leapt to her defense now, he'd be doing it for the rest of their lives. Gossip would circle the ton about the mésalliance he'd made, and everywhere Chantal went, she'd be snubbed.

Only the sheer force of her personality could conquer this treacherous battlefield of lies and whispers. And so he watched, his heart thumping so loudly he could barely hear, as the love of his life proved whether she would thrive or fail as a politician's wife.

In that moment, the petite Chantal towered over most of her guests. One by one, she stared them down, looking at John Whitmore last. Pain flickered over her porcelain features, and her accent was strong when she said, "Forgive him, *m'sieur. Vraiment,* he is but a boy, too quick to defend his pet."

Whitmore relaxed enough to nod shortly.

Chantal's tone went steely. "However, you know nothing of my son's birth, or his parentage. What right do you have to call him an interloper in my own home? He has as much right here as any heir this house has ever seen." Her gaze shot daggers at these lofty dwellers of the upper ten thousand. "Indeed, as many of you suspect, blood will tell. Tony will make a wonderful earl one day, and not because he went to Eton with your sons. The world was his classroom, the stage his playground. I make no apologies for it." Her chin high, Chantal gently drew Tony toward the door.

Shame made the more circumspect of the guests look away. But the gossipmongers bridled at Chantal's boldness. Vince saw their expressions and tensed to add his own brand of persuasion, but help came from an unexpected source.

Bartholomew Canfield tossed his half mask onto the table before him and moved to the center of the room, coincidentally blocking Chantal's retreat. She stopped, glaring at him. He gave her a smile that accented his dimple and cupid's bow mouth.

With that unerring sense of the dramatic Canfield had perfected to high art in the Commons, he pulled a stiff piece of paper from his capacious frock coat pocket. "Not quite the thing I'd intended to do publicly, old chap," he said to Vince. "But the time, I think you will agree, is right." Bowing slightly, Canfield offered the piece of paper to Vince.

Relief tingled through Vince from his neck to his toes, making him weaker than usual. His limp was genuine when he elbowed his way to where Chantal, Tony and Bartholomew stood. "Your agent found it, then? Excellent. Thank you, sir." Vince took the paper and read it.

Collective breaths were held. No scrape of a chair disturbed the quietude, no cough or whisper sounded as Vince read. Curiosity, however, was evident in the goggling eyes and craning necks.

Only John Whitmore, who sagged back into his chair and watched with dread, moved.

Even Tony and Chantal strained to see the paper, but Vince held it so only he could read it. His shoulders lifted in a sigh when he finished.

The irrepressible Robbie, as usual, voiced the general feeling. "Well, man, what bearing does such an official-looking document have on this matter?"

Vince smiled slightly. "It's only a marriage document.'' Vince let the disappointed whispers circulate before he added blandly, ''Dated 1815, on the Continent. Where Chantal followed me so that we could wed secretly before I went into battle.'' Vince spoke behind his hand to a servant, who disappeared quickly.

The whispers became a buzz of excitement. Chantal's teeth showed in her gasp, but she closed her mouth quickly, nodding her agreement under the crowd's stares.

At the obvious skepticism from some, Vince stood straighter and passed the document to Robbie, explaining while his friend read silently, ''The little chapel where we wed in Belgium was destroyed in battle before the document was recorded. We quarreled and were separated on the battlefield. Since Chantal and I reunited, it's taken me weeks to track down the parson and the soldier who witnessed our marriage, and to have the documents redrawn. I waited only for proof before declaring to the world that Tony is my son.'' Vince pulled Tony under one arm, Chantal under the other.

Chantal stared up at her husband, glowing brighter than the gaslights. For a long moment, the handsome soldier and the lovely dancer were the cynosure of all eyes, but they neither noticed nor cared.

Sighs of envy came from some of the younger ladies.

Robbie set the document on the table, nodding his agreement. ''Everything's right and tight. You old close-mouthed, stiff-rumped . . . who would have thought?'' Robbie hauled Chantal close and bussed her right on the mouth.

Congratulations and relieved clapping came from most quarters. Even the Countess Lieven unbent enough to nod at Chantal.

John pounced on the document, read it and set it aside
with distaste. He glared at his uncle, making it plain
whom he considered the author of the document. Bartholomew gave him a look that would have made a
lesser man quail. John merely helped himself to a large
brandy from the sideboard.

The servant Vince had sent away burst back into the
room. Vince took the tiny portrait from him and passed
it around. "My grandmama. Many of you have heard
of her—Callista Raleigh. Look at her, and look at Tony,
and you will never doubt again that Tony is my son."

The last of the doubters stared at the two faces and
had to agree. The pall on the festivities lifted. The orchestra struck up in the ballroom again. Couples flowed
gracefully from room to room. Under indulgent stares,
Chantal gave Vince a quick kiss and a look of promise
before the Countess Lieven hustled her from the room
to meet some of her cronies.

Reluctantly, Tony let the servant lead him back upstairs. He obviously wanted to stay.

The party continued, merrier than before. Food over-
flowed plates; champagne bubbled gaily.

Vince led Bartholomew to a quiet corner of the drawing room. "Thank you, sir. You averted a tragedy."

Bartholomew snorted. "Not certain I agree, lad.
Chantal deserves better than these social climbers."

"But how did you obtain it so quickly?" Vince lowered his voice to a whisper.

Shrugging, Bartholomew spread his hands, as if to
say—What else is money good for?

Vince chuckled, but then his smile faded. "When do
you plan to tell her the truth, sir?"

Bartholomew jammed his hands in his pockets and

321

searched the room for his nephew. John sat in a shadowy corner, untouched by the revelry, watching them. Even in the shadows, his eyes gleamed.

Vince knew a fanatic when he saw one, but he told himself that Bartholomew knew John for what he was.

Or did he?

Bartholomew looked at his nephew with a fine blend of melancholy and regret.

"In my own time, my boy. When it's . . . safe."

Vince stiffened. Surely Bartholomew didn't believe Chantal would be in danger from John once her parentage was acknowledged? "Do you suspect John of something, sir?"

Bartholomew shrugged. "Nothing I'm ready to discuss. But I admit I am extremely disappointed in the boy. His actions tonight did not surprise me. I was, in point of fact, rather expecting them, which is why I brought the document. I imagine he was my sole heir for so long that he's become accustomed to believing he should remain so . . ."

"Does he know about Chantal?"

The shrug was less ready this time. "I suspect so. He has been . . . different of late."

Vince hesitated, wanting to tell him of Robbie's suspicions, but without proof he had no right to blacken John further in his uncle's eyes. Vince was furious with John for the scene he'd caused, but Tony had given him provocation and John was more than a trifle bosky. However, the man's behavior still bothered Vince.

Why had John financed Chantal's academy? Why would he not sell his interest to Chantal's husband at a tidy profit? Why would John try to blacken Chantal's standing with the ton?

Round and round the questions went, chasing their tails in his head until he was fair dizzy. When he could answer them, he'd understand John's actions, and why they made him so nervous.

The sounds of laughter and music and clinking cutlery faded to a dim roar in Vince's ears. Distinctly, he heard the beating of his own heart. Blood surged through his veins, the tinny taste of fear an unpleasant reminder of how quickly lives could change. He'd witnessed the fragility of life too many times not to value it now. Especially Chantal's life.

Deep gray eyes watched inimically from the shadows, sending the furious worries on a faster quest for answers just out of reach.

Unbidden, a grisly image filled Vince's mind until he had to clutch his head to shake it away.

Annette, her throat slit from ear to ear, cut down by an unknown assailant at the happiest time of her life.

Like her daughter?

Chapter Eleven

When the last guest wished them good night and the footman closed the door, Chantal flung her arms about Vince's neck. "Oh, *cheri,* forgive me for doubting you. I should have known you could never deny Tony, any more than you can deny me." In his ear, she whispered, "However did you manage to forge this so-clever document?"

The vision in his study still haunting him, Vince clasped her close and rested his cheek on her sweet-smelling hair. "It was less my doing than Canfield's. He is one of the smartest men I've ever known, and he knows how to grease a palm where it does the most good."

Chantal pulled back to peer up at him. "But why is he so interested in us and our affairs?"

Vince shrugged. "Dashed if I know. He and I have always admired one another."

Chantal sniffed, but her skepticism was spoiled by a wide yawn. She tugged him toward the stairs. "Hmmm, well, in any case, I am grateful to him. And quite . . . fatigued with John. Drunk or not, irritated or not, he should never have been so rude to my son. And so I shall tell him on the first opportunity."

Vince had to grasp the newel post as that same blinding vision made him stumble. "Chantal, I do not think it wise to antagonize John further. He is . . . being investigated currently, and I do not wish him to have cause to harm you. I . . . have a sense he can be dangerous."

At the top of the stairs, Chantal turned to offer him a hand onto the landing. "Nonsense. I have known many men like John. All bluster, little substance. Cater to his arrogance, and he remains happy." In their bedchamber, she slanted him a provoking look. "Like most men."

He snatched at her, but she danced away to the other side of the bed. "Are you calling me arrogant, wench?"

In that feminine, French way uniquely hers, Chantal slanted her head to one side and nibbled on a fingertip as she appraised him from head to toe. Her gaze lingered on the bulge in his white breeches. *"Oui.* But at least in your case, you have much to be conceited about."

Vince dived onto the bed and caught the hem of her skirt before she could scoot away. "Oh I do, do I? Would you care to show me which attribute, specifically, you admire?" He dragged her down onto the bed and planted himself atop her.

With a simple possessiveness that took his breath away, Chantal cupped his aching need in one hand and

325

drew his head down to hers with the other. *"Certainement."* Delicately, she squeezed. When he inhaled sharply and thrust into her hand, she kissed his eyebrow and pushed him off. Laughing, she stood. "Why, you have enchanting eyebrows, dear sir. Did you not know?"

Growling with mock ferocity, he jumped off the bed to pursue her. She feinted in one direction, and his clutching fingers caught only a sleeve of her dress when she dodged the other way. The bodice slipped to her waist. She barely paused to shrug out of the dress, leaving her deliciously petticoated and stockinged, and himself besotted and resolved.

A merry chase ensued. Around tables, over chairs, the dignified earl and his countess scampered like children. A vase full of flowers toppled, shattering on the wood floor, but Chantal merely jumped over it, her petticoat hiked to her hips, her lovely dancer's legs enticing him. As he ran, Vince flung off his clothes. His jacket knocked a lamp shade askew, sending gyrating shadows over the room that mimed their every movement.

And finally, when Vince was down to his unmentionables and Chantal was down to her chemise and stockings, she let him catch her. She knelt in the seat of the wing chair before the vast mirror and beckoned him with her eyes. Vince tried to ease her up into his arms so he could carry her to the bed, but she shook her head and pulled him behind her, leaning over the chair back.

Vince's heavy breathing almost choked him. He glanced at the bed, and back at his wife. It wasn't proper to take her like that, as if she were the veriest trollop.

But her eyes, dark purple now, met his in the mirror, reading his struggle with temptation.

"I am told that men want trollops in the evening, angels in the daytime. I do not want you ever to be bored with me, Vince. Come, *cheri.* I confess to a certain curiosity, as well." Waiting, pliant for his pleasure, she leaned over the back of the chair, still watching him in the mirror.

Desire struggled with suspicion. Where had she learned such tricks? Had she been unfaithful to him after all? No proper English noblewoman would ever proposition her husband so. She did her duty in the dark, her night attire efficiently buttoned to her neck, then pulled down properly when the deed was done.

And within a few years of marriage most of the ton's proper husbands were unfaithful to their wives. . . .

The struggle was brief; desire won. With a little gasp of need, Vince propped his knees between hers in the chair, lifted her chemise, freed himself and plunged deep. The chair and Chantal groaned in concert. Vince immersed himself, pulled free, dipped into her well, over and over until the chair scraped against the floor. Chantal pushed back to meet him, moving his hands from her hips around to her breasts.

Fitting himself as tightly within her as the position would allow, Vince paused. He looked at her in the mirror. Her eyes were closed, her cheeks flushed, as she concentrated on the intimacy of him filling her. But when he pulled her chemise down and cupped her breasts in his hands, her eyes opened.

Vince held her gaze in the mirror. Kneading her fullness with one hand, he teased her tender, flushed lips with a fingertip. She licked his forefinger and drew it into her mouth, sucking gently. Vince's heart leapt to meet her. The feelings coursing from her to him and back, like some subtle but unbreakable bond, might have been explained explicitly by many men.

A beautiful woman ringed him, succulent. She was open for his pleasure, pulsing deep inside as her own need grew. Her beautiful breasts were ripe for his plucking.

Staring at his ballerina in the mirror, even in the sheer physical pleasure of the moment, Vince knew that this intimacy had a deeper source. This woman was not just a vessel for his pleasure; he could not pour into her without mixing his own essence with the mysterious wellspring of joy that was Chantal. She was inexhaustible, a fount of pleasure and bubbling vitality that he could drink to his fill only to thirst again in a few hours. She was the source of his joy in life, in his manhood, in family.

Without her, he would wither and die.

And so, even as he could remain still no longer, Vince took in full measure all she offered. But, conscious of the ineffable gift they could grant only to each other, he gave in return. . . .

His fingers reached around and found her, rubbing her little button in concert with every hungry lunge. And when she stiffened against him, her still suckling mouth biting his finger, he plunged a final time and filled her with his own vitality.

They slumped onto the chair back, still glued together, until Vince finally managed to ease away. His knees felt rubbery, but he staggered with her to the bed. He peeled off their remaining clothes and drew her naked into his arms.

And yet, even in that poignant moment, doubts grew in reverse proportion to their slowing heartbeats. How could she love him so well and have spent the last ten years chaste? He had to know. Because he felt so close to her, he finally found courage enough to tiptoe into the forbidden zone they'd staked out between them. He took a deep breath. "Chantal, have you . . . known another besides me?"

Immediately, her drowsy posture stiffened to alertness. "What do you mean?"

He cleared his throat. He wasn't this nervous the first time he made a speech in Parliament. "Ah, that is, well . . ." And then, in a rush, "Innocent women know naught of the lovemaking skill you've shown. And since you did not learn it from me . . ."

Alertness became anger. She pulled away from his embrace. "Tell me, my fine earl, how many men do you think I've bedded?"

Too late, he decided to leave the subject for another day when they weren't so tired. He slid over to her, trying to pull her under his arm again. "Never mind. It doesn't matter."

She swatted his hand away and huddled on the edge of the bed. "It obviously does. How you could ask me such a question in light of what we have just shared—"

His own irritation stirred. She was protesting a bit too much. "Such skills do not come naturally to sheltered women." He bit his tongue, wishing he'd put the sentence differently.

She snatched at the term. "But then, I wasn't sheltered, was I? I was left to fend for myself and the child you helped create."

Kicking the heavy down cover aside, he reared up on

329

his knees and caught her shoulders to pull her up to face him. "The child I knew nothing of! The child you cheated me of because of fears you would not even voice, much less give me a chance to address. All because of my busybody, interfering mother—"

She scrambled off the bed. "Your mother was not solely to blame."

He towered to his feet. Somehow their very nakedness made the raw vulnerability of this moment more dangerous. "Explain that remark."

Chantal stabbed a finger in the air toward him. "You never invited your friends to meet me. You never took me off the estate. Even our wedding was intended to be private. When your mother made it so painfully clear that I could never be a good politician's wife, the fears I'd been stifling could no longer be ignored." She bowed her head. Her finger dropped. "I feared you were marrying me because we had been . . . intimate. That you'd grow bored and impatient with me when I couldn't perform as the perfect politician's wife."

Vince surged toward her, but she put a chair between them, her head lifting proudly again.

"You little fool," he gritted between his teeth. "Why in God's name did you never tell me how you felt?"

"I wanted to. But then *Maman* died, and there was no time. You were going away to battle, and I feared being a distraction to you—"

Vince laughed harshly. "Distraction? Do you know how nearly I died because of your cowardice?"

Her eyes huge, she covered her mouth with both hands. As if compelled, she looked at the ugly scar on the outside of his leg.

Once out, the words were like signposts warning of

danger ahead. But this journey had already been too long and perilous for him to turn back now. Only when they made it through the tortuous path that had divided them could they forge ahead to a peaceful future. Jerkily, Vince stalked to his robe and pulled it on, tossing her own heavy velvet dressing gown to her.

Her eyes still wide, as if she sensed the rigors ahead, she dressed herself. Vince was in no mood for niceties. He shoved her into a chair before the fire and knelt to add another log to the feeble flames. "Sit, listen. When I'm done, you can nag at me to your heart's content, but 'tis high time you understood how thoughtless and selfish you were."

Then, with one arm on the mantel, he stared down at the glowing embers, thinking how like their relationship the slumbering fire was. Banked, but fiery hot beneath the surface coolness. Dark, but touch an ember to life and it sparked, casting a glow that warmed everything within reach. Stoked, the fire could become a blaze, consuming all before it, leaving a brave soldier burned to the essence of his being—a heart—and his ballerina love singed to ashes.

The fiery image gave him strength to touch old wounds still raw beneath the superficial healing. "I was like a madman when I found you gone. I enlisted everyone to search for you—the magistrate, the vicar, every country squire and bumpkin within ten square miles. And then, when we found a woman matching your description had taken the stage, we followed your trail to London, where we lost it. We concentrated on all the packets leaving for the Continent. I assumed you'd returned to France. When that turned up nothing, and I had to leave for Belgium, I set the runners to search.

They kept in touch with me by packet, and when they found nothing . . .'' He gripped the mantel so hard he broke a fingernail to the quick. Idly, he tore the nail loose and licked the blood away, not noticing the way Chantal winced at his casual handling of his own pain. He stuck the wounded hand in his dressing coat pocket.

"Suffice it to say that my fear of dying somehow became all mixed up, feeding upon my fear of never seeing you again. At first I was too busy on the field to mourn you, but with every packet that gave me no news of you, my anguish increased. Were you starving? Were you cold? Had you been violated? Were you even still alive?'' His soft monotone somehow accentuated the pain he'd suffered, for he still found it difficult to speak of. "I had no answers, no hope, no surcease.''

Tears misted those purple eyes he'd almost died for, but he was lost now in his own memories. She shrank back a bit more with every ruthless sentence, but the monotone was beginning to rise in volume.

"War is a curious leveler. It brings out both the worst and the best of mankind. It makes the cowardly brave, the brave cowardly. I saw soldiers risk their lives to carry men they'd never met to safety. I saw others turn and run when their comrades were being gutted. And I, you might ask?'' He gripped the mantel with both hands now, still refusing to look at her. "I was the worst of the lot.''

Her voice husky with tears, she said, "No, Vince. You're the bravest man I've ever known—''

Hissing a denial, he whirled to face her. "Brave? I led my regiment into the most dangerous part of the battlefield, against direct orders. My men were slaughtered like cattle. Shrapnel rained down upon us, but still

I led them up that battery, determined to take the cannon that was wreaking such destruction. Because of my bravery?'' He spat the last word, as if it were an epithet. ''No, my charming wife. Because of you.''

She covered her eyes, sobbing, shaking her head.

The veins on his neck standing out with his torment, Vince jerked her hands away and hauled her to her feet. ''You will listen. I didn't lead my men on that suicide mission to save lives. I did it to lose one. My own.'' He began to shake her slightly with every sentence. ''My best friend was blown to bits before my eyes. Because of you. I will limp for the rest of my life. Because of you. I lost the best part of myself at Waterloo. Because of you. The part that believed in the inherent good in man—and woman—the part that loved and laughed and knew happiness because it gave so eagerly to others.'' Chantal's hair was flying about her shoulders now, so hard was he shaking her.

She didn't try to pull away. Her head lolled on her shoulders; her eyes remained fixed on his tormented face. Like a rag doll, she took his fury, accepting it as her due.

And then his eyes focused on her again. When he realized how hard he was shaking her, he gave a moan of self-disgust and tried to turn away. She caught his hands and pulled his head to her shoulder, running her fingers through his thick, disheveled hair. ''Finish, my love.''

''I . . . I searched for you even after I returned, with no sign. A year or so later, I finally gave up. Many times I considered blowing out my brains, but there was no one to take over my estates except a remote cousin whom I despised. Duty, after awhile, became its own reward. And then, when I took up my seat in Parliament, I found a spark of interest in life again. But women? There were transitory relationships. I seldom kept a mistress more than a month. I didn't just fear being hurt again. They . . . were not you." And he subsided against her shoulder, spent.

Shaking hands still stroked his hair as if he were a child. "I'm sorry, I'm sorry, I'm sorry. I never meant to hurt you so. If I had known, if I had understood—"

"And the nightmares. They've become less frequent over the years, but—"

"I know. You've had them since we've been together."

Taking a deep breath, Vince pulled away to cradle her face in his hands. "Now mayhap you understand. If I am arrogant, or overcautious, I have good reason. You were my best childhood friend, my first lover, my last love. If anything, anything ever happened to you again, I think I should go mad."

She kissed the words away. "Nothing shall." She nibbled at her lip, obviously wondering whether to tell him something. Instead, she led him back to the bed, removed his robe and covered him. "Sleep, my love." She removed her own robe and climbed in next to him. With her mouth in the hollow of his throat, she whispered, "And no. I have never known another lover. But I was a dancer. I was around very experienced women. French women. We talked. My . . . forwardness comes out of love for you, the need to make amends and to be a good bedmate for you."

Vince hugged her convulsively. "I'm sorry for doubting you. I should have known—"

"The only mistake you made was not telling me

sooner. If you'd told me all this when we first met again, I would not have resisted so long. I will never forgive myself for hurting you so. I took the money because I had no choice. I suspected even when I left that I was pregnant, though I did not know for sure. I ... did not want my child to grow up lonely and ostracized, as I had been. I see now that I was wrong. My only excuse is that I was young, and confused. I ... can think of only one thing I can give you that no one else can. One thing that will help us forget the pain of our past."

Vince's heart thudded against his chest. Did she mean ... He lifted his head. "Yes?"

"I ... carry your child, Vince." At the blaze of manly pride and joy in his eyes, she hid her face against his shoulder, blushing. "A life for the life you lost. Tony has ever wanted a brother or sister. And you need a baby to spoil and coo over."

Vince hauled her out of bed to whirl her about the room. "God is just, after all! You are the most beautiful, perfect countess a man could wish for, and I ..." He took a deep breath. "I adore you, Chantal. I always have. I always shall." There, it was out. He held his breath, setting her from him, his heart pounding against his ribs. This night would mark a turning point in their relationship. They would finally know the happiness that had been stolen from them. Some of his joy faded when she remained silent, staring at the carpet. Did she not love him, after all?

When he took a step toward her, her color deepened, making her amethyst eyes sparkle against pink satin skin. "I ... know. And I never forgot you, never quit loving you. You believe me?"

Ah, so that was it. He pulled her back into his arms, sighing his happiness against the top of her head. "Of course I believe you." Feeling drunk with happiness, Vince veered across the room to the secret drawer in his dresser. He pulled out the velvet pouch and shook the ruby ring into his palm. Unable to speak for the lump in his throat, he took the ring to Chantal, knelt before her, took off the ostentatious diamond and slipped the ring into its proper place on her marriage finger. He put the diamond on her right hand.

Then, still kneeling before her, he cleared his throat and managed, "I intended to give this to you on our wedding night. You wear my heart, my one and only love. Treat it tenderly."

Chantal lifted her hand, turning the exquisite ruby from side to side. Even in the dimly lit chamber, it caught fire. Like their own hearts, it had burned in silent secrecy, awaiting the right moment to flare back to life. She tried to speak, but her mouth trembled with her feelings. She pulled him up into her arms and gave him a kiss all the sweeter for the pain preceding it.

For a long moment they stood thus, clasped breast to breast and heart to heart, awed at the second chance fate had given them. Tears misted Vince's own eyes. He had to clear his throat and make a light remark before he melted into a puddle at her feet. "This means you will obey me now, yes?"

True to form, she stiffened and pulled away. But when she caught the smile playing about his lips, she raised a mocking, haughty brow. "When it suits me."

"Oh, yes?" His teasing smile faded. He led her back to the bed and pulled the covers over them both, kissing her tenderly. "Then sleep with me and be my love. Now and forever."

She snuggled against him, yawning. "*Oui*. Forever. God willing." She was asleep on the words.

His emotions raw with wonder and joy, and fears he could not quell no matter how hard he tried, Vince cradled her long into the night. She'd qualified her vow of forever. And she'd told him precious little of her own life in those ten years. She was still hiding something, even after her vow of fidelity.

What? Assured of her love, he told himself it didn't matter. He pulled her closer, vowing to protect her and the gift she carried. He drifted off to sleep, beginning to believe that happiness *was* a state of mind. They'd both paid dearly for this moment. He would savor it to the fullest.

But Vincent Anthony Kimball, Earl of Dunhaven, had yet another lesson to learn.

Happiness was more than a state of mind. The step between redemption and ruin was both short and slippery, dependent upon too many things out of his control.

Love could move mountains; could it stop death?

The night of the ball did indeed mark a turning point in their marriage. More secure in their relationship, Vince became less possessive, calmly accepting Chantal's outings. He even bit his tongue on the rare occasions when she decided to teach at the dancing academy. Her condition would soon make the lessons impossible, so he refused to make an issue of them. His forebearance won her frequent smiles and deepest passions. About her past, however, she never spoke. Vince couldn't dismiss the nagging fear that some specter she'd thought long banished would return to haunt their fragile new happiness. But for the next few months, he put aside his fears and learned to enjoy life again, for the first time in a very long time.

He kept in touch with Robbie about the investigation into Whitmore's affairs, but if Whitmore was involved in outright subversion or scheming against the government, he was doing so in a very clever manner. And because invitations had poured into the house since the ball, even one from the Countess Lieven herself to attend the sacred domain of Almack's, Vince could hardly claim that Chantal's business was hurting his reputation. Indeed, enrollment at Chantal's academy had greatly increased. Some of the ton's highest sticklers had sent their sons and daughters there to be tutored by the great ballerina. Even snobs, it seemed, were moved by the great romance that had reunited the valiant soldier and his lovely lost lady.

The fairy tale that Vince's young Danish friend had recounted to him so long ago circulated among the ton. Many of the nobility began to inquire about this talented young writer. Hans Christian Andersen, Vince explained, was still in college but had high hopes of publishing one day.

For the next few months, as England shook off her heavy mantle of snow for the colorful raiment of spring, things went smoothly in the Kimball household. Tony studied his lessons with little more than a pout; Hugo enthusiastically took over managing the stables and quit terrorizing the maids; Lizzie became quite the dancing doyenne, both on and off the stage, and her admirers sometimes formed a line outside her dressing room; Bartholomew became a fixture in the house, playing spillikins and chess with Tony, or escorting Chantal on her jaunts about town.

And then, as May flirted with the first warm days of June, a triple threat assailed Vince's hard-won domesticity. The first conflict arose over Chantal's habit of bringing Adeline into the house when Vince was away. Ostensibly, she informed him, to see Tony. She never forced the issue of Vince's estrangement with his mother, but she made her displeasure with his obdurateness plain by subtle remarks.

"Adeline says . . . oh, *pardonnez moi.* I keep forgetting you don't wish to hear how she is. Or that the doctor is seeing her more frequently these days. More soup, *cheri?*"

She'd pretend not to see the worry in his eyes and beckon the maid to serve Vince more soup, whether he wanted it or not. He was well aware what she was doing. She hoped to force him to see for himself that his mother was all right. But when the servants informed him that his mother was fine, he resisted the urge. The way Vince saw it, Adeline had started this rift ten years ago; she would have to make the first step to end it. But the seeds of concern were planted.

Secondly, late one night, Chantal remembered that she'd left Vince's Christmas gift, an expensive diamond bracelet, at the academy. She told Vince she'd only be a moment, that she'd fetch it herself, but she'd been tired of late, and was already very large, considering she was only six months along in her pregnancy. He decided to go with her.

They arrived to find lights blazing from the dancing

salon and the street outside packed with carriages and carts. Vince helped Chantal down, ordering their coachman to wait. Holding Chantal's hand firmly in the crook of his arm, he approached the entrance.

A blast on a coach horn made them both jump. Vince turned to scowl at his coachman.

He gave a sheepish shrug. ''Sorry, guvnor. Jest tryin' out the horn after it was fixed.''

Vince gave his servant a suspicious glance but continued on up the steps. The door was locked, and by the time Chantal fumbled out her key and got it open, they heard chairs scraping and footsteps retreating. When they entered, they found only Whitmore, Renner and two of their more unsavory friends. However, chairs were set up for a good dozen more, and when Vince peered toward the back, he made out a swinging door that was still moving, giving a glimpse of a dark alley outside.

Vince debated whether he should follow whomever had obviously left, but he didn't want to leave Chantal alone with these wastrels, and she was in no condition to run. So he gave each man a hearty smile as false as their own and accepted their vague excuses of a club meeting. However, after Chantal fetched her bracelet and they were on the way home, Vince made a mental note of the day, the time and the people present to share with Robbie. And it wouldn't hurt to have the runners check out his coachman, either. Some skullduggery was afoot at the academy. Whitmore's refusal to sell his stake in Chantal's business took on a whole new light. A dim, sinister light. What if Whitmore acted out of something more dangerous than spite? Vince resolved to set his own investigators on the fellow.

The third event was the most perilous to his family's happiness. Tony had tried to accept his new responsibilities, he really had. But that early summer saw a change in more than the scenery. Vince had attempted to bond with Tony, taking him to Tattersall's, and even to Parliament a couple of times. In the warmer weather, they went boating on the Thames and fox hunting at a friend's house in the country.

Somehow, Tony always managed to get into scrapes. At the estate, he snubbed the landholder's snobbish little boy and went roistering about the countryside with a stable boy he liked more. At Tattersall's, he was almost bitten by a stallion when he gave it a lump of sugar. At Parliament, he scandalized some of Vince's peers, and amused others, by recounting a tale of a boxing match he'd witnessed in Greece. He adopted the dialect of those present at the match, explaining in Greek that the "opponents were two-fisted titans who, like Atlas, had only to shrug to tilt the world on its axis, by God."

Luckily, only a couple of the men understood Greek. However, as Vince hustled Tony off, he heard one of the stodgier lords say in a snide aside, "Odd little blighter. Shows what happens when one mixes with those Frenchies." The man walked away under Vince's scathing stare, but unfortunately Tony had also heard.

The chip on the lad's shoulder, already big, grew bigger. He began sneaking away from his lessons again, telling Hugo one day in the upstairs sitting room in a passionate decree that Vince overheard, "I don't want to be like the good little boys they want me to consort with. They don't know the difference between a Hottentot and a hot house plant. All they care about is themselves. I think they're disgusting! I don't want to be like them.''

Sighing, Vince went on his way, but he was troubled that Tony apparently felt comfortable voicing his feelings to Hugo and not to his own father.

But Vince's greatest concern was his wife. With every week that passed, she seemed to grow larger. Unnaturally so. He told himself that she was small, yes, but that women smaller than she had children all the time with no complications. She ate well, she slept well and her nausea was mostly gone, so he had no reason for his unease. But something in the way Hugo and Lizzie hovered over Chantal, helping her in and out of chairs, seeing to her every need, warned Vince that her old friends knew something he didn't. However, when he tried to question Lizzie and Hugo, they pretended obtuseness.

Their loyalties had been set long before he came on the scene, he realized. But he'd helped create this baby, and he was determined that Chantal would deliver it with the least amount of pain and suffering he could manage. He hired the best doctor he could find, the physician who had delivered more than one Hanoverian offspring.

But Vince found the old fellow's methods both arcane and archaic. With every examination he gave Chantal, Vince's unease grew. Invariably, the examination consisted of the doctor feeling the distended abdomen, nodding sagely and putting his ear to Chantal's belly to listen to the child's heartbeat. "Coming along nicely, Countess. Quite good, quite good." And he packed his black bag, handed Vince an expensive bill and went on his way.

Late in July, when Chantal was only a month away from delivery, Vince's unease crystallized into outright rejection. The doctor came early for Chantal's examination, arrogantly assuming his patient would see him. Chantal was out with Canfield, so Vince met the doctor, glad for the opportunity of a private talk without his wife present. He pulled the old fellow into his study. "Are you quite certain the countess will be able to deliver this child without harm to either mother or baby?"

The graying, dignified physician broke off his complaints about his busy schedule and looked at him dourly. "I am not a magician, sir. I have done all I can. I do not deny that the child is uncommonly large, and her ladyship uncommonly small, but we must trust to God in such matters."

Vince gritted his teeth. "In such cases, where the female is too small to deliver naturally, what are the alternatives?"

The doctor blinked. "Alternatives? My God, man, the child has to come out the same place it went in. What do you expect me to do?"

Infuriated, Vince pulled out his book of cheques and scribbled a large amount. "You are dismissed."

The doctor sputtered, "N—now see here! No one dismisses me. I delivered the king himself—"

"And we all know what a sterling example of humanity he is," Vince snapped before he could stop himself. Now the fellow would probably carry tales, but Vince was too upset to care.

Primitive dread flailed him like a cat-o'-nine-tails. Of

343

late, his nightmares had changed to something even more terrifying than Chantal dying of starvation. Vince had never seen a child born, but he'd heard enough horror tales from his friends to realize that women seldom died in childbirth in an easy manner. When things went wrong, as they often did, the woman suffered horribly.

The image of Chantal writhing on a blood-soaked bed, huge with the child he'd given her, wracked with pain but unable to give birth, haunted him day and night. The fact that Chantal herself always evaded his questions about her delivery of Tony did little to settle his fears.

Resolved to confront his wife now, as soon as she returned, Vince caught the sputtering doctor's arm and led him to the door, flinging it open. Tony went sprawling from his position listening at the keyhole. Vince glared down at his son, but he kept his temper in check until the doctor was seen politely out of the house by the butler.

Then, gripping Tony's skinny arm firmly, Vince pulled the scamp toward his study. "Nothing is more contemptible than an eavesdropper. It's time you and I had a good talk."

Tony dug in his heels. "I don't want to talk to you!"

At that moment, the door opened again. Laughing, her cheeks glowing with good health, her hair shining in the bright July sun, Chantal entered on Canfield's arm. "No, good sir, you have quite the wrong of it. The lady wasn't batting her eyes at my footman. She was batting her eyes at y . . ." She trailed off when she caught sight of the two most important men in her life. "What's amiss? I saw my doctor leaving in a huff."

Tony jerked away and ran to his mother. *"Maman,*

tell him to leave me be! Tell him I'm sick of my lessons, that I'm worried about you, that. . . .''

She caught him as he jolted against her, staggering under his extra weight. She had enough difficulty carrying her own and that of the child inside her. She didn't walk; she waddled.

Canfield steadied them both, ruffling Tony's already tousled hair. ''What's got my favorite little man so discombobulated?'' Canfield had taken to teasing Tony with his own vocabulary, but this time the distraction didn't work.

Tony's bottom lip trembled. He glanced from his father's angry face to his mother's concerned one and finally looked back into Canfield's kindly gray eyes. He took a deep breath and said in a rush, ''My father fears for my mother to have this babe. And Hugo and Lizzie said she almost died having me, and that childbirth is very dangerous to small women, and that—'' Chantal muffled his lips with her gloved hand, but she was too late.

Slowly, her eyes lifted to meet Vince's. Vince had gone a peculiar shade of green. He swayed on his feet, but his eyes glowed with a fire so hot and pure that Chantal might have been immolated if she'd stood closer. She looked away, paling in shame.

Canfield gasped, taking a step back.

Tony pulled his mother's hand away and cried passionately, ''I hate it here! I hate this man. He did this to you! He doesn't love us. Let us leave here, *Maman*, and go back to Italy where we were happy.''

She patted his shoulder absently, ''Mmmm, *petit*,'' obviously unaware of what he was saying. She took a step toward Vince. ''Vince, please, I—''

He spun on his heel and stormed into his study, slamming the door.

Silence filled the expansive foyer. Finally, favoring his stiff leg as if he suddenly felt very old, Canfield caught Tony's arm. "Come along, little man. I have a story to tell you."

His eyes huge as he watched his mother waddle toward the study, Tony resisted Canfield's gentle touch. "But *Maman*—"

"Needs to talk to your papa right now. Come along. You can feed my horses carrots." And jerking his head at a wooden footman, silently ordering him to procure the vegetables, Canfield urged Tony outside. The things about to be said in that study were too adult for tender ears, and Canfield knew it.

Inside the study, Vince stared at the portrait of Chantal, in its proper place on his desk. Compelled, he picked it up. The years had been kind to her. Her face was still as smooth and unlined as it had been then. However, that winsome, wistful gaze had changed to the mystery and confidence of a woman grown. A woman with her own mind, willful, secretive and . . .

Vince slammed the picture back down. Damn her. This was not her choice alone to make. If she'd been honest with him, he'd have taken precautions. They already had an heir. The bloody vision assailed him again, almost knocking him from his feet. He had to grip the desk to steady himself.

After all his vigilance, all his persistence, all his careful plans, he could lose her yet. He brought one hand to his mouth, biting the knuckle to stifle a moan of denial. He started when a soft hand fell on his shoulder.

"Cheri," Chantal whispered in his ear, "surely God

will not be so cruel as to take me now that we have finally found one another again.''

Vince spun and pulled her into his arms. ''Why did you not tell me? Lizzie knew, Hugo knew, even Tony knows, but I, your husband . . .''

The womanly smile that always moved him was upon her lips as she leaned back in the circle of his arms. ''Because I knew you would not let me do this. And I had to. To make amends for the child I took from you. I cannot love you without wanting your child. How many times when Tony was a baby did I change him, or burp him, or feed him, and dream of how you'd look holding him.''

His hands shaking, Vince cradled her face in his palms. ''Do you think I want another heir badly enough to risk losing you?''

''Life is risk, Vince. If I'd married you when I was seventeen, I doubt we would have been happy. I was so young and foolish. But now I'm a woman grown. Love is not receiving; love is giving. Do not hate me for needing to share this gift with you. Even if . . . well, I do not believe God will be so cruel as to take me now that, against all odds, we have found one another again. But even if you have to raise this child alone, every time you look at him, you will see part of me. And I am vain enough to believe that he and Tony will make this world a better place when they leave it. Let them be living proof of our love to pass down to our children's children.''

Tears came to Vince's eyes at the passionate conviction in the face raised to his. Every word stabbed at him with the hot dart of truth. She was right, he knew she was right. She had so much more to offer now.

And he had so much more to lose.

"Chantal," he whispered. But his voice broke, and he had to steady it before he could continue. "I'll scour London until I find a doctor we can trust. I've heard of a radical new way of childbirth that's only been tried a few times—"

Her fatalistic shrug cut him off. "What will be, will be." They both started when the child within her womb kicked vigorously, as if to punctuate her words. Chantal caught Vince's hand and brought it to her abdomen.

The child kicked again against the palm of his hand. Some of his fear eased at the wonder of this new life she carried.

Chantal kissed his cheek. "See? Even our unborn babe knows how much I love life, *cheri*. Never more than during these days with you. It is enough. Now come, we must find Tony." She drew him out of the study.

Meekly, Vince followed. The blind dread had eased enough for him to nurture a frail hope.

The child she carried was an affirmation of life, not death.

Life sometimes needed a little help, however. Tomorrow, just in case, he'd travel to Oxford to seek out the newest methods and their practitioners. . . .

Outside, Canfield held Tony's hand tightly as he walked up and down the street with the lad. "So you see, little man, your mama and papa have loved one another for a very long time. You are here because they loved one another. They were apart for many years, but they never wed others because they never forgot. Has your mother never told you the story of the Steadfast Tin Soldier?''

Reluctantly, Tony nodded. ''Yes. But my father doesn't love me the way he loves my mother.''

Canfield stopped to stare sternly down at the boy. ''Why do you say that?''

''Because if he loved me, he would not make me do so many things I despise. He'd let me play with my friends more, as my mama did before we moved here.''

Canfield sat down on the townhouse steps, wondering how to explain to a child the adult subject of duty. He was still groping for words when Chantal and Vince left the mansion and sat down beside them.

Tony glanced at them, searching each face uncertainly. When he saw them hold hands, some of his belligerence faded. He frowned in thought. ''If you both loved one another so, why did you leave him before I was born, *Maman?*''

Chantal pulled him under her arm. ''Because I was young and foolish. I did not understand how much he loved me. He searched for us for many years, did you know, Tony?''

Nibbling his lip, Tony peeped at his father. He shook his head.

Vince took up the tale. ''And then, when I saw your mama dance in the ballet, nothing could have stopped me from winning my family. You are both the most important things in the world to me, Tony.'' Vince knelt on one knee before his son, bringing them to the same eye level. ''If you hate your lessons so, I'll tell your tutors that we won't need them again until after Christmas. It will put you behind the rest of the boys, but if it cannot be helped . . .'' Vince shrugged.

Tony sighed but shook his head resolutely. "No, Papa. I will study. But may I visit my old friends at the theater soon? And invite some of them here?"

"Of course." Vince stood and held out his hands, helping his son up with one, his wife with the other. "I am very proud of you, my boy. I am sorry I have not told you sooner."

Tony beamed. "Most magnin, ah, manen, ah . . ."

Vince inserted gently, "Magnanimous?"

"Yes, that's the ticket! May I go tell Hugo that we can visit the theater?"

"Certainly, lad. Run along."

Before the words were fully out of Vince's mouth, Tony was gone, the heavy front door slamming so hard behind him that the door knocker rattled.

Smiling, Canfield shook his head. "What a scamp." But his gaze settled on Chantal's huge middle, and his smile faded.

Vince said casually, "I'm going to Oxford in the morning if you'd care to go along with me."

Canfield nodded. "For now, I'll be off." He bowed over Chantal's hand, but Chantal held onto his hand when he would have pulled away.

"Haven't we had mystery enough in this household? What secret do you two keep from me? And why are you always so concerned for my welfare?"

Vince and Canfield exchanged a glance.

Canfield reddened under Chantal's appraisal, blustering, "Yes, well, now's not the time to go into that—"

As if cued, a curricle clattered up the street, dangerously swerving to avoid a pedestrian. Robbie jumped down, tossing his reins to his tiger, and said urgently, "Vince, we need to talk." He gave Canfield a guarded glance. "About that person we discussed earlier."

Canfield froze in the act of descending. Again, he and Vince exchanged a look. Vince held the door wide. The other two men followed Chantal inside.

Chantal glanced at the tense faces, grimaced slightly, but accepted Vince's suggestion that she have a quick nap. Still, even as a footman escorted her up the stairs, she glanced back at the three men who were already heading for Vince's study.

Robbie glanced uncertainly at Canfield as the door closed behind them.

"You can trust Bartholomew to keep his mouth shut, Robbie."

"About his own heir?"

"Especially about him."

Paling, Canfield groped for a chair and sat, suddenly looking his age. "So, it's true. John is involved in subversion."

Robbie nodded grimly, accepting the glass of port Vince offered. Canfield shook his head at Vince's inquiring glance. Vince poured himself a glass and sat down behind his desk.

"I have a man inside this supposed club Whitmore's formed," Robbie said. "Took him some time to gain their trust, but he just came to me to warn me that Whitmore and his ilk plan to blow up the London, Southwark and Waterloo bridges."

Vince set down his glass so hastily that port splashed the papers on his desk. "But good God, man, that will shut off half the commerce into London for months."

"Exactly. In the ensuing confusion, they plan to foment riots against the government."

"Do you have proof of this?" Canfield asked grimly.

Robbie sighed. "Hearsay only, at least so far."

"And the date planned?" Vince interjected.

"My man hasn't been able to discover that. I thought since you know the fellow, Vince, and since they're meeting in your wife's academy, maybe you could sneak in tomorrow night and listen in on their meeting."

"But I thought you said you had a man inside."

"Only the general rabble-rousers. The principals meet tomorrow at eight in the evening, to finalize plans, with only Renner, Whitmore and two others present."

Vince shook his head. "I can't. I have to travel to Oxford tomorrow."

"I'll go," Canfield said. "He's my responsibility."

Robbie cleared his throat. "Ah, but sir, this could be dangerous."

Canfield shrugged. "So? I'm no stranger to that, or to rabble-rousers." He glanced at Vince. "Do you need me to go with you, lad?"

Vince shook his head. "No, I already know whom to see. But Bartholomew . . . John could be treacherous, even to you, if he's undone."

Canfield rose, leaning heavily on his cane. "So can I, with the proper provocation. I've turned a blind eye too long to John and his shortcomings. I shall let you know what I discover, sir." He nodded to Robbie and stalked out.

Frowning, Robbie watched him go. "Do you trust him, Vince?"

"With my life."

Robbie stood. "That's good enough for me. God willing, it won't come to that."

* * *

Upstairs, Chantal watched sleepily, still drowsy from her nap, as Vince packed. "Where are you going?"

"To Oxford. To procure a better doctor for you." Vince sat down next to her, biting his lip to stem his fear at the huge mound of her belly under the covers. "Promise me you will stay home tomorrow while I'm gone."

"I just wanted to finish some bookkeeping at the academy—"

"No!" Vince moderated his tone. "Not tomorrow. Please, wait until I return."

"Why?"

"Must you always have a reason?" Vince heard his own harshness and softened it by kissing her cheek.

She pouted up at him.

He laughed. "My love, now I know where Tony gets that sullen lip."

"What are you and Bartholomew keeping from me?"

"All in good time."

Chantal flung back the covers and set her feet on the floor. "Yes, your time. Very well. I shall visit your mother tomorrow instead."

Vince scowled, but he went to support her as she heaved herself to her feet. "If you wish."

"I do. And I also wish her to be present when I have this babe." She put her hands on her hips and spread her feet. "All in good time, yes?"

How she could look so pugnacious, so adorable and so . . . pregnant all at once mystified Vince. He smiled ruefully. "I can deny you nothing."

"Hmph, well, you do a jolly good job of it when it suits you," she grumbled, tying a voluminous dressing gown over her night rail.

Colleen Shannon

He stopped her with a gentle hand over hers. "Let's eat up here tonight. Just the two of us." His gaze dropped to her waist. "Or perhaps I should say the three of us?"

She teased, "Or four of us?"

He blanched. "Surely you don't think you're having twins?"

"Perhaps." But she laughed at the look on his face and relented. "Probably not. I'm famished. Does Cook have dinner ready?"

"I shall see." Vince rang the bell pull.

That night, the master suite of the townhouse echoed with laugher. The servants listened indulgently to the goings-on, for it had been too many years since their master was so happy. The serving maid lucky enough to fetch the empty dinner dishes rolled her eyes at the cook and the scullery maid when she came back down.

"They was kissing and barely looked up when I went in. Never seed a couple so much in love." She set the tray down next to the washing tub with a clatter.

The cook nodded, gratified, at the empty dishes. "The master never ate so good afore she come. Be it true, what they say, that she might die havin' this babe?"

The maid's proud smile faded. "So I overhears the butler sayin' to his lordship's valet."

The cook shook his head mournfully. "Ain't right. Poor man deserves a bit o' joy after all them grim years."

Both maids nodded. "God willin'."

The next day, on the road to Oxford, Vincent Anthony Kimball proved true to his blood. Like his grand-

354

father Drake, Vince believed that careful plans made as much luck as trusting the will of God. Destiny or not, he would not return until he had the name and address of a physician who could save his wife if there were complications.

Chantal, however, believed in the mystery of fate. At eight that evening, when she was leaving Adeline's, she decided to stop at the academy. The accounts could wait, but somewhere in her theater trunk, she had the remnants of the tisane Hugo had mixed for her ten years ago. It had strengthened her greatly after the difficult labor, and she wanted to get the bottle and see if Hugo could reconstitute the residue. A change in her body, a slight lowering of the child, warned that her water could break any day now, and she wanted to be ready.

Besides, some curious urge she could not name told her it was important that she go to the academy.

Surely Vince wouldn't mind a brief stop . . .

Chapter Twelve

Precisely at seven-thirty, Bartholomew Canfield used the key Vince had given him, locked the acadamy door behind himself and looked for an appropriate hiding place. John would search the premises before the meeting, he was sure. Canfield appraised the open room. Impossible. He went to the office, and it, too, lacked a hiding place except . . . Canfield shoved back the lid of Chantal's huge theatrical trunk. He grimaced, but he truly had little choice. He shoved the trunk against the wall nearest the dancing floor, leaving the office door partially cracked open. Then, folding his fragile old bones inside the trunk, he pulled several filmy costumes on top of his head and shoulders, praying he could hear well enough.

Canfield tried to settle comfortably. He was too old for such contortionist nonsense, and for a moment, the tight dark space brought back childhood memories he'd labored long to forget. Nothing infuriated him more than to be forced to a course of action he didn't want. Then, it was work or starve; now, it was stop John himself or watch his hotheaded nephew, in one stroke, ruin the good name Canfield had labored to establish.

Canfield seldom misjudged his man, in personal or business affairs, but it seemed he'd underestimated John. He'd known that his nephew dabbled at the fringes of the radical crowd, but he'd believed John too sensible to threaten the goose that laid his daily ration of golden eggs. Surely John knew that if he was caught in outright treason, his uncle's favored treatment by the crown would end abruptly and brutally.

And yet, even as Canfield's relationship with the daughter he'd never known grew strong, his fears about his nephew had grown apace. In rare moments, Canfield was troubled by the vitriol in John's mien whenever Chantal and Tony were present and John didn't realize he was being watched.

Thus, Canfield jumped at this opportunity to see for himself exactly how far John had overstepped the bounds. Instinct warned Canfield that if John was bold enough to foment treason against the power of the Crown, he was bold enough to dispense with his competition for the fortune he obviously considered his rightful inheritance.

Canfield tried to settle comfortably against the hard leather bottom of the trunk, but it was useless. With the iron will that had served him well his whole life, he ignored his discomfort and put his mind to an even harder task.

Tonight must answer two questions.

Was John truly organizing violent rebellion?

Was he a threat to Chantal and the boy?

The minutes ticked by, Canfield growing more tense with each second. Images came and went in Canfield's mind. Seeing Chantal pregnant had made him grieve all the more for the love he'd used and abandoned out of the stupidity of avarice and ambition. How many times had he wished he could turn back the clock and start over, divorce his first wife and marry Annette? Guilt and regret were his only company now. Often, he'd wanted to tell his lovely daughter the truth, but fear always stopped him.

When she knew he was the one who'd betrayed her mother, would her smiles turn to disdain? Would he lose the grandchild he already doted on to the ghosts of a past he could regret but not repair?

And most frightening of all, would Chantal die in childbirth, as so many women did, before he had a chance to redeem himself? The parallels between his life and Vince's were already terrifying. They were both Englishmen who'd loved strong-minded, independent French ballerinas; both women had borne their children and raised them alone rather than ask for help. And then, just when he and Vince finally realized wealth could not buy happiness, they were given another chance.

There, Bartholomew prayed, the similarity must end. Vince couldn't lose Chantal as he had lost Annette.

Footsteps on the dancing floor recalled Bartholomew to his purpose. No more maudlin recriminations. Once he'd dealt with John, he'd tell Chantal the truth and hope for the best. Bartholomew strained to listen.

The steps came nearer. The office door screeched open as the gaslights were turned up.

A voice he recognized as Renner's said, "Don't you think you're being overly cautious, old boy? Place was locked up tight as a drum."

"When one plots revolution, one cannot be overly cautious." John's voice receded as he spoke. He closed the office door firmly and walked back to the center of the dance floor. "Now . . . powder and fuses?"

Between the trunk and the closed door, Bartholomew could catch only snatches of conversation, but what he did hear was alarming enough. Moving very carefully so as not to scrape the trunk along the floor, Bartholomew shoved the costumes aside and eased back the trunk lid. He still couldn't hear well. He levered himself out of the trunk, biting back a groan as life returned to his numb limbs, and equally quietly closed the trunk lid. He tiptoed to the door and put his ear to the keyhole.

". . . our man says all will be ready in time," Renner said.

"You have your allies in the Commons ready?" John asked.

"Ready, willing and able. This day has been too long coming. This will not be another Cato Street debacle."

"No," John agreed grimly. "It shall no—" Tense silence prevailed as footsteps approached over the dance floor.

"John, Mr. Renner," Chantal said, "why do you meet here so late? Is there anything I can help you with?"

Canfield groaned and closed his eyes.

John's voice had changed in pitch. "You've done quite enough, thank you very much."

"What do you mean?" Chantal's footsteps backed away.

Frantically, Bartholomew looked around the office, which was dimly lit from a gaslight outside the tiny, high window, but he should have known better. Chantal would not keep a pistol among her possessions.

John's steps followed her. "How fortunate that you should come here tonight. I've been wondering how I could get you away before you delivered another brat."

Chantal gave a bleating scream, and then came the sound of a slap.

John cursed. "Hold the bitch while I tie her up. Providence has smiled on us this night."

Tightening his grip about his silver-headed cane, Bartholomew barreled out of the office. The abrupt light blinded him, but he made out a kerchief dangling from John's hand as he prepared to gag Chantal. Renner was holding Chantal's arms behind her back, but she kicked back at his shins, and his grip slackened. Two other men stood in the shadows, watching but not assisting.

"You disgusting little whelp, unhand my daughter!" Bartholomew had the element of surprise in his favor. He was able to whack Renner over the head, forcing the official to release Chantal. At the same time he screamed, "To me! To me! The watch! The watch!" The chandelier above their heads rattled with the force of his naturally booming voice.

The other two men scattered, one running for the alley, the other for the front door.

Renner was on his knees, shaking his dazed head.

And Chantal? She stared at Canfield, her eyes huge in the bright gaslight, too shocked to dodge as John caught her wrist and squeezed.

"You're not as smart as I thought, are you, little

puss?'' John drawled. ''You had no idea he was your father, did you?''

When Renner started to rise, Bartholomew whacked him over the head again, harder. Renner subsided with a moan.

Bartholomew raised the stick to his nephew. He froze when John pointed a small pistol at his belly. The stick slowly lowered.

''Wise of you, old boy. But you always were too cursed smart for your own good. Just not quite smart enough . . .'' John backed toward the door, still clutching Chantal's wrist, dragging her with him.

Bartholomew changed to a more powerful weapon, the one that had always cowed John: words. ''You knew from the beginning, didn't you?'' *Come, little worm, show me your superior intellect.*

Gleefully, John paused. ''Of course. Before you knew yourself. That day in Covent Garden, I recognized her, of course. But I'd already seen her there once before, when you were not present. That's why I tried to hurry you off. She much resembles her mother. I'd already made my plans before you ever invited her to dinner. One step ahead of you, as usual.''

''And why are you admitting this to me now?''

''I already know you've disinherited me. The moment she showed up, I knew I'd not get a bloody farthing. But I'll get my due. You'll pay a pretty penny to get her back. If I can stop myself from slitting her pretty little throat, just for fun—''

Chantal kicked him and found her voice. ''So, that is why you wished to marry me. You are a pig!'' She ended on a vituperative stream of French that John ignored. He stared at his uncle.

His uncle stared back. Canfield had latched onto something else John had let slip. His brows lowered, ice clouds over chilly gray eyes. "When did you see Annette?"

John shrugged and began backing toward the door again. "On several occasions."

All the color faded from Bartholomew's ruddy face. Like an automaton, he walked jerkily toward the door, ignoring the waving pistol. "It was you, wasn't it?" His words had the sibilant menace of a gravestone being carved, stroke by careful stroke.

Chantal froze at the sepulchral whisper, jerking John to a stop.

John blustered, "I don't know what you're talking about—"

The voice was one pitch higher, but still uncannily soft and even. "You killed Annette. Slit her throat to keep me from marrying her. To protect your goddamned inheritance."

"Such melodrama is not like you," John protested, but for the first time he looked afraid.

Chantal gasped, her gaze flying between the two men. Planting her feet, she ignored John's attempt to pull her to the door. Comprehension began to dawn in her lovely face. If John had been looking at her, he would have realized that danger could come from unexpected sources, but John's eyes were mesmerized by Canfield's inimical gray gaze.

"*Non,*" Chantal whispered harshly. "Say it is not true. *Jamais.*"

Slowly, John turned to her. She blinked at the enmity that suddenly beamed from him, a dark hatred so complete that it had its own curious lambent quality.

"I kissed his ass for thirty years, and you, who've done nothing to deserve a penny, suddenly appear to take it all. Was I supposed to smile and step aside?"

At the partial admission, Canfield growled and darted forward.

John raised the sagging pistol and pointed it at Canfield's heart, his finger tightening on the trigger.

With a nimble swivel of her hips, using all her weight, Chantal pulled free and deliberately raked the many sharp points of the ruby ring across his cheek, clawing John's wrist with her other hand.

John cried out in pain. His arm jerked, and the shot pocked Chantal's mirror instead of Canfield. With a roar, John grabbed Chantal's hand, pulling it from his face. Her ring came off, flying into a corner, but she was too busy grappling with John to notice.

Then Canfield was on him, flailing John with the cane, a profane stream of curses dripping from his lips like venom.

Chantal stood aside, watching stonily as the heavy silver-headed cane fell over and over. But when John sagged to his knees and fell face forward, and Canfield continued to beat him, Chantal caught his arm.

"Enough."

Canfield tried to pull away, tears streaming down his face now.

"No, Papa. Let him live to fight for crumbs with the rats in prison."

Shuddering, Canfield dropped the cane and stared down at his nephew's bruised and bloody head. The boy bore no resemblance to his dead wife now, if he ever had. Sickened at what John had become, and his own apparent part in creating this monster, Canfield turned away and stared into the pure features of his daughter. This lovely legacy Annette had given him.

"It is true, then? You are my father?"

Afraid to speak lest he disturb the fragile acceptance unfurling between them, he nodded.

Chantal blinked, the wonder in her eyes finally crowding out sorrow for her mother. "Why did you not tell me sooner?"

"I—" Canfield cleared his throat. "I feared you would hate me. I loved your mother passionately, my dear, but I was just beginning to make my fortune. By the time we met I was already married, and divorce—" He looked away, unable to finish.

"Divorce would have ruined you," she said calmly. "I quite understand. It is perhaps a legacy in our family that we are foolish when we are young."

He took a sharp breath. Was that forgiveness in those eyes that reminded him so much of Annette? He didn't deserve it. He hadn't earned it.

But oh, how he needed it. . . .

Chantal kissed his cheek. "I have longed for a father my whole life. How could I reject you now when you have been so kind to us?" Something seemed to occur to her and she cocked her head to say severely, "And I don't want or need your money—"

"Perhaps not, but you shall have it just the same. And no doubt do better things with it than I ever did." He kissed her hand, whispering a prayer of thanks in his heart and hoping that somewhere, somehow, Annette was listening.

Chantal seemed to sense his thoughts. "*Maman* would not want me to hate you for things that cannot be changed. She had obviously made her peace with you before she died. She would want you to be a part of my life, and Tony's life, and—'' She broke off with a gasp, clutching her protruding stomach. She staggered and would have fallen if Canfield hadn't caught her arm to steady her.

''Oh dear God,'' he breathed, looking around in panic as if a doctor would materialize in the mirror. ''The pains have started?''

Chantal stood a bit straighter and gave him a wan smile. *''Oui. Ma bebe* does not wait for convenient moments, it seems. But why should he be different from his father?'' Carefully putting one foot in front of the other, she walked to the door. A dim red glow gleamed in the corner, but neither of them noticed.

Canfield supported her arm, ignoring the unconscious men on the floor. ''But . . . it's not time, is it?''

''No.''

The one word sent him into a flurry of motion. He gave Chantal's hovering coachman a dismissive wave and tenderly helped Chantal into his own capacious carriage. ''Carefully,'' he warned his own coachman. ''And the first watchman we pass, flag him down. He's business to attend to.''

The servant set a sedate pace, slow enough that Canfield would have noted, if he'd bothered to glance out the rear window, that the Kimball coachman did not return home. He glanced up the street in both directions and slipped inside the academy, which Canfield had forgotten to lock.

However, Canfield had eyes only for his daughter. She'd relaxed again enough to wonder aloud, ''I wonder if Vince will be back yet?''

Canfield said grimly, ''He'd better be.'' With the

name of a doctor. Canfield glanced at Chantal's huge belly and quickly looked away. Mayhap it was a good thing that the child was a month ahead of schedule.

They paused two streets over to speak briefly to a watchman, warning him to collect the two men at the academy, but were soon on their way again. Canfield shifted his legs constantly, all his senses alert for the slightest grimace from his daughter. She sat placidly, her hands crossed over her stomach.

Her total lack of fear only exacerbated his own.

She patted his tense arm. "I shall be fine, Papa. Now, as to names . . . Vince and I have settled on Francine for a girl but cannot agree on a boy's name. Do you have any ideas?"

Canfield forced his fevered brain to concentrate. "My oldest brother was more like a father to me than my own father. He died in a mine cave-in when I was twelve. His name was Durwood. I should be honored if you'd name the child that, if it's a boy."

She tested the name on her tongue. "I like it. We shall see what Vince has to say."

When Vince finally returned two hours later, he had little to say. His face was white with exhaustion, and it went paler still when he saw the hive of activity surrounding the house. He took one look at the maid hurrying upstairs with clean towels and Canfield pacing in the foyer and knew the truth. He froze where he stood, dread creeping over him in icy waves that buried him under an avalanche of panic.

It was too soon. He had a name, but he'd yet to meet the doctor who had been recommended to him.

Canfield stopped pacing. "Damn you, where's that doctor?"

Vince tried to speak, swallowed and managed faintly, "Bath. I . . . intended to see him tomorrow." Vince pulled a scrap of paper from his pocket.

Canfield snatched it. "Leave him to me. I'll bring him here at gunpoint if I have to." He stalked toward the door, his movements so decisive that he barely needed the cane. "Oh, by the by, tell your friend Robbie that he was right. John and Renner did speak of revolution, and powder to blow something up. The date, I do not know, but the watch should have them in custody now. No doubt they can be . . . persuaded to tell all." Canfield exited, opening the door himself without the hovering footman's aid, and slamming it behind him so hard the windowpanes rattled.

Terror tightening his throat, Vince started up the stairs. The horrific vision hovered like a grisly specter haunting his every movement, but somehow he glued a smile to his face when he entered the master chambers. His wife lay pale but composed against the pillows, a maid dabbing the sweat from her brow. Chantal had obviously just finished a cycle of pains, but she smiled her relief when she saw him.

"That's just like you, to be gallivanting about the countryside when your child decides to be born."

Relieved at the distraction, he took up the badinage. "Chantal, my love, you are ever contrary to begin this with me out of town—"

"Blame your heir, my lord," she responded gamely. " 'Tis sooner than I am ready, to be truth—" She broke off with a gasp, clenching the covers in two white-knuckled fists.

Vince's eyes went blank with panic, but the elderly maid beside the bed caught Chantal's hands and encouraged, "Squeeze, milady. And scream, belike the child will hear ye and come out the quicker jest to see what the clammer be."

But Chantal bit her lip so hard blood came and shook her head, her eyes huge on her husband's face. She squeezed the maid's hands tightly, however, harder and harder until the spasm passed. Then she went slack upon the bed. The maid wet the small towel to dab at Chantal's mouth and brow.

"There now, 'tis no more, no less than other women do. Ye'll come through right as rain, sure as I stand here," the maid encouraged. Sotto voce, she whispered to another maid, who was tearing a sheet into strips, "Get the lord out 'o here so the lady can scream if she wants."

The younger maid shrank away from such a formidable task, but when Chantal sent her a pleading look, she timidly approached Vince. "Please, yer worship, this is women's work. We'll take good care o' the countess 'til the doctor arrives. Come along."

Vince shook his head. "No. I want to stay with her."

The pains gripped Chantal again, but she bit out, "Go, Vince! Please, I don't want you to see me like this," before she arched against the bed.

Helplessness had never sat easily upon Vince's broad shoulders, and he had never felt more helpless than he did at this moment. Seeing Chantal in such obvious pain, when he knew her labor had barely begun, touched a primitive chord within him that made panic vibrate through every nerve in his body. He knew he had to get a grip on himself before he would be any use to Chantal, so slowly, reluctantly, he walked through the door the younger maid held open. "I'll be back," he gritted through his teeth.

The next few hours found him wearing a path in the entryway marble. The knowledge that he was but one of many lords in this old house who'd trod the same trail was no comfort to him. How many of his female ancestors had died in childbirth? He could not remember; his head felt full of wool. But too many. And most of them were larger than Chantal.

Biting his knuckle to stifle a moan, Vince went to his study, started to pour himself a full snifter of brandy, changed his mind and carried the crystal bottle with him, lifting it periodically to slug back several swallows. When the bottle was half empty, his fear was dulled.

He'd not heard a peep out of the bedchamber for the past few hours. He didn't know whether to be glad or afraid of that. He stared down into the glowing amber liquid, and suddenly he felt better because he knew what to do.

Hugo burst into the foyer, smelling of the stables, with Tony at his heels. "It's time?"

Vince blinked and nodded. Why had Hugo grown two heads?

Tony started up the stairs, but Hugo pulled him back. "No, lad, your ma wouldn't want ye there now. Later, after the babe is born. Come along, let me show ye that new game o' sport I seen t'other day. Rugby, they be callin' it, and ye must be a braw lad to play it."

Torn, Tony glanced between the steps and Hugo's outheld hand.

Vince steadied himself on both feet and said gently,

"I shall keep watch, my boy. Go on and have fun. We'll fetch you the minute it's done."

And so, though it was nearly midnight, Tony let himself be dragged out the door onto the greensward of the back lawn. The servants pulled out huge torches to light the vast expanse.

Vince beckoned to a footman and gave him a mission just as the door burst open. Lizzie, her bonnet sooty and ragged, her dress singed at the hem and sleeves, staggered inside. Robbie was equally dirty and equally tired.

Shock sobered Vince instantly. "My God, what's happened?"

"Fire. The academy," Lizzie explained, collapsing into a foyer chair.

Robbie took up the tale, accepting the butler's proffered rag to clean his sooty face. "The fire brigade tried to put it out, but they were too late. Two men matching the description of Whitmore and Renner were seen fleeing the scene."

Vince scowled. "But I thought the authorities had them."

"They were gone when the watch arrived." Robbie flung the towel down in disgust. "And your coachman? Do you know where he is?"

"Come to think of it—" Vince hurried to the back of the house and came back quickly. "He never returned from taking Chantal to the academy. Dammit, I knew I should have dismissed him." Vince pounded a fist into the wall.

A sound they all recognized froze them in horror.

A pistol shot echoed an ugly retort. Vince ran outside, alarmed for Tony, as another shot sounded, breaking the glass beside the door. Vince dived for the ground, rolling for cover as he'd learned to do in the war. Robbie did likewise, waving Lizzie back inside. She slammed the door closed.

Vince lifted his head, but in the dark he could see nothing. Dammit, where were Tony and Hugo? He didn't need to see to know who the assailant was, however. "Whitmore, you fool," he roared. "You should have left London when you had the chance." As he finished speaking, he and Robbie crawled off, to disguise their location.

Two more shots pinged off the front steps, uncomfortably close. Whitmore was good at pinpointing his target by the sound of a voice.

"That's the problem with you bloody lords," Whitmore snarled. "Think you know what's best for the hoi polloi. Well, I have a message for you and your kind. I only hope my bloody uncle is here to receive it!" A crashing sound was followed by a brilliant flash of light. Flames began to lick at the side of the house.

Horrified, Vince crawled to the horse trough, filled a bucket and crawled back to throw water on the flames. They sputtered and went out, but he also apparently revealed his location, for this time the pistol shot whistled by his head.

Vince ducked. Robbie was gone, and Vince knew he was circling behind the source of the powder flash. Keep Whitmore talking. "For such a clever chap, you've really behaved stupidly," Vince taunted him. "Canfield told me he intended to leave you a million pounds even after he found Chantal and Tony."

Whitmore yelled, "He's a liar! He wouldn't have left me a penny. I may be ruined, but I can sure as hell take some of you with me—" Light flared in the darkness.

Dammit, he had another lantern! Vince started crawling back to the trough, but a faint moan sounded. The light was snuffed out.

Robbie's grim voice said, "The only place you're going, my lad, is to gg—" He ended on a moan. The sound of a heavy weight falling galvanized Vince.

Renner! To hell with safety. Vince made a running lunge toward the shrubs near the street, where the voices had come from. He almost stumbled over Robbie and Whitmore, and could just make out Renner running toward a carriage parked down the street.

The Kimball carriage.

Infuriated, Vince spurted into a run. Heavier footsteps joined his. Vince glanced over his shoulder and found Hugo following, his bared teeth shining in the faint gaslighting on the street. Hugo tackled Renner from behind, his huge fists flailing the smaller man into submission.

With a last running leap, Vince stepped onto the bottom step of the driver's seat as his carriage started to pull away. Vince caught the coachman in a choke hold in one arm and used his other hand to grab the reins and draw the panicked horses to a halt.

Even when the horses stopped, Vince still tightened his grip about his servant's throat. He'd trusted this bastard. The blighter could have killed Chantal.

Chantal! He had to get back. Vince squeezed hard enough to stun the fellow. He was climbing down, leaving the servant slumped on the carriage seat, when a noisy clatter up the street foretold the arrival of several watchmen. Lizzie, sooty but unbowed, led them at a full run.

" 'Ere, yer ludship, that's enough o' that," one said, puffing. "We'll take the bloke now."

Tony peeked out of the shed Hugo had sent him to hide in and trotted over to appraise the combatants.

Vince left the three men to the watch and hurried back to the house. Lizzie stayed to help Robbie up. He groaned and leaned on her a bit more heavily than was strictly necessary.

"See that they're locked up tight as a drum," Robbie ordered. "I'll be in to question them on the morrow."

"Aye, sir," the three watchmen said, each shoving a bound man before him.

Robbie glanced at the front door. Lights blazed from almost every window of the townhouse. "Why so much activity? I expected the household to be asleep."

Lizzie's eyes widened. "It . . . must be the baby." She bolted inside.

Inside the house, Lizzie watched Vince slug back brandy as the butler shook his head to Vince's quiet questions. Despite the late hour, most of the servants hovered near the kitchen, frequently peeking into the foyer.

A short, stifled scream split the eerie quiet with the keening agony of an animal in pain.

Vince jerked as if someone had slapped him. The butler shrank into himself, his proud posture abruptly slumping. The servants disappeared, shaking their heads and muttering to themselves.

Rubbing her sooty hands down her dress, Lizzie ran up the steps.

Vince didn't try to stop her. Maybe Chantal would be comforted by her presence, as she was not comforted by his. He could scarcely blame his wife for not wanting to see his face. Her condition was, after all, his fault. Vince took to pacing again, the brandy forgotten in his hand.

Dammit, where was Canfield? Bath wasn't that far. He should have been back before now.

A few minutes later, a new arrival blew through the door. A month, even an hour earlier, Vince might have said an ill wind blew her, but at this moment, the sight of his mother soothed him like a breath of fresh air. The cobwebs cleared from his brain; strength flowed through his paralyzed limbs.

She stopped, hesitant, just inside the doorstep, staring at her son.

The servant who had fetched her glanced between mother and son before he discreetly disappeared. Later, he'd be heard to say to his fellows belowstairs, "Right touching, it were, the way they looked, one at t'other. I knew then that everything would come out right and tight. This old house'd be a home agin."

In the foyer, Adeline took a deep breath. "Vince, I . . . forgive me for what I did. You cannot hate me any more than I hate myself."

In the emotional stress of the moment, words seemed too weak to voice his feelings. He, too, needed forgiving. Faced with the greatest loss he'd ever known, Vince realized that he'd foisted needless pain upon his household out of a juvenile sense of outraged male pride. If Chantal, who was the one who'd been wronged, was willing to forgive and forget, what right had he to carry a grudge and deny his children their loving grandmother? Truly, she'd acted in what she considered his best interests. How could he hate her for that? Of a sudden, the house that had never felt quite right since she left it took on its proper proportions again with her small, commanding presence.

Praying that Chantal would be as comforted as he was, Vince held out his arms to his mother. Tears of joy upon her face, she walked straight into them. She pulled his drooping head to her soft bosom, stroking his hair back as she had when he'd been a boy.

"She'll be all right, Vince," she said fiercely. "I promise. Come now, take me to her."

Vince pulled back when she tugged him toward the stairs. "She asked me to leave. The maids say she won't scream with me there."

"Nonsense. You can stand a few screams. You've heard your share, after all." Insistently, she pulled him with her. "She'll be comforted by your presence. That, I know."

Indeed, Chantal's tired, haggard features softened when she saw them. She took a deep breath, some of the pain fading from her expression. "Thank God," she said simply.

Adeline sat on the side of the bed to clasp her daughter-in-law's hands. "No, my dear. Thanks to you. I . . . have never known a more loving soul than yours." When Chantal's hands squeezed and her face twisted, Adeline took the nails digging into the backs of her hands without a squawk of protest. She tossed a commanding look over her shoulder at Vince, urging him to his wife's other side.

But Vince froze helplessly in the center of the floor. The confrontation with Whitmore had relieved part of his agony, but here, back in this hellish chamber, the damned vision was too close to reality for comfort. The sheets covering the mound of Chantal's belly were dotted with blood; she writhed in a torment he could not fathom, much less ease. His nightmares were coming true before his eyes, except reality was worse. Chantal's attempts to stifle her cries had resulted in a swollen mouth puffy with blood blisters from the many times she'd bitten it.

Adeline waited until the agonized clasp at her hands eased before she stood and rolled up her sleeves. "Where the hell is the doctor?" She washed her hands in a warm bowl of water.

Her uncharacteristic profanity recalled Vince to a sense of calm. "Maybe I should go for him myself. Bartholomew is taking a confoundedly long time." Vince sat down beside his wife and grabbed the rag to tenderly wipe her mouth and brow.

"How long has she been like this?" Adeline demanded, tying a long string of fabric to each footpost.

The older maid, whose straggling hair and worried frown had spoiled her former cheerful countenance, glanced at the clock. "Ah, close to six hours, milady. And . . . no improvement."

Adeline said nothing, but the lines in her face deepened. She handed each end of the fabric to Chantal and said with an encouraging smile, "Pull this during the pains. It may help."

Chantal looped the fabric over her hands just as another pain gripped her. She bowed so hard against the mattress that only her heels and shoulders touched it. A piercing scream slipped out, and the veins in her neck stood out in sharp relief.

The hairs on the back of Vince's neck raised. He patted her shoulder awkwardly. "Scream, my love. As loud as you want. Tony is playing outside."

A groan slipped out of Chantal as another series of pains gripped her, harder. This time, her scream echoed in the chamber. Lizzie, her face scrubbed and shiny, peeked inside the door, but Adeline shook her head and waved her out. The door closed and her light steps receded.

Vince exchanged a helpless glance with his mother. Then, a dim memory surfaced. He searched the room, and finally found one of Chantal's fans. He ripped the fragile frame apart, leaving a thick piece of wood folded upon itself in layers. He carried it to Chantal and held it before her agonized face. "Bite on this, my love, and save your poor mouth."

Gratefully, she closed her lips about the wood. The next spasm seemed to hurt her a bit less as she bit down hard on the fan and pulled with all her might at the strips of cloth.

For two more hours, they worked with her, encouraging her during the spasms, wiping her brow during the calm moments. These, however, grew farther and farther apart.

But every time the maid and Adeline pulled the sheet up to check between Chantal's legs for the head, they looked away from Vince's agonized gaze without speaking.

Vince climbed into bed with his wife and caught her shoulders to pull her back against him. "Don't you need to push, my love?"

"No. . . . Oh God, oh God, it hurts. . . ." She ended on a sibilant hiss of pain, biting so hard into the fan that Vince heard the wood crack. From this position, he could see how huge was the mound of her belly. The

377

child had lowered slightly in her womb, but even in Vince's limited experience, it still seemed much too high.

"Can't we give her some laudanum?" he asked, his voice hoarse.

Adeline's agitated hands folded a towel constantly, as if she could not be still, but she shook her head. "We do not dare. When the time comes, she has to be strong and aware, else she'll never be able to push the child out."

When the time comes . . . Vince stared down at his laboring wife. Maybe it was already too late. His lust was going to be the death of the only woman he'd ever loved. Vince supported Chantal's shoulders, so dazed he didn't realize he was crying until wetness dropped on his hands.

During a brief respite, Chantal leaned her head back against his shoulder and cradled his cheek in one weak hand. In a measure of how exhausted and weak she was, she didn't ask him to leave, or comment at the tears he swallowed for her sake.

She sighed. "I am glad you are here. But oh, poor *cheri*, this is as difficult for you as it is for me. I am sorry to be such a trial to y—" She bowed again, her shoulderblades pressing into Vince, but he welcomed the pain, wishing savagely that it was he who had to bear this instead of her. Had she not sacrificed enough out of love for him and her child?

Would her very life be forfeit, too?

He would curse God for the rest of his days if Chantal was taken from him. No, no, no, no, he repeated endlessly in his mind.

Adeline peeked beneath the sheets again. She looked

very old when she straightened. She shook her head slightly at Vince.

Panic screamed through him. He began to rock, holding the precious weight in his arms while he still could, and this time, no amount of male pride could bank his tears. The baby was simply too large for her small frame. After so long, they should at least see a head. He was losing her. And there was nothing in the world he could do to stop it.

The pain came in unending waves for her then. Vince held her, rocked her, supported her as she pulled at the fabric, but he knew her screams were becoming weaker. Her breath was an unending rasp of agony that found an echo in Vince's heart and mind. His tears were an endless stream now, and even indomitable Adeline had begun to sniffle.

If she died, he'd . . .

New footsteps pounded up the steps. Bartholomew burst into the room, a stranger one step behind him.

"Sorry, lad, had to track him down. . . ." Bartholomew trailed off, staring at his daughter. He went as white as the sheet on which she lay, backing up a step.

The doctor, a thin young man with dark, rumpled hair and intense green eyes, waved him out of the room. "This is no place for you, sir. Leave me to do my job."

Vince cleared his throat, but it was raw from tears, and his voice was husky. "You are Terrence Stanton?"

"Yes, my lord. Now move aside." Decisively, the young man set his black bag at the foot of the bed, pulled back the sheet covering Chantal and examined her. He snapped out questions as he worked, the details of how long she'd been in labor, how many stone she'd gained, all the while gently feeling her belly and looking between her legs. He put an odd instrument Vince had never seen to her stomach, and some type of listening device in his ears.

He draped the contraption around his neck. "The baby's heartbeat is strong, but I see no evidence that it's moved down the birth canal." He glanced at the women in the room. "Do any of you have midwife experience?"

The older maid nodded. Adeline said tiredly, "And I've twice helped in a birthing."

"This will not be a normal birth," the young man warned. "Are either of you sick at the sight of blood?"

Both women shook their heads.

"If I can help at all, please let me stay," Adeline pleaded.

Vince had clambered off the bed at the doctor's command, but Chantal's writhing brought him back. She was lost in her own world of pain now, her usually shiny dark hair dank with sweat, her perfect skin ashen. No wonder Bartholomew had recoiled at sight of her. She did not look like healthy, vibrant Chantal. She looked like a . . . Vince closed his eyes in denial.

The doctor stepped between him and the bed, lowering his voice so Chantal wouldn't hear him. "My lord, your wife is in serious jeopardy. The child is too large for her to deliver naturally."

This confirmation of his worst fears drew Vince to the inevitable conclusion that had hovered over him all night. The words hurt as they came out, but he had little choice. "Can you . . . extract the child somehow and save my wife?"

The doctor shook his head gravely. "No, in most

cases it's just the opposite. When the woman . . . expires, the child can sometimes be extracted at the last moment and saved. But you do not wish this?''

Staring at Chantal, who was barely moving now, so weak was she from the continual pains without respite, Vince shook his head, unable to speak.

"Then we can try only one thing. I have never performed this operation on a living woman, you understand. My colleagues and I have practiced on cadavers, but it seems the only alternative. Have you ever heard the word caesarean?''

Vince's heart leapt to his throat. This was the procedure the dons at Oxford had informed him had been tried in very rare cases. Most women had died, but they knew of one who'd lived. "Yes. Julius Caesar was cut from his mother's womb.'' And the woman promptly died.

"Correct. I have studied for some time the exact construction of a woman's reproductive system, and I believe there is a way to cut the abdomen open, remove the child and sew the mother back up. But it will be very risky. She could die from loss of blood, or infection, or I could cut wrong, or—''

The new worries were more than Vince could bear. He raised his hand. "Enough! Is there any other way?''

His green eyes soft with compassion, Stanton shook his head. "None that I know of. The child would be crowning now if he'd come down the birth canal, and the countess is already very weak. She will surely die in agony if we do not try this.''

"Do it," Vince mumbled through gritted teeth. "Do you need my help?''

"No," Stanton said, folding up his shirt sleeves and

pulling a roll of wrapped instruments from his case. "Yes. Do you have any brandy? I have found, quite by chance, that it seems to help with infection when used judiciously during operations."

The words were scarce out of his mouth before Vince was downstairs fetching the brandy. He snatched it from Bartholomew's shaky hands without a word of explanation and ran back upstairs. The doctor was stirring something into a glass of water. Vince picked up the bottle.

Laudanum. "Is it safe to give her this?"

"It's best that she be totally still, and we want to spare her unnecessary pain," Stanton explained. "Would you give this to her?"

Vince took the glass and tenderly lifted Chantal's shoulders to hold it to her mouth. The fluid dripped down her dry, cracked lips, but she didn't swallow. He shook her slightly, terrified that they were too late. "Chantal, the doctor is going to help you. Please, you must drink this. Wake up, darling."

To his heartfelt relief, her eyes fluttered open. They were dark and blanker than he'd ever seen them, but she blinked and focused on his face with difficulty. When he begged her again to drink she did so, weakly.

The doctor watched her, frowning, and when the glass was empty, he took it from Vince's limp hand. "Go below now, sir. You've done all you can, except pray."

Stumbling, Vince left.

For what seemed like hours, he and Bartholomew strode up and down the foyer. Tony, Hugo and Lizzie joined them, sometimes sitting on the steps, sometimes walking their own worry paths. But the silence from above began to wear on them. Dawn showed through the huge trees outside the house, gray light casting pallid shadows on the gray hope to which they still clung. But their grip grew more precarious with every passing hour. Chantal had been in labor more than twelve hours now, and still there was no word from up above.

The sun battled for dominance with the clouds and finally won the day, but its cheerful normalcy seemed obscene to those who waited. Endlessly.

Bartholomew stared grimly at the bright landscape. "She forgave me, do you know?" he said vaguely.

Vince stopped pacing to stare.

"Just like that!" Bartholomew tried to snap his fingers, couldn't and stuffed his aged hands in his pockets, as if disgusted with his own clumsiness. "Not a word of reproach. Even said she didn't want my money."

"She knows, then? You told her?" Vince asked.

"Aye. Right before . . ." He bowed his head and slumped onto a step.

That, at least, was something. It was right that Chantal knew she was not alone before . . . if . . .

Vince leapt up the steps, unable to bear waiting any longer. He shook off Bartholomew's staying hand and climbed the stairs three at a time. *Scream,* he begged inwardly. *Let me know you still live!*

And then, miraculously, a cry came. Vince's knees buckled at the sound of it. He caught the banister to steady himself

It was a babe's cry.

Down below, Tony's tears dried; Bartholomew's shaggy old head lifted; Hugo bolted to his feet; Lizzie covered her heart, muttering a fervent, quiet thank-you.

Feeling ten years younger and a hundred pounds

383

lighter, Vince ran up the steps into his bedchamber. He stopped, frozen in horror, to see the doctor literally sewing up Chantal's stomach.

Adeline, her face more tired than he had ever seen it, put her finger to her mouth, shushing him. Vince slipped into the room.

The older maid brought him a blanket-wrapped bundle. Vince's knees went weak again when he saw a tiny, angry, wrinkled face capped by a lush thatch of black hair. The baby was fat, and healthy and . . . Vince counted the fingers and toes and noted the testicles . . . all there.

Fatherly pride would come later, he assumed, but right now he had but one thought.

He stood to the side of the bed, watching the needle pierce his wife's flesh. Bile rose in his throat. How could she survive being cut open and sewn up like a blasted fish?

Adeline blotted the blood away, and then the last stitch was in. Stanton poured fresh brandy onto the cut, wiped his instruments and dropped them back in his bag.

Then, his young face drawn with exhaustion, he looked at the earl. "It's too soon to be sure, but I believe your wife will recover. She won't be able to get up for some time, and everything will have to be done for her. She'll be in pain. Give her laudanum for a few more days. . . ." He trailed off as he realized Vince wasn't listening.

Vince had dropped on his knees beside the bed to frame his wife's still, quiet face in his hands. "Chantal, darling, are you all right?"

Stanton patted Vince's shoulder. "Let her sleep—"

But, as if she'd been called back from the shores of death itself by the touch of his hands, her eyes fluttered sleepily. She started to move, moaned in pain and went still.

"Give her the baby," Stanton commanded the maid.

Vince helped arrange the child in Chantal's weak arm. The baby's agitated cries stopped at the touch of his mother's flesh and the sound of her heartbeat. The boy's eyes opened wide and he stared up at his mother with a look that Vince would swear later could only be described as recognition.

Chantal took a deep breath. Her voice sounded rusty. "He's . . . healthy?"

Vince kissed her brow softly, still afraid she'd break in his hands. "And gorgeous. You have given me another heir, my love." *Two is enough. I will never put you through this again.*

The doctor met his eyes and pulled something from his bag. Vince recognized the rolled sheepskins wrapped in tiny pieces of paper.

Accepting them, Vince nodded and said quietly, "I understand. My man below has a bag of gold for you, sir. I will shout your praises far and wide in the Lords and to the ton, if my wife lives."

Pleased color stained the high cheekbones, proving the doctor's youth had been stifled but not buried under professional gravity. "She'll live. I shall be back on the morrow to check on her progress." And off he went.

Adeline watched him go, her eyes wet for the first time that night. "He's an amazing young man. God heard our prayers after all."

Vince watched Chantal open the sheet so the baby could suckle. The angry chirps were replaced by greedy slurps.

"Yes, he did, Mother." Vince sighed, pulling her hand down on his shoulder to pat it. He watched his wife and son, weariness washing over him in great waves. He'd never known a longer, more torturous night, even when they were waiting for Boney to attack at Waterloo. Perhaps he'd rest his head beside Chantal's for just a moment.

His head drooped. Half kneeling, half leaning on the mattress, Vince relaxed, peace stealing over him. She'd live, she had to live, but he'd not leave this room until he knew for certain. He slept before the thought was finished.

Next to him on the pillow, Chantal turned her head. She used her free hand to brush aside his tousled hair. And then she smiled, a smile so luminous with adoration and exultation that he would have wept at the beauty of it. A smile bright enough to defeat the shadows of her own ordeal.

Wiping away a tear, Adeline swept back the heavy drapes, letting sunshine into the room. It chased away the last despair that lurked in the corners, dancing on crystal vases and winking on the yellow diamond Chantal had left beside her bed. It sparkled on the white diamonds on Chantal's and Adeline's eyelashes.

"Poor Vince," they said simultaneously.

And then, laughing in joy, they held hands and turned their faces up to the sun.

Two weeks later, Vince bounded up the stairs to meet his wife. She was able to move around for short periods now, and he was delighted to find her up, nursing the baby in the old rocking chair he'd had brought down from the attic. Adeline had informed him that he and his father had both been rocked in that same chair.

For a moment, he paused in the doorway, his heart pounding with joy at the sight of his wife and child. Just as nothing in their relationship had come easily, Durwood's birth had caused his parents a great deal of anguish. But Chantal was healing nicely, and the boy was a lusty, bright-eyed infant. No doubt Durwood, like his brother Tony, would be a fitting heir to the legacy their father held in his hands. Nothing worth keeping came easily to the Kimballs. . . .

Vince looked down at the wrapped bundle. He'd commissioned this surprise for Chantal shortly after he'd discovered she was pregnant. Now, in the fullness of the joy she'd given him, in celebration of the long years ahead, he'd deemed it an appropriate moment to give her this, despite the fact that she hadn't fully recovered. He walked forward as she lifted the baby to her shoulder to burp him. She turned her head and smiled at him.

His throat tightened. Every smile, every gesture, every intimate moment between them was precious, for he knew how perilously close he'd come to losing her. Young Stanton was already deluged with patients in his new practice, and if Vince had his way, he'd be deluged with many more.

Vince caught the back of the old rocker, bent and kissed his wife's shoulder. "I never tire of seeing you thus," he whispered. She cupped his cheek, sighing her contentment.

Vince straightened as his son grunted at him. Durwood focused on him with muddy blue eyes, waving his fists. Vince stuck his finger in one tiny hand. "Don't like sharing her, eh, old chap? Well, if I must share, so must you."

Walking around the chair, Vince knelt and set the bundle in her lap.

"What's this?" she asked, still patting Durwood on the back.

Vince lifted the baby away, setting him in the day cradle in the corner of the room. The baby gave a wail of protest.

"Just a moment, my boy," Vince said, stroking the velvet cheek with one finger. The baby's waving fist passed his line of vision. His eyes crossed. He suckled his hand.

Laughing, Vince returned to Chantal, who was struggling with the wrapping. He helped her open the parcel.

A beautiful book, its pages gilded, its cover inset with precious stones, fell into her lap.

Like a gift.

"For the gift of love you gave me," Vince whispered, kneeling before her. "Small recompense, but the best I can manage."

Her eyes huge, she looked up. "But isn't this just Drake and Callista's story?"

"Not anymore." Vince turned the pages past the lovely fairy tale of Drake and his Beauty to a new illustration the artist had painted with a skillful hand.

Chantal caught her breath, running her finger over the poignant scene.

A beautiful black-haired dancer, wearing a filmy dress fashioned of triangular pieces of fabric in every hue of purple, her lovely legs bare, stretched her arms with yearning toward a handsome soldier. The young man, brown-haired and blue-eyed, watched her with quiet, steady devotion, his hand extended to her. On the hand was a ruby heart. It had been painted with such skill that it seemed to glow with the secret heart of bluish fire only the best rubies possess.

Chantal burst into tears.

Alarmed, Vince pulled her onto the floor on his lap. "My love, I wanted to please you, not make you cry."

Her sniffles ended as she pulled a clean kerchief from her pocket and blew her nose. "It's just the ring. . . . I wish I hadn't left it at the academy to lose it in the fire."

Vince smiled mysteriously but let her go on without interrupting.

". . . and the dress. I recognize it. It's the one I wore the last time I danced for you before you went away to war. . . ."

He cradled her close, as one holds something very precious. "I know. That image emblazoned itself on my memory for ten years. It kept me steadfast in my belief that we were fated to be together again. Why have you never worn it since returning to me?"

"I lost it in Scotland." When the baby whimpered, she turned her head, but Durwood, as if sensing his parents' need to be alone together, thoughtfully found his fist again.

"Are you ready to tell me now what happened to you all those years ago?" Vince asked gravely.

Chantal still stared at the picture. "Nothing of importance. Those years we were apart are becoming a dim memory to me now. Would you have it matter?"

Vince pulled her tighter into his arms. "No, my

lovely ballerina. And I want you to know that I will build you another dancing academy, if you wish it. You have such a God-given talent that I cannot deny you."

In the brilliant sunlight of a new day, like his grandparents before them, the two Kimballs pledged their troth. The invisible bond between them was as much a legacy as the book their heirs would one day cherish.

That night, Vince carried Chantal down the stairs for her first meal with the family since her ordeal. Bartholomew stood at the head of the table and raised his glass in salute to his daughter and the baby a nursemaid propped in a chair, surrounding him by cushions, near Tony's end of the table.

"To Frenchwomen. The loveliest, kindest women the world will ever see." Bartholomew drank deeply.

Hugo lifted his glass. "To Durwood Kimball, brawest laddie amongst a long line of braw laddies."

Robbie lifted a toast. "To England. And all present who have once again helped save the Crown." With the proper persuasion, Robbie had told them earlier with extreme satisfaction, Renner had broken and given them details of the times and places of the proposed explosions. They had caught the rest of the conspirators in the act of setting the charges at the three bridges.

Lizzie lifted her glass. "To the earl and his countess. The steadfast soldier and his ballerina."

Adeline lifted her own glass, her face shining with pride in her family.

Vince lifted Chantal's hand and kissed the knuckles.

"I shall miss my ruby heart ring." She sighed for his ears alone.

Smiling, Vince pried open Chantal's hand and set

something in her palm, closing her fingers about it. She opened her hand and gasped.

A perfect ruby glittered in the candlelight, shaped like a heart.

"I searched a day but finally found it. The smaller diamonds must be buried, but we can have it reset. I desperately wanted you to have this, to put a happy ending on our own fairy tale," Vince whispered in her ear. "We are one, my love. Fused in fire and pain and tragedy, we still shine and endure. Forever after, you will wear my heart on your hand."

Chantal's eyes misted over. She kissed him.

The adults at the table clapped and made teasing cat-calls, but Tony wrinkled his nose in disgust as he glanced between his parents and the gurgling baby propped near him. He sneaked a glass of wine from the carafe while the adults were distracted.

When the laughter died down, Tony stood and imperiously rapped the table with his knuckles. When everyone was looking at him, he said, "To horses." He sniffed, brushed his nose in disgust and glared at his brother. "And brothers who don't stink."

Ignoring the laughter, he drank deeply of his wine.

A FAERIE TALE ROMANCE

VICTORIA ALEXANDER

Ophelia Kendrake has barely finished conning the coat off a cardsharp's back when she stumbles into Dead End, Wyoming. Mistaken for the Countess of Bridgewater, Ophelia sees no reason to reveal herself until she has stripped the hamlet of its fortunes and escaped into the sunset. But the free-spirited beauty almost swallows her script when she meets Tyler, the town's virile young mayor. When Tyler Matthews returns from an Ivy League college, he simply wants to settle down and enjoy the simplicity of ranching. But his aunt and uncle are set on making a silk purse out of Dead End, and Tyler is going to be the new mayor. It's a job he takes with little relish—until he catches a glimpse of the village's newest visitor.

__52159-8 $5.50 US/$6.50 CAN

Dorchester Publishing Co., Inc.
P.O. Box 6640
Wayne, PA 19087-8640

The Snow Queen

ANNE AVERY

When Boston-bred Hetty Malone arrives at the Colorado Springs train station, she is full of hope that she will soon marry her childhood sweetheart and live happily ever after. Yet life amid the ice-capped Rockies has changed Michael Ryan. No longer the hot-blooded suitor Hetty remembers, the young doctor has grown as cold and distant as the snowy mountain peaks. Determined to revive Michael's passionate longing, Hetty quickly realizes that no modern medicine can cure what ails him. But in the enchanted splendor of her new home, she dares to administer the only remedy that might melt his frozen heart: a dose of good old-fashioned loving.

_52151-2 $5.99 US/$6.99 CAN

Dorchester Publishing Co., Inc.
P.O. Box 6640
Wayne, PA 19087-8640

Please add $1.75 for shipping and handling for the first book and $.50 for each book thereafter. NY, NYC, and PA residents, please add appropriate sales tax. No cash, stamps, or C.O.D.s. All orders shipped within 6 weeks via postal service book rate. Canadian orders require $2.00 extra postage and must be paid in U.S. dollars through a U.S. banking facility.

Name_____

Address_____

City_____ State_____ Zip_____

I have enclosed $_____ in payment for the checked book(s).

Payment <u>must</u> accompany all orders. ❑ Please send a free catalog.

A Faerie Tale Romance

Let Me Come In

LINDA JONES

It's been fourteen years, but Benjamin Wolfe remembers it like yesterday—the day his father was run out of town by Hamilton Pigg. Now Ben is back to give the three remaining Piggs—lovely Cecilia and her sisters—a taste of their own medicine. But Ben doesn't count on Hamilton's daughter being such a beautiful woman, or so stubborn. And suddenly he finds himself questioning—despite all his huffing and puffing—whether it's revenge he really wants, or just for the lovely Cecilia to let him come in.

___52217-9 $5.50 US/$6.50 CAN

Dorchester Publishing Co., Inc.
P.O. Box 6640
Wayne, PA 19087-8640

Please add $1.75 for shipping and handling for the first book and $.50 for each book thereafter. NY, NYC, and PA residents, please add appropriate sales tax. No cash, stamps, or C.O.D.s. All orders shipped within 6 weeks via postal service book rate. Canadian orders require $2.00 extra postage and must be paid in U.S. dollars through a U.S. banking facility.

Name_____
Address_____
City_____State_____Zip_____
I have enclosed $_____ in payment for the checked book(s).
Payment __must__ accompany all orders. ☐ Please send a free catalog.

**WHO'S BEEN EATING FROM MY BOWL?
IS SHE A BEAUTY IN BOTH HEART AND
   SOUL?
WHO'S BEEN SITTING IN MY CHAIR?
IS SHE PRETTY OF FACE AND FAIR OF
   HAIR?
WHO'S BEEN SLEEPING IN MY BED?
IS SHE THE DAMSEL I WILL WED?**

  The golden-haired woman barely escapes from a stagecoach robbery before she gets lost in the Wyoming mountains. Hungry, harried, and out of hope, she stumbles on a rude cabin, the home of three brothers; great bears of men who nearly frighten her out of her wits. But Maddalyn Kelly is no Goldilocks; she is a feisty beauty who can fend for herself. Still, how can she ever guess that the Barrett boys will bare their souls to her—or that one of them will share with her an ecstasy so exquisite it is almost unbearable?

_52094-X   **$5.99 US/$6.99 CAN**

**Dorchester Publishing Co., Inc.
P.O. Box 6640
Wayne, PA 19087-8640**

Please add $1.75 for shipping and handling for the first book and $.50 for each book thereafter. NY, NYC, and PA residents, please add appropriate sales tax. No cash, stamps, or C.O.D.s. All orders shipped within 6 weeks via postal service book rate. Canadian orders require $2.00 extra postage and must be paid in U.S. dollars through a U.S. banking facility.

Name_____
Address_____
City_____State_____Zip_____
I have enclosed $_____ in payment for the checked book(s).
Payment **must** accompany all orders. ❑ Please send a free catalog.